VINE
STREET

DOMINIC NOLAN

VINE STREET

HEADLINE

First published in 2021 by
HEADLINE PUBLISHING GROUP

2

Cataloguing in Publication Data is available from the British Library

ISBN 978 1 4722 8885 1

Typeset in 11/14.5 pt Adobe Garamond Pro by Jouve (UK), Milton Keynes

Printed and bound in Great Britain by Clays Ltd, Elcograf S.p.A.

HEADLINE PUBLISHING GROUP
An Hachette UK Company
Carmelite House
50 Victoria Embankment
London EC4Y 0DZ

www.headline.co.uk
www.hachette.co.uk

Based on a somewhat true story

Carthago delenda est

VINE STREET

Part One

SOHO

2002

I

Birds pick at the dead hedgehog Billie has been meaning to see to for a few days.

'Magpies are back. Eating that hedgehog.'

'Save you dealing with it.'

Voice catching like sandpaper. His breath worsening.

'Don't suppose they'll eat the bones. Maybe they'll bury them.' She turns to him. 'For later. They do that, don't they?'

He shrugs with the corners of his lips, unable to raise his shoulders. Billie opens the bedroom window. One of them looks up from its feast, seeing her framed there with its black crow eyes.

'I think they know us.'

It goes back to what remains of the hedgehog, and she returns to her chair beside his bed and reaches for his hand, a discarded glove beside him. He has no grip.

'I'm going to tell them you're not up for it.'

He stirs, head inching round towards her.

'You're not well enough. I can talk to them, tell them some things. I'll explain about how I was there too, from the beginning.'

Wheezing, he builds up to speak. 'You don't trust me. What I might say.'

'Do you?'

'Seventy years, maybe it'll finally come to an end.' His eyes close. Breath tearing like old pages. 'What does it matter? What can they do to me now?'

2

When the doorbell rings she has made a start on the ironing. There isn't much as there is a girl who comes, but Billie likes to keep her hand in. Stooping to turn off the iron at the wall, she shuffles out to the front door.

'Mrs Cassar?'

Two of them, a man and a woman. She's bad with gauging these things now; at her age it feels as if everyone is at least sixty years younger than her. He looks like he probably has a couple of children, but she is unimaginably young. Billie thinks back to what that was like, the feeling of immortality.

'Yes?'

'Detective Sergeant Rathbone. This is DC Duffy. We spoke on the phone.'

'Of course. Come in, come in.'

She reins back and ushers them into the front room, big floral armchairs and sofas. They take the three-seater and she sits across from them in the two, glad one of them hasn't taken her husband's armchair. The darkened antimacassar frightens people off.

She fights to her feet again as soon as she sits.

'Will you have tea?'

'We had coffee at the station, thanks,' Rathbone says.

Billie lowers herself into the chair once more, sitting back with her knees pressed together, hands in her lap.

'I was doing the ironing.'

'We're sorry for the interruption, Mrs Cassar.'

She waves him away. 'Nobody ever minded ironing being interrupted.'

'We were hoping we might have a word with Mr Cassar?'

Billie wonders if he always speaks in the plural.

'As I explained on the phone, my husband is extremely unwell. They have let him come home, but he is confined to his bed upstairs at the moment.'

'I see,' says Rathbone, his use of the singular somewhat mitigated by a conspiratorial glance at Duffy.

'It's very hard to make plans,' Billie goes on. 'He didn't have a good night, I'm afraid, and he's sleeping at the moment. I have to let him get his rest whenever he can.'

'Of course, of course.' Rathbone nods. 'We're very sorry to hear he's not well.'

'Not serious, I hope,' Duffy says.

Billie smiles. 'He's fond of saying that at our age everything is serious and nothing is serious. He's ninety-one years old, and we've been married for sixty-four of those.'

'Good Lord, congratulations,' Duffy says.

Billie spots the slightly maniacal glint in her eyes; the insistence of youth accompanied by a dreadful fear of those things that have endured.

'Is it possible that I might be of any help?' Billie offers. 'What exactly was it you wished to talk with my husband about?'

Rathbone touches the knot in his tie. 'It's a matter regarding his work, Mrs Cassar.'

'With Kent County Constabulary?'

'We don't think so, no. We believe this goes back to his time in the Met.'

'Oh, perhaps I *can* be of some help, then.'

'I don't—'

'I was a constable with the Met too.'

'Really?'

'That was how we met. I was with A4, that's what they called the women's branch back then. We'd had the volunteer patrols for some years, but they began to realise the value of having us on the force to handle women and children. I was A4, but I was attached to C Division in Vine Street, which was brilliant because even back in the thirties Soho was lousy with bars and clubs and prostitutes.'

Duffy chokes on a laugh.

'They used to send us in to the underground parties all dressed up. Just to observe. Take notes. Never get involved or make arrests. There were worse jobs.'

Rathbone shifts to the edge of his seat, leaning in. 'Mrs Cassar, did you know your husband's partner, Leon Geats?'

'Oh yes. I knew Leon very well. Worked with him before I ever met Mark. All three of us were on a case together in . . . goodness, when must it have been? 1935? 1936? Scarcely seems believable, does it?'

'Have you seen much of him over the years?'

'Leon? Heavens, no. He left the force before the war. I saw him briefly afterwards. He had just been demobbed and looked us up.' She frowns. 'He dropped out of sight after that.'

'Demobbed? We didn't find any record of him serving during the war, which is strange, because he was of the right age.'

Billie shrugs. 'I can only go by what he told me, which, to be frank, was very little. Leon always held his cards close to his chest.'

'There's no trace of him after his time in the Met, you see,' Rathbone says.

'You should check the *Gazette*.'

'*Gazette*?'

'He was mentioned in dispatches several times. But, you see, my husband and I left the city after the war. Leon never contacted us again. I really don't understand, Detective Sergeant – these things you talk about happened so long ago, what is it about Leon that you wish to know? And how is my husband involved?'

'Mrs Cassar, we're Warwickshire Police. A body was found in a field in the north Cotswolds. Two bodies, in fact. We have reason to believe one of them might be Leon Geats.'

Billie's hand went to her mouth. 'Oh God. In a *field*? So he was . . .'

'We're treating the deaths as suspicious. It appears the bodies have been there for a long time. Decades, at least thirty or forty years, possibly longer.'

'Oh no. Poor Leon.'

'We're not completely certain, and making a positive identification is proving tricky. Did Leon have any family?'

'His mother. She passed away just before the war. I believe his father died in the first war. There's nobody alive that I know of.'

'Yes, we have a record of his mother's death, but nothing about her burial.'

'I'm afraid I couldn't help you with that.'

'Would you know if Leon had ever been hurt? Injured in some way that might help us with the remains?'

'No, I don't—oh, yes! Yes, now you say that, that last time I saw him, he did tell me he had been wounded during the war. He broke his leg.'

Rathbone and Duffy share a look.

'We joked about that, because my husband had broken his badly too, which was why he couldn't join the army.' Billie looks to Duffy. 'He was a policeman throughout the war, you understand. Right through the Blitz, we never left London. At that time, the cities were the worst places to be.'

Rathbone claps his hands on his knees and battles to his feet.

'Thank you, Mrs Cassar. You've been very helpful.'

'I'm sorry I couldn't tell you more about Leon.'

'I understand it isn't easy, but I think your husband may still be of some help to us.'

Billie nods. 'It's just so hard making plans with him. I really don't like to disturb him when he's resting. What I can do, I can talk to him about it. I'll have to be careful telling him, though. They were quite close back then and I'm not sure how he'll take it.'

'Of course.'

'I used to be good at taking witness statements, so I'll hold a little interrogation, see if he remembers anything that might be of use.'

'Well, you let us know, Mrs Cassar. And we'll be in touch if we need anything.'

She opens the door, pausing with it just ajar. 'You said two bodies. Have you identified the second?'

'We have, but I'm afraid we couldn't—'

'Oh, no. Of course, what am I thinking? Just so horrible to think of Leon in an unmarked grave with another body.'

'I never said they were in a grave.'

'Oh, I'm sorry. When you said field, I assumed . . .'

'Again, apologies for intruding, Mrs Cassar. Give your husband our best wishes.'

'Oh, all right then. Yes, thank you.'

Billie holds the door open and watches them out to their car, waving them off.

Back in the bedroom, he is waiting for her, eyes alert.

'They found him?'

'Yes.'

'They won't get anything.'

'No.'

'And even if they did . . .'

'Yes.'

Easing herself into the armchair, she stretches her legs out. Noticing him notice, she tugs the hem of her skirt up a little.

'Still got those Joan Crawford legs.'

He chuckles.

From the bedside table she picks up a book, *The Heart in Exile*.

'Now, where were we?'

Behind her, bird's feet clack along the sill outside the window. Billie doesn't turn to see if the magpie is watching them again.

1963

3

Bed's empty beside him, duvet straightened and smoothed out. Voices and laughter float up the stairs. She's brushed down his uniform and it hangs on the outside of the wardrobe.

Washes and shaves. Trousers, shirt and shoes. Leaves the jacket, in case there's a marmalade mishap he never hears the end of. When he gets downstairs, he leaves it folded neatly on the seat of the hallway chair. Used to hang it on the back until it was explained to him about shoulders.

'Morning, Dad.'

Marcia fixes a half-slice of toast between her teeth, pulling a cardigan on as she barrels by in the hall, squeezing his arm as she passes.

'Hey, Marse.'

Says something through the toast and she's out of the house, door banging shut behind her.

'She'll be late,' he says, entering the kitchen.

Billie's buttering toast. 'She'll be fine.'

'Isn't she opening up?'

'It's Thursday.'

'People don't bank on Thursdays?'

'Thursdays she gets a lift from the Connolly boy, so no bus.'

Makes a mental note to look into that.

'He's so creepy,' Charlotte says, spooning up porridge at the table.

He kisses her on the back of the head.

'Da-ad.'

'You'd done your hair? I couldn't tell.'

'*Dad.*'

Billie slaps his arm as he grabs a buttered slice from her. Something passes between them and he tilts his head. She gives him a look like, later.

'You'll be late too,' he tells Charlotte.

'No college today, I'm in the salon. Not on till noon.'

'Oh.'

'But I'm meeting Siobhan in a bit.' She rinses her bowl out and leaves it to dry.

Peckish, he eyes up another slice and Billie sighs, handing it to him.

'Well, remember the rules,' he says. 'No hard drugs or getting pregnant.'

'Not before noon, anyway,' Charlotte says, dancing towards the front door.

Billie starts after her. 'Will you be back for dinner? Lottie, will you be back for—'

The door closes.

'—dinner?'

'Don't think she heard you.'

'She hasn't been hearing me a lot.'

He munches on his toast. 'Hmm.'

'Magpies are back.'

He spies two of them perched on the fence in the back garden. They walk up and down in front of the neighbour's pigeon loft, either sympathising with or taunting their incarcerated cousins.

In the glass of the dresser's hutch doors, she watches him and he catches her. Shaking something off, she gathers up her bag and a cardy from the back of a chair, which apparently is all right for her.

'Popping to the shops.'

'Bill.'

'Need bread. Few bits.'

Hooks his fingers in hers before she can go, and she freezes.

'What is it?' he says.

In her other hand the keys are jangling like she's warding off evil.

Pulls out the chair beside him. 'Sit. Talk to me.'

Her head bobs from side to side, weighing something up, and her fingers break free of his as she goes to the bottom of the dresser and opens the cupboard, pulling out a folded *Daily Mirror* buried beneath the junk of years.

'This is yesterday's,' he says as it slaps on the table.

'I wasn't going to show it to you.'

'You hid the paper?'

She shrugs.

'But I saw it at the station.'

'Page eighteen. Bottom right.'

Licks his fingers and begins to flick through. 'Best place to bury a story, I suppose.'

Opening it out on the page, he reads quietly. A perfunctory piece, probably taken from a local paper, with no real detail. A young woman was found at a quarry near the A40 in the Cotswolds. Yet to be identified, she was catatonic and had suffered a serious head wound. Local police are treating it as suspicious.

He reads it again, slower this time, but he hasn't missed anything crucial.

Billie slides into the seat beside him. 'It's been over fifteen years.'

'I know.'

'A lifetime. Literally, for the girls.'

'I know. I know.'

'Do you?'

'Bill, I'm not daft. But if there's even the slightest chance, then I can't—'

She grips his wrist. 'I *know*. That's why I'm showing you this.'

He reads through the story again.

'Do you think the same man did this?' she says.

'There's not much to go on here.'

'But?'

He shrugs.

'Be careful when you go. Nobody has come out of this very well.'

Takes her hand, brings it to his lips. 'I've done okay.'

She smiles, leans in and kisses him.

'I really do have to go to the shops.'

'Hold on a sec and I'll give you a lift.'

'That'd be nice.'

He gets up. 'Be right back. Left my jacket on the bed.'

In the hall, he scoops his coat off the chair and takes the stairs two at a time. Bottom of the wardrobe there's a beaten old leather satchel, a lockbox inside. He opens it, sifts through papers and pictures to find what he's looking for: an envelope containing two photographs.

A man and a teenage girl in the first, caught in a candid moment, laughing.

Leon Geats and Nell Martin.

He the closest to a father she ever had, and she the first real instruction in family he ever received.

The second picture is different.

Black and white. Poorly developed.

Eyes open but blank.

Jaw hanging slack.

Hair darkly matted, blood from the ear and down the face.

Maybe alive.

Maybe dead.

His partner. Seventeen years ago, and never seen since.

1935

4

The brothers had tried hard, by ferula and scripture, to teach Leon Geats how to be a good man, but ten years later there he was asleep on the stairs of his Soho building at well gone noon, gin bottle clamped between his knees.

WPC Billie Massey kicked his foot, to no response. She shook his shoulder, gently at first and then enough to kill a small child. Geats opened one eye and peered up at her.

She grinned. 'How you doing there, chum?'

'Oh, fine. Just fine.'

'Are you sure? Because you're sleeping on wooden steps two floors below your flat.'

'Helps with the back.' His other eye, gummed with sleep, had to be prised open. 'Tell me something.'

'Anything.'

'Do I have on trousers?'

'In fact, you do.'

'You see? Things can always be worse.'

Sitting up, a phlegmy cough rattled in his throat and the gin bottle was sent clattering down the stairs.

He'd spilt some.

He hoped he'd spilt some.

Trying to move provoked such pain, the only reasonable

explanation was his head was beginning to slide off his shoulders. He held it carefully in both hands so it wouldn't escape with the gin bottle.

'Time d'you say it was?'

'Didn't. Almost one.'

'And what could possibly be so important at such an ordinary hour?'

'Something you might want to look at.'

'Is it eggs? Is it sausages and eggs?'

'Dead woman. Round the corner on Archer Street.'

'Dead? Sounds like detective work. You want to fetch yourself a detective.'

'They're on their way, but she's a pro. We should take a look.'

Geats made another stab at getting up. 'Lead the way, then.'

She looked him up and down. 'You going like that?'

'You don't think . . .'

Billie shook her head.

He looked round. 'Up two, you say?'

She took his arm and led him up the stairs. 'Come on, soldier.'

Geats could remember stopping at the Lyric and having a drink that went down very nicely. He could remember the three or four more that also went down very nicely. What he couldn't remember was how he got the bottle of gin, or ended up on the stairs a couple of flights short of his rooms; but it wasn't so out of character that Billie had even tried feigning surprise at finding him there.

He fished around in his pockets for a key, without luck. Sighing, she produced one from the pouch she'd sewn into the lining of her hat.

'Knew giving you that would pay off one day.'

Leaving his front door ajar, she leaned against the wall outside.

'Archer Street?' he called from the bathroom, splashing water on his face.

'Flat above the Globe.'

'Do we know her?'

'I don't know the building, except for the clubs underneath.'

He padded into his bedroom and threw on the least offensive mufti he could find, then hurried down the stairs with her into the alley the building let out into.

One of those disreputable folds in the city, the Yard fingered its way thinly behind drab buildings in the Piccadilly corner of Soho in such a fashion that the sun never made its way more than halfway down its sooted walls. Mildewed bricks wore the constant shine of damp, the ground a mash of fag ends and flung food.

At any given moment it was home to two or three seedy clubs serving as hangouts for gangsters and fiends, patrons stumbling out in the wee hours and spicing the place with dashed glasses and the odd gutful of vomit.

Directly across from the mouth of the Yard was Archer Street, a narrow road lined with four- and five-storey buildings, its sun-starved pavements in a perpetual cool. It was always busy, as the London Orchestral Association called it home, and musicians cluttered the place with their cases, waiting outside to see if there was any work going, breaking out into impromptu sessions that echoed down the street.

The Windmill Club had its own street-level entrance, with a separate door for the Cairo Club in the basement and the upper floors, with the Globe on the first, and four flats across the two floors above that. Boyle, uniformed constable and giant of a man, stood sentry, nodding as Billie led Geats up to the third floor.

'Charwoman, old French widow, found her,' she said, pushing the door to the flat open. 'She unlocked the door when she arrived.'

There were no signs of the locks having been tampered with.

The door opened into a thin hallway running almost the length of the building. The ceilings were low, but not head-dippingly so. Four doors led off the hall: a bathroom, a kitchen, a sitting room, and the bedroom spanning the full width at the front. Another uniform, a young constable named Everett, stood in the hall and they nodded to him.

Geats wandered into the kitchen, finding a single plate on the small table, crusts of a sandwich abandoned on it and an empty glass fogged with milk standing beside.

He nudged the plate. 'Milk and sandwiches. Seem like a tart's breakfast to you?'

Billie shrugged. 'Milk lines the stomach.'

A coin meter for the electric protruded from the hallway wall. The sitting room was dark but neat. A teddy bear with a yellow checked scarf sat tucked in the corner of a settee with blankets hung over the back of it.

The bedroom was the largest room by far, and housed a big double bed. Thick curtains hung in the windows, but had been pulled together only loosely, shafts of light spilling in. Most of the floor was uncovered boards, a woollen rug either side of the bed and a mat at the foot that had creased over. That was the only sign anything had been disturbed, except for the dead woman draped on the bed.

Her legs hung out over the side, wide apart with feet flat on the floor. She wore a grey jumper and tweed skirt. A faux-silk stocking covered her right leg, the foot slipped into a blue glacé court shoe. Her left leg was bare; other shoe on the floor, matching stocking twisted round her neck and knotted beneath her ear. Other than that, her clothes were not disarranged in any improper way.

Billie stood over the body, head a-tilt to mirror the dead woman's. Her eyes heavy, partly closed, as if maybe just in muddy half-sleep.

'What d'you think your final thought is, when you know it's coming like that?'

'Don't reckon your final thought ever feels final,' he said. 'You always believe you'll get just one more.'

'You know her?'

Geats looked closer. 'Maybe. One of the French ones. Fifi?'

'Where's her patch?'

'Piccadilly Circus, if she's the one. Corner of Regent and Glass-house, and up Regent on the Quadrant sometimes.'

'A Café Royal and Oddenino's girl.'

'Bit of ooh-la-la goes a long way over there.'

Down the hallway a furore broke out with Constable Everett.

'Come on out of th—ow! You little . . .'

Geats ran to the bathroom door, finding Everett on his hands and knees groping around beneath the tub.

'You lose something, Constable?'

'No, I—Goddammit and blast it all to hell!'

He snatched his hand back, blood streaming down from a wound on the back.

'She bit me.'

'She?'

He pointed under the bath. Then, getting up, he slid past Geats into the hallway, clutching his hand to his chest.

Geats crouched down and squinted into the dark, two wild eyes peering out at him.

5

The tub's legs were high enough that where it wasn't flush to the wall, she had managed to fold herself into the gap below the curve. Young, twelve at most, though it was hard to tell through the fear.

'Hi.'

She hissed, turning it into a shriek when the constable's boots came back into view.

'Okay, okay, let's clear the room,' Geats said, pushing the other copper back out into the hallway and closing the door so he was alone with the girl. Sitting on the khazi, he crossed his legs and produced a packet of cigarettes. Fixing one between his lips, he lit it and inhaled, then bent over and offered the pack to the girl.

'Woodie?'

She said nothing.

'Probably not. They're not for little lungs. Especially little girl lungs.' He inhaled again deeply. 'Have to get all that burny goodness in there.'

A little voice said, 'I smoke.'

'Sure, sure. Bet you can fly too.'

'I do.' She scowled.

'Tell you what. I'll light one and leave it here for you. If you're quick, you can come out and get it. Have to be our secret, mind. If the others know I'm sharing my Woodbines, every bugger will be in here mooching one.'

He lit a second ciggy with his father's lighter, a strange brass number, and laid it on the side of the tub, burning end hanging over the edge. It didn't take long for a small hand to reach up from under and snag it, a small girl following it out and scampering into the corner beside the bath. Looked healthy enough, dash of blonde hair over a little snub of a nose and those piercing eyes.

She examined the cigarette closely before bringing it to her lips and sucking, immediately coughing wildly.

'Told you. Not for girls.'

Glowering at him, she realised that in her spluttering she'd knocked the lit end of the cigarette and put it out. She held it up.

'Come here.'

He lit her up and saw she'd noticed the lighter.

'Know what it's made of?'

She shook her head.

'See it has two bits that are fused together? They're bullets.'

She wrinkled her nose. 'No they're not.'

'Yep. Well, they're spent shells. When you fire a gun, this is the cartridge left behind when the bullet shoots out. These particular ones are .303 shells my father collected many years ago in a place called Ploegsteert Wood. You know where that is? No? It's in Belgium.'

'Where's that?'

'It's across the sea. Full of swamps, and Dutch and French who don't want to be Dutch or French. Which is wholly understandable, but still didn't prevent them being invaded by the Germans. Which is why my dad was there, to fight the Germans in a big to-do called the Great War. While he was there, he and lots of other soldiers dug holes in the ground called trenches, and they lived in them for months at a time and fought other men who lived in other holes.'

'Why?'

'Well, that's one of those things that deep down we all know why, but it's so stupid we struggle to put it into words. Anyways, they had cigarettes but the army couldn't provide them with lighters. So they made their own.'

'Did they have to shoot someone first to get the empty shells?'

'I guess they . . . you know, I didn't think to ask. Warning shots, maybe.'

'He give it you when he got back?'

Slowly, he shook his head. 'Friend of his did.'

They sat quietly for a while. A church quiet, a quiet after a storm. She took another smaller puff of the cigarette, stifling a cough, and mostly just held it after that, flicking ash into the tub occasionally. Geats tossed his fag end in and it fizzled out in the wet around the drain.

'That your supper out there, the sandwiches and milk?'

She nodded.

'You were here the whole time last night?'

Drawing her knees up before her, she rested her chin on them.

'You been in the bedroom?'

Nothing.

'Didn't leave your hiding spot, huh? Smart. Didn't see who was here, then?'

She closed her eyes.

'We don't have to talk about that. Been a while since those sandwiches, though. Think you could stand a little food?'

Maybe a slight nod.

'Yeah, I thought so, way you tried to gnaw on the hand of that bizzy. You know, I'm not very good with food. Usually I need someone to make it for me, otherwise I get it all wrong.'

'What kind of get it wrong?'

'Oh, it's a disaster. Shoe and pebble pies. Candle and bullhorn stew. And I don't recommend my newspaper and old hat sandwich.'

She looked at him flatly. 'I'm not a kid.'

'No, I suppose not. But look, I have a friend who helps me out. She knows to put all the right stuff in there. I don't know how I'd get through most days without her. I think you'll like her too. Do you want to meet her?'

A nod.

'Her name's Billie. What shall I tell her your name is?'

'I'm Nell,' she said, as if this was the most obvious thing in the world.

'Well, pleased to meet you, Nell. I'm Leon.'

'Leon.'

'It means lion.'

Her look told him she was sceptical of this.

'What say we go look for Billie and scare you up some scran?'

He held out a hand and she took it, letting him pull her to her feet. Opening the door a notch, he peeked out with one eye and found Billie on her own, so pushed it wide.

'Billie, this is Nell. Nell, meet Billie.'

Billie crouched down, such as her skirt allowed. 'Hello, Nell.'

' 'Lo.'

'It's very nice to meet you.'

Nell slid shyly behind Geats.

'We were just discussing the possibility of some breakfast,' he said.

'The owner of the Globe has opened his doors. There's a small kitchen down there, so I can rustle something up.'

'Can Dolores come?' Nell said.

Geats glanced at Billie. 'Dolores? Who's Dolores, sweetheart?'

'She's in the lounge.'

He edged back into the lounge, keeping the girl behind him. His eyes cut round the room, but he saw no one.

'That's her,' Nell said, plodding into the room and picking up the bear.

'Dolores,' Geats told Billie, pointing at the bear as they headed downstairs to the club.

The Globe was a two-bob dive that had been operating for a few months and wouldn't last much longer than a few more, the kind of place that had opened only because a similar club had failed there before and something had to fill the space. The rear was given over to the dance floor, with a large bar at the centre and tables at the front of the building. It was there that the owner wafted around dishing out tea and toast to grateful constables and a slightly confused old dear sitting alone at a table by a window overlooking Archer Street.

Nell ran over when she saw the woman, who was no bigger than the girl, and they embraced.

'Félicité Plaisant,' Billie told Geats.

'The charwoman?'

'She's worked for Mrs Martin for a couple of years. Quid a week, cooks and cleans.'

'Mrs Martin?'

'That's the victim, your Fifi. Josephine Martin.'

'She has a husband?'

'From what I can work out, she bought one when she came over after the war. Nobody has seen hide nor hair of him, and I don't think he's the girl's father.'

Somewhere a phone rang. Geats popped his head back out into the stairwell. 'That's in the flat.'

Bounding up the stairs, he found the phone in the living room. He lifted the handset carefully, saying nothing.

A woman spoke. 'Fee? That you? Please, Fee . . .'

'Who is this?'

'Oh, I thought . . . Josephine there?'

'She's not. Can I ask who this is?'

'Wait . . . Geats?'

That stalled him.

'Geats, it's me. Leah.'

'Stilts?'

'Yeah. Shit. So it is true.'

'What's true?'

'About Fee. That she's dead.'

'Who told you that?'

'Tart telegraph. Heard it from a girl who heard it from another girl that bizzies were all over her flat.'

'You knew her?'

'Yeah. She was my friend.'

He left that hanging there a moment. 'Stilts, can you come here? To Archer Street? Might be of some help.'

'She's been done, then? Weren't natural?'

'Detectives aren't here yet, but don't look natural to me. Where are you these days?'

'Just round the corner on Little Pulteney. I'll be there in a few.'

'Good. Okay. Stilts?'

'Yeah?'

'Sorry.'

'Yeah.'

Downstairs, the murder detectives had arrived, led by Inspector Proudfoot, whose waistline had far exceeded his sense of civic duty many years ago. His forehead shone from the effort of the single flight he had made it up, and with a thick hand he brushed back the thinning quill of damp hair cast vainly across his pate.

'Geats. What are the Dirties doing here? This is murder business.'

Officially the Clubs & Vice Unit, in Vine Street and throughout Soho the team were known as the Dirties.

'Dead woman worked the streets. Come to see if we knew her.'

'And?'

'By sight only. French, I think.'

'Did I hear the phone?'

'Another brass, calling to see if it was true.'

'You get their name?'

'She's on the way here now. Her, I know.'

Nell sat with Billie, munching contentedly on a sandwich, Dolores perched on a seat beside her, her own plate on the table. The girl appeared oblivious to what had happened, yet just half an hour earlier she'd been biting and spitting like something feral. He wondered what her mother's death would mean, whether she had any other people in her life.

Proudfoot had Geats show him the scene, giving it the most cursory of looks over.

'You find it like this?'

'Didn't move anything apart from the girl.'

'That the daughter?'

'According to the charwoman. Just turned eleven. Name of Nell.'

Proudfoot grunted. 'Mortis set in. Been dead a while. Curtains only half drawn, and the lamps aren't on. Could have been yesterday afternoon.'

'Charwoman was here until gone eleven last night.'

'Hmm. Someone turned the lights off, then. Might be worth a look for prints on the switches.'

Geats considered this and walked back into the hallway. He dropped a couple of shillings into the meter and lamps throughout the flat flickered back on.

'Leccy ran out.'

'Doubt we'd have found any prints but her own anyway,' Proudfoot said. Leaning over the body, he studied the stocking knotted at her throat.

'Reckon she might have snuffed herself, if I'm honest.'

'You're serious?' Geats laughed, then saw his face. 'Oh, you're serious.'

'You don't see it?'

'Sure. Slips off a stocking, ties it round her own neck tight enough to cut off the air, and then calmly lies back and just lets it happen. No struggle, no panic.'

'No struggle is the key, though. Look at the place. No fight took place here.'

'If she thought it was a genuine punter, she could have been taken by surprise. Pulls off the stocking, he takes it from her, playful like, pushes her back onto the bed. Astride her, maybe, so she can't move, then he's round her neck with it and that's that.'

Proudfoot looked about the dresser and the mantel.

'No cash. No jewellery. You find any?'

'Nope.'

'Robbery?'

Geats shrugged. 'Charwoman says she lives hand to mouth, and has some debts.'

'Probably worth asking around the pawnbrokers. She had any jewellery, she might have put it up the flue.' He looked at the body again. 'Still doesn't look like much of anything happened here. Wouldn't surprise me at all if she did this herself.'

Back down in the Globe, Proudfoot spoke with the charwoman, and then with the next-door neighbour, who said there was an American who visited Martin regularly.

A coroner's van arrived to collect the body about the same time as Leah Hines turned up, Geats fetching her from the street. Born and bred in Soho, she went by Dutch Leah sometimes and affected an accent to sell herself as a piece of strange in competition with the French and Belgian girls; or Connie, which was what her mother called her; or Stilts on account of her taste for precarious heels.

He steered her to a small table near the bar at the back of the Globe. Proudfoot was sitting with Billie and Nell, who was staring mournfully at the unwanted crusts of her sandwich as the inspector tried to question her.

Geats shook his head. 'Should just leave it to Bill. Do you know her well, the girl?'

With a scarlet nose and all the makings of a cold after a winter's night on the street, Leah pulled her coat tightly around herself, chin tucked in and talking low. 'Not well. Barely at all. I met Fee in the cells, got pulled in a few times. She rolled her own ciggies, dished them out if you needed one.'

'She have a ponce?'

'Nah. Well, not really, I don't think. There was a bloke came had a word with her once when we was in the pub. He weren't upset or nothing, but he looked serious. She went off with him, but I seen her the next day and she was fine.'

'This fella, was he French too, or a local?'

'Said he was French, but Fee ain't French. Wasn't.'

'She's not—isn't she the one goes by French Fifi?'

'Oh yeah, but she's French like I'm Dutch. Except she was actually Russian.'

'Josephine Martin was Russian?'

'Lived in France for a spell, then came to London. Saw how popular the French girls were and figured she had an accent and what bloke can tell the difference?'

'So, this Frenchie who came to the pub, was he really—'

'Who's this, Geats?'

Proudfoot had hauled himself out of his chair and across the club.

'Leah Hinds. The phone call earlier? She knew the deceased. Leah, Inspector Proudfoot.'

Geats glanced round Proudfoot and saw Billie comforting a sobbing Nell. 'That went well, then.'

'Girl doesn't know much. Couldn't tell us anything useful. I think she probably was in the flat when her mother died, maybe saw the body and went into shock.'

'Yeah, that must be it.'

'You two know each other?' Proudfoot waggled a stout finger between Geats and Leah.

Geats nodded. 'We run the same streets.'

'Probably best you clear off, then. So there can be no question about the witness's statement.'

Geats rolled his eyes where only Leah could see and excused himself. Nell had composed herself and stood by a window clutching Dolores, looking down on the musicians crowding in the street below.

A couple of flautists were duelling. He couldn't get a read on her; she seemed both too young and too old for her age. But maybe that was all children. Geats had no particular experience with them other than having got over being one.

'She has an uncle,' Billie said.

'Mother's brother?'

'Yeah. An Albert Mechanik. Leicester Square. Uniforms are going round there now.'

'Mechanik.'

'Odd name.'

'They're Russian.'

'Really? Thought you said French.'

'That was an act, apparently. Not unusual.'

'Mean anything, them being Russian?'

'Not to me.'

'He a suspect, the brother?'

'That's Proudfoot's domain, but to hear him tell it, she might have killed herself.'

'How the hell—'

'He's not going to fall over himself trying to solve this. If she was working and it was a punter they can put a name to, or if he can put a boyfriend or this brother in the frame, then maybe. Proudfoot's no man-hunter, though.'

Geats hung around as detectives came and went. Proudfoot muscled the investigation so Geats couldn't talk to any witnesses, couldn't open up any lines of inquiry that would cast too much shade on the suicide theory. When Leah realised Proudfoot was leaning towards suicide, she buttoned up and gave him nothing. None of the girls who worked the same streets as Martin would. Geats could already see how this one was going to get crumpled up and tossed.

6

In the Clubs & Vice office, Nell meticulously worked her way through a half-pound packet of Butter Bar biscuits. Her tea remained untouched on the small desk and Dolores kept vigil over her. She sat with her uneasy face half turned from Geats and Billie watching through the window from the main floor.

'Think she'll be all right?' Billie said.

Geats blew. 'She came into one type of sketchy situation, and now some maniac has made it that much harder.'

'You see yourself with kids?'

He laughed. 'I think we should all get out of here as quick as poss and leave no trace.'

Sergeant Pym came up from the desk looking for Geats.

'Got a fella, Albert Mechanik, downstairs.'

'Right. Let him up.' Geats turned to Billie. 'Sit him at a desk out here, and I'll tell the little one what's going on.'

He rapped shave-and-a-haircut on the office door and went in.

'Hey.'

Nell smiled.

He glanced at the empty biscuit packaging. 'We'll have to call you Crumbs, as that's all you leave.'

Gesturing to an empty chair, he waited for her to nod before sitting.

'Your uncle's here.'

'What's he want?'

'Well, he's come to take you home with him.'

'What, for ever?'

'I don't think anything is for ever, but for the time being, yes.'

'I can't.'

'Why's that?'

'Because I don't want to.'

'Not sure what choice we have. Is there any other family you could stay with?'

Nell shook her head. 'I want to go home.'

'You can't live there alone.'

'Yes I can. I can look after myself.'

'I don't doubt it. But how will you get money to buy food?'

'I'll steal it.'

'And what about paying the rent?'

'How much is it?'

'I don't know.'

'I'm sure I can work something out.'

'Is that so? Your uncle says he'll take care of you.'

'He lives in a small, stinky room.'

'Perhaps he can get a bigger, less stinky one. The main thing is there's someone looking out for you.'

'I could stay with you.'

'You could stay with . . . listen, I'm not sure that would be a suitable arrangement for either of us.'

'Why?'

'I work strange hours. Long hours. I can barely look after myself. If Billie wasn't around, probably I'd be in all sorts of trouble.'

'You can both look after me.'

'We look after all of Soho, Nell. And it's a task that keeps us very busy.'

Crossing her arms, she sat in silence.

'Billie packed you some clothes from the flat. And you've got Dolores here to keep you company.'

That earned him a glare.

'Look, he's out there now waiting for you.'

She refused to look.

'I'm sure he's excited about having you come stay with him.'

'I don't take up much room.'

'An undeniable advantage of smallness.'

'And I can do stuff, like clean up and cook.'

'Well, there you go.'

'I wouldn't get in your way. You'd barely know I was there, other than the good stuff.'

'Nell . . .'

'I don't need my own room. I can sleep on the floor.'

'You don't want to sleep on the floor. Come on.'

He picked up the small suitcase Billie had packed and handed Dolores to her, the girl trudging out of the office in front of him.

'Mr Mechanik,' he said. He handed the older man the case.

'Come along now, Eleanor,' Mechanik said. 'Say thank you to the officers.'

'Bye,' Nell said glumly.

'Thank you for all your help,' Mechanik added.

'If anything should occur to you – about your sister, I mean – if you could call the station, or drop in.'

'I will certainly do that, Sergeant.'

'You'll be busy with this one. She's . . . gone.' Geats looked about, but Nell was nowhere.

'Eleanor,' Mechanik called.

The girl appeared in the doorway to the Clubs & Vice office.

'Come along,' he said. 'Let's waste no more of these people's time.'

She allowed him to take her hand but made a show of being pulled along, out of the double doors and down the stairs.

'She'll be fine,' Geats said.

Wandering back into the office, he saw Dolores on the chair Nell had been sitting in. Grabbing her, he jogged after them, catching up in the thin alley leading out to Piccadilly.

'Nell. Nell! You forgot someone.'

Her face was inscrutable as she received the bear from him.

'Wouldn't want you without your friend.'

'No,' she said. 'Wouldn't want that.'

He watched them walk away, Dolores hanging from Nell's hand by one leg.

Back in the station, Billie was cleaning up the biscuit wrapping in the office.

'Caught them,' he said. 'All's well.'

'You know she left it here deliberately.'

'What do you mean?'

'She snuck back in here to hide the bear.'

'Why?'

Billie shrugged. 'Maybe so you'd have to go to Mechanik's place to bring it back? So she'd see you again?'

'I'm sure she didn't . . .'

He looked uselessly at the chair where he'd found the bear.

'No,' he reassured himself. 'She'll be just fine.'

7

Shortly after midnight, in the corner of the Yard that hid the entrance to his building, Geats interrupted ongoing negotiations between tail and punter. He roared, enough to chase them off. Most of the local brass knew by now that the Yard was off limits for street trade, but the presence of the back-door clubs meant the occasional re-establishment of terms was necessary.

Most Londoners bore no criminal malice, beyond the sort of benign liberties anyone would hope to get away with, yet all regarded the police as their hereditary enemy. Geats was an eternal outsider in his building, an alien creature to his neighbours, who stole furtive glances at him in the hallways when they passed, scurrying away without talking.

At the same time, they recognised that his presence kept the barbarians outside the gates, and as such maintained an unspoken accord to help him should the situation arise. As it often did with Clara Geats.

His mother lived on the first floor, two below Geats. The building had been the first place he had found upon transferring to C Division as a green constable, and when his mother's drinking had finally cost her the Whitechapel flat he'd grown up in, he found her rooms in his building. Where better than the Yard for a confabulating alcoholic?

Quietly he let himself into her flat. In the small kitchen opposite the door, he found a note from the old widow he dropped a few shillings to every week to look in on Clara, along with a plate of left-over stew. The kitchen was nestled between the two main rooms of the place: a floral-papered living room overlooking the Yard, and a bedroom that had once offered a view over the lower buildings behind it but now accepted paltry light from the small space left between the building and the new multistorey garages.

Clara was in the living room, sound asleep in her armchair, vanquished pint of gin on the table beside her. The fuss that moving her would entail was too much for the hour, so he draped a blanket over her and left her where she was.

Taking the leftovers, he went up to his own flat, distinguishable from his mother's only in that someone had added a bathroom, saving him from the common facilities each floor had, and he had painted the walls of his living room a billiard-baize green, which sometimes still astonished him. Sitting at the small table by the window looking over the Yard, he spooned up the cold stew by weak moonlight.

8

Proudfoot built a narrative of suicide.

A pawn ticket showed up in a more thorough search of the Archer Street flat, twenty-five quid's worth of rings and necklaces in hock. The same amount had been owed to a dressmaker, who swore blind she'd never received payment, but Proudfoot might have slipped and told her of Martin's death before he'd sorted out the business of the debt.

Statements from the charwoman and other prostitutes were shaped to paint a picture of a woman tired of the life and at her wits' end, little provocation required for her to do something drastic. That lasted until the inquest, when eminent pathologist Sir Bernard Spilsbury suggested that bruising on her upper legs and the side of her jaw was indicative of a struggle, and that he'd never in his life seen a woman tie a stocking round her throat and strangle herself to death.

The new working theory was that she knew whoever had come to the flat, or had let them enter as a potential client, and had come to some business accord before being taken by surprise having removed her stocking. The trail now cool, Proudfoot tried desperately to scare up suspects.

The post-mortem revealed she had a tattoo on her right thigh, 'To my Cesar For Ever Till I Die', a sentiment she'd been around eight years out with, as a Belgian gentleman by that name had been deported back to Ostend in 1927 and nobody had seen him since.

The charwoman said Josephine Mechanik had married an English waiter, Henry Martin, just after the war. Six months later, he had emigrated to America, suggesting he had been paid and his bride had been part of a white slavery route into London from the Continent. Whispers and rumours abounded of a Parisian pimp who she worked for, looking after new arrivals from France and pushing cocaine, but no names were forthcoming, and foreign pimps were ten a penny in Soho. A found cigarette stub generated some excitement for a few hours, until Geats sheepishly admitted it was his.

There was a man she saw sometimes, an American lush by the name of Jimmy Orr, but he was in a sanatorium at the time, trying a cure, which as far as alibis went was pretty tight.

Nell's uncle, Albert Mechanik, was a retired dance teacher who by all accounts lived off Martin's earnings, and had several almost-respectable citizens stand up for him to account for his whereabouts. And anyway, like he told the police, why would he kill the main source of his income?

A court made official his guardianship of Nell, and over the months, as Geats forgot about Josephine Martin, so too did he forget about her young daughter and her scarfed teddy bear, who for one fleeting after-noon had seemed to be his sole concern in the world.

Proudfoot made no arrests, and by Christmas Josephine Martin's file had gone to the bottom of the pile. Just another dead whore whose death would never be accounted for.

1936

9

Mark Cassar picked his way through the hedge at the side of the country lane, pinching his trousers at the thigh to lift them off the ground. The early frost had softened and the earth was starting to churn.

A well-dressed corpse, looked to be in his fifties but carried some pork so it was hard to tell, had been riddled with bullets and dumped. His shoes were clean and his trousers had ridden up his calves; someone had dragged him in behind the hedge by his ankles. He lay less than six feet from a chain-link fence that ran the perimeter of some kind of sanatorium.

'Sergeant Cassar here doesn't like getting his hems wet.'

Nutty Sharpe was crouched beside the dead man, whose hand he lifted with a length of snapped branch to get a better look at the signet ring bearing the initial M.

'Sergeant Cassar buys his shirts on Jermyn Street.'

Minter and Lander smirked. Sharpe's attack dogs, ears always pricked, fangs always bared.

'Can I roll him, Sir Bernard?'

The pathologist made a gesture that Cassar read as, how much more could the scene be messed up? Sharpe made his own gesture, Minter and Lander turning the corpse over.

'One, two, three, four, five holes in the chest, and one in the back makes six. What do you say, Sir Bernard? Someone emptied their piece into him?'

'I might be able to narrow the models down when I get the slugs out of him. Not until then.'

'Sir Bernard doesn't appreciate conjecture.'

'Nor does he appreciate morning calls summoning him to the provinces to look at gunshot victims. Is this even Met territory?'

Sharpe rose nimbly upright. 'No. St Albans have their own city force. But they're not used to things like this, are they, Constable?'

A wily old bizzy had been observing from a few yards, leaning against the fence. He grunted with disinterest. 'First clapped eyes on him, I knew he weren't nothing to do with us, Chief Inspector.'

'Oh?'

'On account of his fancy get-up. Rings on his fingers. Fact he'd been shot. Not a *provincial* kind of killing.'

'Certainly been moved,' Spilsbury said. 'And from the pattern of the bloodstains, I'd say he had been wrapped in something.'

Lander was sifting through the dead man's pockets. 'Nothing here, boss. No papers, can't see any labels on his togs.'

'Cassar?' Sharpe said. 'Thoughts? Observations?'

'No, nothing,' Cassar said, shaking his head. 'Except for that this is a hell of a place to dump a body.'

He poked his head back out through the hedge, glancing up and down the lane. Came back and looked the length of the wire fence.

'You kill the fella. You go to the effort of wrapping the body and driving it out here, drag it through a hedge so it's hidden from the road, and then leave it in full sight of the . . . what is this place?'

'Mental defectives colony,' the constable said.

'In full sight of this place,' Cassar said. 'Constable, if you were dumping a body, given your local knowledge, would you leave it here?'

'Oh no, sir. No, I'd carry on driving up the way, couple of miles north. Place called Nomansland Common. Thick woods and some old gravel pits over that way. You drop a body in the right spot there, it'd remain undiscovered for months, if it were ever found at all.'

Sharpe nodded. 'So, someone's tried to hide the body and made a pig's ear because this wasn't their patch. Not bad, Cassar. Not bad.'

'Shot in one place, driven to the outskirts of town and dumped?' Cassar said. 'All feels a bit Chicago. Feels like gangs.'

Sharpe nodded. 'We need to ID him, and we need to find the crime scene. If this is gang business, we need to know who he's tied up with and whether this is the end of something or just the start. We need to know if he's with the Italians, or the Greeks, or the Jews.'

He looked down at the man. 'He look Jewish? He could be Jewish.'

10

Nude, there was more of the dead man. The room was his.

Saddlebags of fat hung either side of his stomach, skin pale like the underbelly of a whale. He also looked older, mid sixties, perhaps. Spilsbury had opened him up and emptied him out, had removed the bullets and weighed the organs, and those vitals lay in dishes on a steel trolley.

Minter and Lander had remained at Scotland Yard, sending copies of the man's fingerprints to forces around the country and beyond. Cassar had felt the man's suit was French, and since he had a reputation for knowing such things, Sharpe had photostats sent to the anthropometric departments of French and Belgian forces. As a reward, Cassar had accompanied him to the morgue.

Spilsbury pointed to the dead man's face.

'Bruising on his cheek here, and scratches on his chest here, possibly from being grabbed.'

'The scars?' Sharpe indicated the deep seams running down one side of the face and neck.

'Old. Probably decades.'

'Knife?'

'Hard to say, but very possibly. Deep and long, consistent with a slashing motion. They would have bled terribly. Required many stitches.'

'So in all likelihood, he's been in the game most of his life.'

Spilsbury said nothing, never one to be drawn into narratives beyond the physical evidence.

'The shots?' Sharpe asked.

'The one in the back entered at a right-to-left angle but didn't hit anything vital. The other five entered the front, four of them at a left-to-right angle, and one almost straight on. There are also cuts on his left hand and forearm.'

'Defensive?' said Cassar.

'No. No, I don't think so. We found small shards of glass caught up in his clothing and hair. Looks like he crashed into something, put his arm through a pane of glass.'

'The bullet in the back was first?' Sharpe asked.

Spilsbury pursed his lips. 'Considering the evidence as a whole, I think it probably was. He was shot, and fell forward into whatever glass he put his arm through. Then he turned and took the other bullets to the front. The one that entered straight on did so because it passed through his hand on the way, altering its angle somewhat.'

'Which one killed him?' said Cassar.

'Well, that's an interesting question. His collarbone and shoulder were fractured. His left lung was pierced twice. But no other vital organs were hit. It's possible he survived for a while, though the lung would have given him a lot of trouble. Both the lung itself and the chest cavity around it filled with blood. It would have been difficult for him to breathe.'

Cassar pictured the man on his knees, fighting to heave air into his punctured lung. His chest tightening as blood poured into it, rising up and spluttering out of his mouth.

'You're saying he drowned in his own blood?'

'It's not dissimilar.'

'Anything else?' Sharpe asked.

'Well, you were right about one thing.'

Spilsbury pulled the sheet away from the man's waist and they all three stared at the dead penis.

Sharpe smiled. 'Yid.'

II

Without much to go on, the rest of the day was spent chasing other forces for possible identification. Whatever had happened, there didn't seem much chance the man was a civilian. His clothes and jewellery suggested money; his scars souvenirs of his lifestyle; he had six bullets in him; and moving a body and dumping it out of town probably required more than one person.

They made plans to comb the streets of Stepney and Whitechapel. Question the back-room dealers of Hatton Garden.

Stake out the nosh houses on Greville Street.

Minter and Lander exchanged wild theories.

'Shylock murdered on a collection.'

'Yid bookie who crossed the wrong racketeering firm.'

'Jeweller robbed for his smuggled wares.'

'Ponce killed by a rival for his tart.'

Cassar forced himself to laugh along with them.

'Poked his nose in where it wasn't wanted,' he offered, drawing out a long beak in front of his face. It wasn't the first time he'd found himself playing the fool to impress other idiots.

The first real break came the next morning, when Cassar answered a call from the Paris police. Someone had recognised the photograph of the corpse and had matched the fingerprints to their file: one Emil Allard, aka 'Red' Max Kassel.

Born in Riga in 1879, he was a ponce, a white slaver and drug trafficker, and had been deported from France in 1929 having been linked
to a cargo of white women sent to the Argentine. Since then, it was
suspected he had been working at the London end of a trafficking
operation bringing Continental women into England.

Russian pimp.

Frenchwomen.

London brothels.

That meant only one place – Soho.

Their connections were lacking, though. Jewish bookies and Italian
racketeers, these were the scenes the Flying Squad were plugged into.
Ponces ran small operations, a couple of girls at a time, working out of
sight in boarding rooms and alleys.

Being creatures of habit, they sought to corral the case within the
ambit of their own experience, and so spent two days questioning men
who knew nothing. Bookies, boosters, fences, hoodlums, even a few
pimps, but none who had heard of Red Max or Emil Allard.

Eventually it was Sharpe who turned up a name, after returning
from a meeting with an old snout, gin on his breath.

'Jack Isow.' He slapped his hand on his desk to emphasise the point.
'We all know of him. Club owner, runs a churning list of dives around
Soho, most of them bottle parties where negro bands play. He has
dancers mingling with the guests, keeping the gents happy, and some
of these girls are of the Continental variety. So where does he get them
from? Think we should pay a visit to one of Mr Isow's establishments
and see what we can see.'

'We bringing in C Division?' Minter asked. 'They've got a Clubs &
Vice Unit, might know Isow.'

Sharpe shook his head. 'Might know him too well. Vine Street has
always been a cesspit, copping from local clubs and businesses to turn
a blind eye. We'll raid first, get a look-see on what Isow's all about. If
he's running foreign tail off his dance floors, I want it locked down in
a way his C Division mates can't cover for.'

'Where's this gen coming from?' Cassar asked.

'Bern Locke,' said Sharpe. 'Known him donkey's.'

So had Cassar. He knew Locke to be a horse-chanter out at Chelmsford before the course closed, filing down teeth and painting up brows on old nags to boost their price, but knew better than to ask Sharpe how exactly that qualified him to grass on Soho underground bars.

'Two a.m., I want to be knocking on Isow's door. Names and numbers for all the punters. These places attract Bloomsbury types roughing it for a taste of the West Indian scene. Might get lucky and find someone who'll spill if we agree not to tell Daddy.'

Cassar nipped home to change into a fresh suit. He had a hot date at a club.

12

Two a.m.

Soho was just getting started, but Geats had a long head start. Slouched by gin and sitting in his trousers and long johns, anyone's guess where his shirt had got to, he stewed at a corner table watching the hoopla.

Three basements knocked through, Chez Renée's was a gaudy blend of art deco and artificial palm trees liberated from a previously closed club. Mirrors lined the walls to create the illusion of space, but were unsilvering fast, casting cataracted reflections.

Arranged with the usual bottle party rules, musicians drank for free and the place was crawling with chancers sporting dented bones. The wooden floor was unsprung and unpolished, but still they danced.

Women with women.

Men with men.

White with black.

Even the Marxists sidled up to the dancing girls the club employed. A haven for those most comfortable on the margins.

Geats was alone, as he was every night, as if seclusion was a race memory. Nothing escaped his notice.

The two Italians at the bar, Sabini gang foot soldiers who took orders from Babe Mancini and Tommy Mack, hips cocked as if the blades in their pockets were magnetised by the undulating dancers, itching to start a fracas.

The well-heeled gentleman tourist hiding that he favoured one leg, and the pair of ladies with him eyeing up the black musicians, sisters from the aristocratic nose they shared.

The corner-slinker, gussied up in ill-fitting frippery, on the arm of a fresh-faced toothpick in his father's suit. Geats's vagrant gaze settled on them, a glint of recognition but no more than that, no details seeping out of his mind.

Because of the way one thing led to another in his way of thinking, by drinking alone in a dark corner of a busy underground club Geats believed he was giving nothing away about himself. In fact, everyone in Chez Renée's, from the regulars and dancing girls to the trombonists and doormen, knew all there was to know about him precisely *because* he was drinking alone in a dark corner and did so every night he was there.

At dark corner tables he felt like himself, but dark corner tables were also part of his work, and he'd never established quite where the line was. Police or partier, he longed to be one thing or the other, for whatever it was he seemed to be in the eyes of others, he surely was not in his own midnight reveries.

'Sergeant.'

A fresh gin, just what he needed at this point, landed in front of him and the hostess sat down. Simone Calcavecchia, dark eyes and olive skin, Mediterranean by way of the Newtown slums in Cardiff. There was no Renée at Chez Renée's; Simone ran the place for Jack Isow, an independently minded operator who owned several dives around Soho and paid protection to neither crook nor copper, which resulted in not infrequent riots and raids at his establishments.

Geats raised the glass to her. Chatting over the band was futile, so they sat and watched. He recognised some of the players from the scene: Jiver Hutchinson on trumpet; Joe Deniz on guitar; Pops Clare on the double. The trombonist was a suburban white boy in boot polish black-up that shone in what light there was and sweated down his neck in grimy streaks.

The leader wasn't playing. He was tall and lithe, his fluid gyrations mesmerising, hips snapping back and forth as nimbly as his glinting taps.

Simone tilted in close, her words warm on Geats's ear.

'That's Snakehips, baby, and he has what it takes.'

He sure did. A bit-part tinkler on the keys, he answered his real calling on his feet, the band maintaining a precarious clip behind his viperous moves. Dancing broke out between the genteel sisters, who tweaked and paddled with spastic abandon in front of the small stage, and others joined them.

Geats envied their losing themselves in the music, present but not present, allowing the rhythm to break over their heads at something like the pitch of madness. He could never let himself go like that. Closing his eyes, he yearned to embrace the moment unconsciously, but even the inside of his eyelids felt watched.

The number finished and the band took a break, allowing amateurs to come up and jam irreverently, dampening the dance floor's enthusiasm somewhat. Geats opened his eyes and remembered where he knew the gussied-up young woman and her toothpick escort from — constables from a different division, out Shadwell way. Another man had joined them, and Geats recognised him as Inspector Lander, a member of Nutty Sharpe's Ogpu.

Downing his drink, he nudged Simone with his elbow.

'My sense of things is you're about to be raided.'

She followed his eyes to the little confab in the corner between the young woman and the Flying Squad inspector, which had reached some accord. Together with the toothpick, they began making their way to the stairs leading up to the street door.

Unsure whether he'd been noticed or not, Geats folded his coat over his arm, gave up any hope of locating his shirt. 'Nutty Sharpe's boys. Nothing to do with my lot at Clubs & Vice.'

Simone shouted over the music. 'What does Sharpe want with me?'

Geats shrugged. He pointed at another door, near the stage. 'Get to the rear yard that way?'

She nodded.

'You coming?'

She shook her head. 'Take the band, though. Don't want them getting nicked. Need them back here tomorrow, or whenever we reopen.'

Geats held the door open and the band slipped through, taking their instruments with them. Simone was engaged in negotiations with the drummer, offering assurances about the kit in his absence. She also ushered the nasally aristocratic sisters and their spavined friend past Geats.

'Take them too. Daughters from the sort of family who wouldn't appreciate the scandal.'

Through the door was a cloakroom and a small office, and at the end of the corridor a staircase leading up to the ground floor of a building three doors down from the club's main Lisle Street entrance.

'Not that way,' Geats said, steering the others away from trying the front door. 'Flying Squad will be all over the street.'

A rear door led out into a thin, irregular-shaped yard carved out between the rears of buildings on Lisle and Gerrard. It existed to offer the rumour of sunlight to back rooms and was partitioned up with flimsy wooden fences, which Geats flicked aside like matchsticks, moving deeper into the internal warren of the block.

Half a dozen buildings down, he cleared away some panels of corrugated iron to reveal a manhole cover.

'I shall not go down into the sewers,' one sister said.

Geats lifted the cover. 'You're not. It's just made to look that way.'

They were behind what had once been the most notorious illegal dive in all of London, but many years before that, the whole area had been the site of a military ground, and where they stood had been the main gate. Tunnels had been dug out underneath, snaking this way and that, some of which existed still between the sewers and train lines; including one that had led away from the gatehouse.

Kate Meyrick, the late and legendary owner of the 43 Club, had shored up the tunnel and used it both to bring in booze and allow escape to her celebrity clientele, who patronised her place as it was a reliable source of superior cocaine.

Geats dropped down the hole to the earthy chamber beneath, beckoning the others after him. Directing them along a tunnel they had to stoop to pass through, he waited until they were all on their way before climbing up the rude wooden ladder, dragging over the corrugated iron and replacing the manhole cover.

'Pitch black down here,' one of the band complained.

'Here.' Geats passed his flashlight forward and picked out its glimmers up ahead.

'How far?' said someone.

Geats sighed. 'Till you reach the end. About five hundred yards.'

Webs long forgotten by their spiders festooned the passage and caught up in their hair, and the sisters shrieked at the thought of things crawling down their dresses. Geats cast looks back over his shoulder, expecting flashlight beams to slice the blackness, but none did.

At the end of the tunnel, the others waited for him to come to the fore. A rickety ladder had been nailed together from off-cuts, and he tested each rung before resting his weight on it. There were only half a dozen steps, at the top of which he pushed open an angled iron hatch, like a coal hole, leading out into a narrow alley.

He offered a hand, lifting the ladies out and helping their friend, leaving the band to their own devices.

'Where we at?' Snakehips said.

'That's Great Newport Street,' Geats said, pointing out of the open end of the alley. 'Where you headed?'

The band murmured between themselves.

'The Old Florida in Mayfair,' Snakehips said. 'See if we can't catch ourselves a late jam.'

Geats nodded the other way. 'Follow the alley up thataways. You can get through between the tenements and the back of the horse mart. There's a passageway out onto Charing Cross Road. I'm you, I'm going up to Shaftesbury Avenue before heading west, make sure I miss those Flying Squad boys.'

The band sloped off and Geats had the moneyed trio wait in the shadows as he edged out into the street looking for police activity. They were only round the corner from the club, and he could see the blue lights splashing across the terracotta façade of the Hippodrome. He flagged down a High Lot in the street and ushered the party inside, instructing the driver to take them to Smith Square, where the elder sister's fiancé lived. He apparently was an agent of some influence, as promises of Geats's swift advancement through the ranks were made, though he couldn't blame them for not having properly assessed his nature.

13

A couple of weeks after Kate Meyrick was sentenced to fifteen months' hard labour – having bribed a Vine Street sergeant to the tune of a hundred quid a week for the best part of a decade for turning a blind eye to her illegal club activities – Geats capped his first week on patrol with his rookie night-time raid. It was Valentine's Day 1929, and the world was still six months away from sliding into the Great Depression.

The 43 remained open in Meyrick's absence, but was now the number one target for a Vine Street station trying to prove the whole barrel wasn't filled with rotten apples. Geats's excitement for the task was muted somewhat by being posted in the surrounding streets, away from the club itself, and told to watch out for stray runners.

The then Inspector Charlie Garland, who had quickly taken the fresh-faced Geats under his wing, noticed his disappointment and steered him towards the mouth of the alley on Great Newport Street. With a wink he told him to stand there and wait for something to happen, telling him to decide for himself how he'd want to police the situation.

Not knowing what he meant, Geats stood nervously at the street end of the skinny alley for almost an hour, stamping his feet and clapping his gloved hands against the cold. Eventually there was some noise, and peering into the darkness of the alley, he spotted movement in a small yard at the other end. Venturing down cautiously, he found a sad-eyed, husky-voiced Tallulah Bankhead, the most famous actress of her day on London's many stages, clambering out of the trapdoor having fled the 43 with fistfuls of cocaine.

A delinquent of prodigious dimensions, her misbehaviours were the stuff of legend: she was a high priestess of voodoo, practising hierogamous rituals; she smuggled herself into Eton in a laundry bag for orgies with wet-eared blue-bloods and future prime ministers; her tax arrears personally outraged the Chancellor of the Exchequer.

And she was an American to boot.

'Dah-ling, do give me a hand. I'm absolutely filthy.'

Lifting her out of the tunnel, Geats brushed off her gown, spangled with muck and spider webs.

'Yes, oh look, there's a spot there. How marvellous of you.'

A cock of a silk-sheened hip, a flash of vented thigh, and Geats's loyalty to His Majesty was no longer just in doubt, it had evaporated entirely. She incited rebellion within his heart and he worshipped her for it.

'Now, dah-ling, I'm positive I left my automobile around here someplace, but these streets all look the same to me. It's a monstrosity of a thing. Can barely drive myself in it.'

Leaving her in the lee of the alley, cloaked in his tunic, Geats roamed the streets as far as Covent Garden before locating the green-with-cream Bentley, driving it back to collect her. It took very little imploring on her part for him to chauffeur her to her Mayfair house on a crooked little street off Berkeley Square, during which drive she had two cigarettes on the go.

She rewarded him with a kiss, running her tongue along his teeth and nibbling his bottom lip, and a knickerless cartwheel in full view of the street. He floated the mile back to Gerrard Street, where less fortunate patrons of the club were still being mopped up.

The next day, Geats snagged her telephone number (Grosvenor 1658) from an unpurged directory, but venerated her too much to call. Years later, he seethed with jealous rage watching her on the big screen canoodling with Gary Cooper.

14

After seeing the sisters off in the taxi, Geats sauntered across the street back towards the club. Flying Squad had gathered in a narrow court between the Hippodrome and Daly's Theatre, just up the way from the door to Chez Renée's, and were conspicuously interviewing punters dragged out of the club. He watched for a good spell, but decided discretion was the better part of valour.

The night air was cutting and London was as still as it ever got, which wasn't very. Little Newport Street was the southern end of a jinking thoroughfare running up to Shaftesbury Avenue, and he headed that way. Barrels were being rolled into the White Bear public house, run by Frankie Frost, who had spots everywhere from Fleet Street to Holland Park, from Battersea to Highbury, all under the skirts of Darby Sabini's protection racket.

Up the street, outside the dairy supplies store, he saw the familiar shambling figure of a local destitute, Benny Brownlow, draped in rag and raiment. So large God must have been paying attention that day, he was thick-faced with cropped hair, cap clutched in his fist as he stared up at the flats above the store.

'What do, Benny?'

'Sergeant.'

'Everything all right?'

'I seen the Russian. He was a cheroot.'

The owner of the dairy store came out with a broom, and Geats noticed for the first time the broken glass on the pavement.

'Some bother?'

'Morning, Sergeant. Just a broken window on the second floor. It were broke the other night, but a further piece must have come loose since yesterday.'

Geats looked up. Several lights in a second-floor casement were clearly smashed, lead fingers sticking out crookedly.

'And it was broken the other day?'

'Maybe four nights ago? I opened up and there was glass outside, so I swept it away. I figured it was a bird. There was a little blood.'

Geats shook his head, pointing up at the twisted cames. 'Inside out.'

'None of my business, I'm sure.'

'You know them?'

'Only to see. They've never come in the store. Foreign. French, I'd say.'

'They?'

'A woman, mostly. She has a fella who's there a fair bit. And a maid. There are always comings and goings, though.'

The shop was number 35, a door marked 36 leading to the floors above. Geats found it unlocked and went for a dekko. Couple of locked doors on the first floor, along with a small bathroom that smelled like the river at low tide. Bare brick walls in the stairwell, steps worn down like the Scala Sancta. Marks on the walls, stains perhaps, but the light was low and he reminded himself which neighbourhood he was in.

Two more doors on the second, both locked. He knocked and waited. Nothing. He pressed his ear to the wood and jiggled the knobs, but it was late for this sort of off-duty assiduity. What was a broken window on a Soho night?

He trotted back down and shrugged at the shopkeeper.

'I'm dog tired.'

The man nodded knowingly. 'A husband throws something at his wife. Being how they are, she ducks, and here we are.'

'I'll pass by tomorrow. See if anyone's in.'

Benny chuckled to himself. 'The Russian was rolling. Rolled like a cheroot.'

The shopkeeper swept around Benny's split boots, dancing him into the road. 'You're an awful pest, Benny. Clear off now and leave the sergeant to his business. Come back at noon and I'll see to some dinner for you.'

Benny moved on, but Geats caught his elbow and pressed some change into his hand. 'Get you through a few days, Ben.'

Benny held his cap aloft before putting it on and lumbering off. 'You indulge him.'

'You know who that is?'

'Sure. Everybody knows Benny.'

'No. Do you know who he is?'

The shopkeeper's face tired quickly.

'He was merchant navy,' Geats told him. 'Good boxer. Before the war, he scrapped with Black Jack Johnson in his last fight before he took the belt.'

'I've heard the stories. We've all heard—'

'No story. Fought him in Plymouth. Was in over his head, took a pasting in the end, but he was there. What does that tell you?'

The shopkeeper considered this. 'He took one too many to the head, you suppose?'

'Nah. His ship ran into a spot of bother in the war. Spent a few hairy days on deck dodging U-boat attacks, and then a few hairier days on a piece of wreckage after they failed to dodge a U-boat attack. Imagine it, three days and nights floating out there before he was found. Never been quite the same since.'

The shopkeeper whistled as he headed back into his store. 'I thought he was just some mad tramp.'

Geats started off for home again. Even if it were possible for someone to be no more than a mad tramp, it'd take the living of a life to become such a thing.

15

Untied laces wet and frayed, shirt tails hanging loose, Geats swayed into the station on Vine Street. A dingy dead-end stub, what remained of an already unremarkable street mostly annexed by the construction of a grander one.

At the duty desk, Sergeant Pym jutted his chin towards the door to the stairs.

'First floor, Leon. Everyone is gathering there.'

'Oh aye? What for?'

'His Lordship Nutty Sharpe is here. Some big to-do about a body found out in the sticks.'

Sharpe and his Flying Squad had rooted out serious corruption in C Division seven years ago, just before Geats got there. The previous superintendent was farmed out to the wilds of Y Division, policing Enfield and Potters Bar, and the testimony of a constable secured eighteen months' hard labour for the station sergeant after he was thrown off the force. Sharpe had maintained an odd sense of propriety over Vine Street ever since.

Big to-dos were something Geats never wanted to attend, but also never wanted to be left out of. The first floor was given over to C Division's detectives and the Dirties. Wainscot partitions walled off small offices around the extremities, with desks scattered about the open space in between. Uniforms and detectives, almost every member of the division, were gathered around these looking up at a man who stood on a chair holding aloft a photograph as if he was Moses with the tablets.

Chief Inspector Nutty Sharpe, head of the Flying Squad.

'This is the recently departed Emil Allard. Went locally by Max Kassel, or Red Max. Known to the Paris police as a white slaver, trafficking women into Britain from all across the Continent. His body was found Friday morning in a ditch in St Albans, but we have reason to believe he was gunned down the night before in Soho and later moved.'

Geats sidled along a row of office doors at the perimeter of things and found a spot next to Billie Massey. Hair back in a tight bun, a scowl of concentration on her face, she was violent with the taking of notes.

'They promote you to secretary, Bill, old chap?'

Without looking at him, she said, 'Did you sleep in a puddle again?'

Point.

Sharpe pushed on. 'Today we're going to shake a few trees, see what falls out. We need to find the murder scene. We need to know who this Red Max operated with in London. He was a ponce; what women worked for him? Did he have contacts in the clubs? According to the French, he was actually a Russian Jew. The rackets are mostly Italian in the West End, and there's been mounting aggro between them and the Yiddish operators, so who were his associates? We want to look at Jack Isow.'

Geats audibly snorted.

At the front of the crowd, Inspector Lander, looking brisk for one wearing the same clothes he had raided Chez Renée's in just hours earlier, turned to seek out the guilty party. Geats felt his glare wash over him, and wondered momentarily whether Lander had spotted him in the club.

'This has all the hallmarks of a gangland slaying,' Sharpe said. 'The victim was shot multiple times at close range and was then dumped at

the edge of the city. This might have been a warning, either from competing ponces, or by a protection racket.'

Geats peered over at Billie's notepad, flicking back a couple of
pages. 'Has he been like this from the off?'

She slapped his hand. 'Get away. I'll miss something.'

'Nothing of value, if this rambling is anything to go by. Jack Isow,
honestly.'

'He's telling people where their grid searches are.'

'Look, they're pinning a list up on the wall, don't get hysterical.'

The meeting broke up and Sharpe's retinue gravitated around him:
Inspectors Lander and Minter, and Sergeant Mark Cassar. He cut a
fancy figure now in his Savile Row suits, but he had walked the streets
of C Division in a tunic with Geats for years before Sharpe snapped
him up. Lander was in Sharpe's ear, the chief inspector looking Geats's
way.

'Bill, you should push off now, there's a good girl.'

Reading the coming turbulence, she did as he suggested. Geats
decided to make a show of getting away, a corridor being all the better
for a dressing-down than the centre of the office. Sharpe buttonholed
him at the door to the stairwell.

'Something on your mind, Sergeant?'

'No, sir.'

'Really? Seemed as if you had thoughts you'd like to share on who
might be responsible for this shooting.'

'Thoughts on who's not responsible, maybe. You're miles off if you
think Jack Isow is gunning people down.'

'That so? Expert on Isow's operations, are you?'

'His dives are on my patch. He's a villain in name only. Runs bottle
parties and underground jazz clubs. Worst that goes on is a bit of
unlicensed boozing and maybe some fun times in the cloakrooms
with the dancing girls. He's a gangster without a gang. Only muscle he
has is on the doors to toss out drunks.'

Sharpe leaned in. 'There are billiards halls and gaming rooms throughout Soho, some run by Jack Isow. These places are fronts, and the kinds of operations run by Kassel need that sort of legitimisation. Those of you on the streets can't have helped but notice what is happening out there, the trouble between Italians and Jews. The Blackshirt marches aren't helping any. This could well be an escalation of that, targeting people working with the Yiddish gangs.'

The agitations of the populist Oswald Mosley were stirring up trouble between his Blackshirt followers and anti-fascist protesters, that was true, but Geats couldn't imagine anyone giving less of a shit about that than an operator like Isow.

'The only thing Jewish about Jack Isow is the gefilte fish he serves at the Shim Sham.'

'The lip on you. What else passes through them? You cooing in the ear of Isow? Free drinks at his clubs, maybe a girl for your trouble. Lander saw you last night.'

'Bang-up job I did of letting him know about the raids.'

'He saw you chasing the coons out the other door, couple of tarts, too.'

'Wasn't me.'

Lander grabbed his arm. 'Oh, it was you, Geats.'

'I saw the tight net you cast over the street. What would it say about your Flying Squad lads if someone had got through all that unseen? And even if I had been there, it would have been my own time. Even a copper has the right to enjoy himself off duty.'

'Good coppers are never off duty,' Sharpe said. 'I know all about this station, cosying up to villains. I cleared the bad apple out once, I'll do it again.'

A sly smile crossed Geats's lips. 'No doubt there was lots of positive intel to be had last night. Concrete links between Isow and this Kassel. Eyewitnesses, so forth.'

'Wind your neck in, Sergeant. Or we'll do it for you.'

'Sir.'

Lander shoved Geats aside, he and Minter following Sharpe down the stairs. Cassar lingered.

'Money Mark Cassar. Long time no. Still looking dapper.'

'And you're still paddling round in the Soho gutters, Geats. Still not sure if you're one of us or one of them.'

'Oh, I'm not one of you. Don't possess the intestinal fortitude to swallow that much pride.'

'How *did* you get away from the club? Reckon I could talk the chief inspector around. Might see his way to forgiving transgressions if you worked with us, gave us the gen.'

'I'll give you this for free – your boss is off his rocker if he thinks Isow was tight with this Kassel. Some small-time ponce ring with French tarts? That's not Jack Isow's scene. Were you on Lisle Street last night? Then you saw the club, and that's his bottom-rung dive. Wall-to-wall tail, and he don't need some pimp to supply it. What would his angle be with a French gang? You want to root around in Kassel's laundry, you'll be wanting to talk to the French ladies, or them what pretend to be that way.'

'Is Nutty right? You taking garnish from Isow?'

'I can police the clubs because I know the clubs, and the clubs know me. You ever did a real day's coppering in your life, you'd know Isow has a reputation. He don't pony up to no one. He's been telling Darby Sabini where to go for years, and you think he's slipping me the envelope? Leave it out. Christ almighty.'

Cassar bumped him with his shoulder making to leave, but Geats caught his wrist.

'Tell me one thing, friend of mine. You seen the body, this Kassel? He have cuts on him? Hands or his head? Not a knife, but glass?'

Cassar's expression said it all.

'Yeah, thought so. But you keep after Jack Isow. Don't mind me.'

16

The partitioned office that had been assigned to the erstwhile commanding officer of the Clubs & Vice Unit – now retired to the south-coast resort town of Lark – was never somewhere Geats had much use for. He was usually out in the hustle and bustle of Soho, holding strategy meetings with Billie in cafés or milk bars whenever he could. At Vine Street, he preferred the liveliness of the open bullpen, where he and Billie, as the only two surviving members of the unit, had commandeered a desk in one corner.

However, the handwritten sign – *Flying Squad* – hanging from the office door did not escape his attention, and he suddenly felt a nostalgic longing for his old boss's surroundings.

The door was ajar, the room invitingly empty, and he slipped inside for a quick nosy. The coroner's report on Red Max Kassel was on the desk, lying there as if it wanted to be read, and who was he to deny it?

Evidence from the scene where the body was found – fibres caught up in the victim's trousers – suggested it had been wrapped in something and then dragged to the ditch. No wallet or identifying documents. Photostat of the fingerprints had been sent to Paris, where they identified him from their files. Allard had been deported from France on the back of his involvement trafficking white women to the Argentine. He had known connections to organised crime in Montreal and London's West End.

Sitting at the desk, Geats pored over the details of the gunshot wounds, the coroner's remarks about cuts to the victim's hands and forearm, fragments of glass gathered from his clothing and hair, and thought of the house on Little Newport Street. So engrossed was he that he failed to notice Sharpe come in with Lander and Minter, the three of them standing over the desk before he realised.

He met Sharpe's stare. 'I, uh, suppose you're wondering why I called this meeting.'

Sharpe squinted. 'What do you think you're doing, Geats?'

'This is the Clubs & Vice office.'

'It's Flying Squad's office now. Like the sign on the door says.'

'Must have missed that. Door was open, you see.'

'Door was open because until five seconds ago I didn't really have any reason to distrust anyone at this station.'

Geats stood up. 'Anyways, now you're here, there's something—'

'You spying on your own side?'

'I—no. And wouldn't you be the other side, if I *was* spying?'

'Reporting back to Jack Isow. Letting him know what's what.'

'Christ, here we go again.'

Sharpe prodded him in the chest with a wrought-iron finger. 'You forget yourself, Sergeant. I am a chief inspector, and you will address me as such. Is that understood?'

'What's going on here?'

All four of them turned to see Superintendent Dalton in the doorway.

'You causing bother again, Geats?'

'The day does end in a y, sir.'

'We found your sergeant here sneaking into the room to steal intelligence,' Sharpe said.

'That's right, sir. I snuck through the wide-open door and sat at my own desk and did larcen the coroner's report with my own eyes.'

Dalton closed the door behind him. 'We've spoken about your attempts at humour before, Sergeant. Now, what's all this about?'

'Your man here strongly disagrees with my line of inquiry. Says it can't possibly be Jack Isow who's party to the trafficking and pandering of Continental women on his patch.'

'That a fact, Geats?'

'It's an opinion, sir.'

Sharpe shook his head. 'I don't know how things are done around here, but I prefer evidence to opinions.'

'Isow being Jewish isn't evidence of anything,' Geats spat.

Sharpe pointed at him. 'I have reason to suspect a relationship between Sergeant Geats and this Jack Isow that is—'

'I'll stop you there before you make wild accusations you have no way of backing up, Chief Inspector,' Dalton said, raising his hand. 'Geats has worked Soho for years, and more recently has been attached to Clubs & Vice. His job takes him to the less salubrious and more disreputable corners of our division, but he has proved a great font of reliable information from otherwise unattainable sources, and has never given us cause to believe that conduit runs in both directions.'

The kind of unimaginative copper who excelled at the organisational stuff that door-kickers loathed, Dalton nevertheless knew which side his bread was buttered and was therefore seldom shy when it came to demonstrating his station's newly rediscovered scruples by extending every courtesy to a force attack dog like Sharpe.

However, that it was Sharpe who had investigated and rooted out the prior corruption in his station, and now felt that gave him privileges in Vine Street, did not sit well with Dalton. Though he'd shrunk from the streets his whole career, he was a canny, gimlet-eyed operator in the company of beaks and top brass, and ran his nick like a fiefdom. Everyone kissed the ring, even Nutty Sharpe.

'Indeed, Chief Inspector, the reason I wanted to speak with you was to offer you Sergeant Geats's expertise for as long as you are here.'

'Superintendent, I have my own—'

'It'll work better this way, with Geats as liaison between you and me. Things'll run smoother. And I expect his knowledge of local flora and fauna will prove an asset to you.'

'I don't think this is ne—'

'That'll be all, Chief Inspector.'

Dalton left abruptly, the door shutting behind him in a manner leaving nobody in any doubt that the matter was closed. Sharpe eyed Geats like horseshit he'd walked into his own mother's house; grief he'd brought upon himself.

Stalking out of the office disgustedly, he roped Cassar from somewhere unseen and, arm round his shoulders, spoke with him in a simmering huddle. They returned together, Geats unable to interpret anything from their expressions.

'Cassar here tells me you worked together before.'

Geats nodded. 'Soho was our patch when we were on the beat.'

'Makes sense to pair you up again, then. Cassar is the senior partner, so he gives the nod and you do exactly as you're told. The police in Paris reckon Kassel came to the West End, and we can all agree Soho is a hotbed of foreign pimps and their wares. Makes sense we search the area for the scene of the crime, listen out for any chirping birds. That is, unless you have a dissenting opinion on the matter?'

Geats knew a rhetorical question when he heard one.

17

Cassar maintained a silence as furious as his pace as they strode east through Leicester Square.

Geats upped his steps to get level. 'Where we going? I got an idea about a place just up here near Gerrard Street. There was this window, see—'

'I got places, Leon. I got places and I got people, so let's just do that.'

'All right. We crossed Charing Cross Road, though, so this ain't C Division no more.'

'Don't think crooks give a damn about divisional boundaries. And you're with Flying Squad now. Neither do we.'

Little St Andrew Street met six other streets in a circle of misery known as Seven Dials. This had been Minter and Lander's stomping ground in E Division years ago, and from the looks and nods in Cassar's direction, the Flying Squad were still regular visitors.

They stopped at a lodging house for travellers and destitutes and Cassar put a hand on Geats's chest. 'You stay out here.'

'Really?'

'Got someone I need to speak to; don't need new faces spooking them.'

He ducked inside and disappeared up the stairs into the warren of rooms that had no doubt been cut into two or three smaller ones. Geats stamped his feet and huffed in his hands to stave off the cold.

'This is me, the business of people getting conducted in my absence while I stay outside like a dog. Talking to myself.'

Cassar reappeared a few minutes later and set off round the corner.

Geats jogged after him. 'Don't tell me. Nobody home?'

Outside a butcher's on Little Earl Street, they stopped again. A piglet trotted by in the road, chasing an escaping cabbage. A woman hanging out of a window on the first floor of the next building along loudly scolded a man sitting on the kerb. He looked as if he'd given up dreaming of better things to come.

Cassar pushed open the door to the flats above the shop. 'Leon, you—'

'Yeah, I know the score.'

He only had to wait a couple of minutes for Cassar to return.

'We can get a length of rope for me, perhaps. Next place we stop, tie me up outside, leave me a bowl of water.'

'Do you ever just let it be?'

'We're wasting our time with all this. I know much better places to sniff around.'

'Of course you do. God, you're exactly what Charlie Garland always said you were.'

Geats bristled at the mention of his old swami on the force.

'Will never be convinced he isn't the sharpest prick in the room, what Charlie told anyone who'd listen. And here you are, knowing better than everyone else. Better than me, better than all the guys on the case, better than Nutty Sharpe, who only has decades of experience. But he can't possibly know what he's doing, can he, Leon?'

'Oh, I reckon your man Sharpe knows exactly what he's doing. He'll have it all squared away just the way he likes it.'

'You're a clown, Leon. So not only is Sharpe clueless, he's corrupt now? Who's the one running around telling Jack Isow everything he knows?'

'I've never snitched for Jack Isow in my life. And it's a bit rich casting aspersions upon my integrity while you're getting on with all this.'

Cassar hesitated. 'What d'you mean?'

'What do I mean? Do me a favour. The doss-house we stopped at? You were on the top floor seeing that fence who's worked out of there for years. Passes gear through the market stalls. What could he possibly know about Red Max? And up here, where you've just been? The former itinerant quack practising as an abortionist in a shabby little room? I suppose you could be asking about Red Max, on the off chance, but let's not you and I pretend we don't both know you're doing the collections.'

Cassar tried a laugh that came out a squeak.

'Money Mark, still at it. Must have been a real boon for business joining Flying Squad, able to cross boundaries and go where you want. You chaps must be taking dropsy from half the ponces and hucksters in the city.'

'Geats, if you—'

'Oh, shut it. Did I ever spill before? No. None of my palaver. But since we're in this neck of the woods, how about we pay a visit to someone who might actually know something?'

Neal's Yard was a collection of dilapidated warehouses tucked in between two streets off Seven Dials, home to a motley assortment of businesses, some legal and others less so. Above an apothecary, the first floor was occupied by an old Swiss widow masquerading as a Russian occultist, and the two flats on the floor above that by a Brummie ponce running a couple of fourteen-year-old Belgian girls.

'You remember Fluke?'

Cassar shook his head.

'Maybe it was after you went up in the world. This should prove instructive, then. No doubt you'll be able to shake him for tips at some later date.'

Fluke had once kept rooms at the thin end of Little Dean Street, just a bedroom you reached by passing through the kitchen. He had two women, both of whom claimed to be married to him; whichever one picked up the most promising-looking gent got the bedroom for the evening while the other doled out favours by hand and mouth in the kitchen.

Around the time they both realised they could do all of that without Fluke's help was when he moved out, and he'd since crossed Geats's path with two girls he'd bought off a woman who had fled the Germans in Brussels in 1914 and set up in London. Born and bred in Soho, they'd somehow inherited their mother's accent, a phenomenon Geats had never found the heart to question.

He hammered on the second-floor door and a girl shawled in a sheet, either Suzanne or Jeanne, he could never tell them apart, opened it and hurried back to her bed.

Geats strolled in. 'Morning to you, too.'

'What's this?' Fluke was bleary-eyed and half dressed. 'Bloody Geats. Time do you call this?'

'It's the afternoon, Fluke. You want I should interrupt business hours?'

'This not even C Division turf. Dirties got no call being here.'

'Let me introduce my good pal Sergeant Cassar, from Flying Squad. They're no respecters of boundaries.'

Fluke peered fretfully round Geats at Cassar.

'Forgo the pantomime of upright citizenry,' Geats said. 'He knows you're a right scutter. We're here for other things.'

The girls were sprawled on a mattress on the floor by a loading door that had planks nailed across it. The pulley from the old iron hoist arm on the roof swung to and fro in the breeze outside.

Fluke fetched himself a bottle for his morning toot. 'What d'you want?'

'Red Max Kassel.'

Drinking slowly, Fluke eyed Cassar over the bottle, weighing up how buggered he was, or stood to be depending on how this went.

'Know him but don't know him. Know what I mean?'

'Seldom, if ever.' Geats pointed to the girls. 'He anything to do with them?'

'No. They was from their mother. Told her I'd look after them.'

'Paternal figure that you are.'

Fluke shrugged.

'But Red Max is into French cunny?'

'I don't have nothing to do with any of that.'

'His reputation, I mean.'

'What I've heard, yeah. He's Russian, mind.'

'Latvian.'

'What's the difference? Not from bloody Croydon, what I'm saying.'

'What do you know about the women he brings in?'

Fluke shook his head. 'Look, you know me, Geats. I had the wives, right pair of cunts they turned out to be. Now I got these two, full-time job that they are, along with the new wife. But I don't have none of that dance school perfume on me.'

Geats and Cassar exchanged a glance.

'Two things,' Geats said. 'Firstly – wife?'

'She's next door, in the other flat. Sleeping, like. Always bloody sleeping. Thought she'd be a help with these two, but they all just conspire against me.'

'Yeah, proper victim of circumstance. Secondly – dance school?'

'How they move them around, what I heard. Could be bullshit.'

'You know where this school is?'

'Nah. Just what I heard people saying. Like I said, I never had no business with the man myself.'

Cassar cleared his throat. 'This going to break the case open, Leon? Matrimony and unnamed dance schools?'

'Might do.'

'West End's drowning in so-called dance schools. We better get going now if we're going to knock on all fifteen thousand of them and get home in time for our tea.'

Geats kept his thoughts to himself the rest of the day. They made a few more house calls, finding nothing that resembled a murder scene, which for Seven Dials was in itself suspicious, and Cassar threw in the odd question about Yiddish gangs and Jack Isow. He was a detective who understood what it was he was looking for, even if it didn't exist. To him, the distinction was unimportant.

Geats had his own agenda. The flat with the broken window on Little Newport Street was a good bet for the Red Max murder scene. Frankly, he had no real interest in the matter beyond showing up Cassar and Nutty Sharpe in some way, but that was good enough to be getting on with.

18

The first thing Geats saw when he walked into the Vine Street station was a map of Soho propped up behind the sergeant's desk with dozens of red marks on it. The second thing was a line of manacled men squeezed together on a bench, drunks and pickpockets, hoisters and louts. The old fella on the end snored loudly and Sergeant Pym kicked him so hard he fell off the bench, dragging three others with him on the chains.

'Been bringing them in all day. Supposed to be finding me whoever it was done for the Russian ponce, but all I get is this lot, and enough others to fill the cells.'

'I'm going to find the boss,' Cassar called out over his shoulder as he took the stairs two at a time.

Geats ignored him. 'This map where we hit today?'

Pym nodded. 'Chief Inspector Sharpe's idea, to narrow down the search for the murder scene. Men coming in and out of the station can see at a glance where everyone's been.'

Geats squinted at the distribution of the red marks. 'There any rhyme or reason to this, or has Sharpe just kicked down random doors?'

Pym shrugged, like it was business out of his control.

Geats shook his head. 'Nobody found where Kassel was killed?'

'Not so far.'

Leaving Pym to his prisoners, Geats slipped out of the station and made a pass of Little Newport Street. It was getting on and the dairy store was closed, no sign of the shopkeeper who had found the glass. He regretted now not collecting some of it from the ground, in the event that the coroner could make some comparison with the fragments found on the body. The rubbish collectors in their sideloader had almost certainly done their rounds since and picked up any refuse from the shops on the street, evidence lost for ever.

Though it was late, there was a pub at either end of the street and theatres all around, so the place was overrun. Across from the dairy shop stood the Newport Dwellings, a row of four six-storey tenement blocks. Going door-to-door asking for witnesses at that time would only have earned him many punches in the face, but he found his way up to the flat roof of the wing opposite the store and settled himself down for a recce.

All that happened was it got darker and quieter.

Nobody so much as approached the door to the flats at number 36, but as the theatres and pubs emptied out, there were suddenly more people and then no people at all. Night lived at the other ends of Lisle Street and Gerrard Street, where Wardour Street partied until dawn.

The cold air and hard roof gave Geats a bit of a back, and he stood to stretch it out, counting the clicks of his spine. He searched for the tower of St Anne's, with its clock faces set in a copper cupola that looked like a bluebottle's head, but even though it was only a few streets away, he couldn't make it out in the black skies. The moon was barely a sliver, a thumbnail pressed into the night fabric.

With his father's lighter, he read his wristwatch: just before one o'clock. The street below was quiet. Down the stairs, he waited in the doorway to the tenements for a few minutes before quietly cutting across the road and trying the door to number 36. Still open.

As before, only the bathroom was unlocked on the first floor. Flicking the light, he had a closer look than on his first visit. The tub appeared to have been scrubbed recently and rather haphazardly. Leaving the light on, he crept upstairs to the second floor. He knocked lightly and waited. Nothing.

The doors weren't terribly robust, and he braced himself against the rear one and gently pressured it with his shoulder, boots pushing against the opposite wall, until he felt the frame splinter and give. It opened into a small vestibule with two doors: one straight ahead, the other to the right.

The first led to a corridor accessing a small kitchen right at the back of the flat, with a window overlooking a quadrangle behind the King's Head pub. There was very little food – a few tins of bully beef and some canned soup in the cupboard, and nothing on the cold slab.

Faint mewing led him to a box in the corner, and when he opened it, a small face with big green eyes peered out. If the occupants had scarpered, there had been no room for the kitten in the escape plan.

The other door off the vestibule led to a bedroom with a narrow window to the quadrangle. The divan was unmade, silk sheets rolled up and tossed in the corner. Padding along after him, the kitten jumped up on the bed and pawed at his leg. Rich rugs hung from the walls, and thick shades gave the room boudoir lighting. The wardrobes were open and empty of clothes, drawers in the dresser cleared out too. A few shoes were pushed against the wall beneath the window along with a pair of tatty old boots. Picking the kitten up in one hand, Geats brought it to head height and looked it in the eye.

'Bet you saw everything.'

He tossed it on the bed and it ran back, leaping out and hooking onto his leg with its claws. Geats stroked it and pulled it free, placing it on the floor.

Back on the landing, he forced the door to the front room, a much bigger space. A panhandle hallway ran beside the stairwell and opened up into a room the full width of the building, well lit by three windows. Comfortable chairs were arranged around the fireplace, and shelves of books lined the opposite wall. In between, against the stairwell wall, stood a writing desk bureau and a sideboard, upon which was a telephone. Whoever lived here didn't do so hand-to-mouth.

A card table was positioned by the windows and cool air blew in through the broken light in the middle one. Faint traces of blood clung to its bent lead cames. Geats made a study of the floor. The card table had been moved, if the tracery of scrapes from chair legs was anything to go by, and a suspiciously geometrical patch where it now stood was darker than the rest of the floor, as if something now departed had once protected it from the sun. Like a rug, say.

On his hands and knees, he made a close study of the floorboards. Areas had been recently cleaned, and sliding the blade of his boot knife between the boards, he dug out traces of dried blood. There was more around the door handle.

The kitten got onto a chair and mewed again.

'What is it I can possibly do for you?'

Mew.

Geats sighed. Outside, he heard the jangle of crates being loaded onto a milk float.

'Stay here.'

The kitten followed him and Geats had to keep it inside the room with his foot and close the door quickly. Downstairs, he waved at the driver, just about to leave on his rounds. The son of the shop's owner. Geats knew him to talk to, and bought a bottle of milk and a piece of cheese.

In the kitchen, he found a bowl and set the small cat up with some milk and a generous hunk of cheese the size of its head. Whilst it was busy, he nipped downstairs to check the bathroom again. Under the edge of the tub he found a rime of blood, more around the plughole.

'Well, hello there, Mr Kassel.'

In the stairwell, stains had been almost scrubbed out of the steps, and the faint impressions of childlike handprints marked the wall. Recalling what he'd read in the coroner's report, it wasn't difficult to imagine the scene.

If he called Vine Street from the phone in the front room, within twenty minutes the place would be Nutty Sharpe's. Whatever was found would be his. On his own, a full-on under-the-floorboards-and-inside-the-walls kind of search would take all night. If he found something, though, the look on Sharpe's face would be priceless.

The kitten was making a pother in the kitchen, squeaking and scratching at the door. Geats went back there and gave it the eye, but it wasn't for retreating. Pressing the cardboard cap back into the milk bottle, he slipped it into his pocket and headed back towards the landing, flicking the lights off as he went, his new friend padding along behind him.

He was at the door when he heard footsteps coming up the stairs. Easing open the bedroom door, he swept the kitten in with his foot and followed it into the darkness. The feet hesitated on the landing, seeing the door to the front room open, the lights on.

'Hello?'

A woman, accent of some kind. Tentatively she walked into the living room, soles clicking on the wooden boards. Geats emerged from the shadows and quietly stepped out onto the landing. Stealing a glance through the other door, he caught her disappearing round the corner into the main part of the room.

Back to the wall, he sneaked along the short panhandle hallway. In the glass doors of a dresser he could see her round the corner at the bureau. She had pulled down the writing surface, inset with green skiver, and was rifling through the thin drawers and cubbies within, talking furiously to herself in French.

'Hello.'

She reared back in fright, banging against the card table with her hands clutched to her heart.

'My God, you give me the frights.'

French. Maybe Belgian.

'I expect I did.'

'Who are you? What are you doing here?'

'What am I doing here? What are *you* doing here, less than a week after a man was shot in this room?'

Frozen, she stared at him, reaching for some reasonable explanation. She held something in her hand, something she had found in the bureau. He approached her and she stepped back. He showed her his warrant card.

'I'm with the police.'

She whispered, '*Putain.*'

'So, what are you doing here?'

'Madame, she tells me she leaves my card here in the desk for me to collect.'

He held his hand out and she gave him the National Insurance contribution card. It was in the name Marcelle Aubin and had been stamped for the first two weeks of the year.

'This you, Marcelle Aubin?'

She nodded.

'And who is Madame?'

'Madame Bertrand.'

'That's who lives here? She owns the place? Or . . .'

'*Ah, non.* Monsieur Georges, he is, how do you say? He is not owning the building, but—'

'Leaseholder.'

'*Oui.* Leaseholder. Madame, she is renting from him.'

'Madame have a first name?'

'Suzanne.'

'Suzanne Bertrand. And this Georges character?'

'Georges Lacroix.'

'And you? Where do you live?'

She pointed downstairs.

'But you haven't been here the last few days?'

'Madame, she tells me she is leaving and I no longer have a job, or a room. So I find a new room, and Madame says I can collect my card. To be stamped?'

Geats examined the card again before slipping it into his pocket. She looked forlorn.

'What is it you do for Madame, exactly?'

'I keep the house. Cook, clean. Everything.'

'And what is it that Madame does?'

Aubin made a face like, have a guess.

'Anyone else live here?'

'There was another girl, in the room beside mine. They said she was to help me, but she never lifted a finger. Then she left. Madame said she was a dancer.'

'A dancer? You see many of them here, dancers?'

She shrugged, as if he'd asked did they ever have cushions in the flat.

'You were here when the man was shot? Max Kassel?'

She buttoned up.

'Did you know him?'

A shrug of the chin.

'Mind me saying, you don't seem too shook up for someone who was living at a murder scene a couple of days ago.'

'*Ce n'est pas la première fois.*'

'Senna something pas the first? There's been another?'

'No. I don't know.'

'Around here?' He thought about this a moment. 'Jesus. You mean Archer Street? Uh, Josephine Martin?'

'Martin, *mais oui.* Madame Josephine.'

'How did you know her?'

'She was a good friend to Madame.'

'But your Madame was really French? Josephine Martin was not.'

'She came here from France, Madame Josephine. Spoke good French. But was born in Russia.'

'Yes, she was. Just like Max Kassel.'

He was in danger of getting ahead of himself here.

'Okay, Marcelle. We're going to have a longer chat down at the police station.'

'I am under the arrest?'

'If you want to be arrested, you're going in the cells. If you want to have a chat, then we're just going to take a friendly stroll to Vine Street.'

'*Nique ta mère.*'

'Come again?'

'I say, this is nightmare.'

'Quite.'

She got her things together and he led her out into the stairwell.

'Better find the cat.'

'Cat?'

'Found it in a box in the kitchen. Little thing.'

'*Ah, oui. Le chat.* Horrible creature.' She pulled her sleeve up and presented him with several red welts. 'One week has gone since it did this, and it still itches.'

Geats considered leaving the animal to fend for itself, but then heard a tiny mew from upstairs.

'Cat? Come on, cat.'

On the landing above them, he found it rubbing itself against the balustrade, and scooped it up.

'Got it,' he called.

Aubin had a peculiar expression on her face when he came back down. Later, he remembered thinking he should ask her what was wrong. Remembered that being his last thought before the back of his brain exploded.

19

It took Flying Squad a couple of hours to get down on paper their side of what had taken only seconds to happen. It remained unclear who exactly the Frenchwoman was. She feigned having no English, so Sharpe left her in the cells for the night, all the better to soften her up for a little chat.

Just before six in the morning, Cassar walked across the river to his boarding house in Lambeth with the intention of grabbing some shut-eye. The only living soul on the street was the coalman delivering sacks off his cart.

He was certain he never got to close his eyes, not even a blink, before it was loud and bright outside. An alarm clock was unnecessary; his room directly overlooked the sanitary engineering works. It was almost eight when he sat up on the edge of his cot, narrow but still cramped in the bedroom. The rear ones were smaller and faced north, so were cooler in summer and freezing in winter. He'd worn his coat over his pyjamas beneath the blankets, and slipped that off now to dress in a clean suit.

Downstairs, the house was deserted, the other tenants already off to work. A teacher; a newly qualified doctor at St Thomas's; an estate agent; and a young man who claimed to be a novelist but took some perverse pleasure in never being published. Cassar didn't really know any of them, and the hours he kept meant he rarely sat for a meal with them. The only one he'd had anything to do with was Frank, who'd had the room across the landing from him. That had been convenient, but Frank had left hurriedly before it became comfortable.

'Morning, Mrs F.'

Mrs Fewtrell doddered about just inside the kitchen.

'Mr Cassar, up at all hours and down at none. Breakfast has left you behind, I'm afraid. I could find you some toast?'

'That's all right, Mrs F, I have to be getting back to the station.'

'Big case, this one?'

'Homicide.'

'Goodness.' She crossed herself.

Mrs Fewtrell lived in the two rooms in the semi-basement, her sitting room opening into a small yard at the rear exclusively for her enjoyment. She'd have been up and getting breakfast on the table for her four other tenants at seven sharp, no dallying. A short, wall-eyed widow in her early sixties, she was avowedly High Church, and a framed Sacred Heart hung in every room, a crucifix on the hallway wall greeting guests.

Cassar buttoned his coat against the morning chill. The walk back across the bridge was bracing, and it felt as though he'd never stopped, that he'd just turned right back round when he reached the house. He was bloodless, a somnambulist. Sleep was a gift he'd have to wait for.

Nutty Sharpe, on the other hand, was disgustingly revitalised and in clean clothes, though Cassar knew if he'd gone home at all it could only have been for a few minutes, as he lived way out west in Acton, backing onto the railway.

'Boss.'

The office they'd requisitioned from Clubs & Vice was unrecognisable; the furniture had been replaced, so now there was a desk with a chair either side, and a low couch against one wall. It was this that Sharpe pointed at, indicating where Cassar should sit.

The leather strap of an overnight bag crept out from underneath, revealing the point of the couch and the nature of Sharp's sleeping arrangements. Cassar wanted to fill the silence with something, but before he could speak, Minter led in the French housemaid, Marcelle Aubin.

She looked frazzled from her night behind bars, as if she hadn't slept at all, and Minter plonked her down roughly in the chair across from Sharpe. Her eyes darted round the room and she locked onto Cassar, as if seeking something from him, an ally perhaps.

He looked at his feet.

Sharpe read from the insurance card they'd found at the scene.

'Miss Marcelle Aubin. Is that right?'

She crossed her arms, pulling her cardigan tightly closed, and glanced over her shoulder to where Minter and Lander stood, backs to the door.

'Miss Aubin? You following what I'm saying?'

Her voice was small and fragile. 'Aubin. *Oui.*'

'You live there, in the building? Little Newport Street?'

On the collar of her dress there was a single broken line; faint, but undeniably blood. It looked as though she had attempted to clean it off. She clutched her hands in her lap, trying to mask their shaking.

'Miss Aubin, do I need to find an interpreter?' Sharpe glanced past her to his inspectors. 'Or some way of making ourselves better understood?'

Her fearful eyes frantically shot from him to Cassar and back. She didn't speak.

'All right, then,' Sharpe said, standing abruptly.

She leaned back in her seat. Sharpe walked by her, exchanging with Lander and Minter looks larded with occult meaning, and swiftly departed the office.

The wolves closed in.

Lander perched himself on the desk directly in front of Aubin. With her knees pressed together and hands folded in her lap, she made to slide her chair away from him, but Minter was right up against her back and hoisted her forward suddenly, so she was tight enough to the desk that Lander straddled her legs, her face pressed against his midriff.

She yelped, turning her head aside.

'*Qu'est-ce tu fous?*'

Possessed of the kind of shitpan chivalry that would see him happily start a brawl over this but baulk at letting a woman lead an investigation, Cassar balled his fists and tightened up like a spring. Of course, being someone who had chosen to don a uniform for a living, he was also unquestioningly shackled by the chain of command and, more importantly, the need for other men to accept him, so he kept his mouth shut.

Pressed between Minter behind her, and Lander astride her lap, Aubin squeezed her eyes shut. She shrank away from Minter's breath as he leaned close to her ear.

'What'll happen if the boss can't find someone who speaks frog?'

Lander blew out his cheeks. 'Back to the cells till tomorrow, most likely.'

'Busy down there today.'

'Only going to get fuller, too.'

'Might not get a cell to herself.'

'And I didn't see too many ladies down there to share with.'

'No. Might have to bang her up with a few lads.'

'Saw a band they brought in last night. Big strapping black boys.'

'Be only too willing to keep her company.'

They laughed at this.

Cassar did what he did best – nothing. He built obscene daydreams about hurting them; not a coherent series of events, but flashes of violence, of combat where he had proficiency and was quick and adept at meting out punishment.

As quickly as he'd furnished himself with them, they collapsed down into one another like a telescope, leaving him feeling the shame of someone who didn't know what was wrong with them. He looked up and found Aubin staring at him, her welling eyes pleading.

Lander held her chin and turned her face to meet his gaze.

'What do you say? Fancy being a come dish for a pack of darkies putting their clap juice up you?'

'*Qu'est ce qui ne vas pas chez toi?*' she shrieked, tears rolling freely down her cheeks.

Amused, Lander leaned back and apprised her, head at a tilt.

'Seem to be getting awful upset at something you don't understand there, *ma chérie.*'

He lifted his leg over her lap and returned to his corner as Sharpe slipped back into the office.

'Afraid there isn't a person in the building who speaks French, Miss Aubin. Looks like we'll have to keep you in the cells until tomorrow . . . unless we've found some form of common parlance that might help us here?'

Aubin's breath snagged on the sobs she was trying in vain to stifle.

'Would you care to try this again, Miss Aubin?'

'*Oui . . .*'

'Sorry? I couldn't make that out.'

'*Oui.*'

'Oh good. I'm so pleased.' He took his seat again. 'Now, we were establishing where it was you live exactly. Little Newport Street?'

'Not any more, but previously, yes.'

'Were you still there when Max Kassel was murdered?'

She nodded.

'Did you see him shot?'

She shook her head. 'I was in my room.'

'You heard it?'

'Yes.'

'We have the lease being in the name of a Georges Lacroix. That who killed him?'

'*Oui.*'

'He lived there?'

'*Non.* Madame lived there. Madame Suzanne Bertrand.'

'And she worked there too?'

Aubin hesitated before nodding feebly.

'So, Lacroix was there, what? On business?'

'He . . . he was . . .'

'He's a ponce.'

She nodded.

'Walk me through the shooting.'

'Monsieur Georges was expecting Monsieur Max.'

'They worked together?'

'*Oui*. They were often at the flat. Madame said they didn't need me, so I went to my room, on the floor below. Monsieur Max arrived, I heard him walk up the stairs. Then there was shouting, and the sounds of a struggle. I went out into the hall, and then I hear the gunshots.'

'How many?'

'One. And then more, closer together. I could not say. Four? Maybe five?'

'What did you do?'

'I ran upstairs. Madame was on the landing. Monsieur Georges, he called for help, so I went into the lounge. Monsieur Max was on the floor. The window was smashed.'

'He was dead, Kassel?'

'*Non*. He was on his knees. He crawled past me and pulled himself up on the door. Madame and Monsieur Georges were shouting at each other. Monsieur Max got to the stairs before Monsieur Georges went after him. They fell down the steps together. Monsieur Georges, he pulled Monsieur Max into the toilet and locked him in there.'

'And then?'

'He told me to go to my room. I did. There was blood on the walls and floor. I could hear Monsieur Max in the bathroom.'

'Calling for help?'

She nodded. 'Then it was not words. Sounds. Some banging. And then nothing.'

'What did Lacroix do?'

'Someone came in a car. They moved the body from the bathroom, wrapped it in the rug from the upstairs room. They put it in the car.'

'You saw that?'

'When they went down to the front door, Madame asked me to help her clean up. I washed the floorboards in the lounge. I saw the car through the window.'

'Did you know the man?'

She shook her head. 'I could not really see. But he was French. I hear his voice.'

'Would you recognise the car?'

'It was dark. But I hear him say he had to get it back to the garage. That a customer would be picking it up in the morning.'

Sharpe nodded to Minter, who left the office.

'And they're gone now, Lacroix and Bertrand?'

'Madame told me to take a few days, that they would be returning to France and I should find another position. I got work and lodging with a lady in Covent Garden.'

'So what were you doing there last night? Did you lure Sergeant Geats there?'

Wildly, she shook her head.

'No, sir. I did not.'

'You arranged to meet him there?'

'I went to get my card. Madame said she would leave it there. This other man, he was already there. He had broken in, broken the lock.'

'All right,' Sharpe said. He stood, hands flat on his desk. 'Thank you, Miss Aubin. We'll need you to remain here a while longer, but I'll have someone find you something to eat and drink.'

He nodded for Lander and Cassar to come with him, leaving the door to the office guarded by one of his sentries.

Minter found them.

'There's a garage near Soho Square run by a Frenchman, name of Pierre Alexandre. No record here. I've contacted Paris. They're going to dig out his file. I told them about Lacroix, and the name has come up. They think he's in Paris now.'

Sharpe bared his teeth.

'I want this mechanic Alexandre. I want the car. I want everyone involved.'

20

In two unmarked cars they roared across Regent Street into the labyrinth of Soho. The streets narrowed the deeper they went, passing between the grimy brick backs of printing works and hat factories until they exploded out again on leafy Soho Square.

Beside two empty buildings condemned for demolition snaked a thin alley hiding squalid little slum dwellings, some converted to commercial use. Nestled in among them was a garage workshop that cars had to go into sideways-on as the alley didn't offer the width for a vehicle to turn completely nose-in. Pierre Alexandre, in greasy overalls, lay beneath a jacked-up Hillman, feet protruding out into the alley.

Cassar recalled the place from his Vine Street days: a previous owner jailed for supplying cars to a gang of heisters who smashed Bond Street windows and hightailed it in four-seater tourers that they could hurdle into without bothering about doors.

Minter gave the workshop the once-over for weapons and Lander stood over the mechanic's legs.

'Alexandre?'

'Yes, hold on one second, *s'il vous plaît.*'

Lander kicked the man's feet.

Alexandre rolled out from beneath the car. 'Hey, what is your game?'

Lander shoved his badge under his nose and pushed him back against the Hillman.

'Going to take some air,' Sharpe said, wandering out of the garage.

Cassar stepped out too, pulling the sliding doors shut after him. From inside there was a crash and a howl as Alexandre was hurled into something.

Cassar took out his cigarettes, offering one to his boss and lighting for them both. Sharpe sat against the bonnet of one of the Wolseleys. Cassar looked up and down the alley, keeping watch. Neither of them said anything.

Lander loved to rhapsodise as he worked, his voice humming through the garage door, punctuated by Alexandre's high-pitched pleading and wailing. After a particularly loud cry, Cassar reached through the window of one of the cars and turned the engine on, letting it idle.

He told himself the man was no innocent, that Aubin had fingered him as being at the murder scene. That he worked with traffickers and ponces, that he was no different to Kassel and Lacroix when it came down to it. Told himself the man deserved whatever he got.

When the door slid open, Sharpe watched disinterestedly as Minter and Lander dragged Alexandre out on his back by his legs. His face was a wreck and his arms trailed along behind him uselessly, the shoulders ruined in some way. When they dropped him, he rolled onto his front and pressed his cheek to the cobbles, as if seeking solace in their coolness.

'I need help.'

'Don't we all,' Lander said.

'He needs a doctor,' Cassar said.

Sharpe pursed his lips.

'Had an accident with his hoist,' Lander said. 'Slipped and did himself a mischief. Isn't that right, love?'

Alexandre whimpered.

Off a nod from Sharpe, Lander and Minter bundled Alexandre into the back of their car. He howled as they hauled him by his arms.

'Sorting room at St Thomas's,' Lander said.

Sharpe shrugged. 'Give you anything?'

'Said he did the driving that night. Lacroix called him.'

'He know why Lacroix shot Kassel?'

'Some dead whore, killed a few months back. Josephine Martin? Maybe looks like it was about that. She used to handle the new girls they brought in from France. When she turned up strangled, Lacroix and Kassel suspected each other.'

Sharpe looked at Cassar, who shrugged in ignorance.

'If she was a Soho tart, someone at Vine Street will know. What about Isow?'

'He never heard of him.'

'How did he get hooked up with Lacroix?'

'He knew him and Kassel in Paris. Knew their associates. Bumped into them again over here and started doing some driving for them. Picked French whores up from the ports, brought them back here.'

'He know where Kassel lived?'

'Says he's only been to Bertrand's place, and the home of this Martin woman, who lived on Archer Street. But he overheard Lacroix and Kassel talking once, about a top-floor flat on James Street, next door to a pub.'

'All right. Get him off to the hospital and we'll see you back at Vine Street.'

Lander glanced at Minter. 'Himself will be wanting a spot of penance.'

As a Catholic, Minter's spiritual life revolved around guilt as much as God; he was obliged to faithfully confess any and all sins he committed in pursuit of something like justice, and preferred doing so sooner rather than later so they didn't fester.

'Tell him not to dawdle. He can do his contrition in the car on the way back from St Thomas's.'

The two inspectors shot off across the river to see to Alexandre's wounds and Minter's eternal soul, and Sharpe got in the passenger side of his car.

'Bethnal Green,' he said, when Cassar climbed in behind the wheel.

Cassar looked at him dumbly. That was Sharpe's old haunt before he was Flying Squad.

'He told us James Street,' Sharpe said slowly, as if to a child. 'Top floor, next to a pub. I'm thinking he means the Sutton Buildings. Come on, chop-chop.'

Across the city, in the East End, the great red brick tenements of James Street – eight five-storey blocks arranged in three rows, over a thousand homes in all – sat cheek by jowl with the Fountain public house. They searched for the Russian's flat in the block nearest the pub, but managed only to disturb a retired carpenter and his wife, who offered a brief survey of the area's history, emphasising the godawful slums and the lunatic asylum that had been cleared to make way for their home.

The man proudly declared that he knew everyone in his block and most of the others, and there weren't no Max Kassel, though he did know a Hymie Cohen, who lived alone on the top floor and worked in his father's kosher butcher's, but he weren't no Russian.

They spent a couple of hours trying the top floors of each of the blocks, but nobody knew of a Max Kassel or an Emil Allard, and nobody recognised the tastefully staged photograph of Red Max's face post-mortem. Cassar barely said a word the whole time.

Back at the car, he broke his silence. 'More than one James Street. Covent Garden, for instance.'

Sharpe considered that quietly. 'You know, you're not half so irritating when you apply a strict filter to your words.'

This James Street was flush with pubs. Cassar took on knocking duties, maintaining his laconic attitude as Sharpe asked the questions. They walked up buildings next to the Grapes and the Nag's Head and finally the White Lion, finding nothing that resembled the digs of a recently departed Russian ponce.

After the last one, Sharpe made his way straight into the White Lion. 'Jimmy Woolf runs this place. If anyone can point us in the right direction, it's him.'

Jimmy Woolf could not, in fact, point them in the direction of Max Kassel's flat, and had never heard of him. They drove back to Vine Street with Sharpe having caught a dose of Cassar's Benedictine silence.

He was revitalised by a message left on his desk for him to call the French police – Lacroix and Bertrand had been spotted in Paris. Sharpe informed his Continental colleagues that the pair were now officially wanted for murder and that he would travel to Paris forthwith. He told Lander and Minter to pack bags and arrange passage and accommodation for the three of them.

Cassar looked crestfallen. Sharpe pulled him into his office.

'Your pal Geats is going to be a problem. He doesn't seem the type who'll learn from last night; in fact, he'll very probably become more truculent.'

'We did bash his brains in.'

'Clearly a redundant tactic. There's a better way. As irritating as he is, from what you and Dalton tell me, he does know Soho. He might know something about this Josephine Martin business, which could be useful. If we arrest Lacroix in Paris, being able to exert pressure on him with two murders would be handy.'

'He'll know I sold him out last night.'

'And he'll hate you for it. But you can use that. Apologise, grovel if you have to. Getting someone to forgive your trespasses, to have them believe they've bestowed something upon you, is the best way to get them on board. Have a nose into this Martin murder, find how it connects to Lacroix.'

'What if it doesn't?'

'Sergeant?'

'What if Lacroix is innocent of that one?'

Sharpe laughed loudly and skipped out of the station.

21

Geats awoke abruptly from reptilian sleep, gulping for air.

A bottomless kind of ache expanded his head, his mind a dark chamber swarming with crocodiles. Opening his eyes was a battle, followed by a harder fight to make them focus. Found himself face to face with a brick wall, lying on his side. On top of the skull situation, something in his neck hurt like he was on the rack, and moving was completely out of the question for the time being.

His hand lay limply beside his head like it was someone else's, dried blood caked onto it, as well as his shirt and the naked wooden bench he sprawled on, and he supposed it was his own from the way he felt. He let his eyes fall closed again.

He recalled the odd expression on the face of the French housemaid. Had she somehow done this to him? Had she set him up? He'd been jumped from behind, that much was certain.

Somewhere a heavy door closed, and the iron heft with which its lock clunked into place was oddly comforting. A familiar sound. The walls smelled of damp and desperate prayers. Someone was singing, drunken melodies he couldn't quite make out, and then another voice, telling them to shut up for the love of all that was holy.

Geats opened his eyes.

He was in a jail cell. And from the snuffling noises behind him, he hadn't been given one to himself. He feigned sleep, keeping his back to his cellmate, and tried to catch hold of the possibilities racing through his mind.

Had he been found unconscious by police who didn't know any better, tossed in the cell as a drunk? Or had he been betrayed by his own, had his brains beaten in by coppers? Someone involved in the Kassel murder? No, they surely would have killed him, not arrested him.

Without moving, he slid his eyes around as much of the cell as he could see. It wasn't Vine Street, he knew that much. Someone had taken him to another nick.

The door unlocked and let a draught in when it opened. Geats held still, attempting a reasonable facsimile of a half-dead man's breathing.

'You awake?'

He peered over his shoulder, one eye open just a slit. A station sergeant stood in the door holding a tray.

'Tea. Spot of brekkie.'

Sitting up, Geats found his head was even worse than he'd thought, and he promptly threw up in his own lap.

The sergeant stepped back quickly. 'Bleeding hell.'

'Muh,' Geats said, gouts of vomit hanging from his lips.

Placing the tray on the bench, the sergeant mumbled something about getting him cleaned up, and went off, locking the door behind him. Geats examined the tray: cup of lukewarm tea and a bowl of gruel, the origins of which he thought he was better off remaining in ignorance of.

His cellmate pushed himself upright: an obvious drunk, though indistinguishable from Geats as things stood. In his sixties probably, from the looks of it he'd been wearing the suit he had on for at least forty of those years. Scratching himself, he cocked one cheek and farted loudly.

Geats offered the bowl. 'Porridge?'

The drunk took it without question and set about shovelling the mush into his mouth with the small spoon. Geats swilled his own mouth out with the tea and spat it in the corner. Tentatively he touched the back of his head, hand coming away sticky with blood.

On balance, he decided he would like to die.

The door reopened and the sergeant hauled in a bucket of water sloshing about its rim.

'That's mighty obliging, Sarge,' Geats said, looking forward to a wash.

Taking hold of the underside of the bucket, the man tossed its contents over Geats, splashing down his front and legs. The water was freezing, and he howled as he leaped up, hopping from foot to foot. The drunk didn't so much as look up from his bowl.

The sergeant pointed at lumps of vomit still clinging to Geats's trousers.

'Scrape it off.'

Geats stared at him. 'You going to tell me where I am?'

'Marylebone Lane station.'

'You going to tell me why I'm here?'

'You were arrested at a crime scene.'

'At a crime—I'm a bloody police officer.'

The man shrugged. 'Can't help you with that.'

'What do you mean?' Geats patted himself down. 'My warrant card was in my pocket.'

The man shrugged again. 'I expect measures are being taken to establish your identification to everyone's satisfaction.'

'Who booked me in?'

'Flying Squad. They'll be around to see you eventually.'

The sergeant locked him back up, vanishing with the bucket and tray. The old drunk lay down and turned his back to Geats, punctuating his brush-off with another crack of flatulence. Geats reclined, dropping his head gently onto a crooked arm.

Marylebone Lane.

D Division.

Sharpe was keeping him away from coppers who'd know him.

Making some point probably about respect, the chain of command, and general constabulary comportment.

The drunk was allowed on his way, and there followed a long but not-so-mysterious delay in officially identifying Geats as a sergeant of the Metropolitan Police. His watch having been taken from him, he had no idea of the time. The small, high window in the cell let out onto a deeply shadowed yard, making the gauging of the sun's passage possible only in dramatic lurches. It was daytime, and then it was not.

After nightfall, the sergeant returned for him.

'Finally figured out who I am, have we?'

'Come on, we have to get going.'

Geats got up unsteadily and scuffled out of the cell.

'Where we off to?'

'Vine Street. Put these on.'

The sergeant handed him a pair of bracelets. Geats stared at them.

'You're going to walk me into my own nick cuffed?'

'You're a prisoner.'

'I'm a solemnly sworn and warranted officer of the peace.'

'That remains to be seen.'

In protest at this injustice, Geats chose not to converse with the sergeant, holding his tongue through the short drive back to Vine Street and the conspicuous walk up to the first-floor office, where Cassar was waiting. Along the way he saw Billie, who held up the kitten like a tombola prize. He wondered if she had been there to witness him getting clonked out cold and dragged off in a Black Maria.

Never had he been more certain that the peripety of life most closely resembled the formula of a joke, culminating exclusively in the clemency of death.

The Marylebone sergeant uncuffed him and signed him over to Cassar, the really crucial thing now being not to break the chain of custody. Geats dropped down on the couch and looked round the office.

'Where the hell's all our stuff gone?'

'Christ, you're a mess. Look like the wrong end of a train crash.'

Geats touched his head, still tender and oozing a thick plasma that had matted most of his hair into wild styles. A dried blood filigree patterned his face where it had run during his spell of unconsciousness with the crocodiles. His shirt collar was a dark crimson, with a matching bib down the front.

'Take you all day, did it, letting them know who I was? Not only a sergeant, but your former partner.'

Cassar sighed, not in the mood for jousting. 'I had better things to be getting on with.'

'Yeah, not like you wasted anyone's time banging up a fellow officer.'

'You were interfering with a crime scene.'

'Bollocks. I was finding the scene of your murder. You didn't have a clue.'

'We didn't have a clue because you didn't tell us.'

'I tried. I told you yesterday – was it yesterday? I told you that I had an idea of where to look. But oh no. You were all about marching around going through your list of local shitehawks to collect your taxes from.'

'All right, all right. Leave it.'

Superintendent Dalton rapped loudly on the open door.

'What's all this I hear about you from Marylebone, Geats?'

'Misunderstanding, sir.'

'Look at the state of you. Your head.' Dalton glared at Cassar. 'Who's responsible for this, Sergeant?'

'It was a confusing situation, sir, I don't—'

'And Sharpe buggers off to France, leaving one of my men in the cells of a different nick? This is unacceptable.'

'It's fine, sir,' Geats said.

'It's a bushwhacking, is what it is.'

Having fumed at the nature of his assault just a few hours earlier, Geats now bristled at the armchair general's sneering at the cowardice of such a sneak attack.

'Oh, I don't know, sir. There's something to be said for a well-executed bushwhacking. A certain professional courtesy. We all have to die sometime, and I'd rather not in my final moments be faced with the stark realisation that life and death are not, after all, the same thing, especially when there's nothing to be done about it.'

'Foolishness,' Dalton said.

'Better to be blissfully unaware of one's end and go out silently with dignity intact; something that passing decrepitly in a befouled bed does not offer.'

'How hard was he struck?' Dalton said.

Cassar shrugged. 'Comparing before and after . . . hard to make firm conclusions.'

'Tell Sharpe I won't stand for this sort of hooliganism. He'll report to me as soon as he's back.'

'I'll tell him, sir.'

Dalton considered Geats momentarily and left shaking his head.

'Sharpe's in Paris?' Geats said.

'Lacroix was seen there. He's gone to fetch him.'

'With Minter and Lander? What did you do to get left behind?'

'Shut up.'

'Any idea why he killed Kassel?'

'Funny you should say that. What do you know about a Josephine Martin?'

'You're onto that, then.'

'You'd connected them already? Christ, Leon.'

'I connected them last night about three seconds before someone bashed my brains in.'

'If there was anywhere you could afford to take a good hard crack . . .'

'Was it Lander? I bet it was Lander, the miserable son of a whore.'

Cassar emptied an envelope, spilling Geats's watch, lighter and some loose change across the desk.

The lighter was in two pieces, which Geats held up. 'What the hell?'

'Lander thought it was a weapon of some kind.'

'My dad made that.'

'I know. Sorry.'

'Bloody mess, the whole thing.'

'How did you find it?'

'Oh, it was lovely, ta very much. Had a whale of a time. Accommodation at Marylebone was particularly nice, had a lot to recommend it.'

'The flat on Little Newport. How did you find the flat?'

Geats explained in short order how he had located the murder scene, chancing upon the broken glass and putting it together with the coroner's report of cuts to the victim.

Cassar thatched his fingers on his belly. 'This Benny Brownlow character. He's a defective?'

'The war did something to his mind. Boxing probably didn't help none.'

'He involved in that scene?'

'With the Frenchies? No. Old Ben just wanders the streets. Sometimes he's paid muscle for bookmakers. Bring him along, make folk more enthusiastic about paying what they owe. Guns aren't his thing, though.'

'We should speak to him, get a formal statement. He might remember more than he told you.'

Geats allowed that. 'What he says is like half a code or something. You can't always expect him to make the kind of sense you want.'

'Where does he bed down?'

'Nowhere permanent. Doss-houses. Derelicts. Hell, he likes a view of the stars if the weather permits it.'

'Did you work the Josephine Martin case?'

'I went to the scene, me and Bill. Martin was a pro, but I didn't really know her. Proudfoot took over and made a right bollocks of it. Had her killing herself, until Spilsbury tore that apart at the inquest. After that, no suspects really emerged.'

'She was Russian, like Kassel.'

'Yeah.'

'Why didn't you mention her before?'

'Because I didn't even give her a second thought until that maid brought up her name last night. And because Sharpe was busy looking for Jews in the light fixtures and braining coppers going about their lawful business.'

'Maybe this Martin was Jewish. Consider that?'

'Christ was Jewish, so I guess anything's possible.'

Getting up from the desk, Cassar sat on the couch beside Geats, looking at him sheepishly.

'Look, last night. That didn't go—'

'You could have just asked. Could have just said, "Where you going, Leon?"'

'You wouldn't have said.'

'Well, you could have knocked on the bloody door of the flat and said, "Aye-aye, what's all this then?" instead of having them do me like that.'

'What I'm apologising for. It was out of order. Look, can you help me? With this Martin thing?'

'How?'

'I don't know the case. Proudfoot, I'm guessing, is still as useless as he ever was.'

'Not wrong there.'

'While Sharpe and the others are off in France, if I could shake something loose on Martin, it'd go a long way.'

'Pfft.'

'Wouldn't hurt you either. I know you couldn't give a damn about promotion, but Flying Squad isn't an enemy you want.'

'There was someone I was thinking about having a chat with. Probably won't catch them for a couple of hours yet, mind, but you can buy me a few medicinals in the meantime to make up for last night.'

Cassar glanced at his watch. 'Now?'

'Well, if you need your beauty sleep, Sergeant . . .'

'All right. Let's go.'

Billie was waiting downstairs on the bench in the lobby, the kitten stuffed inside the front of her coat, fast asleep. Getting up, she made Geats bend down so she could prod and poke at his wounded head, leaking still.

'Has nobody looked at it?'

Cassar chuckled. 'A few looked. Some even pointed and laughed.'

'It needs a wash.' She sniffed. 'Most of you does.'

'A drink is what I need.' Geats sighed. 'And we have police work to do.'

'By way of a pub,' Cassar said.

'What work?' Billie said.

Geats glanced around the lobby. Opening the door, he held it for the others and they exited into the skyless trench that was Vine Street, squeezed between the station and the Piccadilly Hotel.

'Proudfoot tanked the Martin investigation. He was happy for it to go down as suicide until the pathologist banjaxed that theory, and by then he'd let it go cold and just shuffled it to the bottom of the pile. He worked J Division coming up, Proudfoot. Been here years, but still doesn't know Soho at all. Doesn't know who to ask. But he took a half-arsed witness statement from someone we can follow up on.'

'Who?' said Billie.

'Trifle previous for her to be out touting yet, but she's usually found at Cambridge Circus.'

'Leah?' Billie said.

Geats nodded. 'Stilts, yeah.'

Cassar looked confused. 'Who is this now?'

'Local brass. She knew Josephine Martin. Called her flat the day she was found. I had her come along for a chat, but Proudfoot jumped in. I doubt she told him half of what she knows, but she might tell us. Well, Bill, anyway.'

'Me?'

'How many times have you interviewed her or taken a statement after she's been nicked?'

'Half a dozen, probably more.'

'She knows you. Knows you're not a Proudfoot. She'd have known right there what he was all about.'

'She'll probably be getting up about now, getting ready for work.'

'Exactly. Time for a few drinkies first.'

Billie blew her lips. 'I know where she lives.'

Geats considered her mournfully.

'No drinks, then? No rowdy conversation, no banging of tables, no great toasts of our age?'

She took him by the arm.

'Come on, Leon.'

22

Most of the south side of Little Pulteney Street was filled by the St James's Residences, a series of eight red-brick tenements built over shops, with more tucked in behind accessed by an archway halfway down the street. The alley it led to was a stranger to the sun, the rear of the blocks dressed in grime and grey. It was a world of wrought iron: railings protected the so-called light wells and entrances to basements, and balustrades guarded stairs to upper floors.

This was never Cassar's thing, knowing where the locals lived. He'd fought hard to get into Flying Squad because he wanted to catch real villains, and since he'd been taken under Nutty Sharpe's wing he had – bank robbers, counterfeiters, smugglers, murderers. In a couple of years, he thought he'd accomplished more than he had in twice as long on the beat around Soho. Yet something about the way Geats and Billie were at home in the streets made him feel inadequate.

In a garret flat on the top floor, Leah Hinds grouted powder onto her face in preparation for her night's work. She looked Geats up and down. It was as if he took some demented delight in not cleaning up the blood or his wounds, daring people to look at the ghastly mess.

'Wondered what would happen when you met someone bigger and meaner.'

'You don't know what state they're in,' Geats said.

'Better than you, I'd wager.'

'Yeah, well. Jumped me from behind.'

'Know the feeling.'

'Who you mooching off to stay here, then?'

'I'll have you know I have a gentleman friend.'

'Thought you were an independent,' Billie said.

'He's no ponce. He's a conjuror.'

Geats laughed.

'He does tricks at restaurant and bars. Does all right out of it. Has impressive sleight of hand.'

'No doubt,' Geats said. 'All the better for forking into pockets with.'

'Look, I haven't got long. Need to be out on the Circus in an hour or so.'

'Thought it would be better to annoy you off the clock,' Billie said.

There was a banging at the door.

Leah sighed. 'Jesus, I told him what the score was. You lot stay here.'

The flat was part of a larger layout now divided into several abodes; the front door opened into a small windowless kitchen and dining room, with a table and an electric stovetop cooker with cabriole legs in the corner.

Leah greeted a small, worried-looking man at the door.

'Stanley, I told you to make yourself scarce.'

'You're not out yet.'

'I'm about to go.'

'Leah, I don't want—'

'Stanley. We talked about this. It's how it is. Go down the Caprice, they always let you set up to do some tricks. Earn us a few bob.'

'Until when?'

'Three. At the earliest. I'm keeping it locked up until then.'

Shutting the door, she returned to the only other room, the dormered bedroom where the others waited.

'That's Stanley.'

'Your conjuror?' Geats asked. 'I could feel the magic.'

'Shut up.'

'You lock him out?'

'He has a habit of coming in, sad puppy look on him, when I'm with a punter. Doesn't improve the mood any.'

Cassar had melted back against a wall, but Leah caught him watching her in her dresser mirror.

'Who's your pal, Geats?'

Cassar gripped his own lapel. 'Sergeant Cassar, Flying Squad.'

Leah winked at Geats in the mirror.

'Hanging out with the Sweenies, is it? That count as going up in the world or down?'

Geats flopped down on the double bed, gazing at the ceiling. 'We were wondering about Josephine Martin.'

'What happened to the other one who was dealing with that?'

'Inspector Proudfoot? It's still his case, but it touches on something we've been working. I thought maybe . . . look, I know Proudfoot didn't cover himself in glory.'

'He said Fee snuffed herself with her own silk stocking. I mean, have you heard the likes?'

'She worked for people connected to a gang based in Paris.'

Leah stared at his reflection. 'You really want me to talk about them?'

'Kassel's dead. Lacroix has fled to France.'

'I didn't really know names like that, but I saw the older one in the paper. They said he'd been shot.'

'That's Kassel. Red Max.'

'He was Russian or something, like Fee.'

'You know anything about a dance school? Where it was, maybe?'

Leah laughed. 'I heard mention. Fee never said where it was, and I never asked.'

'So it does exist? Not just a cover for bringing women in from France?'

'There's loads of places like that, posing as legit businesses. Some of them do have lessons and the like, all part of the swindle. Some of them send girls out on "tours", only you ain't working on your feet.'

'You think Kassel or Lacroix might have killed Josephine?'

'Why would they? They taxed every dollar she made, and she was useful to them with the new girls. I know she was growing weary of it and wanted out, but you don't kill someone over that.'

'You know the brother at all?'

'Albert? Yeah. He's a right prick. But what about Nell, is what I want to know. You done anything to find her?'

Geats sat up. 'The girl? What do you mean? She's with this Albert, isn't she?'

'I couldn't believe you left her with him.'

'I . . . he was her mother's brother, who else was she supposed to go to?'

'Not him.'

Billie handed Geats the kitten, which had woken up, mostly to keep him quiet for a few moments.

'Leah, you asked what we're doing to find her. Is she not with Albert any longer?'

'I went round there just to see how she's doing like. Gone. He reckoned she'd upped and run. I ask you, run where? He was the only family she had.'

'You don't believe him?' Billie said.

'If his mouth was open, I wouldn't give nothing that came out no credence. He's half a pimp, that one.'

'Are you saying he has her doing street work?'

'No. I don't think so. I mean, it's not beyond the bounds – I was at it at her age. Nell has an imagination, I ain't denying that, but she's young, and younger still up here.' She tapped her temple.

'What then?'

'I think the pair of them might have been badger baiting.'

Cassar had posed as a punter during C Division days, trying to bust such operations. Ponces used young girls to tempt men into an arrangement before revealing they were just eleven or twelve and threatening to shout for a constable to furnish with the girl's birth certificate unless they were paid off. They'd target classier clubs and hotels, aiming for the Bloomsbury and Mayfair gents who'd do anything to prevent a scandal.

'How old is she?' he asked.

'Eleven,' Geats said. The kitten was licking his little finger and allowing him to groom its head fur with it. 'She could pass for older, mind.'

'Has she run before?' Billie said.

Leah shrugged. 'For a couple of days, maybe. Never months like this. And she used to run to Albert, so I don't know where she'd go now.'

'What do you think he's done?'

'I don't know. He leeched off Fee, took money every week from her. After she'd seen to the men in the gang and then Albert, she barely had anything left for her and Nell. But Albert will have needed another source of income.'

'We need to speak to him,' Geats said.

Sensing the focus starting to drift away from Lacroix, Cassar stepped in. 'There been any bother with the foreign pimps? Some disagreement brewing between Lacroix and Kassel?'

'Told you, didn't really know them. Only the odd thing Fee would say, but she was tight-lipped when it came to them.'

'Was she involved with either of them? Or both of them? One of them got jealous, killed her?'

Leah shrugged.

'How about rivals to them? Other foreign pimps? Might she have been killed as a warning?'

'I don't know nothing about any of that. Look, I have to get going if I want my place on the Circus.'

Geats gave him a look. 'Mark.'

Cassar ploughed on. 'You know Jack Isow?'

Leah laughed. 'Everyone knows Jack Isow.'

'There any bad blood there, pimps trying to muscle in on his girls?'

Leah flashed a look at Geats before replying. 'The dancing girls in the dives look after themselves. Isow don't let no pimps in his places. How would that work? You're out there shaking a leg with a young lady, and then have to break off and have a chat with her squire to fix terms? There'd be trouble all over the place. In the clubs, you're paid to dance with the gents. You want to come to some other arrangement, that's your own business, and some of them have separate cloakrooms for just that. But there ain't a broker involved.'

Geats got up from the bed, almost tossing the kitten back to Billie. 'Listen, that's been helpful, Stilts. You get lagged and need a hand, ask for me or Bill.'

Cassar let Geats shove him out of the room, watched him hang back a moment, handing over a few shillings. Down in the street, Geats turned on him.

'What the hell was that?'

'What?'

'Isow? Foreign pimps?'

'We have to look at all—'

'Christ, you're no better than Proudfoot. Just bootlicking Sharpe, hoping for treats.'

'Look, Sharpe made it clear I'm senior partner here, so if I want—'

'Your rank isn't worth a pinch of shit to me.'

Billie stepped between them, wide-eyed kitty in her hands. 'We have two murders and what looks like a missing eleven-year-old girl, so if you two could possibly hold off whatever this is until after, that'd be great.'

The kitten mewed.

Cassar turned away to simmer down. Geats had always been able to needle him, had a gift for being a weasel while being right at the same time that infuriated him. He *was* asking questions for Sharpe rather than following where the investigation was going, and in truth, without Geats they'd be nowhere at all.

He raised his hands, *mea culpa*.

'This brother of Josephine Martin's, you want to take a run at him tonight?'

Geats shook his head. 'I'm beat to hell. My head's killing me and I spent last night in a cell. I could do with some human kip.'

He looked at Billie, something passing between just the two of them.

'Well, I'm this way,' she said. 'Catch you both tomorrow.'

'You local?' Cassar said. 'Can I walk you home?'

'That's all right. I'm just round the corner.'

'All right.' He turned to Geats. 'Vine Street, first thing, then.'

Geats half saluted him. Cassar watched him lumber off, gingerly prodding his head, which probably needed stitches.

23

Geats idled in the mouth of the Yard. Residents knew him, and drunks falling out of the clubs figured him for a maniac, what with the blood and general demeanour, and let him be.

Where he was in the shadows, Cassar walked right by him without noticing. A few minutes later, Billie came up Archer Street.

'He suspect anything?'

Geats shook his head. He'd signalled her discreetly to give Cassar the slip; they'd always worked in concert as a team.

'Mechanik has rooms next to that French church off Leicester Square.'

'Before we go anywhere, we need to clean your head up.'

'Come on. That can wait.'

She gripped his arm. 'Well I'm not going anywhere with you until we wipe some of this blood off.'

She spat on a handkerchief and dabbed at his face.

'That is disgusting, you know that?'

'I know it gives you some strange amusement, strolling round looking like you just fought a bear in a sewer, but Mechanik won't be impressed. A change of clothes really wouldn't—'

'Bill.'

'All right, all right.'

A place of perpetual motion, Soho was alive around the clock, but never more so than at night beneath the arc lights. Everything changed: the cut of the stone, the shadows they cast, the nocturnal glimmer of eyes and skin.

They came in the north end of Leicester Place, the square at the other end, cinema and theatre crowds dispersing into the surrounding streets. Feeling queer suddenly, Geats stooped against the back wall of the Empire, then hunched over with his hands on his knees.

'You all right?'

He held up a finger and then vomited. Freeing himself of another couple of puddles of watery goop, he spat away strings of bile.

'Jesus. You need a doctor.'

'I'll be fine.'

He stood upright, wiping his mouth on his sleeve, and leaned against the wall. The world had donned a new shimmer, sashaying this way and that, and it took a moment to adjust the roll of his eyes to this new way of moving in order to keep placing one foot in front of the other. When he had a handle on it, he took a few unsteady steps across the street to Mechanik's building.

'Leon . . .'

'Let's just do this, and then I'll deal with it.'

Mechanik lived in a single room on the third storey of a thin building next to the French Catholic church. The ceilings got progressively lower each floor you went up until they were barely above the door frames. He welcomed them in as though they were old acquaintances, offering them the two chairs either side of a small table by the window.

'Coffee, officers? I cannot drink it myself this late, I would be awake all night. What is more, up and down the hallway to the lavatory every hour or so too.'

'Thank you, Mr Mechanik, but we're fine,' Billie said.

He looked curiously at Geats, pale with sweat sheened across his face, blood on his clothes.

'Been an interesting day,' Geats said.

'Those are the ones your memory knits together in the end.'

Mechanik perched himself on the ungenerous cot pushed to one wall, rubbing his knee as he sat. He moved with a stiff limp, a cane leaning against the door frame.

'Have you news on Josephine?'

Geats studied him. For living in such humble surroundings, Mechanik was well groomed. A small, neat beard and moustache, his hair carefully swept back. His clothes looked expensive, but old, slightly shabby now: cuffs frayed, loose threads on the sleeve. Trying to keep the habits of a man who had once lived better than he currently did.

'Mr Mechanik, do you know a man called Max Kassel?'

'Max, yes. Although, he was Emil Allard when I met him.'

Admitting to knowing Kassel right off the bat flummoxed Geats somewhat.

'I see. What was your relationship with him?'

'Relationship? No, that would make it sound as if we were close in some fashion. We were not.'

'You knew about his . . . uh, arrangement with your sister?'

'Sergeant, I know exactly what it was my sister did for a living. I did not judge her. I could not judge her, for she gave me an allowance. Since my knee, I cannot easily work.'

'What was it that you did previously, if you don't mind me asking?'

'I was a dancer. More properly, a dance instructor. I was never good enough to make my name on the stage, but I was not a terrible teacher.'

'Where did you teach?'

'Oh, in St Petersburg originally. Then Paris. This is where I met Emil at first. He knew a young woman I was instructing. Later, I bumped into him in London, quite by chance.'

'By chance? You didn't meet him through Josephine?'

'Oh no. I did not involve myself in Josephine's affairs. I was happy to gratefully accept whatever money she could spare for me, and not ask questions. No, I met Emil, or Max as he was then calling himself, in a dance studio in Covent Garden.'

Red Max in a dance studio. Geats could feel the case begin to solid-ify beneath his feet.

'Do you remember where this was exactly?'

'I do not know the precise address, but it was one of those little places off Floral Street. This was some years ago now, you understand. The premises have been taken over by a theatre school since, run by a woman with a lopsided face. Stroke victim, perhaps.'

'Kassel was a dancer too?' Geats asked.

Mechanik smiled. 'Oh yes, once a very keen one.'

'When did you learn he was involved with your sister?'

'Josephine mentioned some people she knew, and I deduced she was talking about Emil.'

'Did you have any contact with him?'

'No. We were not friends. Not even casual acquaintances. He was a man I met through our shared interest in dancing, but I meet so many people that way. It was coincidence that Josephine also knew him.'

'It was just coincidence that you met your sister's pimp in two sepa-rate dance studios on different sides of a sea?'

'You read too much into this. Certainly, it is no coincidence that a man such as Emil, a procurer, would also be interested in the dance scene in whatever city he was operating in. Where better to find flights of shapely young women? Sergeant Geats, what is it you really wished to ask of me? I read the newspapers, I am aware of Emil's demise.'

'Did you know his business partner, Georges Lacroix?'

'By reputation only.'

'Through your sister?'

'Josephine spoke of him, but his was a name known in certain cir-cles in London. I had left Russia several years before my sister, before the war. I thought Paris was where I would make my name dancing. I have roots there. I love the city. After the war, I secured passage out of Russia for my sister, and we decided to go to London together. I was fortunate then to have several communities from which to draw help and support. I am Russian. I am French. I am Jewish.'

'And what do the French of London tell you about Georges Lacroix?'

'That he is a trafficker. Of women. Of narcotics. That he is a dangerous man. Something Emil appears to have discovered to his cost, no? Of course, Lacroix is not his real name.'

'No?'

'He changed it because Roger Vernon was a loud and notorious name. One he could no longer live with. You know of Devil's Island? It is a penal colony, an island ten miles off the coast of French Guiana. A savage place. Disease is rife, violence is an everyday occurrence. Regardless of sentence, very few make it home from there alive. He was jailed there for robbery, but nine years ago escaped with six other men. He was the only one whose corpse did not wash up across the straits on the mainland. After making it to Panama City, he boarded a ship back to Europe. Such a man is not to be misunderstood.'

'Do you think he could have killed your sister?'

'When your detectives interviewed me after Josephine's death, when they thought I might be a suspect, I told them this – why would I kill the person who, quite aside from being the only family I had in this world, provided me with my income? On purely selfish terms, that would not serve my interests. Josephine worked for this man, earned money for him. What purpose would him killing her serve?'

'My experience, people often act completely contrary to their own interests.'

Mechanik chuckled. 'I suppose I cannot argue with that.'

'Do these circles of yours have anything to say about Red Max?'

'You know Emil was deported from France?'

'For trafficking women to the Argentine, yes, I know.'

Mechanik set his face equivocally. 'He was not a good man.'

Billie, who until this point had been listening quietly and scratching the kitten between its ears when it poked its head out of the side pocket of her coat, suddenly piped up.

'That's not quite right, though.'

'Excuse me?'

'Just now, when you said Josephine was your only family. What about Nell?'

Mechanik's brows rose, and he sighed deeply. 'Forgive me, you are quite correct. *What about Eleanor?* A question I have asked myself every day recently.'

Billie gestured around the room. 'This is a confined space for any two people to live in, let alone a man of your age with a young girl.'

'Constable, I have not seen Eleanor for some weeks now.'

'How many weeks?'

'In truth, she was not here more than three or four nights.'

'Where did she go?'

'I do not know. She was prone to running away for short spells . . .'

'Did she not come to you when she ran away from her mother?'

'She did. She did. And as you point out, that was not a particularly convenient arrangement.'

'Nell is eleven years old. She's your niece. Are you not concerned for her?'

'You ask me this? Young lady, what is it you know of Eleanor? You met her just the once, on the day her mother was murdered. What can you tell of a person when that is your only contact with them?'

Geats interrupted. 'Mr Mechanik, I think what the constable means—'

'I understand. I do. Eleanor is young, she has experienced great tragedy. But I have known her all of her life. And I can tell you, she was a handful when she was little more than knee-high.'

'We've heard you were running a bait game with her,' Geats said.

'What is this, bait game?'

'Come on, Mr Mechanik, let's not play pretend.'

Mechanik smiled, working his knee hard with his knuckles. 'Who has told you these things?'

'Oh, you know. *They.*'

'Ah, yes. *They.* I am familiar. *They* can be very helpful, especially after the fact. *They* who met my sister while in the cells for whoring. I know *they* all too well.'

Geats hoped he hadn't got Leah into trouble. 'Is it true?'

'It most certainly is not.'

'You have no idea where your niece is?' Billie said.

'I am ashamed to say, I have not. Since my sister's passing, I have struggled to feed even myself. I rely on the generosity of friends, and hope maybe to gain a few hours of employment instructing dance, but with my knee . . .'

He fought to his feet, staggering on his bad knee, and hobbled to his wardrobe. From the bottom, he tugged out a small cardboard suit-case and hauled it onto the bed.

'Eleanor's,' he said, opening it.

Inside were a few items of children's clothing, a couple of books and a stuffed doll.

Billie got up to go through the case. 'She left all this?'

'She took some things. The clothes she wore more often. Her coat. A small leather case that contained photographs of her mother. Her favourite teddy bear. Yellow scarf with black checks.'

'Dolores,' Geats said.

'Quite.'

'Sounds like she never meant to return,' said Billie.

Mechanik glanced round the room. 'Can you blame her?'

He hobbled to the door and held it for them, grimacing.

'What happened to your knee, anyway?' Geats said.

'I am a dancer, Sergeant Geats. My life happened.'

Geats glanced down between the stairs folding back on themselves around the walls of the well to the hard lobby floor.

'Maybe want to get yourself somewhere a little closer to earth.'

24

Geats breathed loudly through his nostrils, sucking up as much of the chill night air as he could, hoping it might clear out his system. Billie eyed him closely.

'I'm fine.'

'You've never been fine. But right now your head is literally still bleeding, you threw up in the street, and you're breathing like a wheezy old squeezebox. So let's agree things are less than optimal.'

His eyes bulged and lips pouted as he dragged in another couple of buckets of air. Blowing it back out, he seemed to renew himself.

'You think he knows where Nell is?'

Billie shrugged. 'I don't know. I don't have a read on him.'

'No. Wily old fox.'

'You worried for her?'

'I keep thinking about what you said when she hid the bear in our office. That she wanted it so I'd have to come round here with it.'

'Maybe I was wrong.'

'She asked to come live with me.'

'Really?'

'Said she'd be no bother. Hardly know she was there, and that she could cook and clean.'

'I'm trying to picture that . . .'

'And now she's vanished.'

'Yeah.'

'That's on me.'

'You couldn't have known what was going to happen.'

'If I'd listened to what she was actually saying, maybe I could have.'

'She couldn't have gone to live with you.'

'No, but she didn't have to go to her uncle. Something could have been arranged.'

She touched his arm. 'Leon . . .'

'We need to find her, Bill.'

'All right.'

'It's late. Let's get you home.'

When Billie had joined the force a few years earlier, she'd left her family home in Bermondsey and moved into a hostel run by a Catholic convent near Warren Street, but the sisters weren't always understanding of the odd hours and odder company she kept working for the Met.

Superintendent Dorothy Peto, who ran the women's branch, had arranged for her to take a room in the house of a prominent benefactor, the wife of a sitting MP, on Sackville Street, less than two minutes' walk from Vine Street.

Geats accompanied her through Piccadilly Circus, stopping a few doors short of her home.

'Probably best nobody sees me.'

'Not looking like that, anyway.'

'What about him?' he said, looking at the cat.

'It's a her. She was grooming herself on the desk this afternoon, gave everyone an eyeful. Didn't you, madam? She does need a name, though.'

'Tallulah.'

'I'm not sure I should encourage this fantasy that you met Tallulah Bankhead.'

'I know this is difficult for you to accept, but she kissed me. On the mouth. It was pleasantly obscene. And she's surprisingly acrobatic in high heels.'

'If we call her Tallulah, will you promise never to mention this delusion ever again?'

'On the lips, Bill,' Geats said as he walked off. 'Most indecorously.'

25

A few loiterers, cigarettes gummed to their lips, bristled when Geats swanned through the Yard. He stopped off at his mother's flat. Clara was awake and had been listening to tangos and foxtrots on shellac discs that had found their way to Britain from the east on the wave of the diaspora. The gramophone had wound itself out and she stared inscrutably at its silence. Other records littered the floor; she'd had out some klezmer and some Gershwin, and her favourite of all, the great Kiepura.

'Matka, how are you?'

She didn't look at him.

'Have you eaten?'

She shrugged him off and sipped from her gin. That day's bottle had a finger left, at most.

'Look at you, thin as a rake. You have potatoes? I'll make latkes.'

A curl of her lip. 'You'll make someone a lovely wife one of these days.'

Well used to his mother's sneers, he rolled up his sleeves and got to work. Finding two softening potatoes in the kitchen, he peeled and quartered them before feeding them into the hand-crank grater. He squeezed out the starch and beat the eggs and added the salt. Shaping the mixture into fritters, he dropped them into hot oil until golden brown and served them with mizeria made with onion and chives.

Clara picked at them, pushed them around her plate, occasionally licked a finger. Geats had all but cleared his plate before she noticed the blood on his shirt.

'Leon, your head.'

'It's fine.'

'We'll need a bowl of soapy water with a clean cloth. And bring my tea tin.'

He did as he was told, returning to find his mother settled in her armchair. He placed the bowl carefully on the table so it didn't slop, and opened up the tin with her medical supplies. A drunk always had stuff on hand for cuts.

'Matka . . .?'

'Make sure you wash it thoroughly. And dry it properly before you dress it.'

'Right.'

In the corner stood a Biedermeier tabernacle mirror with console table. He adjusted his chair so he faced it and cleaned out his wounds, scrubbing at his scalp to remove the caked blood from his hair. Patting it off, he applied Dakin's and bandaged it lavishly, then returned the tea tin to the kitchen and washed out the bowl.

Troubled by a mild but persistent cough, Clara treated it by emptying the bottle of Gilbey's into her glass and putting on an early Isa Kremer, recorded for a Turkish label. As ever, it was a fine line as to whether the liquor turned her wistfulness to melancholy.

She patted the floor in front of her armchair.

'Come here, Leon.'

Like an obedient pet, he sat beside her legs, back to the chair, and she ran her fingers through the hair sprouting up between the bandaged halo.

'So much like him,' she said, stroking his cheek.

The only good picture they had of his father stood on the sideboard, taken the day he left for France by a neighbour with a leatherette box camera. In it, he stood proudly in his uniform. He had been a phantom presence in Geats's life, something his mother would admonish him with. As a small boy, he'd suffered night terrors, which had greatly inconvenienced Clara's attempts at sleeping off the gin.

'Your father wouldn't have stood for your nonsense,' she would tell him.

But Geats had to believe that he would have.

Now, Clara's other hand rested on his shoulder and he reached up and squeezed it.

'You're about the age he would have been, had he made it back.'

'Matka . . .'

She kissed his head and wrapped her arms round his neck, laying her cheek on his hair. He could feel her breath on him.

'This is how he would have looked.'

Unknotting her fingers from his, she lifted the needle from the gramophone and drained her glass. He looked up at her, but she was gazing at the photo.

'Sometimes I feel God mocks me with your face.'

26

Upstairs on the landing outside his room, Geats paused for the briefest of moments before slipping the key back out of the lock. He turned to the shadows at the far end of the gloomy corridor, where an irregular staircase reached up to the garret rooms.

'Are you going to come out of there?'

The figure stepped down from the flight, a man in a grey suit with his hat pulled low.

'I thought you'd be up earlier, Leon. You don't normally spend so long with Clara.'

Geats's knife was strapped to his leg, and he didn't want to make a show of reaching for it. Clenching his fist around the keys, he let one protrude between his first and middle fingers, and offered the stranger only an unhelpful silence.

'I thought we might talk,' the man said.

He wasn't from the streets, but he wasn't police either. Yet he was *something*. Educated, mannered, well dressed. An air about him of the officially unofficial. The kind of person whose authority was of the arbitrary and unquestionable variety. A gangster of the future.

'About the Kassel affair,' he added.

Geats smiled, and the man caught it and smiled in turn.

'That amuses you?'

'I just wonder what sort of person refers to the grubby murder of a grubby pimp as an "affair"?'

'Your wound is dressed.'

They stood in silence again, the man fluent in such forms of communication. He produced a packet of cigarettes and lit one, offering them to Geats with a minuscule gesture. Geats shook his head, although the taste of the smoke made the offer inviting.

'Interesting clubs you frequent,' the man said at last. 'Some kind of friend to the negroes and the homosexuals?'

'No. It's the reds I go there for. I'm a jazz-loving Bolshevik. That what this is, a shakedown? If so, you picked the wrong man, and the wrong place.' He jerked a thumb over his shoulder to the slim hallway window over the Yard. 'We're three floors up. Could be you go back down a sight quicker than you came up.'

'Have you found the dance school?'

'Look, I don't know who you are—'

'Yes you do.' The man glanced down the main staircase. 'Invite me in.'

'You armed?'

'I can be armed wherever I am in seconds.'

Geats didn't move.

'No, Leon, I'm not carrying a gun. I work in an office, for heaven's sake.'

He opened the door and let the man follow him in.

'Living room's that way. Get you something?'

'Appreciate an ashtray, if I'm permitted to smoke.'

Geats found one in the kitchen, also retrieving his knife from his ankle and slipping it into his pocket. The man was sitting in one of the two armchairs, and Geats placed the ashtray on the table between them. At the table by the window, he flicked on the lamp.

'I get to know your name?'

'You can call me Harrison.'

He raised the sash window a crack to let air in and smoke out, before sitting in the other armchair with his hand in his pocket.

'You've been following me, Mr Harrison?'

'Not so much. More like a picture I build up from various different sources. People talk to me. Most people.'

'Special Branch?'

'I'm not Scotland Yard.'

'Do they have a name for where you work?'

'Oh yes. Many different ones, depending on what is required.'

'How about we make this easier and you tell me what you want.'

'Max Kassel, as he was calling himself, was a person of great interest to me.'

'A ponce. Mover of narcotics. A street hood in a suit.' Geats leered at his guest's tailoring.

Harrison laughed. 'Yes, very good. Kassel brought people into the country. Some he made legal with marriages to Englishmen, others he provided with false documentation. Often he used a combination of the two.'

'How do you mean?'

'Providing women from various places with papers that made them appear to be French nationals, who he'd then marry off in England and get bona fide documents for.'

'Like the way Josephine Martin was really Russian.'

'For example.'

'You're worried about Russians coming into the country.'

'Among other aliens.'

'They're all women, though.'

'To be frank, I suspect most countries would generate far better levels of intelligence if all of their agents were women. But not everyone shares my opinions on that.'

'What do you want from me?'

'What do you know of Kassel? His past.'

'Nothing, really. Running women to the Argentine, that sort of thing. Worked with a fellow called Lacroix, who was a bit tasty by all accounts.'

'Kassel worked with criminal gangs in London and Paris, and Latin America, as you say. He had been involved in white slavery since before the war. He also ran operations in British Honduras, organising brothels for the timber cutters, and in Montreal too. It was there that he grasped his real power. There was a man called Bouchier, a pimp and a gangster who went by the nom de guerre Le Marseillais, even though he was from La Rochelle. It was said he ran the biggest white slavery operation in western Europe, criss-crossing the Atlantic between dozens of locations. Bouchier had taken care of his biggest rivals, and thought he would rule the enterprise for many years. But in 1930, he was shot dead on the street in Montreal.'

'By Red Max?'

'So the tale goes. Whether it is street mythology or truth, who can say? I expect these things usually are a little of both.'

'Sounds like you know considerably more than me.'

'There are things I know, and there are things I do not. Places are like music, Leon. The hills harmonise, the streets sing. And in Soho, you know the tunes. You hum them in your sleep. You can kick up a fuss where I cannot, know who to ask questions of when I do not.'

'Exactly what sort of fuss and what kind of questions?'

'I was only just on Kassel's trail when Josephine Martin was murdered.'

'You know who did it?'

'No. I didn't know Martin at all. I only connected them because I had a tail on Kassel and he went to Archer Street and then fled when he saw the police. He and Lacroix were quite frantic after that, so I surmised that the dead woman was known to them. Their behaviour changed; they lay low for a few weeks. This was frustrating. You see, a contact I have in Paris had told me of the dance school scheme, and I had hoped they would lead me there. Any records or paperwork they might have kept would be a gold mine.'

'In terms of locating the aforementioned Russians.'

Harrison smiled tightly. 'I think we're getting off track with the Russians. Are you familiar with the Abwehr?'

'Funny-looking chaps. Some sort of little burrowing creature.'

'I believe your superintendent is a great admirer of your sense of humour.'

'Christ, the files you people keep must be a rollicking good read.'

'The Abwehr. German military intelligence. Their role has mostly been defensive, but last year the Nazis renamed the Ministry of Defence the Ministry of War, and their goals changed accordingly. We believe they are ramping up the recruitment of spies in European nations, and attempting to place their own agents abroad. Obviously we keep a close eye on anyone connected to the embassy, but they've been working on more creative methods. Kassel's pipeline is a weakness they have identified. I was tasked with monitoring him, but then he was murdered, and you and Flying Squad have been rampaging through my case with your big elephant feet.'

'Why don't you ask Nutty Sharpe for help?'

'Chief Inspector Sharpe isn't someone you ask for help.'

'You don't trust him.'

'I don't trust anyone beyond trusting them to be themselves.'

'And what makes you think me being myself is going to be of any help to you?'

'I don't care about the murders, I only want the pipeline between Paris and London. Who they've brought in. Any records there might have been. You understand, we're in a precarious position. We haven't recovered from the Depression; nobody's sure how Baldwin is going to work out as prime minister; the king is dead, and this new one, with his American good-time Gertie, is trouble; the Italians are in Abyssinia; the Germans have taken the Rhineland; things in India are far from rosy. Any passage that alien agents can use to get into the country unnoticed needs to be plugged up.'

'And if I find something?'

Harrison popped a card onto the table between them, an address printed on it.

'I don't know where that is.'

On the back of the card he scribbled a rude map.

'Come see me there if you want to help out. I can be a valuable friend to you, Leon.'

27

Long before it was light, Geats was back at Vine Street, hunched over old occurrence books at Nutty Sharpe's desk, searching in vain for any historical mentions of Max Kassel or Georges Lacroix, or of anything that looked like the activity of foreign pimps. Of the former he could find none, and of the latter the material was so voluminous as to be useless without further refinement.

There was simply too much to wade through on paper; what he needed was a human guide, an organic index to the written record. At what he judged to be an early but civilised hour, he made a phone call and then rushed out to Fratelli Camisa, the Italian grocer's on Old Compton Street, and bought a dozen fresh mushroom arancini.

From there he hailed a High Lot to Hammersmith, so they would still be piping hot when he arrived at the quiet, leafy road near the waterworks. Charlie Garland had the door open before he reached it, and embraced him warmly. Retired three years, he looked good for it.

The house was large, and echoed of children now moved on. His wife Polly made tea, and Charlie showed Geats to an upstairs room he had converted into a study of sorts.

'Where you set about the critical endeavour of retirement,' Geats said, admiring the mahogany desk.

There were two armchairs in the dull early light of the west-facing window, and they sat with their tea and arancini, something Charlie had bought in Soho whenever the opportunity presented; going out of his way when it did not.

'Leon Geats. They haven't got you yet, then.'

'Not for want of trying,' Geats said.

Garland paid close attention to the bandages around his old pupil's skull. 'Friend or foe?'

'Hurts me that you should feel it necessary to ask.'

'It was another copper, wasn't it?'

Geats bit off half a steaming rice ball and did his best to chew around the burning heat. Where he himself was a bullshit trapeze artist, foxtrotting around Soho by the skin of his teeth, Garland had joined the force in the first year of the century and done three decades of service. He'd signed up for the army at the outbreak of war and returned home four years later in one piece, if not exactly of sound mind.

Picture the ginger love child of Rasputin and Rembrandt's Abraham, and that was Charlie Garland. Geats didn't believe he'd ever seen the man's mouth through his hellish moustache and soup-catcher. Punctuating silver tufts lent hauteur to the long burnt-orange growth, and he had been well known by police and villains alike for his unruly brush of red hair – less red now than it had been – and his stern sense of morality.

The Carrot-Top Jesus.

The Taproot Redeemer.

Salvātor sativus.

Nearing retirement when Geats was sworn in, he had thrown himself into teaching the young man what he knew, something to give back to the force before he left. If the sergeant who sat with him now wasn't exactly what he had foreseen creating, Charlie being a strict Anglican and man of towering faith, he was at least a man who understood the streets in which he worked.

'Guess who I find myself working with again?' Geats said.

'Amaze me.'

'Mark Cassar.'

'Money Mark. Still looking every bit the dandy?'

'Oh indeed. With the added accoutrement of his stripes courtesy of Flying Squad.'

'I heard Nutty Sharpe had snapped him up. He never had the depraved feel for the streets you have, but he's a far more ruthless political animal.'

'He'll need to be. He's ranging with wolves like Lander and Minter now.'

Charlie almost spat on his own floor in disgust.

'Lander I can understand. He's a savage, but he's upfront about it. Minter, though . . . your father was a papist, so perhaps you understand him better than I ever could. His desperate need for absolution after the things he does.'

'The big G Catholics believe in isn't God; it's guilt.'

Garland snorted. 'Your guilt has always been of the Jewish variety. How is Clara, anyway?'

'Let's not get uncivilised at this hour.'

'And what an hour it is. Can only be a case dragged you from your pit with the sun so low. What are you on, this business with the dead pimp? Riddled with bullet holes, the paper said.'

Geats told him about the annexing of his corner of Vine Street by Sharpe's mob, and the connections he'd drawn between Red Max and Josephine Martin. 'Way I heard it, Kassel made his big power play by murdering a pimp by the name Bouchier in Montreal, six or seven years back, and that completed his takeover of the trafficking out of Paris. He was deported from France, but hooked up with this chap Vernon, now calling himself Lacroix, who's supposed to have escaped from Devil's Island.'

Garland chuckled. 'If I had a farthing every time a park bench claimed to have got off that island . . . I don't know Kassel or Vernon, though. If they were operating when I was in Soho, they kept out of my line of sight.'

'Bouchier went by Le Marseillais on the streets.'

'Huh. Now that name I do know. Castanar and Micheletti mean anything?'

'Only from you. Legendary feud between French ponces.'

'Juan Antonio Castanar. Dago, but he'd been a dancer in Paris so was as good as. Claimed he'd worked with Pavlova's company, but found pimping easier and more rewarding. Ten, fifteen years ago, Soho was infested with these French pimps, *souteneurs*, part of what the Parisian police called the Apache underworld. French passed laws to run them out of the city after the war, so they all settled here.

'One of the chiefs was a fella name of Martial Lechevalier. He was one of the first to realise that the French and Belgian tarts who came to London to escape the Germans were very popular with the locals; figured he might as well start bringing more over. Also realised that those who had married Englishmen and then hit the streets couldn't be deported if they were nicked, on account of being natural-ised Brits.

'So, he cooks up this marriage caper, bringing girls over and paying some jobless oaf to marry them and make them all legal. Tacked what he paid them onto what the girls owed him for bringing them here, and then they paid tax to him for the foreseeable. He never really kept a stable of women like a brothel, just had them in debt to him like a racketeer.'

'Exactly the same as Kassel and Lacroix.'

'Yeah, this was the original clever French ponce. So clever, he got himself carved up with a razor outside the Regent Palace Hotel. This is '23, '24, something like that. Never stuck it on anyone, but best bets were one of a pair of up-and-coming pimps – Castanar and Micheletti. These two hated one another. Micheletti was a little Algerian chap, quick with a blade, which is why I always fancied him for Lechevalier. He also cut up Castanar one night in the 43 Club, left him with a railway down his face.'

'What happened to them?'

Charlie tugged lightly at his fiery beard. 'What happened to them? Darby Sabini, that's what happened. They'd been doing well, running prostitution in Soho between them. Castanar and his crew rolled out of the Union on Frith Street. But they also had a dance academy. See, bringing over these French birds weren't enough for Castanar. He started seeing how he might catch a few local doves too. Offered classes, no money up front. Idea being that there was loads of work waiting for them and they'd pay off the fees in no time. So the girls signed up, got dancing lessons, learned a few moves, and then it turns out there's no work. They can't get in stage shows or nothing like that, and suddenly they owe fifty, a hundred quid for lessons.'

'Uh-oh.'

'Exactly. But then nice Mr Castanar, he has a solution. What if the girls go on a tour with a new dance company he's setting up? Or what if they agree to dance in a nightclub he has a stake in? What could the girls say? They couldn't refuse, they owed too much. So they go along, find out this dancing isn't exactly of the ballroom variety, and after that they can't tell their friends or family because they'd be disowned as whores. Hell, some of them were even sent abroad. White-birding, we called it.'

'Where's Sabini in all this?'

'Castanar signs up this girl, Anna. She's English, but the daughter of an Italian immigrant in Clerkenwell. This man, he goes to Darby Sabini when his daughter goes missing, tells him he's heard from one of her friends that she's going on an overseas tour for Castanar, but he thinks there's something fishy about it. Sabini knows all about Castanar, and don't appreciate him spreading his net over to the Italian quarter. Has a sit-down with the Spaniard, arranges for the girl's safe return. About this you'll hear dozens of different stories, most popular being that she'd been shipped off to the Middle East and spent a month on her back in a tent in the desert. Ask me, more likely she was in a two-up two-down in Chingford. Regardless, she comes home, the father is happy, all's more or less well.'

'But . . .'

'But Darby Sabini has decided Castanar needs to go. He doesn't want an all-out war in Soho, though. It's not his turf, and he doesn't want in on the whoring. He just wants the dago gone. He waits a few weeks and then firebombs the dance studio, burns it out. Puts it around on the street that Micheletti did it. Castanar buys this, and it all boots off between him and the Algerian, who he already wants to kill for slicing up his face. They both get nicked on various assault and rioting charges and are deported.

'While later, in Paris, they bump into each other in a bar and Castanar shoots Micheletti. At least, he's convicted and jailed for it, but he always claimed he never did the shooting. That a man called Le Marseillais did it and put the gun in his hand.'

'Bouchier.'

Charlie nodded. 'Starting to make sense in a grand way now, isn't it? Bouchier clears up the two vice kings of Soho in one go, and then gets himself murdered in Montreal a few weeks later. Since then, I guess Kassel and Lacroix have been top dogs in Soho. And were clearly pretty good at it, as we didn't know they existed until one of them killed the other.'

'I've heard about Kassel having a dance school. This studio of Castanar's . . .'

'Right near you, son. Archer Street.'

'That's where the Martin woman lived.'

'Pieces are all slotting together.'

'I don't know of any dance school there, though.'

'They never advertised it outside or nothing. Put ads in the paper to get girls, but the sign on the door would have said something innocuous, or made it sound like a management-type company, so they didn't get any walk-ins. You know how the street is always crawling with musical types. Strictly by appointment only.'

'Josephine Martin was murdered in her flat on Archer Street. And her brother said he didn't know where Max Kassel's dance studio was.

But if Kassel and Lacroix cleaned up in the aftermath of Castanar and Micheletti, chances are—'

'They took over the same place. Across from the back of the Apollo it was, next to that place where all the starving artists live. First floor.'

'The heart of the beast,' Geats said.

28

The usual congregation of musical sorts kicked about in Archer Street outside the London Orchestral Association. A few doors down, Geats slunk into a street-level vestibule that housed a door to the upper floors of numbers 10–11, but found it locked. The sign on the wall showed no name assigned to the first floor. In the neighbouring building an arched passageway led through to a yard forming the corner of Archer and Rupert, including a rear door to numbers 10–11 that was propped open by a wooden box.

Upstairs, he broke into the dance school, an operation that was exactly as sophisticated as pressuring the double doors until one of them splintered and snapped around the mortise lock. There was no external indication of the place's function, but the door opened into a large open space with polished wooden floors and bench seating along one wall. The room was otherwise empty.

A door in the opposite wall led to a small antechamber accessing two further rooms: a small lavatory with basin, and an office, which had a cot bed. A large desk sat in front of the window over Archer Street, the wall beside it lined with four-drawer steel filing cabinets. They were locked, but Geats forced them easily enough with his boot knife.

Inside were rows of files with photographs: headshots of ladies who had presumably attended the school, going back four or five years.

Some files were empty, others contained copies of the same pictures. Flicking through, he found a few faces he recognised: women who did street work, a few club dancers. Many he did not know, and some of them appeared very young, the soft features of pre-pubescence.

Some files also included official-looking documents, birth and marriage certificates. This was the stuff that his new spy friend Harrison would salivate over, but it wasn't a whole lot of use to Geats. What he really wanted was some trace of Max Kassel's home address.

Frustrated, he slammed a drawer shut in one of the cabinets. A section of plaster fell from the wall behind. Separating the office from the studio, it was a lath-and-plaster job sporting other bare patches and a few spots where the naked wooden laths had snapped, threatening darkness behind.

Tilting the cabinet forward, he peered down the back. Someone had broken through the wall, stripping away the laths to fashion a square hole accessing the space between the wall studs. Walking the cabinet forward on its corners, he cleared it away from the wall and looked into the hole.

Something had been dropped down between the studwork, behind the remaining laths. He stuck an arm in and felt about; shoulder deep, his fingers brushed against some kind of box. It was low down and wedged in there pretty good, and took some tugging and pulling before he got it out of the hole. It was a box for a pair of glacé bar shoes, tied with twine.

One big sweep of his arm cleared the desk and he set down the box. The twine unknotted with a single pull. He lifted the lid.

'Christ.'

Inside were photographs of a different kind. Young women modelled in front of sets dressed in exotic scenes, some in lingerie and some in considerably less. A few were posed with more mundane vulgarity. Flicking through, there were girls he estimated were not yet in their teens.

In a flurry of rage, he dragged the cabinets away from the walls, finding holes behind each one, and with his hands ripped the laths away from the studwork. There was one other box low down in the wall like the first, but if there had been more, they had been removed.

The scope of Kassel and Lacroix's activities was coming into sharp focus, but there wasn't much there that could help Geats find out who murdered Josephine Martin. Perhaps he could track down some of the women in the files, interview them. There was such a churn of faces on the streets that he doubted most of them would still be in Soho. He wondered how many were even still alive.

He took a selection of documents from the cabinets and put them in one of the shoeboxes, tying both back up. Stacking them neatly, he wrapped them in a blanket he found on the cot and left with the bundle beneath his arm. He knew exactly who could help him with this.

29

If Harrison was who Geats thought he was – an operative with British intelligence – then the resources at his disposal would dwarf those of the Met. He'd know what to do with the documents.

Examining the card Harrison had given him, he followed the crudely drawn map on the back and found a covered alley on Great Windmill Street, tucked in between the Trocadero Hotel and St Peter's Church. Its mouth was obscured; the entrance was crooked, so you entered from the side and turned into the alley, the stone cut in such a fashion that it was difficult to see there even was a passageway until you were actually in it. All his years in Soho, Geats had never known it was there.

The alley led through to a cobbled court completely hidden from the main streets, standing somewhere between the Trocadero and Lyons Corner House, dead centre of the block between Shaftsbury Avenue and Coventry Street. Harrison's address was one of two large but dilapidated red-brick buildings with copper-fronted mansards. They stood there as if they'd been forgotten while other city streets had been built around them.

Crumbling steps led up to the front entrance on the upper ground floor. The door was ajar. It was large inside, but the tall, narrow hall-way had been stripped of its wainscoting and paint, leaving a rustic impression.

'Second floor,' Harrison shouted down from upstairs.

Geats took the naked steps and hesitantly looked for an open door on the second floor, finding Harrison in a cavernous room that spanned the front, six windows in breadth. No better decorated than the entrance hall, it was at least furnished, and expensively so.

Heavy mahogany desks lined one side, covered in paperwork and photographs and other evidence gathered by Harrison. A fire crackled in the hearth in the opposite wall.

'An office, you told me you worked in.'

Harrison shrugged, glanced around as if unsure what Geats might have expected.

'I never even knew this street existed,' Geats went on. 'Which is embarrassing for a copper whose beat for seven years has been Soho.'

'Sink Street doesn't exist until you need to know it exists. Tell you the truth, I was beginning to think I'd have to employ alternative methods to get you on board.'

'I found the dance school.'

'Oh?'

Geats placed his bundle on the nearest desk. 'Records. Photographs.'

'That's all of them?'

'God, no. Cabinets of the things.' He wrote down the address on one of the files. 'I'll need to report that I've found it, though. So you'll have to be quick with whatever you need from there.'

Harrison nodded. He made no move to look at what Geats had brought him. 'The photographs . . .?'

'Some are just pictures of the women. Like you'd have on a passport, but bigger. Not glamorous or anything. But I found two boxes filled with . . . other kinds.'

Harrison gestured to the wall. 'Like these?'

Geats saw pictures of a naked woman draped on a chaise longue, which he recognised from some of the photographs he'd found.

'Yeah. Exactly like that. They're from the same source?'

Clearing a space on a desk, Harrison removed the blanket and opened the boxes, spreading the documents across the sage skiver.

'Let's see what you have, then.'

As he pawed through them, Geats surveyed the information pinned up on the bare walls.

'This is good,' Harrison said. 'These files, all the names. This is good intelligence.'

Geats couldn't hear him.

On the wall was pinned a photograph that had stopped him dead in his tracks, yet the more he stared at it, the more it made a depraved kind of sense to him. He pointed at it.

'Where did you get this?'

Harrison followed his finger. 'Ah.'

'What the hell is it? And where did you get it?'

'I believe it is Eleanor Martin.'

In the picture, Nell wore a school dress and lay on a bed, propped up by pillows. Garish make-up smudged her lips and around her eyes, like a girl who'd got into her mother's cosmetics. She clutched Dolores, her scarfed teddy bear.

'There are more?' Geats said.

Harrison nodded.

'Worse than this?'

'Yes.'

'Show me.'

Harrison opened a drawer and handed Geats a thin sheaf of photographs. He went through them carefully.

'I'm going to find whoever's behind this. And then I'm going to kill every single one of them.'

'Leon, look—'

'Don't bloody Leon me. She's eleven. And there are others just as young in those boxes. I thought you were after alien spies, but this . . .'

'Kassel and Lacroix in all likelihood had no idea that agents were using them to get into the country. They were just ponces. Whore taxers.'

'And child slavers.'

'That too.'

'*Just* . . .'

'I mean to say, they were unaware of any broader aspect to their own operation. They weren't knowingly working for foreign states. They were criminals. Pornographers. Pimps.'

'It's the criminals, pornographers and pimps that I want.'

'I know, Leon. This is in the spirit of reciprocity.'

Geats looked at the pictures again.

'She looks almost asleep. You think they doped her?'

'There's a photographer, Kassel and Lacroix used him frequently. He paid them for models; they forced girls to pay off their debts to them by posing. Sometimes they forced them in other ways.'

'How did you come to get them?'

'They came in packets bought from an outlet in Soho.'

'An outlet?'

'My gift to you. The Domino Milk Bar.'

'Babe Mancini.'

'You're aware of the basement attractions at the premises?'

Geats nodded. Babe Mancini and Tommy Mack were small-time hoods on the fringes of the Sabinis' Italian mob, muscle for protection rackets. More recently, they'd fronted the money to open a milk bar in Gerrard Street, these enterprises being all the rage since they attracted a young crowd, kept late hours and didn't require a licence as there was no alcohol. The main source of income was somewhat more occult: a basement lined with various coin-operated machines. Sabini was losing his grip on the touts at the racecourses, but electronic amusements allowed him to control the odds without needing a venue.

'They deal in smut down there too.' Harrison handed him a sheaf of completed witness statements testifying to the purchasing of indecent images in the basement below the Domino.

'These witnesses . . .'

'They'll hold up in the real world,' he said.

He went on talking about the detail in the statements, and then how he would visit the dance school and arrange for photostats to be made of the records there so the originals could eventually be 'discovered' by police and entered into evidence at Vine Street.

But Geats wasn't really listening.

Neither was he really paying attention when, within the hour, three men unloaded the filing cabinets from a van and wheeled them into the building; or for the next three hours as they helped Harrison photostat the records, cranking out three copies a minute as they worked through the drawers.

Instead, he spent the time scouring Harrison's material for any sign of Nell, finding a couple of dozen photographs of the girl in all. He thumbed through the cabinet files searching for more, but found none.

Returning to those he had, he examined the sleepy expression on Nell's face in the photo. He studied the set behind her. He committed every detail to memory so that he'd recognise them if he ever saw them in other pictures.

When Harrison told him that the cabinets were on their way back to Archer Street, Geats took the witness testimonies and left with barely a word.

There was work to do.

There were heads to crack.

30

Before he had even sat down, the phone in the Clubs & Vice office rang twice. Both times asking for someone Cassar had never heard of: two different unheard-of parties. The third time it rang, he took it off the receiver and left it.

He'd dropped in at New Scotland Yard first thing to see if there was any word from Sharpe in Paris. There's wasn't. Got waylaid talking to other Flying Squad chaps, making the latest on the Soho side of the murder case sound like more than the big ball of nothing that it was, and eventually tipped up at Vine Street well after midday.

That was when he found out Geats hadn't been seen, and worse, he and Billie had gone to question this Mechanik the night before, without him. There were also stacks of years-old occurrence books on the desk.

Billie was out in the main bullpen, still accompanied by the bloody cat. It rolled over on a desk, following a square of warm sunlight.

He caught her eye. 'Nothing?'

'Nope. Pym said he was already here when he got in, and he left in a hurry around eight.'

'Leon was *already* here at eight?'

'Maybe he came back last night and never left.'

Cassar didn't dismiss the idea. Seemed more likely than Geats rising with the sparrows.

'Come on. Get your coat.'

Billie stood. 'Where we going?'

'Strategy meeting.'

She looked at the cat.

'Put it in the office,' he said.

She lifted the kitten off the desk, whispering in its ear, for all the good that could do, and carried it into the office, shutting the door.

'Is it going to be a permanent member of the Dirties?'

'Took her home with me last night, but when the maid came into my room this morning, she started sneezing and coughing. Eyes streaming.'

'Allergic?'

She nodded. 'Have to tell Leon he needs to take her.'

Cassar smiled. 'Just as long as I'm there when you do.'

They walked through Piccadilly Circus to the Lyons Corner House.

'Strategy meeting?'

He shrugged. 'What's better for strategising than cha and pastries?'

On the first floor, they were shown to a small table in the middle of what looked like thousands. Business was brisk, nippies darting this way and that with trays of tea and cake. Somewhere in a corner, a band played light music.

Billie removed her hat, hiding it on her lap beneath the tablecloth, but left her coat on.

'You can take it off. Even coppers are allowed tea.'

'I know.'

Still she didn't remove it. Way she glanced about, it was as if she was anxious about being seen in her uniform in a place like that. Their waitress arrived. Cassar ordered a brew and Bakewells, and looked at Billie expectantly.

'Iced coffee, please. And have you a cake or pastry with lots of cream?'

'I think I'll be able to find something,' said the nippy.

'Iced coffee?' Cassar said, when she'd left to fetch their order.

'Why is it blokes can go into a pub and start faffing about with half of this and half of that like they're mixing nostrums, but a woman fancies a refreshing beverage and it's faces being pulled like they ordered gutter juice?'

'I—'

'Think twice before whatever you're going to say. I get enough off Leon, but at least he's funny.'

He thought twice.

'Should have got milk for the cat,' she said.

Loosening his tie, he shrugged his coat off onto the back of his chair. It was new, a sporty double-breasted number with pointed lapels and a wide belt, tailored so its lines narrowed below the waist. He had hoped it could be a topic of conversation, but now he was struggling to think of ways things could be going worse, and the tea hadn't even turned up.

She looked amused at his discomfort.

'You don't know how to deal with women, do you?'

'Don't know how to deal with anyone, truth told. Mother used to say I was one for my own company.'

'They live in London, your parents?'

He shook his head. 'Flu got her when I was eight.'

Immediately he wished he'd never mentioned his mother at all.

'Oh Mark. I'm sorry.'

'Dad did pretty well, just me and him.'

'Is he still . . .?'

'Five years ago. Lungs.'

She touched his arm, resting her hand there just above his wrist. As any kind of intimacy usually moved him to paralysis, he knew he would have to keep his hand nailed to the table, struggling on awkwardly with the other to both eat and drink if she hadn't released him before their food came.

'He was Maltese. From Malta.'

'And your mother?'

'Scottish. She was in Malta for . . . well, her father worked for a shipping company, and what with the Suez, Malta was a convenient stop-off point. When she grew up, she worked for them too. They worked together for a long while. Dad, my dad that is, was a builder. He got work when they constructed the breakwater at the Grand Harbour. They went down in diving bells, air pumped to them. When it was finished, six years' good work, he had enough money to take Mum back to Britain. Her family were dead, so they came to London. She was already pregnant; made in Malta, born in London.'

Christ, that was more than he'd ever told anyone about himself. He looked at the surrounding tables for a moment, as if someone might have eavesdropped his potted history, concerned what they might think if they did, though he had revealed nothing remotely scandalous.

Their orders arrived and he thought it best to get Billie talking, having eked out what desultory conversation he possessed.

'Uh, what about you?'

'No, I'm not Maltese. Or from Malta.'

'A Londoner? From London?'

'A Stopfordian. From Stockport.'

'Really?'

'Born there, anyway. Then Mum moved to Darlington. She was . . . well, unmarried mother was how they put it, so she cleared off with her little bundle of shame. Out of sight, out of mind. Married George when I was four. Don't really remember too much before that.'

'He's your stepfather, then?'

'One of those situations that suited both of them, as his first wife had just died, leaving him with two children. Mum'd been working for them at the house. Gave it six months and they married. Constable, he was. Where I get it from.'

'Was?'

'Oh no. He's still alive. Just retired. Runs the local Conservative Club.'

'And you ended up down here.'

'Came to work. Wasn't much up there, and through the Conservative Club George knew these two sisters in Kensington. Spinsters. I worked for them a spell before joining the police.'

'He must be proud.'

'I think so, although the sisters were mildly put out. His eldest, also George, is a copper too, but up in Darlington. He—'

She stopped abruptly and laughed.

'Look at you.'

'Hmm?'

'You've got . . .' She pointed, before producing a handkerchief and wiping a smudge of jam from his face. He angled his chin to help.

'Thanks.'

'Messy devil. You seen the time?'

'We should get back. If himself is there, he'll have complaints. You haven't touched your cream cake.'

'It's for Tallulah.'

He grinned. 'Tallulah? Leon's not still on about—'

'Only at every opportunity.'

He took care of the bill and got a bag from the nippy for the cream cake.

'How much do I owe you?' Billie said, as they exited out onto Coventry Street.

'Strategy meeting refreshments are the senior officer's responsibility.'

She nodded at his new coat as he slipped it back on.

'But I fear I might be denying some gentleman's outfitter your hard-earned guineas.'

'It's new,' he said, very pleased it had been noticed, even if she was teasing him.

31

The statements Harrison gave him secured Geats a quick warrant from a magistrate cosy with Superintendent Dalton. Neither Cassar nor Billie was in the Clubs & Vice office, but Tallulah was sitting on the desk. She got up, stretched, and mewed loudly. As he moved closer, she leaped from the desk and clung to his coat, digging her claws in and swinging there until he grabbed her in one hand.

'What are you doing here?' he said, holding her up to his face.

Mew.

'Glad we got that cleared up.'

'Where the hell have you been?' Cassar folded his coat and placed it on the couch, leaving him still wearing his usual expression of annoyance. Billie loitered in the doorway looking diffident.

Geats held up Tallulah like he was showing Billie a lamp. 'How come the cat's here?'

'She can't stay with me. The maid's allergic, apparently.'

Tallulah mewed.

'She's hungry.'

'I got something for her. We went to the . . .' She looked at her feet.

'The what?'

'We got tea at the Corner House,' Cassar said.

'You two?' Geats said, amused but then something else.

'I got a cream cake,' Billie said brightly, holding up a bag.

She took Tallulah and sat on the couch. Cassar eyed her and then the cat, and lifted his coat from beside them, draping it carefully over the back of the desk chair. He brushed something invisible from the wool.

Scooping up a dollop of cream from the cake, Billie offered it to the kitten, who licked her fingers furiously and demanded more.

'She likes it.'

'Of course she likes it,' Geats said. 'It's cake and it's bigger than her.'

'You said in the office first thing.' Cassar checked his watch superiorly. 'It's almost five.'

'*You* said in the office first thing, and I was here at bloody five. Where were you?'

'Five? You were not.'

Geats pointed to the occurrence books. 'Who do you think was looking at them? I've been following up on something. And I found the dance school.'

Cassar frowned. 'How?'

How, not where. Always about him being behind and not the case getting ahead.

'Saw Charlie.'

Geats told them Garland's stories about the French pimps back in the day and the dance school on Archer Street, and made up a load of codswallop about a snout pointing him in the direction of the Domino.

'We're supposed to be working this together,' Cassar said. 'In fact, you're supposed to be helping me. This is Flying Squad's case.'

'Which is why I'm here now, telling you about it. Figure you'll be able to muster more constables for a search of the dance studio. Meanwhile, I'll lead Clubs & Vice on a raid of the Domino. That way, you get any intelligence on Kassel's operation, and I get to crack some skull.'

'Effective division of labour.'

Placated, Cassar went off to make phone calls and organise the search. Billie eyed Geats with suspicion.

'What?'

'Why'd you give him the school?'

'Because he'd have acted all put out for about a week. Besides, Mark was never much in the door-kicking department.'

'Whereas you . . .'

'I love putting in a door.'

'Uh huh. You got a team together?'

Geats nodded. 'Need a canary, though.'

'How dressed up can I get?'

'It's a milk bar, Bill, not dinner at the Savoy.'

'I think it might take a few goes to get right. We should probably start with the gowns.'

'Nothing says evening wear like a dairy-based beverage sucked through a straw.'

One floor up, in a glorified broom cupboard, was Costume, a small room lined with clothes rails full of garments and togs confiscated over the years on raids of various houses of disrepute. Billie often glammed up for their undercover sorties in Soho's more discerning clubs. There was everything from rayon guinea gowns to home-made evening dresses cut from paper patterns to tailored silk with intricate panels and net insets. She perused the rails and took a few garments behind a coromandel folding screen, Geats standing against the door to deter any nosy parkers hoping for a peep show.

As canary, she would head into the milk bar and make sure there wasn't an army of Sabini henchmen waiting for them inside; if all was clear, she would come out and give the prearranged signal – a clenched fist behind her back – and Geats's team would bring the thunder.

'Ooh, I think I know just the thing. We got it at that high-class place on Pall Mall. The one the minister was at, pants round his ankles. I think maybe I've already worn it, though. To the Shim Sham.'

Geats sighed. 'Let's see.'

'Okay.'

She walked out in a sheer silk faille gown in perfect jade, backless with a low fluted skirt.

'What do you think?'

'Muh,' Geats said.

'Oh, you've seen it before,' she said, doing a turn.

Geats nodded weakly. It could have been tailored for her.

She grinned. 'Go on, chum. Show me what you've got. What would you say if I walked up to you in one of your clubs wearing this?'

Geats swallowed thickly. A bottomless sensation crept up on him and he tried to clear it through his throat.

'I might have seen it before, but every time I clap eyes on you is like seeing something new.'

'Leon . . .'

'Well, don't come over none. Just what I *would* say.'

Backlit, her face was a mystery. 'Uh huh.'

Walking back behind the screen, she gave it some hip, and returned a few minutes later in a frilled blouse with a more sober pleated skirt hanging just below the knee.

'More suitable, I think,' she said.

He adjusted himself.

'We should go. I need to kick down some door.'

32

Soho thrummed in the early evening.

That couldn't be helped: raiding the place at dawn, they'd find it empty, and going in later in the evening risked a more belligerent crowd.

He wanted the smut peddlers.

He wanted Babe Mancini and Tommy Mack.

He wanted to slap chains on everyone in the Domino Milk Bar and burn it to the ground.

But he'd have to be content with cracking some head.

Not wanting to advertise their intentions by leading a police car gymkhana up to the front door, the vehicles arrived piecemeal, some parking up at the east end of Gerrard Street outside the King's Head and others looping round from the north and sliding into Macclesfield Street, round the corner from the target.

On the ground floor, the Domino operated just like any other milk bar: a café that sold soups and sandwiches as well as milkshakes and ice cream. A dozen or so tables were scattered around inside, usually filled with young people. A huge electrically lit domino hung aslant in the window, a single flashing pip one end and three the other, signalling the street address of 13.

Geats and Billie were squeezed into the back of a Wolseley with Constable Boyle, who was napping as he did immediately before any operation. Tallulah stretched out insouciantly along the back of the bench seat, though she watched everything with crocodile eyes. Slipping out, Geats pressed himself against the corner column of the store that had dual fronts on Macclesfield and Gerrard. Pulling on his gloves, he made fists and felt the leaden loads tighten against his fingers. He unsheathed his billy club, giving it a drum major's twirl.

Billie came up behind him, winking as she walked round into Gerrard Street. The Domino was the second shop in, and she quickly disappeared inside. Geats waited, peering round the corner. Felt like he was holding his breath for a lung-busting period.

This was his London.

Slim buildings ganged together like stakes in a palisade, crummy hallways and dank cellars, their grubbiness proof the city's old stones were still teeming with life.

Door-kicking.

Head-breaking.

Winding up the gangs.

He'd always believed he was destined for something else, though couldn't imagine what, and so treated life as an endless series of altercations that he undertook with blithe disregard for his or anyone else's fate until his true purpose should make itself known. As far as plans went, it didn't feel like much, but he never had been much in the long-term department.

Down the other end of the street, he could see his men edging round the corner of the pub, itching to go. He raised his club in the air like a flag, bringing them under starter's orders. Billie marched out of the Domino and crossed the road, and without breaking stride formed a fist behind her back.

Geats brought his club down, and within seconds, a squad of bull-headed coppers were piling into the bar to a chorus of shrieks and scattered tableware. Geats ambled along at his leisure, pausing outside to watch through the window. The shop wasn't his concern; names would be taken, the staff would be spoken to, but most people were probably in there with the honest intention of enjoying a tasty beverage with friends.

The downstairs was his purpose.

A path was cut between the upturned tables and he strode in, Billie falling in behind him, through a door into a rear room and down a staircase that descended back towards the front of the building.

In a well-lit room they were greeted by several rows of coin-operated gaming machines – cards, dice, roll-down marble races, glass-topped horse-racing carousels – and men queuing to slot pennies into them. Geats's eyes watered from the smoke festooning under the low ceiling.

An old boy stood in the corner with a big cash box to give change of a bob, or a pound note for those who took themselves seriously. Geats put a finger to his lips to hush him.

Billie pointed to a door through to a rear room, and Geats nodded for her to take it with a couple of uniforms. His focus was on the doors to the two vaults that stretched side by side beneath the pavement and street, both closed. The other constables started quietly rounding up the gamblers and leading them upstairs.

Geats yanked open the first door, finding a small bespectacled creature hunched over a desk fitting photographs onto the flexible cards of a Mutoscope reel. He lunged forward and clamped a gloved hand over the man's mouth before he could object.

'A word out of you and I'll lock you up and forget exactly where for a week or two. Right?'

Eyes like saucers, the man nodded.

'Mancini and Mack. They in the next room?'

He nodded again.

'I'm going to let go, then I'm going to leave you here. A single peep from you and I'll do damage you won't walk away from the same. We understand each other?'

The smallest nod in the world.

'Good.'

In the main room, he pulled the old man with the cashbox aside.

'Right, here's what I want you to do, Dad.'

Geats and a couple of other constables positioned themselves by the door as the old chap gave a knock.

'*What?*'

'Need some loot. Fella here, big spender, only has a fiver. Need some ten-bob notes or I'll be giving him all me brass.'

The door opened, and as quickly as Tommy Mack's face appeared in the gap, Geats drove a loaded fist into it, sending him sprawling backwards. Babe Mancini tried to hold up his pal, but Geats had his club out, shooting it forward like a sabre in the tight space, jabbing him in the ribs.

On the floor, Mack's nose was smeared across his face like a dropped pie, and Geats had hold of Babe's collar, hauling him out into the light. He struggled, but Geats was powerful and had him from behind, an arm clamped round his throat, twisting punches into his back with his other hand.

'Where them kidneys at, Mancini? Eh? Let's be having them.'

Ramming in three four five shots, Geats let him fall. Babe walked himself round in a circle on the ground, not knowing whether to arch his back or bend over double, such was the pain.

The vault they'd been in had a couple of stools and a table with a bottle. Boxes were stacked behind that. Stepping over Tommy Mack, Geats found more packets of photographs and material for the Muto-scope reels.

'Watch them,' he told Boyle, who was alert now and looking for any reason.

The rear room of the basement was darker than the gaming room, lit only by ensconced lamps with sordidly coloured shades. A dozen hand-crank Mutoscope machines stood against the walls, their elec-tric lights flickering from under the lens hoods. Above each one was hung an uplit poster teasing its contents, going well beyond what the butler saw.

If Geats had expected Billie to follow demurely in his steps, he had been mistaken. To the horror of the mortified punters, she was running the crank of one of the machines, head bent to the viewer.

'This the sort of thing you like?' she asked the man she'd pulled away from it. 'Bunch of drunk lords giving a maid the three-of-one?'

'No, no, no . . . I thought it was going—'

'If you say you thought you was going to see the sights of gay Paris, I'm liable to forget myself entirely.'

She looked them in the eyes.

She gleefully jotted down their names.

She gave every impression of being the exact type of fire-and-brimstone termagant who'd report their lewd evenings to their wives down to the last detail. Leading them out in a sheepish column, she winked at Geats. He liked her hammy winks, the twitches of a madwoman.

Tommy Mack was sitting on the floor, hems of his shirt untucked and scooped up to his face to stem the bleeding. Babe Mancini leaned against the wall outside his vault, beneath the pavement lights, clutching his side.

'I'll piss blood on account of this, Geats.'

'I sure hope so.'

'What is all this? We haven't started a riot in your province in months.'

'You're spreading filth.'

'Since when has that been a crime in Soho? Who set you on us? How much they offering? We're reasonable men, Geats. We'll beat it.'

Geats banged him again in the kidney.

'You couldn't afford me.'

On one knee, Babe huffed, 'You prick.'

Geats watched them hauled off by the constables, but kept the photographer for himself, shoving him back into his vault.

'What's your name?'

'Fowler.'

He held up one of the pictures of Nell.

'All right, Mr Fowler. Remember her?'

Panic in his eyes. The fear of not knowing.

'It's your set, though,' Geats prodded.

Fowler nodded.

'This would have been November time, probably. Maybe December. Young girl. Doped.'

Nodding like he couldn't stop.

'You have the negatives? Other prints?'

His eyes slid to the wall behind the desk, lined with drawers.

'Point.'

He did.

Geats released his grip and opened the drawer, flicking through envelopes arranged by date. They contained brown Kodak 120 negatives cut into strips of four frames. He opened a dozen, checking them against the light, before he found Nell. Forty or fifty images in the envelope.

'This it?'

'I only remember the one shoot with her. I do so many, though . . .'

'Yeah, we'll get to that. You put her into one of your moving reels?'

'I just took pictures because she was—'

'Was what, squire? Passive? Sedentary? Dormant? Doped out of her fucking gourd? Yeah. You sell any of those prints?'

'I think so. I couldn't say how many.'

A cardboard tray sat on the side with packets of printed pictures.

'That what you were selling tonight? She in any of them?'

'No.'

'You remember who brought her to you?'

'I don't deal with any of that.'

'She didn't knock on your door and ask to model, though, did she?'

He shook his head.

'Max Kassel?'

'Oh God.'

'Tell me what you know.'

'Nothing, really. He'd turn up with a girl from time to time. I'd pay him for a session. He was a reliable source of models.'

'At your studio? Where's that?'

'My home. In a warehouse off Marshall Street.'

'Near the baths?'

'Yes.'

'You ever go to him? See where he lived?'

'No.'

'So you know nothing.'

'No, but . . .' He hesitated.

'But what?' Geats pushed.

'One of the models—'

Geats scoffed.

'One of the *girls* told me she'd been at his flat on James Street.'

'Yeah, only the several hundred James Streets in this city.'

'She said she was at the school right round the corner, that it was in Marylebone.'

'The trade school?'

Fowler nodded. 'What I took her to mean, yes. That has to be worth something.'

'We'll see,' Geats said stolidly.

He lugged the man out of the small dark space and handed him into the arms of waiting constables. Returning to the vault, he had a flick through the circular reel Fowler had been working on: a young women bending over with her skirts hitched up, offering hallowed glimpses to an eager gent, the whole thing built round a gag about him dropping petals. Not the saucy teases the machines were shipped with; Darby Sabini's boys had clearly been producing their own blue loops. The darkroom must have been back at the man's pad on Marshall, as the vault only contained stacks of developed photos and frames ready to be loaded into Mutoscope wheels.

He left it to the constables to collect the evidence and strolled out into Gerrard Street, galvanised by the hum of violence.

'Saw Mack and his new nose.' Billie was leaning against a street light, arms crossed.

Geats looked around before carefully pulling out the packet of negatives from his pocket and showing her one.

'Jesus, that's Nell.'

'Yeah.'

'You knew?'

'Fella who told me about this place, the samples he gave me. There were several of Nell. I didn't enter them as evidence.'

'Why?'

'Why? Bill, there's only me and you give a shit where this kid is. She turns up in filth shots, she'll be officially labelled a whore and that'll be that for her. Wherever she is, we need to find her quickly and pull her out quietly if she's going to have any kind of life different to that of her mother.'

'I wonder if Cassar got anything at the dance school.'

'He won't have.'

'How do you—oh. Of course. You went there yourself before.'

'Might have had a gander.'

'Thought you gave it up too easily.'

'There are records of girls who were enrolled. Maybe some of them were Continental girls brought over. And there were pictures. Like these ones.'

'Nell?'

He shook his head.

'This hasn't really got us anywhere, then.'

'Wouldn't say that. Photographer gave me a good idea where Red Max's flat might be. Fancy a stroll, take a peek in the windows at Selfridges?'

33

James Street was the other side of Oxford Street, technically D Division, so it was an excursion they were to keep under their hats. Standing on the corner across from the Lamb & Flag, they smoked Woodbines. On the top floor of the skinny building next door, no lights were on.

They watched for half an hour, but nothing changed. The door to the flats was locked, so Geats showed his warrant card to the owner of the Italian café below and got him to open it. The man said he hadn't seen the occupier of the top flat for a while, but didn't know him well.

It became immediately apparent it was Red Max's place, because someone had already forced the door and ransacked it. Like any life, comfortable or otherwise, once it was spilled all over the floor it was unimaginable that it had ever looked at home in its circumstances. The atmosphere of the place was breached, all context lost. What had once been belongings was now merely evidence.

'What do we do?' Billie said.

'Search.'

'For what?'

'Whatever the people who beat us to it were looking for.'

'What if they already found it?'

'Does this look like a mess the making of which was halted by discovery? No, it looks pretty total to me.'

'Looking for something we don't know, in a place already torn apart. Brilliant.'

Billie saw chaos, hissing and harrumphing that they'd never find anything. She righted upturned furniture and searched through its nooks and crannies, as it was obvious someone else already had from the slashes in the cushions and fabrics. She sifted through heaps of books, lying like dead birds with their covers spread.

For Geats, they had arrived at this place on the back of having been at other places, having learned things that had led them there, and it was freshly endowed with inheritances from those previous places. That was the nature of police work: you never looked at a place with brand-new eyes.

Rather than searching the flat top to bottom, he tackled the problem from the other end and set about looking for where he himself would have hidden something valuable or confidential. What tiny spots could be expected to have escaped unseen from prowling eyes?

He groped around pipework in the lavatory and kitchen.

He fingered the skirting and flooring for loose boards.

He dug his hands into jacket pockets searching for telltale signs of needlework where something might have been sewn into the lining.

Then he found, between the satin liner and cowhide sweatband of a vindictively stomped bowler, a ticket for the cloakroom at the Grosvenor House Hotel. He held it aloft like a winning pools coupon.

'You think that's it?' Billie said.

'It's still here, so they didn't find it.'

'Worrying, how your mind works.'

'Mayfair. Walk there, cab back?'

Tallulah mewed loudly and tried to hop out of Billie's pocket.

'Hold on there.' She lifted the kitten out and placed her on the floor, whereupon she raced to a corner behind a naked inlaid mahogany pedestal plant stand, squatted, and splattered the floor.

'And that's why you don't feed them their body weight in cream.'

Billie shrugged. 'She's yours.'

Tallulah reappeared from behind the stand and sat in the middle of the floor grooming herself.

'Think I'm shoving a shit-licking cat in my pocket, you're mad.'

'Hey, you rescued her.'

'Christ.'

Tallulah riding his coat pocket, ticket in his breast, they walked through Mayfair towards the Grosvenor on Park Lane, where people liked to imagine the rich stacked themselves in front of Hyde Park to live lives of great satisfaction. Geats swung his arms and raised his chin boldly, the world suddenly ready to hold true before this measly ticket somewhere over his heart.

No sooner had he opened himself up to optimism than he was shanghaied by dizziness and dank nausea again, the lasting legacy of his bushwhacking at the hands of Nutty Sharpe's boys. Resolving to walk it off, he was barely aware of Billie talking to him or the cat making a fuss in his pocket, so firmly was he concentrating on maintaining his guts and suppressing the pounding headache he now feared was a new normal. The effort contracted the circumference of his perception; he saw only the pavement a few yards ahead of his feet, the damp air his nose cut through. Anything beyond that, its existence was equivocal until the sensation passed as the Grosvenor hove into sight.

It looked like a bank had got together with its pals and formed a queue. The lobby dripped with swank, and with his bandage and defiantly Soho threads he felt it was only a matter of time before someone asked just exactly what he thought he was doing there.

'We mustn't let on we're police,' he whispered.

'Leon, we're not in uniform.'

Pressing his nose to the glass, he peered through the front door towards the desk.

'For crying out loud. Give,' Billie said, hand out.

Following her inside, he pressed himself into a cranny beside a fluted column and watched her give the ticket to the attendant at the cloakroom desk, who handed over an umbrella without any fuss.

Trying to remember what it was to walk unsuspiciously, he trailed her back out of the hotel and into the first taxicab waiting outside.

Geats trilled his consonants. 'Vine Street, my good man. The world awaits.'

Billie was already playing with the brolly.

'Bad luck, miss,' the driver said, looking round. 'Shouldn't open them inside.'

'Are we inside?' Geats said.

Billie reached up under the folds of the canopy, running her fingers along the ribs and stretchers.

'I'm not opening it,' she said.

'Technically, I'm saying. Would the metaphysics of fortune differentiate between being inside a building and inside a vehicle?'

'There's nothing here.'

The umbrella popped fully open as if of its own volition, surprising everyone.

'Oh!'

She laughed with havoc, losing all rein on herself as the tip of one rib found its way into Geats's ear, unable to contain a snort that erupted.

'Sorry,' she said, covering her mouth.

Geats had always found the abandon of a good snort exciting, but instead said, 'And what about bus shelters? Or bandstands? Are they covered by the vagaries of luck?'

'Don't think there's room for it to open fully back there,' said the driver, a worldly denier of realities.

Its panels were in autumnal colours and a badge nailed to the wooden handle commemorated the silver jubilee of the late king.

'Got the king on it,' she said.

'New one or the dead one?' the driver enquired. 'Bless his soul.'

That unreasonably set Billie off again.

'Dead one,' she chuntered through swallowed laughs.

Geats plucked the tip from his earhole.

'You've a scratch,' she said, reaching for it.

Her cap-sleeved blouse offered a view of a hitherto unnoticed skelter of beauty marks inside her upper arm, and as her finger grazed around the inner rim of his ear, some fervid speculation was unavoidable. It was excruciating, but he maintained a brave face.

'And if one had a house,' he said, 'and one removed the front door so as to leave the structure open to the elements, would that be a loophole to indemnify against cosmic caprices? Or is the nature of the building, of its *insideness*, more radical than that?'

Closing the umbrella, she stood it on the floor between them.

'Leon, what the hell are you rambling about?'

'I feel there should be rules.'

34

Cassar had wallahs from Scotland Yard going through the documents discovered at the dance studio on Archer Street. Feeling pretty chipper, he sent a young WPC out for grub for the whole squad, and later sat with his feet up on the desk eating fish and chips from a cone of paper.

Geats appeared, brandishing an umbrella and perspiring heavily. He dropped onto the couch and seemed to shrink into the back of the seat. Tallulah mewed and he set her on the floor, where she raised her snout in expectation to the waft of battered fish.

'Where you been?' Cassar garbled through a mouthful. 'Where's Billie?'

'She's right . . .'

Geats looked up expectantly but found no Billie.

'Raid was over ages ago,' Cassar said.

'We were at Max Kassel's flat.'

Cassar dropped his feet from the desk. 'What?'

'He found something in a hat,' Billie said, sauntering in, back in uniform and holding a cone of chips.

Geats got up and craned his neck round the door, peering out into the main floor. 'Fish and tatties all round, is it?'

Cassar pulled loose a hunk of battered cod and popped it in his mouth. 'You found something in a hat?'

'Cloakroom ticket for the Grosvenor. Got myself this.' He held up the umbrella.

'What is it?'

'A cricket bat.'

Cassar rolled his eyes.

'George V,' Geats mumbled. 'Some kind of sick joke?'

He slid the runner up so the canopy opened and locked into place.

'No!' Billie and Cassar cried together.

'Come on. How much worse can things possibly get?' Geats twirled the umbrella and collapsed it again. 'I don't know. Maybe he left it there by mistake.'

Out of the corner of her eye, Billie scrutinised his clamminess, his dove-grey skin. 'What's wrong with you?'

'That's a longer conversation.'

She let it go at that, but in a fashion that told him she had noted his pallid look, and sat beside him. He nicked a chip.

'The brolly?' Cassar said.

Geats regaled him with the glorious details of their day, culminating in the discovery of a souvenir rain-stopper.

'I'll have the boys go to Kassel's flat,' Cassar said. 'Give it a thorough going-over.'

Geats shrugged. 'Someone had already been pretty thorough before we got there.'

The heady sense of promise the cloakroom ticket had offered had left him now, and they seemed as far from finding Nell, or her mother's killer, as they'd ever been.

'Found some records at the dance school,' Cassar said. 'Young women who'd been "enrolled". Might be able to track down some of them, see what they know.'

Billie finished her chips, balled the paper and tossed it in the bin.

'Now what?'

Geats stood up emphatically.

'Now we get drinks.'

'Your answer to any stymie,' Cassar said.

'Business and pleasure. I want to check out Chez Renée's after you boys raided the place.'

'Colossal waste of time that was,' Cassar muttered.

Geats tromped out of the office, calling over his shoulder, 'Grab the cat, Bill.'

The weather had taken an abruptly British turn, and against a cold stinging rain they huddled beneath the umbrella and arrived dripping at the door on Lisle Street, closed but not locked. They were halfway down the stairs when the doorman, a large Trini called Garfield, appeared at the bottom.

Geats threw up his hands. 'We come in peace.'

Garfield's expression remained unchanged, but he gave the nod and stood aside. The club was almost empty and lay in testing darkness. Figures moved dimly on the stage, fooling around, not even jamming, tinkering with their instruments before settling down to play. Dusty tapering shafts fell from the street lamps above, sifting through the pavement lights and providing the only source of illumination.

The tables – those that were intact – were vacant, pushed up against the walls. Perched on a stool in the middle of the dance floor, as if she'd been waiting for them, was Simone Calcavecchia. Hostess now to a Waterloo of a club; needle of her barometer spinning, registering isobars of rage. Smashed tables and chairs were neatly heaped behind her in a pyre. A swept pile of broken glass, fag ends and assorted wreckage of an authentic night glinted in the murk.

Geats found the switches for the overhead lights and clicked them impotently.

'You didn't pay the bill or something?'

Simone slid off the stool and prowled towards him.

'You, you jelly-boned bastard.'

'Now, Simone . . .'

Her usually pristine hair squalled above her head, and he noted she wore the same gown he had seen her in several nights ago when the raid went down. He backed up slowly.

'You're upset.'

Eyes fixed on him, she extended a finger in Cassar's direction.

'I can explain him,' Geats said apologetically.

Their relationship had always been dressed in indifference and mild disregard, but now, foul-eyed and abominable, he suspected she might be working on stronger feelings. The finger curled down into a fist and struck him on the chin.

He staggered back, complaining, 'I'm a wounded man.'

His companions wisely stepped away from the skirmish.

'I spent three nights in the cells. Came back to find my club smashed up, thanks to your friend over there.'

Geats surveyed the mess, glancing at Cassar.

'You lot smashed the place up?'

'Not this enthusiastically.'

'No, they only smashed half of it,' Simone said. 'When Garfield and I were in the cells, the Italians paid a visit and finished the job off.'

'Oh.'

'Oh? I'll give you—'

'Wait! I slept in the cells too, and I bet my story's better than yours.'

He tilted his bandaged head, accentuating his point.

A sardine stain had bloomed up through the white gauze. She reached out and flicked it hard, and it smarted, her hands reaching for his face as he recoiled. He engaged his arms with hers and turned her round, holding her back tight against him in knotted stillness.

'He didn't know about the raid,' Cassar offered. 'We don't trust him.'

'I'm going to let go,' Geats said. 'Let's not have any more nonsense.'

She shook herself loose and brushed a wild coil of hair from her face.

Geats retreated, palms up. He showed the others to a tenuous table in a nook, where they sat beneath a disarray of fake palm trees, the odd frond torn off and missing thanks to the raid. Walking back to the small bar, he waited for Simone to man it.

'Your pals took the booze,' she said. 'Italians smashed the glasses.'
Geats looked around thoughtfully.

'You know old Ben? Benny Brownlow, fella on the streets?'

'Everybody knows Benny.'

'Hire him.'

'How's that?'

'He used to box. Like, against-world-champs box-for-real box. Served in the merchant navy. He has his problems and comes across a bit simple, but if you give him a task, he'll do it. He's diligent, built like a boulder, and can hand out naps with his fists. Keep Garfield working the door, get Benny to watch the premises at night. Let him sleep in one of the back rooms.'

'You're serious?'

'If the Italians are chancing their arm again, he'll be useful.'

She toed a box beneath the counter.

'Lift that up for me.'

He did as he was told, and she took out several bottles of champagne, two pints of gin, various syrups and a lemon. Some cloudy old glasses hid in there too.

'Pulled these from the kitchen at the Shim Sham,' she said, meaning Jack Isow's premier venue, only two hundred yards and a world away. Everyone wore evening dress there.

'You won't survive the night on this.' He glanced back at the table. 'Not sure you'll survive us.'

'Truck's coming.'

He considered the bottles. 'What can we do here?'

Didactically, she threw together the gin and simple syrup, adding a dash of lemon juice, poured it into three wide-lipped glasses and topped them up with bubbles and thin coils of citrus rind.

'That's my girl.'

Carrying the drinks at a precarious tilt, he landed them on the table with minimal spillage. Cassar neatly folded the new coat he'd been peacocking about in and placed it on the fourth chair. A look between Geats and Billie, that vicarious passing of mockery and schemes they had.

It irked him. He turned his glass. 'What the hell is this?'

'Get it down you, sans complaint. Cheers.'

The band had coalesced into a jamming session that was threatening to break into tune. Cassar had never been at ease in places like this – no, that was a lie. He'd never spent enough time in places like this to find out if he could be comfortable. Billie looked to be enjoying herself, though she still wore her thick woollen coat, the kitten standing up in the side pocket and peering over the edge. She'd been the same in the Corner House when they'd had tea, as if she didn't want people to see her uniform.

'Gonna boil in that thing,' he said. 'There's nobody here.'

'Someone might come.'

'There is nobody who comes to this place who won't know us for coppers on sight, uniform or no.'

Geats raised his glass to that, drinking and smacking his lips loudly.

Sighing, Billie stood up and unbuttoned the coat. Lifting the kitten out, she just about threw her at Geats, who held the creature up like she was a cherry bomb. She removed her tunic too.

Geats examined the animal with mild disgust, but she curled up in his lap and purred contentedly, apparently unaware of his feelings. Two stevedores clobbered down the stairs, crate of drinks under each arm, bottles rattling as they dumped them on the bar top. They stared daggers at the group, curvature of their arms and chests beneath their shirts a threat to all life.

Cassar leaned towards Billie conspiratorially.

'Told you.'

Cassar fetched more drinks, returning to the table with the rest of the bottle of gin, barbed glares from the labour washing over them as he refilled their glasses. He was beginning to feel good: the warmth of the gin inside him, the hot basement more appealing than his cold room in Lambeth.

Opportunists had entered the club and in exchange for drinks helped Simone clear the debris. After, they sat with their glasses, an adventurous few even making tentative eyes at the dance floor. Simone hustled her girls out of the back to provide partners for any intrepid hot-steppers.

Couchant on the table, Tallulah looked out over the cigarette smoke of the slowly enlivening floor like a tourist on a pier. She closed her eyes for a spell and reopened them, ears pricking up to God knows what over the band's cacophony.

More drinks followed.

Knowing Geats was as likely to dance as he was sprout wings, Billie took Cassar's hand. 'Come on.'

'What?'

'I need someone to dance with.'

'No, I can't . . .'

She gripped his arm with surprising strength, yanking him up upright. The band played swing, and though he knew nothing of dancing, the gin was getting good to him and he let himself be taken along by the rhythm. He watched the other couples and shadowed what they did, snapping Billie back and forth with a single hand, the pair of them jittering across the floor.

When the pace slowed, they closed up and danced arm in arm. Two men glided round in a foxtrot, slow-slow-quick-quicking in and out of other dancers, until they split and cut in on them, one sweeping Billie off her feet and the other clutching Cassar and following his lead. The rolling of their hips to the swelling rhythm was the nearest Cassar had ever experienced to God's presence in his life.

At a drunken pitch, sweat flying from his hair, it dawned on him that he was utterly unafraid; that this was the most liberated he'd ever felt in somewhere that wasn't a small, dark boarding room.

Geats, of course, demurred from the action and watched from the edges. When the band took another break, the others returned to the table to find he had refilled their glasses. Cassar drank deeply from his, and Geats topped him up again.

There followed exuberant rounds of toasts.

'To the travelling philosophers of Soho.'

'To Napoleon and Josephine.'

'To King George V,' Billie cried, holding aloft the umbrella.

Sitting back, she fiddled idly with the brass cuff of the handle, screwing and unscrewing it. Eventually it came loose from its thread, revealing something beneath.

Watching her closely, Geats leaned forward.

Tallulah rearranged herself, back to the band with typical feline ambivalence.

Billie slid the handle of the umbrella off, removing a folded slip of paper rolled around the shaft.

'Leon.'

He nodded, staring intently. She unfurled the scrap and flattened it ambitiously on the table. A sucker for promise, Geats felt hope returning; everything lay before them then.

'It's nothing,' Billie said. 'A list.'

Geats ran a stubby finger along a line.

Elizabeth R. – Jones – £110

'What do you suppose these are? Debts? Payments?'

'Let me see,' Cassar said.

He read and reread it.

'Women on the left. Then just a surname. And an amount.'

'Not small amounts,' Billie said.

'No. I thought maybe records for local prostitutes, but these amounts make no sense. They'd cover a hell of a lot of services rendered.'

Billie worked her way through each line, mouthing the words as she read, as though shaping them in her mouth might lead to understanding.

'Oh.'

'Oh what?' said Geats, craning his neck.

'You don't suppose . . .'

She pointed at a line.

Eleanor M. – Fluke – £150

Geats shook his head. 'I don't—'

'Could that be Eleanor Martin?'

'Nell?'

Cassar spun the sheet round to read. 'Fluke. Wasn't that your boy in Seven Dials with the two Belgian girls?'

'Oh Christ,' said Geats.

And all at once it dawned on him in the most sickening way, like recognising a body in the morgue.

'Fluke said he had a new wife.'

Cassar read the sheet again. 'You think—'

Geats didn't think, he *knew*, and he was already up and running for the door leading to the stairs.

35

Outside, the rain pummelled people back into doorways and beneath overhangs. Geats was drenched seconds after he hit the pavement, tromping east out of Soho.

A third of a mile at most.

Blinking away the downpour and mentally sketching the alleys and yards that ran between the wheel-spoke streets of Seven Dials, he opted to stick to the main thoroughfares for simplicity's sake.

Ducking through the covered passageway into Neal's Yard, he was breathing loudly, treasuring every gasp of air. The rain masked his perspiration. Leaning against the brick wall of the passage, he allowed himself a moment before charging into the yard where Fluke had rooms above the apothecary.

The upper floors were accessible through the shop, which had stable-style doors.

They shrank beneath his boot.

On the second floor he shouldered the door of the room Fluke had said his wife was sleeping in, pain searing through his arm as he went two, three times before the frame cracked and gave way, stumbling into an empty room.

No bed.

A few tea crates and an old wardrobe.

The other door off the hallway creaked open behind him.

A tiny face peeked out, one of the Belgian girls, Suzanne or Jeanne, but she couldn't get it closed quickly enough before he slammed into it, throwing her back into the room.

'Where is she?'

'You can't come in here like this,' she wailed, accent faltering.

'Jimmy!' the other one screamed. 'Jimmy!'

'The girl, this new wife of Fluke's. You tell me where she is.'

'There is no girl,' said the screamer.

Hands behind her back, shoulders twisting this way and that, the first one sidled suspiciously into Geats's line of sight. He made to sidestep her, and she mirrored his movements as if initiating some game.

'What are you play—'

'Cop bastard!' screamed the screamer, waving her arms about her head.

The first sister again matched his attempts to bypass her, resulting in Geats lifting her by the waist and pivoting her to one side to see what she was so clearly attempting to conceal.

On the floor mattress sat a teddy bear.

Yellow scarf with black checks.

'Dolores,' he whispered.

He picked up the bear, squeezing it gently.

He had stood in that very room days earlier, completely unaware that Nell had been somewhere in the same building. Stood there and listened to Fluke prattling on about how he didn't know Kassel.

Choked with scolding rage, he spun in wide-eyed fury when the door banged open wide.

'What the hell's going on?' Fluke roared.

His face contorted when he saw Geats, saw what he had in his hand. Turning on his heel, he tore back into the other room. With one of the sisters wrapped round his leg, Geats waded after him, the room empty when he got there. He grabbed the girl by the chin and showed her the teddy bear.

'I find anything has happened to the girl this belongs to, I'll upend your miserable fucking existence.'

Recognising a genuine threat when she heard one, she let go of him and sculled backwards out of the room, calling for her sister.

The cupboard door was ajar and Geats slapped it open, expecting to find Fluke cowering. Instead, he discovered it was backless, with a hole knocked through the wall behind into the neighbouring building.

Ducking beneath loosely hanging bricks, he stepped into a dim room not much bigger than the wardrobe.

Somewhere a door clattered shut.

Tracing a route after the noise, he ran out of the room and charged along a snarl of narrow corridors, squinting into warrens of tiny rooms divided off by haphazard wooden partitions.

Feet clattering on steps guided him to a flight up to the next floor and to a larger room.

A place of greater darkness.

The way Geats understood the world, one thing always led to the next, and could ultimately lead one anywhere. But walking into that room, he knew he had always been heading towards it.

The corollary of all his human endeavour.

He was untypically calm in the face of it.

'What is this?'

'It's perfectly legal,' said Fluke, standing in front of a bed. 'She's of age.'

'She's eleven.'

'I—no. No, sir, that is not so. I have a birth certificate, and she is sixteen. I have the explicit permission of her guardian—'

'Mechanik.'

'Yes, Mr Mechanik. The girl's maternal uncle, and out of avuncular concern and love he arranged for her to be wed to me . . .'

He trailed off as Geats approached him.

'Eleven. She's eleven.'

Fluke pulled a knife, though he looked more bewildered by it than did Geats, who grabbed his wrist and twisted until the blade hit the floor. He punched him, and again twice more as he fell sideways, maintaining his grip on the man's wrist so he hung slackly by his arm.

Then he let go, dropping him with a dull thud.

He approached the bed slowly. The girl, Nell, was motionless. Fluke pushed himself to his knees, sobbing.

'This isn't necessary. This is uncalled for.'

'Geats!'

Billie's voice somewhere in the building.

Fluke clasped his hands together, back bent in supplication.

'If there has been some misunderstanding, some awful error, then I throw myself at your feet, sir. I have documentation and all legally arranged paper.'

He pointed vaguely at a ramshackle chest of drawers in the corner.

'I ask you, how was I to know if parties previously unknown to me set out to deceive?'

Geats knelt on the bed, the girl not stirring.

He held a finger beneath her nose: the faintest draught of breath, or was he imagining it?

Lowering his head to her chest, he sensed her inhaling air so thrifty and shallow that it didn't move her at all.

He laid Dolores beside her, hooking her arm round the bear.

Touching a finger to her lip, he pulled it back to reveal tiny white pegs, gaps between them at the back. Her eyes opened gummily, dull and halting and tardy to find his. Some narcotic stupor.

Softly, almost telepathically: 'Her teeth are still coming through.'

He stood up from the bed.

Fluke closed his eyes slowly. 'This is uncalled for.'

Lofting him round the neck and between the legs, Geats heaved him into the air and swung him like he might a hay bale.

It was an act of ecstatic remission.

It was an act of grace.

Fluke crashed through the loading door overlooking the yard and plummeted four storeys onto the hard stone that cut off his shriek.

Nell watched, torpid but blinking with fascination.

'Leon?'

Billie stepped shyly into the room. She saw Nell.

'Oh my God.'

She rushed to the bed, but the girl recoiled wearily from her, sliding carelessly off the bed and swimming nakedly across the floor to Geats, balling herself up behind his legs.

Snatching the sheet from the bed, he swaddled her with it, wrapping her arms and legs up in a cocoon. Kneeling beside her, he let her nuzzle her way under his arm and settle there, finding some measure of safety.

'What's wrong with her?' Billie said.

He jerked his chin at the bedside cabinet, the variety of bottles and packets strewn upon it.

'Laudanum,' she said. 'Cocaine.'

'Keep her down, bring her up.'

Billie's eyes roamed from the empty bed to Geats and the girl, to the smashed loading door, flapping out into space.

The question she didn't ask was answered by a sudden howling from below. Moving to the door, she looked down at the Belgian sisters kneeling at Fluke's side, throwing their heads back in grievous bellows.

Tallulah mewed as if in response.

Billie lifted her from her pocket and scratched her chin. Finding focus, Nell watched closely. Billie lowered Tallulah carefully onto the floor and she padded over to the girl, rubbing up against her. Extricating an arm from her truss, Nell scooped up the cat and held it close, peaceful enough for Geats to leave her momentarily.

In the drawers Fluke had pointed to, which scraped out crookedly, he rooted through the papers inside.

'Birth certificate. Says she's sixteen. Like the records we found at the dance school. Did a good job, paper feels old.'

Cassar appeared in the doorway, breathless. 'Found a phone at a restaurant. They're coming from Bow Street.'

The chorus of lamentations from the yard attracted a crowd, people gawping up at the hole Fluke had flown through. Neither Cassar nor Billie asked Geats what had happened, and between them Nell sat calm as could be with Tallulah in her lap.

They could almost believe nothing had happened at all.

36

There was no fuss.

Fluke's death was recorded as a misfortune whilst trying to flee arrest; a distortion of the facts implicitly agreed upon that coasted through all official scrutiny as the man's life was tolerably worthless.

Nobody asked any probing questions of Geats's account.

He offered scant detail.

Billie knew, though, and it troubled her. Perhaps only the memory of the young girl, the wretched state they found her in, permitted her to let it be. Or at least file it away in some uninspected recess of her mind.

In the morning, Sharpe called from Paris to say that Lacroix had been apprehended and was being interrogated. He maintained that Lacroix was his birth name, not Roger Vernon, and denied he had anything to do with Kassel's death. The investigation drew lines between Kassel and Lacroix's trafficking operation and Albert Mechanik and Josephine Martin. Proudfoot had been clumsy in his attempts at fingering Mechanik for his sister's murder, even though he'd made no real attempt at breaking his alibi.

Nell was taken to Great Ormond Street. Her various wounds and infections were treated, though the doctors were more concerned by the effects of her forced narcotics use.

Geats was first through Mechanik's door, booting it clean off its hinges, but he had cleared out, probably right after their previous visit. Inquiries failed to locate him.

The case stalled.

Geats spent a few nights in the empty flat below Josephine Martin's, watching the dance studio across the street, hoping someone might return.

Nobody did.

There was nobody left to return.

In Paris, Sharpe located Georges Lacroix's father and brought him in to see his son, whose belligerence finally crumbled. He confessed that he was the escaped convict Vernon, and that he had shot Max Kassel dead.

He claimed it was over a debt, a story Suzanne Bertrand backed up, but police suspected it was personal: Marcelle Aubin and Pierre Alexandre claimed Kassel and Vernon were both in love with Bertrand.

Vernon and Bertrand denied any knowledge of Josephine Martin's death, and neither believed Kassel had been responsible. They didn't know where Mechanik had fled to. The French refused to extradite Vernon or Bertrand, so Sharpe and his hounds returned home, murder solved but justice to be unsatisfactorily meted out by a Parisian court.

Flying Squad removed themselves from Vine Street, the Kassel case officially solved; Josephine Martin was just another dead whore, and none of their concern.

Nell was released from hospital and the courts placed her in the care of the Waifs and Strays, in lieu of finding a respectable family who might adopt her. She ran away the first night, vanishing without trace.

Geats spent his time trawling the streets of Soho, fixated on finding out who had strangled Josephine Martin. He spoke to working girls on the corners, and dancers in the dives, seeking leads on rough trade, men with a propensity for violence.

He may as well have asked for men who required oxygen to breathe.

The beat coppers of the St James and Holborn divisions agreed to keep an eye out for perverts and deviants, but they were awash with them. It was the world they navigated.

Erosion set in.

The passing weeks diminished Geats's will.

He spent more evenings at home, cooking in Clara's flat and listening to her records and her complaints about Tallulah, who she nevertheless permitted to stay with her when Geats offered to shut her in his own rooms. Occasionally he drank in Renée's and saw Cassar there; the best-dressed cop in London cutting up the dance floor with the blacks and the Trots and the fairies.

Soho scabbed over its wounds and everyone forgot about Josephine Martin and Max Kassel. Everything began to go back to normal.

He should have known better.

He should have known they had no idea what they were dealing with.

Deeper than the wounds, the blood of the place was poisoned.

Part Two
STRANGLER

1963

37

Can smell it on himself again.

Almost twenty years, he believed he'd put it behind him. The odd sojourn to a hospital or care home, purely on the off chance.

Nothing about the women.

Nothing about *him*.

Now here he is, sitting at a table in an Oxford library, combing local newspapers from the past week. There's more detail, but not nearly enough.

The young woman was found sitting in a wheelchair in the centre of the pit in a quarry that hadn't been cut in years. She was dressed in a dark woollen skirt and a man's black shirt. Her hair was fashioned into waves, as if from the 1930s. She had suffered a gunshot wound to the head that doctors believed had happened several months prior and been treated crudely, though not without expertise.

The prognosis for any kind of recovery was not good.

'Mr Cassar?'

The librarian is young, excited by her work. She has another paper in her hand.

'This week's copy of the *Oxford Times* has just come in. It has a short piece on the woman.'

'Thanks.'

He scans it quickly. Nobody has come forward to identify her, and Oxford City Police CID have been brought in.

'Down the street.'

'Sorry?'

'I saw the detectives handling the case talking on *South Today*. They were standing outside St Aldate's Police Station, just along the road there. You know Christ Church?'

'Sure,' he lies.

'Maybe a couple of hundred yards further on.'

Thanking her again, he gathers up his belongings and steps out onto St Aldate's. He glances up and down the street, fifty-fifty chance of going the right way. Right is where he came from, the town centre, shops and cafés. He tries to remember if he saw a college, but the whole place looks like one big bloody college. Looking left, he spots an octagonal tower standing prominently over the street and heads that way.

If Christ is to be found anywhere.

The Jurassic wall of the college's quad stretches out a hundred yards or more along the road. With its corner turrets and stone balustrades, it looms like a fortress, but he's sure that's just his paranoia.

38

Late summer hangs heavily in the CID offices.

Detective Inspector Madison is a man who suffers heat, shirt blooming darkly beneath his arms and down his back. He wipes his forehead with a sopping handkerchief and folds it damply back into his pocket.

'This is not official then?' he says.

'No. It jogged something in my mind, and I thought to look into it a little deeper.'

'Something in Kent?'

'From before. I was Met.'

'Cassar. Cassar. Cassar. I know your name from somewhere. Stories on the grapevine, a long time ago.'

'Soho. The Strangler.'

'You were one of Nutty Sharpe's boys.'

'In another life.'

'Whatever happened to old Nutty?'

'Retired when he heard about making money. Ran book at the dogs.'

Madison laughs, then frowns when he sees he's the only one laughing.

'You serious?'

'First of the great independents. He cleared the old Jews out, and war cleared the old Italians out, so Jack Spot and the East End boys left him alone.'

'He still about?'

'Oh, he's still about. Been drawing his pension now for as long as he was ever a copper.'

'And deserves every penny, no doubt.'

'Don't we all.'

Madison rubs his mouth, wipes the sheen from his upper lip.

'We don't know a lot. Don't even know if there was a crime. Surgeon who treated her said, angle and nature of the gunshot wound, she might have done it to herself. One idea, she's tried to do herself in, mucked it up, and afterwards whoever's caring for her decides it's too much.'

'Left her in a quarry, though?'

Madison shrugs. 'Makes no sense, I know.'

'Her injuries had been treated? Local hospitals . . .'

'No. Nothing. We checked everywhere for a hundred miles, nothing like that in the last year.'

'Someone treated her at home, then?'

'Begs the question why you wouldn't take her to a hospital. My guess, more likely she's from somewhere else. Someone dumping their problem out of sight, hoping nobody finds out who she is. We're contacting other hospitals, other forces. It's a process. This case of yours . . .'

'Someone staging suicides. That was a theory, we never closed the case. Long time ago now. Like I said, something just fluttered away in the back of the mind, you know how it can be.'

'Course, course. Listen, best bet, I'll put you with my bird dog, Detective Sergeant Helm. Old friend of Nutty Sharpe's, least I can do is give you the afternoon. Have Helm lay out what we have, see if anything shakes loose.'

'Appreciate that, sir.'

'Least I can do. Least I can do.'

39

Helm drives, a little Lancia saloon; his own vehicle.

'Was me dad's. He passed, and I figured I'd sell it, but never did.'

Probably he explains this to every new passenger.

'The boss says you was with Nutty Sharpe. Worked the Strangler?'

'Back in the good old days.'

He can feel Helm watching him out of the corner of his eye.

'Must have seen a lot over the years.'

'Hopefully not much more. The pension beckons.'

'Just running down one last job.'

'That's what I'm telling myself, anyway.'

They drive for forty-five minutes to the disused quarry on the edge of the Cotswolds, near Burford. The arena is grassed over, cut faces rearing up on all sides with the curious architecture of limestone. Shrubs and small trees finger over the cliff edges.

'She was there,' Helm says, pointing. 'Just sitting there, right in the middle.'

'Who owns the place?'

'Well . . . it hasn't been worked for some time, and it's changed hands more than once since then. Fella from Stroud is the rightful owner just at the moment, though the way he tells it, he got it as part of some other company he bought to get his hands on a type of digger trucks they had.'

'Not a sought-after locale.'

'Don't think there's much call for limestone these days.'

'What's your take on it all?'

He snaps away with his camera as Helm tells him.

'The boss – I mean, he's a fine copper and all, but . . .'

'He likes a straightforward explanation.'

'You got it. And there's nothing wrong with that. He's got me for more daring lines of inquiry.'

'And how would you dare?'

'I don't buy the idea that she's a failed suicide and someone has abandoned her because it's too much work. It's an all-right idea, in that it absolutely could happen. But it don't fit here. The doctor who examined her, he says that she was most likely shot several months ago. Knows it's not a long time, on account of how the wounds haven't scarred like that yet, but it definitely wasn't too recent neither. Plus, there's no hospital records to support that. The doc, he says the medical work done on her was from a trained hand, but not done in the proper circumstances.'

'What's that mean? Not at hospital?'

'Yeah. Like, she was shot in the head, and the bullet goes through.' He shows with his fingers to his own head. 'In here, out here. High angle.'

'Consistent with a suicide.'

'Yeah, if birds did that sort of thing.'

'It's not common.'

'Pills and wrists, I find. But there was no surgery, see. No real attempt at fixing the damage inside, the doc says. Wound was professionally staunched and dressed, but the skull was damaged and there was nothing done to support it. Beggars belief she's lasted this long.'

'No decent responses to the photo of her that went out?'

'Usual larks with the crazies who like getting involved, but nobody knew her. And that's the other thing, isn't it? She has to be someone that won't be missed.'

'You have theories.'

'Casual thoughts, anyway. She's young, but not so young you could call her a runaway.'

'Thing I worked, they were tarts mostly.'

'Would explain a lot.'

'Not from round here, though.'

'No. Folks who live this way wouldn't put up with that. They'd have the army out dealing with it.'

'In Oxford, what are the likely areas?'

'We have a fair lively evening scene. The town centre, what we call the Bunny Run, there's a good few girls on the prowl there. North of Queen Street and south of Beaumont. East of Gloucester and New Inn Hall Street and west of Cornmarket and Magdalen. But thing is, we know all the faces there. We all muck in here, vice and murder. Not enough of us to specialise like you old city boys. I've spoken to the ladies, and they don't know the girl.'

'Anywhere else roundabouts?'

'More recent, down Cowley with the blacks and the wogs coming in. I don't know that way too well, so it's possible. And you never quite know where you stand with anyone from Northampton. But her photo went round police in those stations.'

'A city's more likely.'

'London, maybe. But Birmingham, what I thought.'

They drive back to Oxford for a spot of lunch with their pints, with nothing new having come out of the adventure. The woman was definitely shot, was possibly a prostitute, and other than that, it's a long shot connecting her to anything.

Helm grabs a satchel off the back seat when they arrive. He gets the drinks in and they take a booth in a quiet part of the pub. He produces a file from the bag.

'Have a gander at that, Sergeant Cassar. Only, mind the locals peering over your shoulder, as the medical photos are in there.'

Taking the file from Helm, he examines the shots of the head wounds, the livid scars showing evidence of neat stitching.

Helm winks. 'Next one's a splash of vinegar on the chips.'

The woman is naked and prone on an examination table, buttocks and backs of her thighs thick with bruising and dark welts.

'Ring any bells with your situation?'

'Yeah,' he says. 'Yeah, I might have seen something like this before.'

1936

40

Geats ripped the fascist's ear in half at dusk after they had exchanged words regarding their mothers, neither of whom was present. This would later be remembered as the uneventful portion of the evening.

It was March, and the British Union of Fascists were parading from Tower Hill to the Royal Albert Hall, where Oswald Mosley would address a crowd of bootlickers only marginally bigger than the anti-fascist protesters gathering outside. Street lights flickering on cast a shine across the sleet that had fallen throughout the day, and the route had attracted comically straight lines of toadies gleefully waving in the arrival of authoritarianism with Nazi salutes.

Coppers from four divisions patrolled the streets, the fascist procession being led by mounted police advancing at a regimental pace and flanked by constables walking alongside the Blackshirts as though arraying them-selves to their cause. They were cheered and jeered in equal measure.

Not that Geats could in all honesty have claimed to be making a political stance by his intervention; it was just that he felt a natural affinity to the underdog.

They had reached Leicester Square, about halfway along the spec-tacle, when a single communist broke the lines and charged at Mosley. He was met not only by policemen making judicious use of their trun-cheons, but by a black-shirted gang with staves running amok with apparent impunity.

And so, it was sympathy for the dangerously outnumbered that prompted Geats to yell at the nearest philosopher, their trading of maternal slights followed by Geats swinging him viciously by the ear into the gutter, tearing the top half of the appendage away so it hung in a bloody frond. Barely pausing for breath, he collected the man's discarded staff and, with his own club in his other hand, set about ruffling a few more brilliantined partings.

Within seconds he was hemmed in and then swallowed by a crowd of Blackshirts. Brandishing his weapons above his head, he thrashed and struck out and continued the fight until he was lifted off his feet and borne along backwards by the surge, arms pinned. The pressure squeezed the breath from his lungs, and as he tried to keep his head above the tumult, a hand found its way into his open mouth, dragging him down into the dim space between knees and boots, and briefly the thought crossed his mind that this might be it.

The chaos was short-lived, however, and order was restored by dark figures on horses prancing among the melee in high-kneed piaffes. Geats was dragged from the mob, having lost his clubs but still throwing punches and kicks, and led by fellow officers behind the lines of chirping onlookers into the field at the centre of the square, which the police had cordoned off as their own staging post, overseen by Sergeant Pym (having started a few riots in his time, he was considered by Superintendent Dalton to be a likely expert in suppressing them).

Billie, administering first aid to anyone who required it, sat on a bench indifferently mothering the half-eared fascist. In truth, his injury was beyond her medical capabilities, requiring stitches at the very least and possibly more complicated surgery.

Elegantly dressed women who had been marching with the Union paused to lament the bloodshed, and Geats found himself face to face with two he recognised: the dancing sisters with the aristocratic noses whose escape from Chez Renée's he had facilitated through the tunnel.

The younger one, less elegantly dressed in full Blackshirt uniform with leather gloves, ran her fingers along his arm.

'Hello again, Sergeant.'

'Madam.'

She gave him a wink before moving off. Watching her depart, he became aware of Billie standing at his shoulder.

'Madam, is it?'

'What am I supposed to call her?'

'Seemed quite friendly, if you ask me.'

'I didn't.'

'You do attract some odd admirers.'

'I don't even know who she is.'

'You don't know who the Mitfords are? They certainly seem to know you.'

'That was a Mitford? I helped her out of a jam once, but we were never formally introduced.'

'That's Unity Mitford, Leon. At the very least, she dines with Hitler. The older one was Diana, Mosley's fiancée.'

'How about that.'

'You know what you should do – invite her back home to meet Clara. That would go splendidly.'

'Tea and rugelach?'

She laughed, nudging him in the side with her elbow. 'Pete Everett was asking after you.'

'For what?'

'Said he had one of your weird ones.'

'He still around?'

'I had to patch up a bump on the head he got.'

They wandered around the enclosed field, finding Everett leaning against the iron railings of the entrance to the underground lavs. The young constable had his hands wrapped round a steaming cup of tea, head swaddled in bandages.

'Got clobbered by one of my own,' he complained.

Geats nodded. 'Know the feeling.'

'Boyle thought he was hitting one of these Marxists, but he missed and give me what for instead.'

'Well, it's the thought that counts. You got something for me?'

'Arrest, week before last. Young woman found in the streets in a bit of a state. Incoherent, under the influence, I figured. Running about in not much more than her bloomers. Took her for a tart and brought her into the cells.'

'Doesn't sound too odd.'

'I didn't think so either. First thing in the morning, though, it became clear she wasn't a tart. Young governess for a family in Blooms-bury, daughters of a well-to-do under her guidance. Had a free weekend and wanted a night on the town. Says she don't remember anything, not even where she was drinking.'

'You believe her?'

'She certainly wasn't in good shape. Daffy in the head as she was, I could believe she'd been doped. I asked if there was any staff she trusted at the house where she was governess – my thinking being, if her story was true, I didn't want to land her in it with her employers. She said the cook there was friendly. I got a number and called, asking for this lady, and she come down the station and identified the young woman like she said, a governess. All things considered, me and the sarge thought it was best to let things go at that. We didn't make no record of it.'

'What do you think happened?'

'Someone's slipped her something, haven't they? Young girl, new to town, don't know many folk. Goes out to a pub, makes some new friends, and someone thinks she's a bit likely. Either pours a few too many down her, or gives her something that ain't what he says it is. Walks her back somewhere and tries it on. Maybe has tastes she don't share and matters get a mite frantic.'

'She escapes half dressed and in a daze.'

'Seems the likely course of events.'

'Any sign of strangulation?'

'No.'

Geats shrugged. 'Suppose I can follow up—'

'Sergeant Geats! Sergeant Geats!'

A grubby-faced boy of ten or so flew down an alley from Lisle Street, holding onto his cap. Geats tilted his head.

'You one of Simone's boys?'

A human telegraph network of likely young lads ran between Chez Renée's and Jack Isow's other joints, spreading the word when things were getting urgent.

'She needs you,' the boy said.

'For what?'

'Spot of trouble at Renée's.' Obscurely, he added, 'Old Benny's taking care of it, but she said you should come pronto.'

'What kind of trouble?'

'Italians.'

'Yeah, they would choose today.'

The city simmered nicely; tensions between Blackshirts and anti-fascist protesters were spilling over into incidents between the wider Italian and Jewish communities. Traditional alliances between Italian and Jewish gangsters were dissolving. The gangs were flexing, trying to extort club operators for racket money; mob soldiers who had fled debts or feuds in Sicily ran the streets for the Sabinis now, and their intentions were clear. Jewish impresarios were targeted, and ructions broke out at the Shim Sham and other venues as Jack Isow refused to bend to them.

The club was round the corner, and Geats and Billie ran after the boy. The doorman, Garfield, waved them on down the stairs.

'This gone be a mess.'

Geats saw at once that he'd walked into the midst of a fiasco.

Two Italian thugs were on the floor in the kind of heaps the body only arranges itself in when its switch is flipped with no prior warning. A third was standing with his hands out, trying to placate Benny, who for his part was calm as could be. Seemed to be looking off someplace nobody else could conjure, fingers drumming against his thigh to the rhythm of the music in his mind.

'You police?' the Italian said, strong accent.

Geats grinned. 'Uh huh.'

'*Questo non ha le mani, ha dei macigni*. He is to kill me.'

'What he say?' Geats asked Simone.

'I got the kill bit . . .'

'You're Italian, aren't you?'

'I'm from Cardiff.'

'What were you doing here?' he asked the Italian.

The man shrugged. 'We came for drink.'

'That right?'

Simone pointed to one of the men out cold on the floor. 'Fat boy here was making speeches. Jews this, Jews that. Then he started in on the threats. Offering his services to protect the club, telling me what could happen, undesirable elements and so on. I told them I got protection. I told them I got Benny.'

'They saw Ben?'

'No. He was out back. He heard his name and came through. The other one here,' she pointed at the shorter unconscious hood, 'he tried making some type of joke.'

'Looks like Ben had a few thoughts about that.'

'Spilled him on the floor like a dropped cocktail. Fat boy tried to grab his wrist and he poured him out too.'

Geats considered the third man. 'Something tells me you don't usually do the talking.'

'*Cosa?*'

'I'm saying you're not the brains of the operation.'

'*Non sono io la teste?*'

Simone shook her head. 'I don't believe this is a brains kind of operation.'

'I make call for Signor Sabini,' the Italian said.

'Don't think that'll improve matters much,' said Geats.

The Italian shook his head ruefully. 'He is not to be happy with you.'

'That a threat? Sounds an awful lot like one.'

This fresh round of menace stirred Benny from his reverie. Taking his cap off, as though paying respects to the departed, he busted the man in the chops before anyone else could blink, let alone move a muscle to stop him. About spun his jaw back behind his shoulder.

Geats probably wouldn't have done anything even if he had known what was coming. Whole situation tickled him, and honestly, he was enjoying himself something fierce.

'This is going to be a fine story to tell,' he said.

'All the makings,' Benny added, fatally.

When the Italians came round, Simone kept Benny out back somewhere, in case he should feel they needed more sleep. Fat boy who had been in charge, he just couldn't shake it off.

'It a bomb?' he said, sitting up on the floor.

'Not a million miles away,' Geats agreed.

'I shouldn't be here.'

'I'll say.'

The man let his head hang between his knees. Geats could see his understanding of the circumstances had been shattered into pieces and he was having no little trouble trying to fit them back together.

'Who else got hurt?'

'Mostly just you and your buddies here.'

The man looked at the two other Italians. 'And you said it was a bomb?'

'Okay, that's enough punches to the head for you today.'

Lifting the man up under his arms, Geats set him upright. The Italian staggered a few steps and steadied himself against the bar.

'You want some water or something?' Geats offered.

'I think I'm needed somewhere.'

'Most of us do like to think so.'

The fat Italian held his head in his hands as his friends battled to their feet. Geats and Garfield helped the three of them up the stairs and out into the street, not one of them confident of exactly where they were or what they were supposed to be doing.

'You have yourselves a pleasant evening now,' Geats said, waving them off.

As he watched them stumble away, two uniformed constables charged out from Leicester Square, hotfooting it towards Wardour Street, followed seconds later by a third, soles slapping the pavement.

'Hey!' Geats yelled.

They ignored him, but he spotted a bandaged head on their trail. 'Everett!'

'Geats, they've got a murder. North end of Lexington.'

'Bill!' Geats hollered, drawing Billie up the stairs from the club.

Grabbing her arm, he ran through Soho, finding police Wolseleys parked across the Broad Street end of Lexington, lights going.

Boyle had beaten everyone there and hovered outside the door up to the flats above number 47. He looked ill. Geats eyed him questioningly, the giant man shaking his head.

Rushing up to the second floor, Geats found Proudfoot standing in the door, glimpsed alarm in his expression.

'Jesus,' the detective said. 'He's done another.'

41

In a kitchen with a bed in the corner, people gaggled round the body, basking in it, warming their hands at the shared hearth of horror. She was on the floor, a handkerchief tied tightly at her throat, face swollen not only from strangulation but from prior uncontrolled violence. The air was fetid where she'd soiled herself in her final throes.

All wedged in the small room, tramping through the evidence: constables, detectives, pathologist, photographer, the doctor who had been called before the police.

Having found the body, the woman's fifteen-year-old stepson now sat in the second of the tiny flat's two rooms, on the bed his father had shared with the dead woman. He wasn't really a stepson; they weren't husband and wife. Legally the man was still married to the boy's mother, who he hadn't seen since she was committed to a sanatorium for lunatics after giving birth. Catholic, he couldn't divorce.

'Boy says she's French,' Proudfoot said. 'Marie Cotton, goes by her middle name, Jeanette. Also known by her maiden name, Cousins. She married an English fella when she first came here, but it didn't last. Any of this sounding familiar?'

'You think she's one of Red Max's girls?' said Geats.

'I dunno. But there's a pattern emerging. Someone's killing foreign whores.'

'Where's the partner?'

'Some wop.' Proudfoot checked his notes. 'Carlo Stephano Lanza. Chef at the Florence on Rupert Street. Got people fetching him now. They'll check his alibi before they break the news to him.'

'What's the son's name?'

'Remo. Remo Lanza.'

'Mind if I . . .?'

'All yours.'

Geats led the boy out onto the landing, where it was quieter.

'Remo, was anything else disturbed?'

'Disturbed?'

'Moved around, or missing. As if thieves had been through the place.'

'I don't think so. To be honest, I found her lying there and immediately went for the doctor. I didn't notice anything.'

'Would there be any valuables kept in the flat? Did she have jewellery? Or any cash?'

'She has a box with a few bits, but nothing special. If there is any money, it'll be with her bank book in the sideboard drawer. Just inside the door there.'

Geats stepped back into the flat and opened the drawer. A few letters addressed to the deceased, but no bank book.

'You sure she keeps it here?'

The boy came and looked. 'It's always there, other than on payday. Then she takes it with her and pays her wages straight into the bank.'

'She has her own account?'

'Oh yes. She would never let Papa handle the money. She paid her wages in and dealt with the rent from the front room.'

Geats pointed at the door across the landing.

'This here?'

'It's part of the same flat. We rent the whole floor, but since there's separate doors on the landing, Jeanette sublet the front room for extra money.'

'Anyone living there now?'

He nodded. 'Dot.'

'Dot? Who's—'

'Leon?'

Billie was on the stairs below the landing.

'Hold on, Bill.'

'It's urgent. And relevant.'

'All right. Thanks, Remo. I'll be back in a bit.'

He followed Billie down to the street.

'What is this, Bill?'

'Someone you need to speak to.'

He followed her round the corner to a bus garage next to the long-quiet Lion Brewery, where they found a young woman waiting whom Geats half recognised from the streets.

'This is Dot Neri,' Billie said.

'Dot? Same Dot rents the front room up there?' he said.

Dot nodded excitedly. 'Coz it has its own door off the landing, Mrs Cotton, she lets it out. I got it cheap about a month ago. I needed a new place on account of my fella's wife coming back from the country after a spell of the nerves. She was—'

Geats cleared his throat.

'Yeah, sorry. She was a cow, though. Anyway, I met Remo in a pub, see. He said they had a room going and it's handy here as you've got Oxford Street and Regent Street an easy walk. Plus, the room smelt something awful, so she knocked some off the first month. Just wanted someone in there.'

'Smelt of what?'

'Dead rats. They had a bit of a problem a while ago, had to smoke 'em out. The previous tenant, she had some trouble with him. He ruined a mattress and left the place in a mess; where the rats came from, I think. Reckon a few got stuck or died of whatever, under the floor like. So yeah, there was a bit of that in the air. I had to perfume the place real strong when I got a punter. But it's gone now. And it's a nice room, three windows. Biggest place I've ever had. And Mrs Cotton, she's just lovely. Was lovely. God.'

'Did she . . . you know?'

'What? See punters? God, no. Mrs Cotton was a respectable lady. She done cleaning work in some posh office. And Remo and his old man work kitchens.'

'When did you last see her?'

'About five? I was just going out to work and I give her a cup back. She'd made me tea. Just lovely.'

'You been back since?'

'Come back about seven, with a bloke. I had a few earlier, but they just wanted the old cotton gloves in an alley. This one wanted a full sit-down meal. Didn't see or hear nothing of her, though, and was back out by quarter to eight. Am just now returning to all this.'

A neighbour took her in for a cup of tea, and the dead woman's partner, Lanza, arrived under the watchful eye of two constables. They ushered him upstairs and minutes later a scuffle broke out, culminating with one of Proudfoot's men tumbling down the stairs. Lanza was incandescent with rage, several constables needing to restrain him for Proudfoot's sake.

'Asked the man where she worked, where her patch on the streets was,' Boyle explained to Geats. 'Didn't take it well. Him and his son insist she weren't a pro. They've been living as husband and wife for seven years. She works as a cleaner, different restaurants and the like usually, but at the moment for a barrister in Mayfair.'

Lanza broke loose again, murderous with sacrificial loyalty to his woman's reputation, seasoning his ire with punches and clubbing blows until his son bundled him into the back room and shut the door on the detectives. Proudfoot came down the stairs, hat dented and raincoat collar torn.

'Unseemly, fighting with that poor woman lying there. For his own good we'll let him calm down.'

Geats nodded understandingly.

Another car pulled up. When the rear window lowered, Superintendent Dalton's face emerged. His presence at a crime scene was almost unprecedented. Catching Geats's eye, he nodded for him to come over.

'Get in.'

Geats got in beside him and waited. Dalton inhaled deeply through his nose. He stretched out his moustache and picked some lint from his trousers.

'Don't want to cause a fuss, having the men see me here.'

'No, sir.'

'Is this the work of the same man?'

'I don't know, sir. She's French, and she has been strangled.'

'Prostitute?'

'Husband says not.'

'Well, he would.'

'They rent a room out to a working girl, and she says the victim wasn't a pro.'

'We have to get moving on this one. Can't afford to get behind like we did with the Martin woman.'

'No, sir.'

'I'm calling in Nutty Sharpe. Possible repeat killer. We need the best on this, Geats. Damned press are going to be all over us.'

He glanced over at the detectives milling around outside the front door.

'You can tell Proudfoot.'

'Yes, sir. Thank you, sir.'

Geats got out and Dalton's car glided off. Across the street, Proudfoot watched it go and glanced back at Geats, his face forming a question.

'Fuck you very much, sir,' Geats muttered.

42

Geats was a crooner.

Cassar listened to him plead his case to Nutty Sharpe, who was back squatting in the Clubs & Vice office, concentrating less on the words themselves than the smooth lining of their vowels. The rounded edges of the consonants. The man could make rats and mattresses sound like hymns.

He was surprised when Sharpe gave his story the time of day.

'You don't think it's the same killer?'

Geats shrugged. 'Could be. But I don't think so.'

'They were both strangled, Sergeant. In their own homes.'

'Like the celestial alignment of nine planetary bodies, two women are strangled to death in their own homes. By God, what astronomical odds would you give they both died at the hands of men also?'

Sharpe's eyes cut fleetingly to Cassar.

'Christ, it's just like conversing with Sherlock bloody Holmes. Don't come the clever one with me, Geats. I've seen more dead women than you've had long nights in that fairy bar of yours. You stroll about the place like you're the only one can put down a case, as if I got to head Flying Squad by winning it in a raffle. But who killed Josephine Martin? Did I miss you solving that one?'

'I don't think they're connected. Sir.'

'We don't know that. Basic policing, Geats. They're both foreign, both living in poky Soho flats, both—'

'Jeanette Cotton wasn't a tart. Long record of employment, lived with Lanza for years just as any husband and wife might, and nobody who knows her has said otherwise. More importantly, no girls on the streets knew her to be a pro. Hell, she let that front room of theirs to a tart, and she's adamant Cotton wasn't on the street.'

'Both strangled, was my point. And it doesn't mean—'

'It's a lazy assumption.'

'I was going to say it doesn't mean that someone else didn't *think* she was a tart. Frenchwoman of a certain age, maybe sees her out in Soho, follows her home. If it is someone who has a taste for foreign tarts, then it would be an understandable mistake. Now, I agree with you: everything we know about her says she's a citizen. But that doesn't mean I don't examine the possibility that two similar cases, literally round the corner from each other, aren't connected.'

Acknowledging the merits of that, Geats remained tight-lipped.

'A personal motive would seem more likely, though, given the violence,' Sharpe went on. 'There was anger to it, and she wasn't displayed like Josephine Martin. You got the details of the former tenant, the one Mrs Cotton had this mattress hoo-hah with?'

'From a letter.'

'Letter?'

'Found in the dresser in the bedroom of the flat. A reply from the former tenant, a James Allen Hall. The girl who rents the front room told us that Hall left the mattress soiled with Vaseline and excrement.'

'A homosexualist?'

'Neighbours said they saw men and women going in there, so I don't know. But he wrote back to her from an address in Charing Cross.'

Sharpe nodded.

'And there's one other thing. Jeanette Cotton has her own bank account. Looks like the passbook is missing, though. The stepson, he says it was always in the sideboard drawer, unless she was paying her wages in. It wasn't there, or on her person.'

'Robbery?'

'The boy says she always pays the money in immediately. Impression I got, she saves her wages and the rent from subletting the front room, and they live off Lanza's wages. Remo said she didn't leave cash around the place. I sent WPC Massey to the bank. They're going to contact us if anyone produces the passbook.'

'Good. Fine. In that case, you go to Charing Cross and see what this James Allen Hall has to say. And take Cassar.'

'Me and Billie can handle it.'

'I need WPC Massey. Inspectors Minter and Lander are going to be talking to the local brass, and your constable is good with that sort of thing. Something of a diplomat. You're with Cassar.'

43

Craven Street was tucked away in the lee of Charing Cross station, a toothpick street between the Strand and that part of the Embankment where coal barges moored by the railway bridge. Georgian terraces built for merchants and solicitors had succumbed to the needs of the day, and single lodgings were rented out by the week.

James Allen Hall lived in a back room on the second floor of one such house. They found him slightly drunk, wild-haired and gum-eyed as if disturbed from a nap. His lodging was small and awkwardly shaped, with a fireplace on a slanted angle and one narrow window overlooking a tiny yard and the back of the buildings on the street behind. It had a powder room just off, though, where Hall had stowed a small cot, freeing the main space for an armchair, a table with two unmatching chairs, and a hotplate on a dresser.

Cassar took the lead and Geats didn't object.

'James, you know a Jeanette Cotton?'

'Miserable sow. Kicked me out, didn't she. Hence I'm here.'

'How do you know her?'

'She give me a room to let when me and the wife had a bit of bother.'

'Bit of bother?'

'Beat her black and blue, didn't you?' Geats said.

Dot had filled him in on how Cotton had told her all about Hall, that he used to live next door on Lexington until his wife threw him out.

'I never gave her nothing she didn't ask for. It was only meant to be temporary, like. Few weeks in next door and then I'd move back. Now look at me.'

He gesticulated around the room as if his surroundings explained the wretchedness of his life, rather than the other way round.

'Mrs Cotton believes you owe her money,' Cassar said. 'For a mattress.'

'That weren't me.'

'What wasn't you?'

'That damaged the mattress.'

'You're aware it was damaged?'

'Three quid she says she wants for it. Outrageous. You know what she charged me for that room? Pound and two a week. She's only paying one and seven and six for the whole gaff.'

'The mattress, James.'

'I used to sublet, didn't I? There are people just want a night here, a night there. Couple of crown each time. That's fair, isn't it? Given I used to spend the night outside, and they were doing only the Lord knows what.'

'You sublet a sublet? Neighbours say you used to have visitors. Men. Sailors and soldiers, often.'

'That's what I'm telling you. It was the others what did that. One morning I come back, the key's left on the ledge on the landing like I used to tell them, and I go in and he's left the place in a right state. There's blood and shit all over the bed, which is done for. Couldn't believe it.'

'And who was this fella you let have the room?'

'I dunno.'

'You don't know who you rented your home to?'

'He took it a few times. Chap I seen down the pub, see. He was in the army, an officer. Brigadier. That's all I knew him by, Brigadier. Listen, I know I left in a bit of a palaver, and she's chasing me for the money and what have you, but is all that worth you coming here look-ing for me? Am I under arrest for a beshitted mattress?'

'Where were you yesterday? Last night, to be exact.'

'Nowhere, really. Around.'

'James.'

'I had a few jars on the Charing Cross, then went to the pictures.'

'Where? Which cinema?'

'Nipped across to the Pavilion. The new Eddie Cantor was on. Now, I'd never say he was as good as Chaplin, but the scene with the gunman—'

'Did anyone see you?'

'I'd conjure hundreds if not thousands did, walking through Charing Cross and Leicester Square. Here, what's yesterday to do with the mattress?'

'Anyone who'd remember you?'

'How many people you suppose remember *you* on any given day?'

'You will.'

'That's because we're chatting.'

'Did you chat to anyone?'

'And because you're police, and you don't forget that in a hurry.'

'In the pub, did you talk to anyone?'

'I worked my way through a few of them, see. The Garrick, the Bear, the Crown, the Porcupine, the Stores. Only had a tipple in each one, so can't say as anyone would place me there.'

'And the cinema?'

Hall shrugged. 'I bought a ticket, but it was the evening show. It was almost full.'

'Ticket?'

He stared at each of them, then fetched his jacket from the bed, rooting about in the pockets.

'Here.' He handed over the retained half of a torn green ticket.

'No date,' Cassar said.

'That's what they give me.'

'Printed number,' Geats said. 'We'll check.'

'Why do you need to know about yesterday so bad?' said Hall.

'Mrs Cotton was murdered last night,' said Cassar.

Hall grinned, then looked from one to the other and blanched. 'You're serious?'

'Killed in her flat on Lexington.'

He thought about that for a moment. 'Good.'

'Good?' Geats said.

'Trouble she caused me. I mean, I never killed her, never would, but can't say as she didn't have it coming. You want to talk to her fella, though. Carlo. The rows them two used to have. Mouth on her. Surprised he didn't do her before now.'

'You ever see him get violent with her?' Cassar asked.

'No, can't say I did. In fact, more likely she'd bash him with something, way she was. You know what French birds are like.'

They left him to his squalor, Geats pausing at the door on the way out. 'This Brigadier, what pub did you meet him in?'

'The Argyll, as I recall. Used to enjoy a pint in there.'

'On Little Pulteney Street?'

'At the corner there. It was only the once, mind. After that, he'd knock and ask if he could have the place. Usually he caught me in the street outside the flat.'

'Ever see him anywhere else?'

'Few dives around Soho occasionally. Nowhere on the regular.'

Back out on the street, Geats shook his head and lit a cigarette, as if to steel himself.

'Believe him?' Cassar said.

'Story sounded both too specific and too vague to be made up.'

'Beat his wife, though. The violence fits.'

'Yeah. We'll run down this ticket stub.'

'And the Brigadier? We gonna look for him?'

'Oh, sure. Have a nosy around all the pubs and clubs from Little Pulteney to Broad Street, ask for the Brigadier in each one. Can't imagine that we won't wrap this up before sunset.'

44

That evening, Geats hung around the centre of Cambridge Circus, leaning against the iron palisade of the public lavatories at the other end from the entrance gate. Just along from him, a blind man sat on a folding chair with his case open on his lap, receiving a few flicked pennies.

The women patrolled the outside of the junction, luring punters from the Cambridge, the Granby, the Scots House. Geats watched a small bespectacled gent buy rejuvenation tablets from the news-stand before hurrying across three streets to the far side of the Circus to engage a lady who wouldn't have seen his purchase.

He waited almost an hour, approached only twice: a young man who gave him a meaningful look before heading down the steps into the lavatories, and a new girl who didn't know any better. She crossed the road specially to speak to him, but two older women clucked around and steered her off, leaving him to his own thoughts. They knew him as a copper who didn't interfere with their work so long as they spoke to him occasionally about any recent happenings.

When Leah arrived, he pushed himself off the fence and crossed the road, standing close to a police call box. She was on the other side of Charing Cross Road, the tallest out there with her heels. When he caught her eye, she was hidden for a moment by a bus with a Canadian Apples advert posted on its side, and was still looking at him when it passed. She nodded down the road and he followed her until she crossed over to join him, pulling him into an alley leading behind the Sandringham Buildings. They huddled in an acute cranny and he palmed her a ten-bob note.

'I saw Nell,' she said.

'Oh yeah?'

'Today. Getting off a bus. Coming from the East End, looked like. Walked on into Soho. Had groceries with her.'

Geats's jaw tightened. 'Resourceful, that one.'

She side-eyed him. 'Tell me she's okay.'

'I had to guess, I'd say she was doing all right.'

'Geats—'

'You don't have to worry about her, Stilts.'

'Fair enough.' She jutted her chin out defiantly. 'I don't know nothing about this new one. The tart on Lexington.'

'Wasn't a tart.'

'Why you asking me about her, then?'

'I'm not.'

'Well, what *do* you want?'

'Jesus, Stilts.'

'It's nippy. I've no mind for an evening of knees-up in the alleys. I want to find a job and be in the flat where it's warm. Don't even mind if he fancies a spot of backgammon.'

'The Brigadier.'

'Who's that?'

'Doesn't mean anything to you?'

'Brigadier? No. Soldier? Don't see too many of them round here. Get a few boys off the ships in the docks. And the odd keelman runs up from the coal barges. The muck and dust on them – gets everywhere.'

'Someone who calls himself the Brigadier, though. Nobody like that?'

'New one on me. I can ask about, see if I hear anything from the girls.'

'Yeah.'

'Should we be worried, Geats?'

'Worried?'

'Two women strangled, streets from each other. If there's someone out here targeting us . . .'

'I don't think they're connected.'

'Oh, well. If you don't *think* so, there's nothing to worry about.' Her laugh was tinged with mania.

'Your friend Josephine, that looked like business. Especially with Kassel being killed right after. This other one looks personal. Or possibly mistaken identity.'

'She was French?'

'Yeah. But there's nothing to suggest she worked the streets. Josephine ever tell you about rivals? Other foreign pimps?'

'Foreign pimps? In Soho? Are you having a laugh? We walk back to the Circus we'll fall over five of them.'

'Yeah, but I don't mean a ponce living off his girl. Something more organised. Running girls into the country from abroad, like Red Max and Lacroix . . . what? You're thinking about something.'

'There have been a few spots jumping up here and there. Flats. Foreign girls living together. A few of them were busted for running brothels, but now they're operating out of one flat and all living in another. It's clever, coz it's trickier to prosecute.'

'Got any addresses I can look at?'

'Couple. Know who's looking after them? Old mate of yours. Queenie.'

'Queenie Gerald? Come on. That cock won't fight.'

Geraldine Gaynor was a Soho legend. Before the war, a raid on her Haymarket brothel, where she was found giving a bath to a seventeen-year-old girl, became a point of contention for Keir Hardie and the Pankhursts, and was discussed at some length in Parliament (where some of her regular clients sat).

Upon release from her (un)surprisingly meagre three-month sentence, and blooming in her notoriety, she would stalk the streets of

Soho in sparkly shoes and sequinned stockings with a mardy parrot squawking from her shoulder.

Before Geats ever received his uniform, Queenie had begun her descent down the Soho ladder, from her original disorderly house catering to peers and gentlemen through increasingly less salubrious accommodations on Regent Street, Long Acre in Covent Garden, and a small flat off Oxford Street. When Geats came across her, she was a decade past her infamy and sharing a basement room near Dean Street with a struck-off midwife who had once entertained a lord in her nurse's outfit for Queenie.

'Hand on heart,' Leah said.

'Last time I saw Queenie, she was getting out. Lined up some old boy with a title and a great pile out in the fens. Liked livening up county council meetings by challenging other gents to duels.'

'He came to his senses. Though, she sued for breach and he had to pay her off handsomely. Then dropped dead six months later, so you wonder if he shouldn't have just enjoyed it while he could. She's back keeping house now, has kept several actually. There's a place in Kingly Court, and she told me she had rooms in a house just behind Golden Square.'

'And she's working for foreigners?'

Leah shrugged. 'What I heard.'

He got details of the addresses as best as Leah could remember and took a walk to Golden Square. The house was on Lower James Street, thin and cramped between taller buildings, anaemic next to the grand red brick of the square.

He knocked and the door was opened by a woman of about fifty, wearing a modest button-up tweed suit.

'Hey, Queenie. Where's the parrot?'

45

Given her previous more infamous digs, Geats was half expecting some kind of high-class joint, lords' bastards lounging in panelled drawing rooms smoking cigars and quaffing brandy. No such luck. The front room was empty and stripped bare, and the back room beyond the stairs housed a lonely-looking drop-leaf table with two ladder-backed chairs. Copies of *Woman's Weekly* and *Home Chat* lay open, *London Life* tucked beneath them.

He took a seat. 'Thought you were out, Queenie.'

'I'm not on the game,' she said primly.

Crow's feet at her eyes, jowly rumours around her mouth. No gay make-up or working clothes. This dour, matronly woman before him was nothing like the Queenie Gerald he remembered prowling the neighbourhood.

He pointed upwards. 'If I were to take a wander and have a nosy about upstairs . . .'

'You most certainly will not.'

A door opened above them somewhere, followed by footsteps on the stairs. Geats listened for another set of feet, but they never came.

'Girls don't go out and fetch punters, then? They're sent here?'

'Geats, what do you want? How did you even find me?'

'Mutual acquaintance.'

'Who . . . oh. Leah.'

'I'm not looking to bust the place, Queenie.'

'No. No, you wouldn't be. Just want me to spill my guts.'

'You know about the killings?'

'The French tarts?'

'Actually, one of them wasn't a tart at all, and the one who was wasn't French, so—'

'Geats, the length of this conversation has already exceeded my interest in it.'

'I just need to know if you hear anything. Rough trade, or anyone with undue curiosity about foreign girls.'

Queenie laughed. 'Undue curiosity? If that doesn't sum up every punter we get in here, I don't know what does.'

'Thought you might hear more than most. Number of girls you come into contact with, here and Kingly Court and wherever else.'

She hardened her face. 'Leah said quite a lot.'

'Not so much, really. Only what you told her.'

'Me and my big mouth. One too many in the Crown when I bumped into her. That'll learn me. I don't know anything about your murders, Geats. Are you sure you're not tying together two things that only have in common the killing of women?'

'No. No, I'm not sure.'

'Well, then.'

He looked about the place, as if inspecting the coving and fireplace for original details. 'Who was it who set you up here?'

There was a knock at the door.

'Wait here,' she said, disappearing down the hall.

He put it on his list, finding out whose coin was behind the place. The discovery of more previously unknown pimps organising on this scale in Soho, so soon on the heels of Kassel and Lacroix, was threatening to dent his professional pride. He thought about his new friend Harrison, and his intelligence connections – but he didn't want to approach him until he had more information to go on.

After showing someone upstairs, Queenie returned, but only as far as the doorway.

'Time for you to go.'

Geats smiled and got to his feet. 'Nice catching up, Queenie.'

'Uh huh.'

'Keep me in mind if you have any incidents. We need to stop the killing.'

46

Led by his nose to the bakery on Great Windmill Street, he picked up one of the day's last loaves and ducked into an off-licence for a pint of gin. At the Yard, he ran up to his rooms and lit the fire, before heading back down to check on Clara.

'Matka?'

A pot bubbled on the stove. Clara sat gingerly on the edge of the seat of her armchair, a towel round her shoulders. She glared at him.

'Tell her to leave me alone. She's such a pest.'

Nell hovered behind her brandishing a pair of scissors.

'The more you fidget around, the longer this will take.'

'I am perfectly happy with my hair.'

'You look like a witch.'

Clara fixed her stare on Geats. 'Will you let her talk to me this way?'

'What's cooking?' he said, avoiding the issue of his mother's hair.

'Soup,' Nell said.

'What kind?'

'Chicken.'

'Chicken? Where did you get chicken?'

'She went out,' Clara said.

Geats looked at the girl. 'Nell . . .'

'Went out and came back with a whole chicken,' Clara added.

'You're not helping, Matka. Nell?'

'There's a man keeps chickens in the yards behind his tenement off Whitechapel Road. He'll sell them to you if he knows you. I got dill, too.'

'Well, so long as there's dill.'

Geats went to the kitchen and leaned over the pot, inhaling deeply. It did smell terrific.

'I got bread on the way home, so . . .'

He poured a gin and brought it out to Clara, who was pulling the faces of someone trying to curl their ears out of the cutting zone of a maniac.

'I assume you didn't bring the chicken back alive?' he asked Nell.

'Pinkie necked it and put it in a box for me.'

'You see the delightful tales she comes back with?' Clara said.

'Who's Pinkie?'

Clara tutted. 'Shimson Pincus. The poultry man she just told you about. Best back-street shochet in the East End.'

Geats's Jewishness was a mystery to himself, and everyone else's was even more arcane, but he was glad it stitched small conspiracies between his mother and Nell.

'No one has ever before commented on the hairs on the back of my neck,' Clara said.

Nell narrowed her eyes as she worked. 'You have the mane of a wild horse.'

The three of them ate at the small table, Nell periodically wiping soup from her chin. The bread was good and the chicken better. Nell stole sips of Geats's wine until Clara told her she was not to drink it, but that the gin was fine.

'Oh, really?' Geats said. 'The gin is kosher?'

Clara considered her glass and shrugged. 'I cannot back that up.'

After dinner, they sat and listened to Clara's records and she sang. Nell sat quietly on the floor, bristling glumly. Geats couldn't tell if she disliked the music or Clara or was just tired, so he made their excuses claiming it had been a long day. Upstairs in his rooms, he tucked Nell into what had been his bed.

'I saw Leah today. Your mother's friend.'

Nell grunted, knowing what was coming.

'Said she saw you.'

'I got out of sight before she could catch me.'

'You got . . . Nell, that's not the point. What did I tell you about going out?'

She sniffed.

'I'm thinking about you. I don't think you're ready to be going out and about, and certainly not as far as Whitechapel.'

'I'm fine.'

'Come on. The dreams?'

She looked away from him.

'God knows, staying locked up all day with Clara is too much for anyone. I'm not saying don't go out at all, but use your brain. You know where all the women work, the ones who might know you. Get off the bus a stop early or a stop late, walk home down the narrow streets.'

'That sounds safe.'

'Daylight, Nell. I don't ever want you out at night. Fair?'

Her bottom lip jutted out.

'Fair?'

'Fair.'

'If anyone found out you were here . . . I'd have questions to answer. And you'd be whisked off to the orphanage.'

He said goodnight, pulling the door to, and bedded down on the sofa in the living room. Although still drinking, he hadn't been drunk since Nell had escaped the Waifs and Strays and turned up at the Yard like he'd told her to do. She still hadn't spoken much about what had happened with her uncle and Fluke, but was spending the days looking after (and profoundly irritating) Clara.

Later that night, he awoke to small sobs down the hall.

Quietly he warmed milk in the kitchen and took her a cup. Neither of them spoke as she sipped it and lay back down. She didn't tell him of what she dreamed, and he didn't push. He recalled the alarming dreams of his own childhood, of being trapped below deck in a vast and dark wooden ship, of wandering its passageways and never finding a way out. The fear that took hold within him, the desperate need to feel safe and protected. Holding her tiny hand, he sat with her until she dropped off and stayed there to make sure she was settled in peaceful sleep.

He would give her space and kindness, and be there if she ever did want to talk. Though if he was honest, the thought of anyone trusting him that much mildly terrified him.

47

Dalton pinned the cutting from the *Daily Mirror* onto the wall of the Clubs & Vice office.

'This was page five this morning. We do not want it creeping out onto the cover.'

Sharpe had called the meeting and handed proceedings over to the superintendent, who wasn't one to subscribe to the theory that the only thing worse than being talked about was not being talked about. The article outlined broad similarities between the Martin and Cotton cases without explicitly suggesting that they were the work of the same killer. The foundations were clearly being laid, though.

Minter and Lander hovered by the door. Cassar sat on the sofa, Geats slumped beside him. This was the kind of meeting in which he wouldn't even dream about sharing his thoughts on the matter at hand.

'My men have been interviewing a lot of the street workers in Soho, asking about rough trade,' Sharpe said. 'And with the Cotton woman, there's a personal dispute that we're also looking into.'

'You don't think it's the same killer?' Dalton saw a glimmer of hope.

'We're not ruling anything out.'

Lander piped up from the corner. 'They were both strangled. Both in their own homes. Both foreign.'

It was unusual for any of the squad to go against Nutty Sharpe's line of thinking in front of top brass, and Cassar smirked when Lander shied back against the door under his chief inspector's glare.

'I'm saying, sometimes a thing is what it looks like,' he said.

'Either way, let's move quickly on this, gentlemen,' Dalton said. 'If we can, establish that they are separate killers. If we can't, then catch the maniac.'

He left, and Sharpe divvied up the tasks. 'Minter, Lander. Continue the interviews, and take Geats's constable so you don't scare the local wildlife. Geats and Cassar, where are you with this mattress business?'

'Fella was at the cinema,' Cassar said. 'Or he has a ticket, anyway. Cinema confirmed it was from the showing at the time of the killing, but nobody remembers him.'

'I want you to go back through reports for the last few months. Anything that looks like it could have been a sex attack. Go back before the Martin killing if you have to.'

Cassar sulked. It was grunt work; a menial task any constable could have done. Geats, on the other hand, searched through the most recent occurrence books furiously.

'Must be here somewhere.'

'What?'

'Constable Everett told me that a couple of weeks back he found a young woman half naked in the streets. Thought she was drunk, but talking to her the next morning he got the idea maybe she'd been doped. Can't remember exactly what he said. Though, thinking about it, maybe he told me he didn't make an official entry.'

'You think our man is slipping them something?'

'I don't know, but it would give us something concrete to go out and look into. Unless you want to sit here with these books all day?'

Cassar stared at them gloomily. 'Let's find Everett.'

Sergeant Pym told them the constable was covering a Mayfair beat, and after some marching around they located him sitting by the drinking fountain on Berkeley Square.

'Katherine Farrier. I didn't make no mention of her in the station records, Sarge,' Everett told Geats. 'If it's down on paper she was picked up in an indecent state . . . it's like officially branding her a whore. I mean, she was a proper lady, I thought. The cook attested for her. Didn't see the worth in ruining her.'

'No, you did right, Constable. Where was it you picked her up?'

'One of them narrow courts that run between Little Pulteney and Peter Street. She was huddled down on the ground there.'

'You remember much about who came to vouch for her? You said it was the cook where she worked?'

'Do better than that. I made me own notes. Got the address here somewhere.' He flicked through his pocketbook. 'Yeah, here it is. Gordon Square.'

48

They had a look-see at the place, a five-storey Georgian townhouse on the east side of the square. From a phone box outside the Catholic church opposite, they called the number Everett had for the downstairs and explained that they wanted to pay a visit without upsetting the family of the house, to which the housekeeper reluctantly agreed to avoid any scenes.

Slipping down the exterior steps to the basement, they were let in the trade entrance and the cook made them tea in the kitchen. The housekeeper, Mrs Henshell, explained that Katherine Farrier was no longer employed there, and had returned home. A stern Scottish woman, she hovered over them in stony silence as they drank.

'Miss Farrier here long?' Geats said.

The cook shook her head. 'Few months.'

'She get on with everyone?'

'Governesses are neither fish nor fowl.'

'How do you mean?'

'They're staff, but they're upstairs, not downstairs. I didn't have a lot to do with her.'

She glanced at Mrs Henshell. As long as the housekeeper was there, she wasn't going to give them anything. Cassar gave Geats a look and he caught on, putting his cup down and staring at Mrs Henshell, keeping it up until it became awkward.

'Well, if you'll excuse me, I have matters to attend to,' she said, her keys rattling as she departed.

It made little difference: the cook remained tight-lipped. She admitted to vouching for the girl at the police station and taking her home.

'Nice girl, bit on the quiet side, but then that's probably a virtue in a governess. Only from out Essex way, but she'd never been to the city before. Thought Colchester was bright lights.'

'She tell you what happened?' Geats asked.

'No. And I didn't enquire. Whatever it was, it had happened and we were past it, so no point dwelling.'

'How much longer did she stay?'

'Couple of weeks. She'd spoken about a fiancé, in her home town. Went back to him, I suppose.'

Thanking her for the tea, they left. A few yards down the road, a young woman in maid's clothes hurried out of the house after them, leading them out of sight round the corner.

'Told them I was posting a letter,' she said, 'so can't be long.'

'You worked with Miss Farrier?' Geats asked.

'I'm Jenny, the maid. I work for Mrs Henshell mostly, but Katherine used to join us for meals. The older ones, they don't like the governesses. Always freeze them out. But Katherine was nice. Sometimes I'd pack us lunch and we'd eat in the square, or the new park where the foundling hospital used to be.'

'She tell you what happened to her, Jenny?'

Jenny nodded. 'She was awful shook up when Cook got her back. She went right to bed. It's not all of us live there, you see. We're day workers. Mrs Henshell, she has a room. And Katherine, on account she come from far away. I brought her up a hot milk, made sure she was all right. She didn't go out much, as a rule. I took her to a pub a couple of times, and we was meant to go that night but I had to cry off as Mum weren't well. Well, apparently she decided to go out on her own. We used to drink in Soho, as I know the pubs there better.'

'You live there?'

'Foubert's Place.'

'Drink in the Shakespeare?'

She grinned. 'Yeah, that's where I took Katherine. She went there that night too. Said she got drinking with a girl in there and they decided they was going to speak with accents, like they was French girls.'

Geats and Cassar shared a look.

'She said they went on somewhere else, said it was a club. She didn't remember where it was. It weren't like her, going out to a place like that, but I think she'd had a lot to drink. She said she started to feel unwell and they left with a man who Katherine thought was taking her to a doctor. She weren't the type to go off with a man otherwise.'

'But he didn't take her to a doctor?'

'No. He didn't. She weren't real clear on what happened, but she said she thought she was . . . well, that maybe he give her the cane. And she lost her dress in all that fuss.'

'She remember the other woman's name?'

'Bella, she said. Just Bella.'

'Okay, Jenny. You've been a big help, thanks very much.'

'I should head on back. If anyone could get lost in the posting of a letter . . . that's what Cook'll say to me.'

Geats smiled. 'You run along.'

'I can see if Essex Constabulary have anything on a Katherine Farrier,' Cassar said when she was out of earshot.

'If this girl's gone home and got married, I don't want to wade into her life unless it's absolutely necessary.'

'What else do we have to go on?'

'Bella,' Geats said. 'Reckon I know exactly who Bella is.'

49

It was early, but Simone fixed them drinks.

Cassar necked his quickly; it went down a little too easily. The band was jamming and his toe tapped out the beat. He'd been spending more and more evenings in Soho, enough that he was thinking about moving from Lambeth. In the clubs, taken by the music; it felt like the only place he allowed himself to be himself.

'You going to nick her?' Simone asked Geats. 'I don't need that happening in here.'

'Not going to nick her,' he said.

'Because she'll probably give you six different reasons to take her in just by standing there.'

'I know.'

'I don't bring any of that stuff in here. Too much hassle. But the customers like a bit of a toot from time to time, so . . .'

'Simone, I just said I wasn't going to arrest her. Not in here, anywhere.'

'It's just—'

'She slips you a cut. I'm not daft. Nobody does anything in here without you knowing.'

'Bella's the only one I allow. Used to dance for me, until she hooked up with Gerry O'Brien.'

Cassar knew O'Brien. Another bottle party impresario, like Jack

Isow, but he moved half the cocaine in Soho through his joints. A former chartered accountant, he used his financial nous to launder his profits, and cruised town in a Rolls-Royce.

'I see her here most times I'm in,' Geats said. 'She keep regular hours?'

Simone shrugged. 'Likes to dance, and our bands are better than Gerry's. She'll be in here before midnight, but how long she stays is down to trade. These days she usually ends up at Never Been Kissed.'

Cassar made a face. That was a new one on him.

'Old location, new name,' Geats said. 'Behind Golden Square.'

There was a thin mews Cassar knew with warehouses and back premises that was home to several dives.

'Where Nero's used to be?'

Simone nodded. 'Number 16, hence the name. "Sweet sixteen and never been kissed, two red lips I couldn't resist."'

Geats turned to Cassar. 'Guess we might as well wait here for her.'

Cassar tapped the bar next to his empty glass and Simone topped him up. He was already rolling his hips. His suppleness was by now one of the great attractions of Chez Renée's, the dancing copper with dark wild eyes. That he was Flying Squad was laughed off by Simone's dancers and the regulars who haunted the basement, for his feet moved with grace, his arms with the sweep of a diving kestrel. He danced with women, he danced with men. He danced with blacks, he danced with queers. He danced and he drank and he soaked his shirt through.

He could feel it coming on.

'Come find me when Bella turns up,' he told Geats.

Geats nodded. He found the safety of a dark corner and drank alone, a furtive eye on every coming and going. And so he noted the arrival of the two sisters he had seen trailing the fascist Mosley through Leicester Square, whose escape from the Flying Squad raid he had handled. Back in the underworld for more excitement. So too did they notice him, conspicuously snaking across the dance floor until they were cavorting about near his table, making big eyes at one of the saxes.

Idle gossip around the station was that Mosley was in with old Adolf, and the sisters partook in debauched orgies with Nazi soldiers at Goebbels' house, yet here they were working themselves into dripping concupiscence with Benzedrine tablets and strapping saxophonists.

When the band broke, he watched the pair chatting to the tall musician by the door beside the stage. Simone opened it and waved them through delicately, Snakehips Johnson along with them, not a soul but Geats noticing. Guest musicians there for the free drink and a jam had started up on stage, and Cassar was dancing with two gents who were in there every night. Leaving him to his frolicking, Geats slid out the side door.

He caught Simone coming back down the stairs and she couldn't help herself glancing back over her shoulder.

'Oh yeah,' he said.

'What?'

'Whatever's going on. Spill.'

'That ain't none of your concern.'

'Making it my concern.' By the crook of her arm, he led her back upstairs and in a sneak she took him to the fourth storey, where a hole in the floor allowed him to peer through a false light fixture into the room below.

'What the fuck is this now?' Geats whispered.

Snakehips was on his knees before the saxophonist, whose kecks were round his ankles, inspecting his manhood like he might a cut of meat or fresh fruit he was weighing up for the buying.

'Snakehips's father was a doctor, insisted he went to medical school. He dropped out when the jazz got hold of him, became a bandleader,' Simone said. 'He clears the men for the ladies, and gets paid a pretty penny for doing so.'

'Clears them?'

'Makes sure they're clean.'

'Clean? What, for . . . you know?'

'Uh huh, honey. For you know.'

Geats pressed his eye back to the peephole.

'Incredible. And Snakehips don't mind?'

'The girls pay well. Truth told, he never needed much convincing to handle prick.'

Snakehips made himself scarce and the saxophonist was removing the rest of his clothes when Simone pulled Geats away and shut the hatch over the hole.

'Hey.'

'Hey yourself. I don't run no peep show.'

'This is police business.'

'No, this is none of your business.'

Downstairs, Cassar let the men he was dancing with buy him a few more drinks. Just looseners, nothing that would knock him off his game for later. Simone mixed up revivers – shaking together gin, aromatised wine, lemon, Cointreau and a splash of absinthe – and they went down smooth as honey but giving a kick that Cassar took onto the dance floor.

A hundred dancers became one undulating wave, Cassar and his two friends lindy-hopping as a trio among them and of them, like a chain snapping this way and that, all high knees and bent elbows. They swept round the floor, shifting shape and style in desynchronised harmony, the music melting into one endless number of hopeful passion, the saxes and trombones and trumpets and bass and drums, and body on body, skin to skin, they held each other to the sweet black music, these three white men, and in that moment and in that place, underground in a grubby West End cellar, they lived their lives how they were intended to be lived.

When the band broke, Cassar was both breathless and euphorically relaxed. Something passed between his two friends, a glance carrying an inkling of treasures to come, and they dragged him off out through the side door, and he was happy to be dragged.

In a dim and shabby hallway, a woman held court in a glittering floor-length gown that exploded out beneath the knee and twisted

round in a spiral, pooling in a thick fur hem. White carnations gar-
landed her bust, shoulders draped with perfect snow-white furs. The
boys paid her, and it wasn't until they stood in the cloakroom that
Cassar realised she must have been the Bella he was waiting for, and
his friends unfolded a little paper wrap torn from the pages of the
Bible and made small heaps of the powder it contained on their hands
and pressed them under his nose. Cassar inhaled deeply, and when his
friends asked him how it made him feel, he told them it made him feel
like more.

More dancing.

More laughing.

More life.

His belt was unbuckled and a hand he was fairly certain wasn't his
own gripped his prick and tugged in concert with his thumping heart,
and when he came, it did a lap of his body on the way out and he
gurgled with pleasure.

Tumbling out of the cloakroom, he ran into Geats coming down
the stairs from God knows where, and the man grinned at him as if he
saw straight through him. Cassar tried to point out Bella, but she was
hurrying away and Geats already knew the score.

He patted Cassar on the back. 'Best you stay here and let me
handle her.'

Cassar nodded vigorously, an ample contribution to the proceedings, and went looking for his friends, who were on the dance floor
where everyone and everything awaited.

Geats trotted back up the stairs he'd just come down, and out onto
the street through a door further down Lisle Street from the club
entrance. A Rolls-Royce was parked up and he hid in the doorway
until Bella glided up to the car.

'Hello, Bella.'

'Bloody hell, Geats.'

'One of two things can happen. I can frisk you, and we'll have a
nice long chat down Vine Street about what I find on you in the way

of cocaine and opiates. Or we can sit in the car and have a parley, and then go our separate ways.'

'You arrest me, I'll be forced to confess I sold narcotics to a police officer.'

'What police officer?'

'Your friend the dancer.'

'No idea who you're on about.'

'People saw him, Geats. They know.'

'You'll be surprised how little people know when they're sitting across from me in a courtroom.'

She sighed and nodded, opening the rear door of the car.

'It's not a Wolseley, but it'll do in a pinch,' Geats said, clambering in.

'You working for Isow now, that it?'

'I'm not. I was in there waiting for you. It's not about your business.'

'What then?'

'Katherine Farrier.'

'Who's that?'

'Young woman, governess for some posh family in Bloomsbury.'

She looked blankly at him.

'Believe you had an interesting evening with her at the Shakespeare a few weeks ago.'

'Oh,' Bella said, looking up and down the street. She pulled a curtain across her window. 'I can't be seen talking with the likes of you, Geats, so we'll take a quick spin.'

She signalled to the driver, who pulled off and began to circle the narrow streets of Soho. She almost looked at home in the car, with her silk gown and diamonds clustered at her throat. Almost, if it wasn't for the worn-out look in her eyes.

Bella Gold, daughter of Russian Jews who came to London at the turn of the century. She'd grown up in Stepney, where her father was a cap-maker, an industrious, well-respected man. Bella inherited none of his work ethic, and had been on the club scene since her early teens.

Shacked up with Gerry O'Brien, one of the first bottle party operators, she sold heroin to the Soho set, morphine to the Chelsea socialites and cocaine to both.

'Katherine, that was her name?'

'You don't remember?'

'Ran into her in the street, I'm not sure I'd know her.'

'How's that?'

'I'm a little foggy on that night. Gerry found me hiding in the bushes across from his place later. Apparently a taxi had dropped me off.'

'You have no recollection of that?'

'Not much, no.'

'What *do* you remember?'

'Vomiting.'

'Before that.'

'I went to the Shakespeare, sell a bit of salt. Have a few beers. We were doing French accents, on account of how the gents hang on every word the foreign tarts say.'

'This was you and Katherine? How did you meet her?'

She shook her head. 'She was in the pub. I don't know. Probably she was on her own and I bought her a drink. I'm always picking up strays.'

'Potential new customers.'

'There was a group, fellas mostly, but I didn't know them. We left to go to someone's flat.'

'How many of you was this?'

'I remember thinking we left as a whole gang, but then there was just the three of us.'

'You, Katherine and a man?'

'He liked the accents. We'd kept them up, but were falling about laughing. Something was wrong, though. Reckon the drinks had been spiked, as everything hit the rocks.'

'Where was this flat?'

'I don't know. Soho. I remember seeing the chimney of the old brewery, but I don't know which street.'

'And the man?'

She shrugged. 'When we were inside, I was scuppered. And I snort heroin, Geats. Whatever he'd dropped on us, it was pharmaceutical. I knew a girl used to offer gin from a flask to punters, a little hocus she mixed up with ethanol and chloral. Robbed them and left them on a bench; they'd wake up a right old mess.'

'Katherine was found in the streets in her underwear.'

'He had a strop.'

'Like for a razor?'

'I do remember that. He had her out of her dress and over his knee, said she was misbehaving. Gave it her, proper strokes across her bum and thighs. God, you could hear her screams for miles, I'd bet.'

'How'd you get away?'

'She was panicked. Wild-eyed. I've been dealing with mardy punters all my life. Know how to handle them. But it was like swimming. I couldn't quite move or talk as I wanted. I was making him promises, hoping to get her back in her frock, but the second he let her up, she was off out the door. He was all over me. He smelt clean, but like too clean, you know? Like bleach. He was on my back, trying it Greek style, and that really is for the French whores. I don't do that. I remember struggling and getting away. I think he might have let me. Didn't want the noise, the fuss. Gerry said he heard a taxi out front, and when he looked out, he saw me in the bushes. I had a dress in each hand, hers and mine. No cash, so the driver obviously fleeced me.'

'You've no recollection of what he looked like?'

'There were several gents in the pub, but honestly, I wouldn't know none of them if you paraded them in front of me this instant.'

'What did Gerry make of all this?'

'Thought I'd drunk myself into a state and dishabilled another strumpet. He took me back to my flat so I didn't interfere with his kip.'

'Always the gentleman. Where are you these days?'

'Connaught Village.'

'Moving up in the world, Bella.'

'Surely.'

'Higher you go, longer the fall.'

The Rolls turned round Piccadilly Circus.

'Drop you somewhere, Sergeant?'

Geats pointed at Great Windmill Street, and the Rolls glided up the road and stopped outside the Yard. He stepped out, holding the door open.

'You ever see him again, this man?'

She shrugged uselessly.

'Hear any stories about rough trade?'

She laughed. 'There are always stories. You call them rough trade. We call them men. And the military ones can be the worst. Soldiers and sailors.'

'What do you mean?'

'Yeah, I remember now. In the pub, he said he was an officer. Had us call him Brigadier.'

Geats stared at the back of the Rolls as it peeled away. For a moment, he wondered whether she'd actually said it. An aperture opened somewhere in his mind, light flooding the place.

The Brigadier.

Now he was cooking.

50

Geats found Nell asleep on the couch in Clara's flat. He heard his mother in the bedroom, trying to cover her coughing, but let her be. Gently he lifted Nell in his arms and carried her up to his place, tucking her into bed and closing the bedroom door.

In the living room, he unfolded the blankets out on the sofa and was about to undress for sleep when there was a knocking at the door. He stood perfectly still; it was late for someone to drop by. He'd left the hallway light on and anyone outside could see that; there was nowhere to hide.

They knocked again, more insistently. The bedroom door opened silently, Nell's face appearing in the crack, eyes wide – with excitement as much as fear, he thought. He pressed a finger to his lips and she nodded. Slowly and quietly, they crept down the hallway towards one another, keeping to the wall away from the door so their shadows wouldn't show beneath it, and met at the bathroom.

He nodded towards the tub and she climbed in, easing herself down in the old tin. From behind the high-level cistern, he retrieved a bundle of rags, unwrapping the revolver hidden within. Checking it was loaded, he cocked the hammer.

Another three bangs on the door.

Geats edged along the hallway. Taking a grip on the latch with one hand, gun in the other, he quickly pulled open the door and grabbed the knocker, barrel up their nostril as he pressed them against the wall.

It was a kid, a boy of nine or ten.

Clamping a hand over his mouth, Geats ducked low and chanced a look out onto the landing at knee height. Nobody out there.

'You're a runner at Renée's,' he said, releasing the boy.

The boy nodded. 'Miss Simone, she said to come. Your friend is in a spot.'

'Bloody Cassar.'

Sending the boy off, he wrapped up the gun and put it back behind the cistern. Nell watched him wordlessly.

'We did that pretty good,' he said. 'Kid had no idea we'd rumbled him.'

She nodded her head purposefully.

'That happens again, we do it exactly the same.'

'Got it.'

'All right, then.'

He lifted her from the tub and she clung to him, so he carried her back to the bedroom and put her down.

'You get some sleep. I have to pop out for a moment as my partner is getting himself in a mess. I'll be back before you know it.'

Kissing the tip of his thumb, he pressed it onto her nose, and she giggled.

The staggered route to Renée's was maybe a two-minute run that Geats made in four, finding Simone in the street outside the club, frantically waving at him.

'What?'

'Come on, your mate's getting into it.'

'Cassar? With who?'

For a terrifying instant, he pictured his partner somehow infuriating Benny and getting his jaw snatched off his face with a sharp right hook.

'With other coppers.'

'What? Which coppers?'

'Some of those Flying Squad boys who raided the place.'

Geats about fell down the stairs two at a time and careened into the club. Space had cleared near the bar, and Cassar was lurching drunkenly towards Minter, with Lander laughing in the background.

'What's all this noise?' Geats demanded.

Minter leered at him. 'You come to take your boyfriend home, Geats?'

Geats looked warily from Minter to Lander. 'What are you two doing here?'

'Following up. We were interviewing whores about the killings. What you should be doing, by rights. Led us here.'

'Where's Billie?'

'Who?'

'WPC Massey.'

'Christ, you might need a nursemaid, but we don't.'

Geats grabbed Cassar's arm. 'Mark, let's go.'

'You want to watch him, love,' Lander said. 'He was dancing with another fella behind your back.'

Cassar barrelled forward crookedly, but Geats caught him across the chest and turned him round. Ignoring the snipes from Minter, he led Cassar back up to the street.

'He needs what's coming to him,' Cassar slurred.

'We all do. We all do.'

Hailing a taxi outside the Hippodrome, he lifted Cassar into the back seat, falling into the vehicle with him.

'Where you pair off to?' the driver said.

'It's just him,' Geats said. 'Gimme a sec.'

He dived into Cassar's pockets looking for coins, retrieving enough to give the driver to ferry his friend to Lambeth. Pulling Cassar up in the seat, he let him slump into the corner in a doze.

Out of the back window, he caught sight of Minter and Lander exiting Chez Renée's, laughing it up on the street. Sliding into the crowds pouring out of the Charing Cross Road pubs, Lander headed west and Minter came towards the taxi before rounding the corner into the quieter Little Newport Street, where Red Max had been killed.

'See this one home safe,' Geats told the driver.

Then he stole into the back street.

51

First thing, Geats was in Vine Street telling Nutty Sharpe about Bella Gold and the Brigadier. The man didn't look sold on the idea, but other matters started to overtake him, and he was happy to give Geats the day to look into it just to get him out of his hair.

'And fetch Cassar to help you. He hasn't shown his face yet this morning.'

Minter had turned up, arm in a sling and face like a sack of weeping beets, with a fantastical story about a gang jumping him until he fought them to a standstill.

'There was at least five of them,' he claimed. 'With staves.'

'Surely one had a knife,' Geats said.

'Wouldn't surprise me. It was all a blur.'

'What they do to your arm?' Sharpe said.

'Shoulder popped when I hit the cobbles.'

Lander was distraught, partly at his comrade having been laid out, but mostly because he'd missed the ballyhoo.

'We'll find them tonight,' he said. 'We'll lie in wait and ambush them. We'll beat them into the ground.'

'Great stuff,' Geats said. 'What did they look like?'

Minter was perched on a desk out on the main floor, half of the station gathered round him, hand of his good arm splayed out on his knee to make a show of his bruised and bloodied knuckles.

Proof of his valiant struggle.

He adopted a pained look. 'I didn't see. They jumped me from behind.'

'What sort of unscrupulous lout bushwhacks a man from behind?' Geats said, rubbing the scar on his head.

That was when Minter caught sight of Geats's own knuckles, also scraped and bruised, and suddenly realised exactly what had occurred.

Geats stared at him, but Minter avoided his eyes. He'd sought medical attention at some point: the arm had been professionally treated and the damage to his face well looked to. The knuckles were the only thing that hadn't been dealt with. He must have done them when he got home, beaten them raw on a stone wall, because they were undamaged when Geats had left him face down on the cobbles of Little Newport Street.

52

Even from his room at the back of the house, Cassar heard the nurses fluttering about outside their dwelling across the street at some god-forsaken hour. He ignored them. Ignored the industrial hum from the sanitary works too. The vigorous banging at his door was quite another matter.

'Uh?'

His mouth was pasted to the pillow.

'It's Geats.'

'Get fucked.'

'One way or another, I'm coming in.'

Shawling himself in his blankets, Cassar hobbled to the door and unlocked it, retching as soon as Geats pushed it open.

'What is that awful smell?'

'That was my question,' said Geats, putting a plate of kidneys and bacon on the top of the chest of drawers. 'Spot of brekkie.'

'You got Mrs Fewtrell to make food out of hours?'

'Told her you'd been undercover on a crucial assignment last night, getting yourself in a rather delicate state in the name of law and order and the protection of this fair city's denizens.'

'Really?'

'She wasn't buying a word of it, but appreciated the endeavourous lying to abet a good pal, and fetched up some leftovers with tea and toast.'

Cassar sat circumspectly on the bed.

'I can't possibly eat.'

'Not before washing up, anyway. You smell like sweat and hand-jobs.'

He dry-retched again.

'Where's your ablutions?' said Geats.

'On the half-landing.'

'Chop-chop.'

The water was cold and would never remove the tastes from Cassar's mouth in a million years. He scrubbed all over and nicked himself shaving. He returned to find Geats popping slices of kidney into his mouth.

'S'good.'

Cassar felt himself green again.

'Eat the toast,' said Geats.

'I couldn't.'

'Yes you can.'

'I'll throw up.'

'No you won't.'

And he didn't.

'Leon, last night . . .'

'Good evening all round.'

'Minter and Lander.'

'Yeah, well. Some prick always turns up and ruins it.'

'I don't think I can go to the station.'

'Good job we're not, then.'

'Where we going?'

'Tell you on the way.'

Dishevelled in the passenger seat of the police car, he tried to focus on distant objects so as not to feel sick as they drove, and Geats recounted Bella's story about her and Katherine Farrier accompanying a man back to a Soho flat.

'Guess what he had them call him?' Geats said.

'What?'

'Brigadier.'

'Christ.'

'Bella wasn't sure where the flat was, but if this Brigadier is the same man Hall mentioned—'

'Or is Hall.'

'Or that. Then they walked to Lexington, to Jeanette Cotton's flat. Bella said she saw the smokestack from the Lion Brewery. It's right round the corner; I noticed it the day we found the body. And the alley where Everett found Katherine Farrier is only a short walk.'

'You like it as a story, then?'

'I like it as a story.'

'Let's pass some time with Mr Hall.'

53

Hall was asleep in his room on Craven Street and took an age to open the door.

'Don't you people ever work civilised hours?'

Geats pushed him back into his room.

'Put some clothes on, Hall.'

They sat at his small table, and when he returned from the powder room where he slept, Cassar glared at him as he made for the arm-chair. He leaned against the wall.

'This Brigadier chap who rented your room,' Geats said. 'Tell us more about him.'

'I don't know more about him.'

'About your interactions with him, then. How many times exactly did he take your room?'

'Exactly, I'd be pressed to say. Half a dozen, something like that.'

'Just for the one night each time?'

'No. He asked for three nights once. Paid me two quid, which was almost two weeks' rent, so I agreed. Plus, a mate of mine, his wife had gone away to see her old mum, so I could kip at his.'

'When was this?'

'That'd be the last time, with the mattress business.'

'He had it three nights, and when you came back there was blood and shit in the bed?'

'Yeah. Got me thrown out. On top of that, he steals my suitcase.'

'He—what?'

'Had a suitcase. Weren't big, but it was nice. When I went to pack my things, on account of that loopy French tart getting all disagreeable, it was gone. Had to carry everything in a sack.'

'An indignity, man like yourself.'

'Right?'

Cassar got up and took Hall's coat from the hook by the door, throwing it at him.

'Come on. You're accompanying us for a few hours.'

Returning to Lexington Street, they woke Dot Neri in the front room of the flat Jeanette Cotton had been murdered in.

'Jesus, Sergeant. Happy to help, but I've only been asleep an hour or so. Had a long night.'

'Sorry. Need a quick look round the room.'

She opened the door wide and plonked herself down on the bed.

'Who's this?' she said, peering at Hall.

'Fella you replaced.'

'The mattress-shitter?'

'I never shat on no mattress.'

'Dot, you find anything here that this one might have left behind?'

'Other than the stench of dead rats, you mean?'

'Rats?' Hall exclaimed, as if he'd never heard such slander. 'There weren't no rats here in all my time.'

'Something stank the place out,' Dot said.

'You find a suitcase?' Geats asked.

'No. What sort of suitcase?'

Hall held his arms open. 'It was about this big.'

'Where'd the smell come from?' Cassar said.

Dot made a face. 'Under the floor. We figured they died down there.'

'You ever look?'

'For dead rats? No thank you.'

Cassar edged round the room, testing the boards with his foot.

Beneath a small table between two of the windows a loose one creaked. On his knees, he swiped aside the rug and shifted a dresser from the ends of the boards.

'Leon.'

Drawing his boot knife, Geats slid the blade between the boards and prised one up. Couldn't see much in the gloom, but reached in there and had a feel about.

'Something here, wedged between the joists.'

They worked quickly, pulling up more boards and exposing a suitcase jammed in there tightly, the corners squished with the effort.

'This your case?' Geats asked Hall.

'Why's it in the bloody floor?'

'Not your doing, then?'

'Like I said, it was missing when I come back here after the Brigadier had his three days.'

'There's something in it,' Cassar said, trying to lift it out. 'Won't budge.'

He and Geats both took hold and pulled, but the buckle gave way where it had been damaged stuffing the case into the confined space, and the lid tore open.

Dot shrieked.

Geats stepped back.

From the hair and size, it was probably a woman, her body folded up in some evil contortion to fit the case, bones broken and joints dislocated. Her feet were up around her ears and she had decomposed in some strange manner, appearing newly mummified.

Cassar threw up on the floor.

'Fucking toast,' he said.

54

Spilsbury unknotted the body and set about reading its remains. The killer had liberally covered the body with slaked lime.

'Presumably under the misapprehension that it was quicklime and would therefore corrode the body,' the pathologist said. 'Lime stops decay, so she's pretty well preserved all in all.'

Cassar peered over the body. 'Cause of death?'

'Strangulation, looks like. Damage to the throat, though it's hard to tell if this is bruising or not.'

'You tell it was manual or done with something?'

'The damage isn't consistent with fingers or hands.'

'The Cotton woman, same flat. She was killed with a handkerchief.'

'No way of being that precise.'

'How long ago?'

Spilsbury blew his lips. 'With the lime, almost impossible to say with any certainty.'

'Can you say whether it's weeks or years?' Geats said.

'I think we are looking at weeks, or possibly months. Not years.'

'Any other wounds?'

Spilsbury nodded, and waved one of his assistants over. They turned the body onto its front.

'See here?' He pointed to the back of the thighs.

'Jesus,' Cassar said. 'Whip? Or a cane?'

'Yes. I'm yet to identify the instrument.'

'Try a razor strop,' Geats said.

Spilsbury considered the wounds again. 'Yes. Yes, quite possibly. He must have been in a frenzy; they are significant wounds.'

'Sexual assault?'

'Again, I can't speak with complete confidence, but there is nothing that stands out like the other wounds. No visible trauma. There is one thing that might help someone identify her, though. At some point in the last few years, she underwent abdominal surgery. See, the scarring is still visible here. Her appendix was removed.'

'So we looking at the same killer?'

'That is your domain, gentlemen. I can only provide you with the evidence.'

55

They drove back to Vine Street and reported to Sharpe. Hall had been released; Bella Gold couldn't identify him as the man she and Katherine Farrier had gone to the Lexington Street flat with the night Katherine was whipped.

'I don't think Hall is our man anyway,' Geats said.

Elbows on his desk, Sharpe steepled his fingers. 'But the man who attacked this Miss Farrier, you do believe he's the killer?'

'Too much connects them not to be,' Geats said. 'The whipping. The location. The fact separate witnesses stated he went by "Brigadier". It's the same man, I'm sure.'

'And did he kill Cotton, too?'

'What we're thinking,' Cassar said, 'is that he got wind of the fact Cotton was trying to get money out of Hall – extort money, really; she was threatening to out him as homosexual if he didn't pay for the mattress – and killed her to stop the attention.'

'Is he?'

'Is he what?'

'A poof.'

'I—does it matter?'

'Could be charges to be laid,' Lander said. He was leaning against the wall behind Sharpe, Minter beside him. 'Get something out of this mess. Nice little case to put down. One less brown hatter roaming the streets.' He stared at Cassar.

'I think the streets deal with that sort of stuff themselves,' Cassar said. 'I hear about nancy boys getting jumped outside queer clubs all the time. Where was it you were set about, Inspector Minter?'

'We're getting off track here,' Sharpe said.

Geats stepped in. 'Or maybe the Brigadier came by the flat and Cotton tried to get money from him directly for the mattress.'

Sharpe thought about that. 'And he murdered her to shut her up?'

'It's too much to believe that two women were strangled in the same flat within weeks of each other and the deaths were unconnected.'

'Does the Martin woman tie into this?' Sharpe asked.

Geats shook his head. 'I don't think so.'

'It's obviously the same killer,' Lander said.

'Not obvious to me. No connection between the victims, and there's enough personal business in both their lives to explain their deaths. Cotton with this mattress and another body beneath her floorboards. Martin with the French pimps.'

'Lacroix was adamant that neither he nor Kassel killed her,' Lander said.

'And I believe him,' said Geats. 'But I still think that's a completely separate case to this.'

'Tell the press that,' said Sharpe. 'They're out there interviewing tarts, getting them to say they were terrified.'

He slapped down a copy of the *Daily Mirror*. The front-page headline read: *Maniac's Three Soho Women Victims! Girl's Friends Fear to Talk!*

Geats looked at the ceiling. 'Dalton's going to have the raging shits.'

'Your superintendent was certainly not impressed, that is true, Sergeant. We need to find this Brigadier character, and quick. Because telling the press there are two whore-killers on our streets isn't going to do much to placate them.'

56

Geats and Cassar worked the streets; they dragged in ponces, humili-
ated punters, turned clubs upside down.

Dillic walked among the women, looking for the prattle prattle on
rough trade whose tastes ran to whipping and the odd throat-squeeze.

They got nowhere.

At night, Geats maintained his keen interest in the business affairs
of Queenie Gerald, intent on discovering who these new foreign pimps
were in his neighbourhood. After he left Vine Street, he dressed like a
vagrant and hid in plain sight on the streets, following Queenie from
place to place, mapping a network of four Soho properties where she
nursed a stable of Continental girls.

The off-street ponces were getting better organised and more elaborate; the obvious fronts, like the milk bars, were being replaced by
more clandestine enterprises. If things of this scale were operating
right under the police's noses without them getting a whiff, then what
else might be out there?

The scheme was well isolated – no matter how tightly he followed
Queenie, Geats couldn't figure out whom she was working for. She
kept a room in a nice flat the other side of Oxford Street as the paying
guest of a spinster of similar age who, from what Geats could ascer-
tain, was under the impression that Queenie had a secure income
from capital left by deceased relatives.

No gentlemen called there, and she didn't stop off anywhere else, other than the odd evening in a public house. The buildings on Kingly Court, however, were a labyrinth of dark hallways and rooms where he couldn't keep her in sight.

Needing to learn more, he scrawled *There is nothing hidden that will not be disclosed* on a sheet of paper, tied it round half a brick with twine, and lobbed it through a first-floor window of the house near Golden Square. Police and rival pimps they had a playbook for, but a troupe of radical Nonconformists was something else entirely.

Scampering away in his tramp's rags, he hid in the shrubby wilderness of the square's gardens and waited. It didn't take long for muscle to arrive. They were dark-featured and some bore familial resemblance, but Geats recognised none of them. A second car carried an older gent with bespoke threads and an air of authority; when he peered this way and that along the street, so too did the others, as if the culprit might make themselves known. They all disappeared inside and the drivers turned the cars round to face back the way they had come.

Invisible, Geats walked right by them and lingered at the corner of Brewer Street. A few minutes later, the car with the fancy one rounded the corner and passed him, and he took off on foot in pursuit. The pavement was slim and only got slimmer, here and there Geats stepping out into the road with the traffic to avoid pedestrians. Running made him realise how untroubled he was by anything resembling athletic prowess.

The car quickly got away from him, but a delivery van was holding things up and he almost caught them up by Wardour Street, his lungs on fire. Catching a glimpse of them turning a chicane from Wardour onto Old Compton, he took a risk and cut through an alley leading to Dean Street.

He was done when he got out the other side, breathing like he was raising well water with a holed bucket. Dray horses stood idly at the corner of Dean and Old Compton with their noses in bags, their coalman owner brooking no dissent from cars piling up behind. Geats watched as his quarry eventually turned onto Dean Street and pulled up outside Rendezvous, a Franco-Italian restaurant run by a raging fascist by the name of Martini. The dapper older gent waved at the doorman and went inside the tiny lobby that hid the doors to the restaurant and also the flats above.

Geats ensconced himself in the mouth of the alley and stood watch, waiting for the man to reappear. An hour passed with no sight of him. A messenger boy on his green GPO motorcycle was idling at the kerb, coming to the end of his shift, and Geats showed him his card and palmed him a few bob, sending him into the building with a telegram for a Mr Smith.

The boy returned a few minutes later and wheeled his bike into the alley out of sight.

'Only the top floor is a flat. Marshall's the name on the door. Edward Marshall.'

'He suspect you?'

'Nah. I showed him the slip, had Flat D on it, but there ain't no flat D. I told him there must have been a mistake, probably a different street or a different number, and he seemed fine with it.'

'Edward Marshall. That's good.'

'He didn't sound like no Edward Marshall, though.'

'How'd you mean?'

'Speaks good English, but he ain't from here. I ran messages to an Egyptian chap for a while, and this Marshall's not so different.'

57

Next morning, Geats fobbed off Cassar at Vine Street, telling him he was going to run down a few snouts, sort of thing best done alone, and went to Sink Street.

From the outside, the building looked abandoned, no lights or movement or any signs of life. He rang the bell and waited fully three minutes before the door opened.

'This some tactic? Seeing how serious I am about seeing you.'

Harrison said nothing, but led the way up the stairs to his large but spartan office. As they went, Geats told him about the new foreign pimps who might be running a fresh pipeline into the country, how he'd followed the dapper gent to his flat in the name of Edward Marshall, and also about the body in the floor.

'Looks like there might be a sex killer after all. This one in the floor was his first, and then he killed Cotton because she was blackmailing him over the mattress.'

'Maybe,' Harrison said. 'Where's the body?'

'The one from the floor? Westminster Mortuary, at the coroner's court.'

'No leads on her identification?'

'Not much. Nothing on her in the way of paper, but she had scarring across her middle. Appendectomy, the pathologist said. Might help us if we find someone who knows a missing girl.'

'I told you about the Abwehr.'

'Nazi spies.'

'There's a particular one I've been tracking. A woman.'

'Yeah, why you were monitoring Kassel.'

'Well, we think she successfully got into the country before Kassel was killed. With his murder and the subsequent arrest of Lacroix, it's possible the Germans might believe she has been compromised.'

'You think they'd kill her?'

'That would be preferable to her falling into our hands. The agent we think is here, she underwent emergency surgery a while back. Appendicitis.'

'Jesus. Does that mean the Brigadier is a spy too? Someone they sent to deal with this woman? Or a double agent?'

'Well, he certainly could be more than he seems to be. I doubt they have another high-level agent operating here without our knowledge. It's more likely they'd hire someone suited to the task. A bravo. Someone who knows the local scene, knows how to make one thing look like another.'

'Kill a spy and make it look like the strangling of a prostitute. What do we do?'

'First things first, we need to steal that body.'

58

Two a.m. and Whitehall was quiet.

A mile from Soho but may as well have been a million. Wide leafy avenues, moonlight bouncing off the limestone like desert pumice. Harrison drove the van, unmarked and painted navy or black.

Geats sniffed, signalling his intent to reopen the discussion they'd been having for hours.

'I'm still not a hundred per cent copacetic with this.'

'It's war, Leon.'

'We're not soldiers here. We're resurrectionists.'

'Life is war. Whether you appreciate it or not, dark forces are aligning against this country, and every so often that means men like you and me are forced to scuttle about under the cover of night doing things best not discussed in polite company.'

'Like nicking corpses.'

'Like that. Look, we simply cannot risk someone identifying this woman and causing more of a fuss than there's already been.'

'She going to get a decent Christian burial?'

'What do you care? You're half a Jew, schooled by Jesuits, and as godless a heathen as England's fine dirt can bear.'

'Doesn't mean I believe the departed shouldn't be treated with respect.'

'She will be taken care of.'

Geats grumbled beneath his breath.

Down Whitehall they drove, past the buildings of state, until it became Millbank, and he caught glimpses of the river through the trees. Though he'd spent almost every day of his life no more than a mile from it, he still found it hard to believe that such a powerful and mischievous presence slouched through the centre of the city and he so rarely saw it.

They turned away from the Thames, up Horseferry Road to the mortuary. Harrison drove into the alley to the side of the building and backed the van up to the loading doors.

A security guard let them in, Harrison with a two-pole canvas stretcher under one arm.

'Why do I get the impression this isn't your first body-snatching?' Geats said, their footsteps echoing along the hard corridor.

'Here,' Harrison said, producing keys and trying a few before Spilsbury's office door opened.

He turned the lights on, the door not even closed. Geats wasn't sure whether it counted as a break-in; Harrison appeared to be able to go wherever he wanted in the city, no door remaining closed to him.

'Photos, files, anything on the dead woman.'

'He was working on it,' Geats said.

'Hmm?'

'The file. It's on his desk.' He held it up.

'Well, well. How's that for providence?'

'We must truly be on the side of the angels.'

'Don't you ever forget it.' Harrison took the file and flicked through. 'We have the file, photographs . . . ooh, pictures of the scars. Now for the body itself.'

'This is going to cause a fuss. They're not just going to brush off a body going missing, one central to a multiple murder investigation.'

'Yes, but that's the lesser evil. If the Abwehr sent someone here to kill an agent, it's better that they don't know that we know that. It's better that they think we don't know anything about it at all. That way, they might try to open another conduit into the country.'

Harrison knew his way round the place as if he went there every day, leading Geats to cold storage.

'This is her. Grab that trolley there.'

Geats rolled it over and Harrison laid the stretcher out atop it.

The way the body had been folded up to fit in the case, coupled with the mummification process of the lime, meant Spilsbury had had to cut it in two in order to examine it properly.

'Grab the legs,' Harrison said, lifting the upper half of the body beneath the arms and heaving it onto the stretcher.

Geats held the legs and lower torso at arm's length. Covering the body, they carried the stretcher back to the loading doors and slid it into the van. All told, they were in and out in less than seven minutes.

'Not bad, Geats. Might fashion something worthwhile out of you yet.'

'The guard,' Geats said, thinking about how Sharpe would be quite beside himself when he found out the body was gone.

'Don't you worry about Baxt. He stood up to the Boers in captivity at Waterval. Nutty Sharpe won't worry him.'

'What do you want me to do with the investigation?'

'Solve it would be nice.'

'Difficult without a body.'

'There are other angles. If they killed her because she was Abwehr, that means they more than likely knew how she got in the country.'

'Kassel and Lacroix.'

'Exactly.'

'Did they know they were bringing agents in?'

'I shouldn't have thought so. But they were the ones who knew the names of the women, and the names of anyone they married them off to.'

'They gave her fake papers?'

'Possibly.'

'You think that's what the Martin killing was about? Someone trying to find out where the German spy was?'

Harrison shrugged.

'Christ. So the cases that we originally thought were connected and then worked out weren't connected are actually connected now after all. That's brilliant. I'm going to look a right apple-knocker telling Sharpe that this Brigadier is a suspect for Martin after all.'

'If he is the killer.'

'We've tied him to Cotton and the dead spy.'

'He might be the person looking for them; doesn't mean he gets his own hands dirty. That kind of operator, he'll have people for that sort of thing.'

'What kind of people?'

'Probably served somehow. Army, navy, police maybe. Physically capable. Someone who knows the streets and can move through them unseen. Anyone like that come up?'

Geats grumbled.

'You're thinking of someone,' Harrison said.

'Benny Brownlow. He was merchant navy, and a professional fighter. He knew about Kassel, saw them bringing his body out.'

'He didn't report it?'

'He kind of did. Benny never came all the way back from the war. His ship went down and he was found clinging to wreckage out at sea. Doesn't always make himself fully understood.'

'Could someone make themselves understood to him? Enough to have him do this kind of work?'

'I don't know.'

In truth, what Geats was thinking was that he himself fitted his own suspicions better than anyone.

Harrison parked up the van outside the Gaumont on Haymarket, which was being gutted and renovated. Geats slipped out.

'What are you going to do with her?'

'Don't worry about that. Just deny all knowledge of it, if asked. I'll be in touch.'

Geats went to close the door, but Harrison stopped him.

'Oh, Leon? Your phoney Englishman with the foreign accent? Edward Marshall? He's Maltese. Eugenio Messina.'

'How'd you find that out?'

Harrison smiled, and Geats again thought that the man was like a ghost, able to walk through walls into any room in London.

'Being Maltese gives him rights here, but I'll dig deeper into what he was up to before he arrived in London. Meanwhile, look into him. But keep it between us; don't put him on paper. Might be he's useful.'

59

Sharpe splashed annoyance on his face and stalked through Vine Street looking for people to shout at inconsequentially. Stories spread quickly.

Body-snatchers.

Sexual deviants.

The killer returned to collect his wares.

The one that got the most traction was that spooks with official papers had raided the morgue at the hour of the wolf, removing every trace of the unidentified body. There was an official cover-up on the go, intelligence services shutting something down.

Nobody could say who first conjured up that idea.

Geats shrugged when asked what he thought.

'The victims were all foreign,' Sharpe mused.

'Not Katherine Farrier.'

'He let her go,' Sharpe said, as if proving something. 'And he thought initially she was foreign.'

'This foreign tart theory, how does that track with an intelligence cover-up?'

'Well, it's a cover-up, so I guess we'll never know.'

'You honestly believe that?'

'I honestly believe it's strange, the body being stolen. It might not change things in terms of who we're looking for – the Brigadier is the main suspect – but we have to consider what his motivations might be.

And whether he *is* tied into the Martin killing after all. Finding him is our priority.'

'We've already turned Soho upside down and shaken everything out.'

'Do it again and see if anything new falls out.'

Geats and Cassar pounded the streets, rousting pimps and prostitutes from their pits and questioning them, many of them for the second or third time. The work suited Geats – it made more sense for everyone to split up and speak to more people in less time, which meant he didn't have Cassar looking over his shoulder. Making token efforts at working the case, he broke it off in the afternoons and looked into Eugenio Messina instead.

If the ponce went out during the day, he was always back at his flat above Rendezvous in the late afternoon, dressing for the evening. One night he did the rounds of the four houses of prostitution he was operating. The next he dined with a woman who Geats had seen working the houses, much as Queenie Gerald did. She seemed to live at the flat with him. The third day, Geats followed him to the City, where he looked at several properties on Queen Street, apparently making plans to move up in the world.

Geats left him and returned to Soho, checking on the brothels. Dressed in his vagrant gear, he mooched around the streets. At the place off Golden Square, he sat himself at the corner of a building across the road and blended into the background, watching silently.

He must have nodded off, because his leg being kicked woke him, a suited man looming over him.

'Get off me.'

'You move from here.'

The man kicked out again, and Geats pivoted onto one knee and kicked back, through the man's ankle. He landed in a heap, swearing in a foreign tongue.

Clearing his head, Geats glanced back towards the brothel and saw two men talking casually to a third, the sight of whom turned him towards panic. Though his back was to him, the man's arm was clearly in a sling; it was Inspector Minter. Not wanting to be recognised, he turned away from them sharply, only to find himself nose to nose with the man he'd kicked over.

'You're quite right,' Geats said. 'I should be going. Apologies.'

The man grabbed his arm when he went to walk away, and Geats brought his knee up hard into his crotch, doubling him up. Pushing him over into the street, he moved off.

'Hey,' one of the other men called out.

Geats didn't break stride, didn't look back. He crossed the road and disappeared round the corner into Golden Square. The instant he was out of their sight, he tore into a sprint, arcing round the next corner out of the square and running for Piccadilly.

Feet slapped the pavement behind him.

'Stop him!'

Geats brushed by people and hoped they followed their usual instincts of doing absolutely nothing when this sort of palaver entered their lives uninvited.

He passed the Regent Palace Hotel and headed down Air Street, under the archway in the Quadrant and out into Regent Street. Not stopping for traffic, he flew across the road and under the smaller arch leading to Vine Street.

Pausing behind the Piccadilly Hotel, round the corner from the station, he looked back. Nobody was following. Not wanting anyone from Vine Street to recognise him in his tramp's get-up, he tucked in his chin and shambled past the station and out onto Piccadilly, hurrying back to the Yard.

Nell was in the kitchen.

'How's Clara?'

'She pretended to go to bed so I'd leave and she could drink in peace.'

'Sounds about right.'

'I've made stew.'

'Excellent.'

'You're all sweaty.'

'Yes.'

'And you smell.'

'I'll do something about that.'

She nodded primly and returned to her pot. Geats washed up and shaved the growth he'd let build up over the past few days, dressing for dinner.

'What did you do today?'

'Clara taught me cards.'

'Oh God.'

'We played the Bishop's Buttocks. And she thinks you should pay me for looking after her.'

'Yes, I can't imagine why she thinks that, so soon after introducing cards into the mix.'

'She thinks many things.'

'You know what I think?'

She shook her head.

'I think at some point we should look into a school for you.'

Tallulah appeared from her box under the window, stretched and yawned extravagantly.

'Who'd look after Loolah?'

'Oh, she'll be just fine. She's anyone's for a scrap of food.'

As if to illustrate his point, the kitten rubbed herself up against his leg until he fed her some meat from his bowl.

'She should see a doctor,' Nell said.

Geats picked up the cat. 'Looks all right to me.'

'Not her. Clara.'

'The cough?'

The girl nodded.

'Good luck getting her to see sense there.'

'She goes out to the bathroom and runs the taps to cover the noise.'

'I'll talk to her.'

'She's very annoying, but I don't want her to die,' Nell said.

'That makes two of us.'

60

The call came first thing, a few minutes after Geats got into Vine Street: another dead woman in a flat. Sharpe immediately assumed control, and Lander accosted Geats in the corridor, taking a firm grip of his arm.

'Nutty wants you and your best boy down at the scene.'

'Oh? Where will you be?'

'We'll be there in good time. Take that dove Massey with you. Good for ministering to women and children at murder houses. Kind of work real police have a horror of.'

Geats shook free his arm.

'I see any real police, I'll be sure to bear that in mind.'

'Don't get tetchy, love. This is your territory. You're in the streets, and of the streets. So if it's street slag got done in, only stands to reason you'll be more use down there than we would.'

He collected Cassar and Billie, and the three of them walked to Old Compton Street, uniforms congregating outside the Camisa brothers' shop. Boyle stood across the road, helmet in one hand, sipping from a flask in the other. Geats caught his eye, and the big man shook his head.

'Bill, stay down here,' Geats said. 'Find out which of these people knows anything, who found the body.'

'No way, I'm not—'

'Can't have too many people in the crime scene, Constable,' Cassar said, following Geats's lead.

On the second floor, a constable stood by a door that had been splintered off its hinges. Inside, a woman lay on a bed with a counterpane draped over her face, blood sopped right through. Her skirt was pulled up over her waist, no underwear, and her stockings rolled neatly down to her ankles. She had been put on display. She wore her shoes still, high pointed heels.

A flat iron had been tossed onto the floor, stained red. Blood pooled on the boards beneath the bed, more dripping, where it had soaked straight through the mattress.

Geats ducked back out and called the uniform on the landing. 'She found like this, head covered up? Or did whoever find her do it?'

'He says she was like that, fella she lives with. He's downstairs. Door was locked and apparently he don't have a key to his own place. Fetched help to break it down.'

'Some girls do that, if they got night business. Saves their fella walking in on it.'

'You'd figure he'd have found a better way in. He's some kind of magician. Does tricks in local clubs, sometimes on the streets.'

Cassar took hold of the corner of the counterpane between finger and thumb and lightly tried to lift it. It was embedded into wounds in several places.

'Put it over her face before he beat her,' he said. 'Perhaps he knew her and couldn't bear seeing her face as he destroyed it. Didn't want to see her eyes.'

'Probably trying to keep blood off himself,' Geats said.

Cassar looked round at the mess. 'Don't suppose it worked.'

The fabric tugged away in increments where it had been driven into the flesh, like string from a roasted joint. Her head was horrifically misshapen, the skull and facial bones fractured, and Geats had to squint until he realised he was seeing brain matter escaping from the side. The jaw was badly broken and dislocated, the tongue severed.

'She bite it off?'

Cassar peered into the mouth.

'No. Too clean. Someone severed it with a blade.'

A length of electric wire flex was wound tightly about her throat.

Cassar acted out what he saw with his hands. 'Gets it good and tight round her neck, and while he's strangling her he pulls the sheet over and bashes her with the iron.'

'Not afterwards, with the iron?'

'Amount of blood, I'd say she was still alive. When he started anyways. And when he did the tongue, maybe.'

An open cupboard had been built into a nook beside the chimney breast, its cretonne curtains pulled aside. Geats saw dresses and gowns and an array of heeled shoes and boots. Retreating in horror, he stumbled backwards over the corner of the bed.

'Jesus.'

Cassar looked round. 'What?'

'Boyfriend's a magician or conjuror? Locked out of his own flat? And look at those boots. The heels. It's Stilts. It's Leah.'

61

Cassar looked at the dead woman.

'That whore we spoke to? Her place was on Little Pulteney, though.'

Geats leaned over the body, but the face was beyond recognition. He glanced round the room again.

'It's her, I'm sure. Leah Hinds. Look around for something.'

Cassar lifted an envelope from the dresser.

'No, this is Constance . . . Hinds. Damn.'

'That's her,' Geats said. 'Sometimes she went by Connie, sometimes Leah. This can't be coincidence.'

Cassar fetched the constable at the door. 'The partner found her? He say anything yet?'

'Not much. Too upset. He's in the grocer's, he ain't going nowhere.'

Geats shook his head. 'He didn't do this.'

'How do you know?' Cassar said. 'There's rage at work here.'

'Sure, but look at her. Dress hiked up, stockings pushed down. She was ready for work, was with a punter. He's got on top of her and pulled the counterpane over her head and beat her bloody before she knew what was happening.' He turned to the constable. 'Underwear?'

'Floor of the cupboard. Wet and filthy.'

'See? She's on a shift. Had one or two out in the alleys, and then finds someone paying to come back. There's no sign of a struggle. She's laid out for business. She been robbed?'

The constable shrugged. Cassar found a handbag on the floor.

'Ten, twelve bob. French letters.' He held up the envelope containing rubber sheaths.

Geats nodded. 'Not robbed. This is a message.'

'For who?'

'For us. For the streets.'

'Doc's here,' the constable said.

Sharpe had sent for Spilsbury, this being the fourth body now. They left him to his work and went down to the shop. Billie stood in the doorway to the storeroom out back. Geats smiled.

'Listen, Bill—'

'I know. It's Leah.'

'Yeah.'

'I spoke to Stanley.'

The conjuror sat on a stool holding a steaming cup of tea courtesy of one of the Italian brothers who owned the shop. He looked smaller than Geats remembered.

'What did he say?'

'Leah was up to her usual. Told him to keep scarce until at least two in the morning. He saw a mate of his – we've got someone going round there now – and came back at around four, but found the street door locked. Said he wandered the neighbourhood for a bit, until the cafés opened. Had a spot of breakfast and returned again at half seven.

'Shop was open by then and one of the brothers unlocked the street door for him. The flat was still locked, and he got no response to knocking. He'd eaten with a labourer at the café, so he nipped back there and asked him for a hand with the door. They shouldered through and found Leah there on the bed.'

'The labourer is here?'

'Boyle's talking to him outside.'

'Good.'

'Geats, was it . . . Stanley was shaken. Was it bad?'

He nodded.

'I don't need protecting from that stuff,' she snapped.

'Christ, I do. That was the most awful thing.'

'Did she suffer?'

He nodded. 'I think it was a message.'

'What do you mean?'

'Her tongue was cut off. Her mouth was smashed to bits. Like it was a warning: don't speak to coppers.'

'Because we talked to her? That was weeks ago. Months, even. Why kill her now?'

'Because—' Geats cut himself off.

He wanted to say, because he'd spoken to her again recently, because last night he was maybe spotted outside the Messina brothel. But he'd told nobody that he had spoken to Stilts. He'd told nobody other than Harrison that he was even looking at Eugenio Messina. Nobody knew.

No.

No, that wasn't quite true.

One person knew that Leah had spoken to him.

Queenie Gerald.

He was considering how he might tell all this to Cassar and Billie when something even worse occurred to him. Leah had told him she'd seen Nell alive and well. If Leah had been killed by people protecting Messina's interests, then those people almost certainly also killed Josephine Martin as a strike against a rival's operation.

The sole witness to that killing would be of some interest to them.

'Something I need to do,' he muttered, walking away quickly.

Billie spread her arms out. 'Leon, what? Where are you going?'

But she was calling after a ghost.

62

Hurrying to the end of the street, Geats was running for all he was worth as soon as he was round the corner, dashing through stubby Winnett Street and across Rupert, charging down the centre of Archer Street, cars veering out of his path. He skidded onto the cobbles of the Yard and burst through the doors into his own building, blowing hard as he dragged himself up the stairs.

Clara's door was shut and locked. He messed around with his keys and went in, finding her sitting in her armchair reading the paper.

'Leon, what is this foolishness?'

Hands on his knees, he sucked in great gulps of air.

'And where's that girl of yours? She was supposed to be here hours ago to fix my breakfast. Might as well wait for lunch now, though I bet the neighbours can hear my stomach.'

'Nell's not here?'

'Lazy girl never came down. There was a big tzimmes up there earlier. No doubt her causing some variety of trouble.'

'Matka, Jesus Christ.'

'There will be none of that talk, thank you very much, and wha— where are you going?'

He fled the flat without closing the door. His legs were jelly on the stairs and he gripped the banisters. Peering over the top step to his landing, he saw that the door to his flat was open. He fought to get his breathing under control, but someone was expanding bellows beneath his lungs. He felt exposed without a gun. Just his fists, his hard head and his boot knife, which he drew.

He threw himself into the flat, landing in the hallway in a crouch he hoped would let him launch explosively at anyone he saw, but his legs were so shot he toppled over against the wall.

The living room looked clear. Blade held like a sabre, he turned to see a hand on the floor poking out from the bathroom.

A large hand.

A man's hand.

The knuckles were bruised and scraped.

'Nell? Nell, it's Leon.'

Down the other end of the hall, his bedroom door was closed.

He could hear a small noise from the bathroom, a rhythmic clicking.

Quieter. 'Nell?'

To himself, he whispered, 'Jesus God, please be alive. Please be fucking alive.'

The frame around the lock on the front door was splintered where it had been kicked in, the damage indicating it had taken a few good boots. There were two bullet holes he could see in the hallway wall opposite the bathroom.

On his knees he crawled as quietly as he could to the bathroom door. The hand on the floor stretched into an arm and the face of Minter came into view, pale as a sheet. His other hand clasped his gut, blood seeping between the fingers at an alarming rate. He was pulling in little bird-breaths at irregular intervals. His eyes flitted around and found Geats, but he didn't move his head or speak.

Geats had run through scenarios with Nell in case anything happened, and he had always stressed to her the importance of remaining quiet. What would she want to hear from him?

'Nell, it's me, Leon. I'm making my way to you.'

The clicking was louder.

'I'm coming in, Nell.'

He sheathed the knife. With a hand on the door frame, he craned his neck round.

There she was, sitting in the bath with the revolver held out before her, pulling the trigger over and over. The hammer re-cocked automatically, cycling through the empty cylinder.

'Nell, sweetheart, it's okay.'

Slowly getting to his feet, he stepped gingerly over the sprawled Minter and gently placed his hand on the gun. Nell let her grip relax and he eased it out of her hand. The cloth it had been wrapped in lay in the bath, with spare rounds that had rolled down towards the plughole. Gathering a few up, he loaded them into the cylinder and snapped it shut.

Two more bullet holes in the bathroom wall beside the door.

'You wait here one second, all right?'

She nodded.

He slipped out into the hall and moved silently to the bedroom door. Readying himself, he loosely gripped the handle and threw it open, following the Webley into the room.

Empty.

Closing the door again, he quickly went down the hall and made sure about the living room, finding nobody there either. Returning to the bathroom, he shut the front door on the way and de-cocked the revolver, putting it in his pocket.

He opened his arms. 'Come here.'

Tearful, she folded into him and he lifted her out of the bath, pressing her face to his shoulder.

'Don't look at him. Keep your eyes shut.'

He took her to the living room and nestled her down in the winged armchair, kneeling before her.

'You all right?'

It took a second for her eyes to find his. She half nodded.

'What happened?'

Her eyes welled up, silent tears breaking down her cheeks.

'You know what? Let's not worry about that just now. You've done brilliantly. Here.'

He grabbed his blanket from the back of the sofa and threw it round her shoulders. He pulled her tight to him and she wept freely into his neck.

'You're just fine, you hear me? Just fine. Now, I need to have a quick word with the chap out there. You stay here for a moment and I'll fix this right up.'

He closed the door behind him as he went into the hallway. Minter was still breathing, tiny hiccups of air that sounded as if they were winding down. His hand was doing a piss-poor job of slowing the blood from his gut.

'What are you doing here? You came to murder a child? A fucking child?' Barely containing his rage, Geats kept a lid on his voice.

Blood seeped from the corner of Minter's mouth. He mumbled something inaudible, just air on his lips. Geats knelt beside him.

'You got something to say?'

'Ĭn nōmine Pătris ĕt Fīliī ĕt Spīritūs Sānctī . . .'

'You can stop that noise right now.'

'Please . . .'

Minter's eyes dropped to his chest. Geats unbuttoned the man's shirt, a bloody and shredded mess, and found a pair of gunshot wounds above the navel. A cross hung on a chain. He took Minter's hand and pressed it onto one of the dark punctures, bringing his other hand down from above his head and positioning it over the other.

'Press down on them.'

The man's voice was faint, barely there at all.

'You Catholic?'

'Father was. Mother's Jewish. God hisself probably don't know what that makes me.'

'Will you listen?'

'You come here to kill that girl?'

'Will you listen?'

Geats nodded.

'Bless me, Father.' Minter coughed, a pathetic rattle that brought up blood. 'I have sinned.'

'What you do?'

'Killed a woman. Killed her.'

'Who?'

He squeezed his eyes closed sharply, pain overcoming him.

'A common whore, but . . . a child . . . of yours.'

'Name her.'

'Leah . . . Leah Constance Hinds.'

'Why'd you kill her?'

'She told a copper . . . what we're doing.'

'What were you doing?'

'Nobody can know. Best that way.'

'Was she the first you killed?'

'No.'

'You kill Josephine Martin?'

He raised his eyes, as if realising for the first time who he was talking to.

'Josephine Martin was a child of God, too,' Geats said. 'You kill her?'

Minter nodded, little more than a shiver.

'Why? Eugenio Messina?'

Another faint nod.

'To what end?'

Minter forced a smile.

'Always the same end . . .'

His breath caught and he fought to suck it in.

'. . . for everyone.'

'Messina squeezing Kassel?'

Minter nodded. 'Scare him. Scare his girls.'

'Trying to shut Kassel and Lacroix down.'

He grinned, blood rimming his teeth. 'Worked too well.'

'They turned on one another. And then you were brought in to investigate yourself. Jesus. Sharpe in on this?'

Minter frowned, shook his head.

'No?'

The residue of the bloody smile on his lips. 'Sharpe . . . smeared . . . Isow.'

'Jack Isow, yeah. Why was that?'

'Italians.'

'Sabini? They want Isow's clubs? Sharpe's taking dropsy from them?'

'Dogs.'

'Dogs?'

Something vacated Minter's eyes momentarily, whatever spark it was that was recognisable as human life, before washing back in slightly duller than it had been.

Geats held his chin. 'Dogs, Minter?'

'He's retiring . . . Wops letting him . . . run book.'

Geats almost laughed. 'Nutty Sharpe is going to be a bookie at the dog tracks?'

'Clear the . . . Jew bookies first.'

'One hand washes the other. And Nell? Why her?'

'Witness.'

'She never saw you. She didn't know anything.'

Minter shrugged, as if such details were beyond his purview.

'What about the girl in the floor? You put her there? You kill Jeanette Cotton too?'

Minter's brow creased, as though disgusted by the thought.

'No.'

'No?'

'God forgive us . . . the child.'

'Us? Who's us? Lander?'

Minter stayed silent.

'You know who killed the other two women?'

He shook his head.

'This is your valediction, Inspector. Your last chance at reconcilia-
tion. You sure you don't know anything about that?'

Minter's voice barely a whisper now, words slurring into the blood
that bubbled around them. Geats lowered his ear to listen.

'Just the whores. We . . . were going to put it all . . . on him.'

'On him? Who's him? Minter?'

'Are we outside?'

'What? No. Minter?'

What he stared at now, Geats couldn't imagine; black eyes reamed
by the terror and delirium of death. Rage took hold of him again.
Death was a small price, a paltry toll for the things the man had done.

Cupping his chin, he raised Minter's face.

'Are you afraid?'

'Yes . . .'

'Good. You piece of shit.'

Pulling Minter's hands away from the bullet wounds, he let him
leak out, watching until his eyes shone only in the way of wet stones.

63

Geats washed his hands and then shut the bathroom door, screening Minter's body. Bundling Nell up in the blanket, he carried her downstairs to Clara.

'Matka, I need you to look after Nell for a little while. I'll be back as soon as I can, but—'

'Thought the idea was she looked after me.'

'Matka, can you just—'

'Nothing but trouble since—'

'Mother!'

Clara froze, staring at him. She noticed the blood on his cuffs and the knees of his trousers. Looked at the child in his arms.

'Leon, what is going on?'

'Bad things, Matka. Bad things. I need you to look after her. And maybe go over to Mrs Robinson's.'

'I'm perfectly comfortable here.'

'Yeah, well I can't guarantee it'll stay that way.'

'Leon, what have you done?'

'Can you just for once do as I say, and I'll explain later?'

He led them down to the ground floor, where Mrs Robinson lived, the widow who had looked in on Clara before Nell. From his urgency, she understood something to be wrong and took them in without fuss.

Geats pressed a few bob into her hand, saying it was for anything she might need to give them something to eat.

There were phone boxes outside the stage doors of the Lyric, round the corner from the Yard on Great Windmill. He dialled the number Harrison had given him for exigent circumstances, Gerrard 5050. A woman answered, and was maddeningly vague.

'Look, I don't know how all this works, but if you have any idea who the hell I'm talking about, then get him to call me back immediately, because I'm stacking bodies like firewood out here. Gerrard 2721. Thanking you.'

He hung around the box, and less than two minutes later picked up on the second ring.

'Harrison?'

'What on earth is this message about, Leon?'

'I have a problem.'

'What sort of problem?'

'The dead-copper-riddled-with-bullets-in-my-home sort of problem.'

There followed a slight pause.

'Oh.'

Geats told him about Leah's murder, and Lander and Minter working for Messina, and Minter coming to the flat to kill Nell and running into the Webley and his six little friends. With a manic tinge to his voice, he prattled away nineteen to the dozen.

'It's the middle of the day and I don't know how I'm going to get rid of the body as I'm supposed to be working last night's murder, which I don't need to work as I know exactly who's responsible, but I can't prove that with Minter dead and I don't think Nutty Sharpe would listen to me if I told him his inspectors were multiple murderers and Christ, probably he'd . . .'

'Leon . . .'

'. . . bang me up the second I opened my mouth about any of it as Minter said he had some understanding with the Sabinis, so he could be—'

'Leon!'

'What?'

'I'll have the body taken care of.'

'Right. Good. Excellent.'

'And Leon?'

'Yeah?'

'Leave Lander alone.'

'What? No. No, I'm afraid I'm going to have to kill that prick most appallingly.'

'You can't.'

'He thinks he's a man of the streets, but he's nothing. His mistake was leaving me alive when he coshed me round the head. I'll show him how a bushwhacking should be done.'

'Let me put it another way. You won't kill him.'

'What is that, an *order*?'

'I understand your instinct is to go and cut his head off and parade it through the streets, but one Flying Squad inspector going missing is going to be trouble enough; two will raise different kinds of suspicions.'

'He killed two women. He tried to have Nell killed.'

'Leon, let me deal with it.'

'And how are we going to ever put this case down? Whoever killed Jeanette Cotton and your German spy wasn't involved in the Martin murder. But how do I tell anyone that? This investigation is buggered.'

'Investigations can be whatever you want them to be. You just need to tell a good story. Dead prostitutes lend themselves to good stories. It's dead police inspectors where it starts getting tricky.'

'What if Lander comes for Nell? He's going to know pretty soon that everything went wrong with Minter, and he'll want to do something about it.'

'Let me worry about that. You keep your head low. Work the murder of the Hinds girl as if you don't know who killed her.'

'Minter said something. *We were going to put it all on him.* I think they were fitting someone up.'

'Sounds like they have their story ready. All the more reason for you to go back to work. Find out exactly what they're doing. Where's the girl now? With your mother?'

'They're together.'

'I'm sending men to your building. If they're there, I'll leave someone to make sure nobody comes for them.'

'Yeah, they're there.'

'The thing here, Leon, is to compartmentalise. Box off all this stuff, and carry on with the rest as normal. I'll be in touch.'

64

Geats returned to Old Compton Street, where Leah had been found dead. The detectives were gone, as were Cassar and Billie. He walked to Vine Street, but the station was almost deserted.

Pym was at his desk.

'Where's everyone?' Geats said. 'What's happening with this morning's body?'

Pym eyed him like he was a stray dog.

'Where have you been?'

'I had a thing. Where's Cassar? Or Proudfoot?'

'Whole station is out looking for the suspect.'

'Suspect? What suspect?'

'The whore-killer. Someone overheard him talking about it in a pub. Called us, anonymous like. You should be out there too.'

'Who is he? Where are they looking?'

'Sharpe said you'd spoken to him before, said you were certain it weren't him. Probably he'll want a word.'

'Sarge.'

'Benny. Benny Brownlow.'

'Benny Brownlow? Bollocks Benny Brownlow! Ben never did this.'

'All four of them, I heard.'

'He certainly never killed all four of them. That's complete . . . where are they at? The club?'

'Aye. Heard you got him his job there.'

'Christ.'

He fled the station, Pym's musings on exactly what this all might mean for his future prospects and promotions fading behind him. Arriving in Lisle Street, he immediately saw that things had escalated. The place was littered with uniforms, Wolseleys angled across the road, detectives milling around looking thoughtful. Simone was talking to Billie. He spotted Cassar at the top of the stairs down to the club.

'Mark.'

'Leon, what the hell happened to you?'

'Where's Ben?'

'He's downstairs, in his room at the back. It's locked. I've been down and called out to him, but there's no response.'

'We're certain he's in there?'

'We had men waiting. They saw him entering the premises. Simone said he went back to his room and she didn't see him again. That was only fifteen minutes ago.'

'Let me talk to him.'

'Not a chance, Sergeant Geats.'

They turned to find Nutty Sharpe behind them.

'You've already had this man at the scene of one of the crimes once, and instead of investigating him thoroughly, you went on to secure employment for him.'

'He didn't do this.'

'Then the evidence will bear that out.'

A single hoot of laughter escaped Geats's lips.

'Sir, Ben is . . . a handful. It'll be bother trying to get him in cuffs if he feels threatened. Let me bring him out.'

Sharpe shook his head. 'Can't afford you bodging this up again.'

'Sir, look. Ben has been on these streets longer than I have, and never once have I seen him instigate violence.'

'There was the business here with the Italians.'

'He didn't start that, he finished it. That was his job. I'll put my hands up and give you that he's a bit odd. What happened to him on that ship, and in the sea, I'll never know exactly, but he didn't get over it. And he maybe isn't all the way there. But this is madness. He's no destroyer of women. I'd stake my life on that.'

'Then why won't he come out?'

'Probably he's terrified. He doesn't do well with confusion. With people shouting at him or threatening him. You can't expect him to react like a normal person. He's more like a child. Let me handle him, bring him in. Do this right. Ben is a face in these streets. Everyone knows him. He doesn't deserve this. He doesn't deserve to be cut down.'

'We're past that, Geats. Time we took him hard and fast.'

Flying Squad bruisers filed down the stairs into Renée's with Webleys and Enfield rifles. The story was already written, and the final chapter wasn't going to take place in a courtroom. When Geats made to follow, Sharpe laid a hand on his shoulder.

'Sweenies handle this one, son.'

He could hear them handling it from the street.

The shouts.

The door battered off its hinges.

The shots fired.

65

Flying Squad shooters trudged back up the stairs, Cassar in their wake shaking his head.

'Nobody in there.'

'Where the hell did he go?' Sharpe said.

'Don't know.'

'There's no back way out?'

'There's a small yard, but it's completely enclosed. He's not out there. We cleared every room, upstairs too. But you should see what we found in his room.'

They followed Cassar down.

'He's definitely our man,' he said over his shoulder.

'Is he, my hole,' said Geats. 'Ben's no more capable of this than he is of properly conjugating the gerundive.'

'We got the weapon in his room.'

'Bollocks. What weapon?'

'The electrical flex. There's other stuff in there too.'

'Like what?'

Cassar showed him to the small room Benny slept in at the rear of the basement, beside the office. It had been a storage room, and still had boxes of stuff piled against one wall, a cot against the other. A single bare bulb lit the windowless space, casting harsh shadows.

A wooden cupboard stood at the far end, its doors flung wide open so they almost touched both walls. Photographs were pinned to their insides, images Geats recognised only too well; the same ones he'd confiscated from the smut operation beneath the Domino Milk Bar. The same ones Harrison had first shown him.

'You motherless fuck,' he whispered.

Cassar pointed. 'That's the child, Josephine Martin's daughter. She's still unaccounted for, so we're looking at him for maybe doing her on top of the mother, and the other three.'

'Jesus,' Sharpe said. 'He's a lunatic.'

'Where's this wire?' Geats said.

'There.' Cassar glanced into the bottom of the wardrobe.

'That's not even the same colour. It's grey.'

'It's wire, Leon. And look here – a leather razor strop. He's our man. He's the Brigadier.'

'This is a fix-up job.'

'Oh, here we go,' Sharpe said. 'By whom, exactly? Who'd want to send some broken-down old prizefighter to the rope?'

'Someone who wants to protect themselves, or protect someone else.'

Cassar smiled unkindly. 'All right, Leon. Always got to be singing from a different sheet.'

'This is a man's life we're talking about, Mark.'

'This is four women's lives we're talking about,' Sharpe said. 'And the girl, too. You want to talk about people protecting people?'

'Like you enjoy pointing out, Chief Inspector, coppers being in the pocket of criminals isn't unheard of. Foreign pimps or gangsters, just as a hypothetical. Bookmakers, perhaps.'

'I think maybe this investigation would be best served by your taking a step back from it, Sergeant.'

Geats couldn't believe what he was hearing. Telling them about Nell might clear some of it up, but he couldn't imagine how he'd do that and keep her safe. Telling them about the missing corpse and the Abwehr intrigue would be even trickier, and about Minter and Lander murdering two women downright impossible.

Leaving Cassar and Sharpe shaking their heads, he ran up to the street and found Billie.

'Bill, this is crazy.'

'I know. And you missed it all. Where did you go?'

'No, I mean it's really crazy. It's all wrong.'

'Did you hear what they're saying about Nell?'

'That's exactly what I mean.'

He pulled her across the road into the shadows of the Daly's stage doors.

'Nell isn't dead.'

'What?'

'I know where she is, she's just fine, so we can strike that one off. And the Martin and Hinds murders are nothing to do with the other two.'

'You don't know that.'

'Yes, I do. The body going missing, that's no accident. Any evidence against anyone for all four of these killings is manufactured, top to bottom.'

'I'm going to need more than that.'

'I can't give you more than that. Not yet.'

He took her hands in his and she looked down at their entwined fingers.

'We have to get Ben before anyone else does,' he said. 'Have to shake this out right. You need to trust me.'

She freed her fingers from his.

'Why? You haven't trusted me.'

'I—'

'Nell's alive and well? When were you going to tell me that?'

'I couldn't . . .'

'Why? You didn't trust me not to tell someone? Who would I have told, Leon? What else do you know that you haven't told me?'

He shrank back.

Billie scoffed. 'Yeah, that's what I thought. And as for Benny, the photos in his room? That was Nell.'

'I know.'

'Just like the ones you took from the Domino Milk Bar.'

'What a *staggering* coincidence.'

'What do you me—'

'Geats!'

'Oh Christ,' he said, as Simone stomped over like she meant him harm.

'This is nonsense, Geats.'

'Yeah, I know.'

'Benny can let his hands go sometimes, but stalking and killing women? No chance.'

'I'm trying to find him before they do.'

'They're saying he killed that little girl now.'

'Simone, I know. But I need to get to him first. They must have let off twenty rounds into that room. They're not interested in taking him alive, but even if they did arrest him, Ben isn't going to do well under interrogation. They'll have him copping to the Ripper murders.'

'He knows this place. Knows it like you know it.'

'I don't—'

'If you were stuck in my club with armed men coming in the front door, where would you go?'

He saw it then.

Benny doing his boxer's shuffle down the street, a creature in his natural habitat; using reflections in windows and angled doorways to keep track of the men following him; ducking into Chez Renée's, nodding to Simone and heading out back; bypassing his small room and climbing the other stairs up to the yard; lifting the manhole cover and clambering down into the tunnel to slip away unseen.

'Shit,' he said. 'Thanks, Simone.'

He took Billie's arm, but she shook him off.

'You got to let me try to bring him in. Let me talk to him.'

'They've got the whole division out here, Leon.'

'Just let me go quiet, like. Anyone asks, I just took off. Not like they'd say that's out of character.'

'Do what you like, Leon. I'm past caring.'

66

Geats hurried away from Renée's, glancing back to see Billie watching him. The look on her face spoke volumes about what she thought of him. Her words lodged in him. He wanted to take her somewhere, try to explain it all, but he needed to find Ben before he fixed anything else. He made for Great Newport Street, where the tunnel beneath the club emerged in a thin alley.

He asked himself, what would Ben do?

Seek to conceal himself for as long as possible; he wouldn't come out on Great Portland Street, but would follow the alley the other way, past the humming substation, and north around the tenement blocks to where the rear of the horse market could be accessed, a covered passageway leading out to West Street.

Following this route himself, he came out opposite the St Martin's and Ambassadors theatres and continued on down the narrow court that cut between them, heading for the business and anonymity of Seven Dials.

He was moving quicker than Benny, though, and caught sight of him further up the alley, hobbling past the shopfronts of various tradesmen.

'Ben! Ben, it's Geats.'

Benny looked back in fear and, perhaps panicking, immediately stepped into the rear entrance of the Sheep's Head Tavern. Geats flew in after him, struck by the baked air of the place, open fires roaring in every corner.

He craned his neck, looking over the heads of drinkers, searching for Benny. The front entrance of the pub opened up just south of the bustling hub of Seven Dials, where he would lose him for sure.

Pushing through the door, he would have hit the street running, but a high-pitched laugh issuing from the bar behind stopped him. He turned back just in time to see a stoat-faced rake of a man who had been teasing Benny eat a right hook that popped his synapses. Punters leaped back like a tray of drinks had been dropped.

Geats held his hands up to calm the big man.

'Ben, it's okay. Listen to me. I want to help you. The police are coming, and dead is as good as alive as far as them taking you in. Come with me and we'll get this sorted. I'm here to help.'

Benny was beyond hearing.

With his arms, he swam through drinkers to the rear door. Confusion spread, glasses were tossed and tables flipped; it was like a fire in a theatre. Geats battled through the throng and pursued him out into the court behind the pub again, running back the way he had come.

Benny cut blindly into a darkened storefront; it had formerly been a cat's-meat man but now disguised a back-room joint known in certain circles as a haunt for a brooding variety of scented boys easy to buy drinks for.

There was no other way out of the place, and as Geats stepped into the low light, he came face to face with Benny. Before he could speak, Benny bobbed and weaved and fired a one-two with his right hand: sharp hook to the ribs, with another to the head hot on its heels.

With a sorry kind of luck, Geats was fortunate the first shot landed so well, as the fact that it nearly broke him in half moved his chin out of the line of the second punch, which clubbed him uncleanly round the back of the head.

Dazed, but not completely spilled out, he fought to his feet, arm clutched tight against his screaming ribs, and staggered out of the café. Benny was crossing the street that cut through the centre of the alley, and was back in the shadows between the two theatres. Geats ran with a hitched, lopsided gait, as if he were desperate for the loo, every breath absolute torture on his ribs.

Benny stood still in the alley. In the narrow confines, he filled most of Geats's view, but when he turned round wild-eyed and frantic, a mob of uniforms appeared blocking off the other end of the court.

Their guns were drawn.

67

Cassar heard Geats's yell echo off the alley's stone.

'Ben, it's all right. Come with me, and we'll get this right.'

Benny pushed through the stage door of the St Martin's Theatre. Geats appeared injured, or winded. Either way he wasn't moving easily, so when Cassar sprinted from the mouth of the alley, he was first into the theatre after Benny. Behind him, he heard Lander instructing uniforms to block the other entrances.

Nobody was getting out of that theatre.

Finding himself in a labyrinth of narrow corridors and staircases, Cassar ploughed headlong through them, not knowing if he was on the right trail or not. A door clattered closed above him somewhere, and as he bounced off the walls, rounding a tight corner, he saw a narrow staircase off to one side.

Two at a time he bounded up, taking a second flight until he was as high as he could go, in a plushly carpeted room behind the upper circle. The theatre was spread over three tiers, with the dress circle and the stalls below.

The building was sitting empty (awaiting an evening performance of a show about the poet Lord Byron fathering his half-sister's third daughter), the curtain up and stage naked. Other police arrived through doors used by patrons, converging on the stalls below.

'There!' someone cried, pointing up to the domed ceiling.

The upper circle sported steeply banked rows, along which Benny was skipping sideways. With great loping strides he stepped over seats and started making his way down to the front. Cassar plunged after him, leaping over seat backs and barely keeping his balance.

Since the night at Chez Renée's when Minter and Lander had spotted him, he'd been avoiding them and keeping close to Geats. He needed something to get him out from under what they'd seen.

Cassar the dancer.

Cassar the fairy.

If he could be the copper who took down the Soho Strangler, that'd be something. People would look past a lot on account of that.

He'd be proven goods.

He'd be bona fide.

Barrelling over the seats row by row, he heard oohs and aahs from the watching crowd below. Ahead of him, Benny got over the front seats and thumped into the balcony's walnut balustrade, leaning precariously over the edge.

On the big man's heels, Cassar hurdled the last row of seats and slammed into the back of him, their combined weight and momentum tipping them over. He clawed at the balustrade, getting a grip with one hand that was sorely tested when Benny missed it completely and clutched at his legs instead.

With the larger man hanging from him, the two of them swung in a great arc, and for one moment, when Cassar's hand peeled off the balustrade, they were free and defiant of gravity, jowls rising and arms floating.

Then all earthly forces reimposed themselves.

Shaped as if seated in a small boat, Cassar fell straight down, legs crashing into the balustrade of the dress circle beneath and firing him into a front-row seat.

Letting loose a terrible shriek, he gripped his leg and held it up, bent at a ghoulish angle beneath the knee, where it had wrapped itself around the hard wood.

From Benny, he heard nothing.

Somersaulting out into space, the big man hurtled all the way down to the floor of the stalls, landing neatly between two rows of seats. Cassar grabbed the balustrade in front of him and tried to pull himself up. He wasn't sure if he wanted to see over the edge or just drag himself as far from his own leg as he could get, as if distance might temper the pain.

His hands were slick with sweat, face running with it.

Everything was bright, as if his eyes screamed with the hurt in his leg.

He collapsed to the floor.

Through the balustrade, he looked down at Geats staggering towards the heaped Benny and peering at him over the row of seats. Turning away, Geats slumped into a stall seat, head in his hands. His shoulders shook.

From where Cassar was, it looked as if Benny's hair had been thrown out in a great mane, star-shaped on the floor.

But Benny had short hair, and it was just blood and other matter.

68

Geats believed he might be going utterly mad.

After a twisting investigation into four murders – two committed by his own inspectors and the other two by a still unidentified killer – and a stitch-up job on Benny Brownlow culminating in the suspect dying and a police officer being seriously injured, Nutty Sharpe was seeking to dampen the coverage of the case: a multiple murderer would bring altogether too much press scrutiny.

The evidence against Benny was circumstantial at best, so after he was scraped off the floor of the St Martin's Theatre, twin narratives took shape: privately the investigation was closed off and the police's position was that Benny Brownlow was responsible for all the murders. Sharpe prepared to pull his Flying Squad boys out of Vine Street, assuring everyone that good solid police work had been accomplished, and that even if the wider public would never know the full story and that it would never be proven in a court of law, a dangerous killer had been accounted for.

At the same time, in closed-door briefings with the press, Superintendent Dalton assuaged their fears of a maniac stalking the streets of Soho by confiding in them off the record that there had indeed been different killers, with the rather more banal motivations of personal grudges: Josephine Martin and Leah Hinds victims of inter-gang disagreement that had also cost Max Kassel his life; and Jeanette

Cotton and the nameless girl found beneath the floor (the disappearance of whose corpse he successfully kept from the press) killed in a
domestic dispute at the hands of a man the superintendent assured
reporters no longer posed a threat. Soho was safe once more, or as safe
as it had ever been. The press concentrated on the French gang angle,
encouraged by Dalton to cover the pending trial in Paris of Lacroix.

Geats was astonished at how easily the bohemian nature of parallel
realities was accepted within an institution as thuddingly conven-
tional as the Metropolitan Police, but decided the mind of a policeman
was uniquely suited to merging seemingly irreconcilable contradic-
tions into a single higher truth as long as someone of superior rank
told them to.

Cassar was whisked off to hospital with compound fractures to his
leg. There was talk of amputation. Multiple surgeries would be required.
No guarantees were made about the success of his rehabilitation.

Returning to the Yard, Geats retrieved his key from above the door.
The smell of fresh paint hit him as he entered his flat. The new coat on
the hallway wall, along with some hastily filled bullet holes and the
absence of the hallway rug, was the only evidence of Minter's demise.
Collecting Clara and Nell from the widow Robinson's place, he settled
them both in his own flat, telling his mother he wasn't going to brook
any disagreement and she could complain all she liked.

He had prepared the sofa for Nell to sleep on, offering the bedroom
to Clara, but the girl went ahead and stuffed cushions and blankets
into the bathtub, fashioning a nest for herself. Geats had thought she
would avoid the room, but something about the iron tub offered her
some measure of security. She bedded herself down, and despite usually being one to prowl the flat by night, Tallulah was happy to curl up
in the crook of the girl's neck.

Perched on the toilet, Geats sat with her a while. Clara had told
him Nell had barely spoken since he had taken her out of the flat bundled in a blanket, but she hadn't made any fuss returning to the place.

'Will other men be coming here?'

'No, I don't believe so. But after everything that happened, I thought it'd be better for us all to stay together a night or two.'

'So we're safe?'

'Yes, Nell. We're safe. You're safe.'

'What happened to the gun?'

'I've still got it.'

'Are you going to put it back behind the cistern?'

'Eventually. Thought I might keep it closer to hand for a spell.'

She nodded, like that made perfect sense.

'Leon, who was he?'

'A bad man. He was a bad man.'

'Did he hurt Mother?'

He nodded.

'And Leah?'

Nodded again.

'Why?'

'I wish I could give you an answer that would make any sense, sweetheart. Bad men do bad things for bad reasons. Trying to make sense of it don't get you anywhere.'

'Is it a bad thing to kill a bad man?'

'That's one of those tricky questions, but it's not one you have to worry about. He was still alive when I found you. Anything that happened after that isn't your fault. You have absolutely nothing to feel bad about, you hear me?'

She nodded and laid her face against Tallulah, who mewed.

Clara was under the covers when Geats went in to see her. Lightly he sat on the edge of the bed.

'How's the little one?'

'Scared. But she'll be fine.'

'Good. Don't want her moping about the place. You going to figure this out, so I can go back to my own bed?'

He nodded. 'Overabundance of caution. There's no real risk.'

'You lie worse than your father.'

'This work I do, this police thing . . .'

'It's not for you, I always thought that.'

'I—what do you mean?'

'You were a boy, my strong suspicion was you'd grow up to be half a gangster.'

'Matka, what the hell?'

'You were always running in the streets with those boys from the Yiddish gangs, coming back with food or tools or God knows what. I thought as a man you'd have schemes and ruses. First time I saw you in that uniform . . . how much you looked like your father. You always looked like him, but that day it was uncanny. But I never thought it fitted you. Not really.'

'I felt at home doing it. I thought I did, anyways. But now . . .'

'Things change. Everyone becomes something other than what they believe they ought to be. Even you.'

That thought terrified Geats. Becoming anything at all felt like some kind of terminal proposition, let alone becoming something he didn't expect. Perhaps he could live his entire life while he waited to become this other thing. That was more comforting.

He leaned in to kiss her, but she rolled away onto her side, facing away from him.

'Night, Matka.'

Sliding a sideboard across the front door as a barricade, he positioned his armchair in the hallway with a clear line of sight and reloaded his Webley. He hadn't seen Lander since the theatre chase, but at some point it would dawn on him that Minter's mission had gone awry, and Geats wasn't sure what the inspector would make of that.

He was sure of one thing.

Anyone who came to his flat looking for trouble would find more of it than they could handle.

69

They lived through the night.

Geats again begged the widow Robinson's indulgence in letting Clara and Nell spend the day with her. He wasn't going to leave them in either his or his mother's flat before he had spoken to Harrison and knew exactly where he stood as regarded any repercussions for Minter's death.

In Sink Street, he hammered on the door but received no answer. If Harrison wasn't there, someone certainly was; it wasn't the kind of place you left unguarded.

He sat on the front steps for hours. The day never quite reached the ground; the sun climbed over chimney shadows to blind the upper floors and bounce back off the windows onto the eastern façade of St Peter's, this gifted light all that side of the church ever saw. Eventually, around lunchtime, the door opened and Harrison stood looking down at him.

'Haven't I done enough for you already, Leon? What is it you want?'

Geats slowly climbed the steps to the door.

'I want to hit you.'

The makings of a smile flickered across Harrison's lips a split second before Geats smashed him in the face, knocking him clear off his feet. He looked up from the floor, astonished, bloody from a nick over his eye.

Geats adjusted his sleeves.

'That was for Benny Brownlow. He never killed those women. Neat. Tight. Done to last. Your needlework is all over this stitch-up.'

He stepped through the door, pulling it closed behind him. Harrison picked himself up, something cryptic in his expression.

'This isn't the place for a conversation like this.'

Geats followed him up the stairs to the large second-floor room whose fire always seemed to be crackling away. Harrison stood before the flames, his back to Geats.

'Why Ben?' Geats asked.

'Because Benny Brownlow could be made to look guilty. Because you told me about him. And because this business had to come to an end.'

'Even if that meant fabricating evidence to make a murderer out of a man who wouldn't hurt a fly?'

'My understanding, there are several members of the Sabini organisation who are living proof to the contrary.'

'That's different. You play in the streets, you take the beats. Everyone knows the risks, and they walked away with their lives. Ben's dead. He did nothing, and he's dead.'

'And Sergeant Cassar was badly hurt, I understand. Seems that should be your priority.'

'Both of them would be just fine if you hadn't meddled.'

'My meddling saw to it that a dead Flying Squad inspector wasn't found murdered in your home. You're welcome, by the way. Keeping you from the noose, and saving the girl a lifetime in an asylum.'

'He wasn't murdered. He got exactly what he deserved.'

'I suspect Nutty Sharpe would beg to differ. Inspector Lander certainly would.'

'I sat in a chair with a gun watching my front door last night. But I can't do that every night. I need to know what's going to happen with all this.'

'There will be no investigation into Minter. He had debts, you see. Bookies. Shylocks. His room was found a little short of clothes and personal effects. On the run, most likely, having overestimated the power of his badge to protect him from the kind of faces looking for him.'

'You think people will believe that?'

'People will believe anything. They're not interested in the truth, only in a good story. Something comforting that doesn't challenge the way they think about life. I've told you this before.'

'And Lander?'

'You need not worry about him.'

'How's that?'

'Inspector Lander is an understanding fellow. Sees the bigger picture.'

'Christ. You recruited him.'

'He's in with the Messina brothers, and operationally the police don't even know they exist. Could be a very valuable conduit of information. He knows you're off limits, and the girl. It has been made crystal clear to him that the penalty for ignoring that will be terminal. And the same goes for you.'

'Josephine Martin. Leah Hinds. Two women are dead because of him. That we know of.'

'James Fluke. Arthur Minter. Two men are dead because of you. That we know of.'

'That's not the same . . .'

'No. Never is, is it?'

Geats sat heavily in a chair before the fire.

'What about the Brigadier? We still don't know who he is.'

Harrison sat across from him, folding his legs neatly.

'We don't need to. He had a job to do, and he did it. What's of more importance is that anyone who looks hard enough will see that a transient simpleton killed a few women, and the death of an Abwehr agent was mistakenly attributed to him.'

'Jesus, Harrison. There's still the law. That's the business we're all in, isn't it? Law and order. Enforce the one to maintain the latter.'

'That's backwards thinking. Laws are totems of order; you establish

the order first and then write your laws. Regardless, I'm not interested
in law. My job is defence of the realm, however that might be achieved.
The realm was here before our current laws and will remain long after.'

'You are something else.'

Harrison flicked lint from his trousers.

Geats was exhausted. 'I don't think I can go back. I don't think I
can keep on doing this job.'

'So don't. Quit.'

'Become a baker, maybe.'

'Come work for me.'

'As a snoop?'

'I suspect you'd enjoy it, Leon. It would suit your lifestyle choices.
You can come and go as you please. There's no uniform, so your most
terrible mufti would do just fine. And all I need is information. Intelligence. I don't care where, when or how you get it. You know the
streets. You know the gangs. You know the rackets. The ponces and
the prostitutes, the rent boys and the dealers, the lenders and the muscle, the clubs and the back rooms, the alleys and the mews. You know
Soho. I need to know what you know.'

'About what?'

'About all of it. How differently much of what happened here might
have occurred had I had more good ears to the ground in Soho.
French. Italian. Jewish. Maltese. The dark heart of this city connects
us to the rest of the world. And I want to know all of it. You won't have
cases, you won't have to chase thieves or hunt murderers.'

'I like chasing thieves. I like hunting murderers.'

'Well, you won't need to meet standards of evidence. Or plant any
if you can't. You'll just live the life and tell me whatever you hear, and
then together we'll work out what has to be done from there.'

Geats felt sick.

*Everyone becomes something other than what they believe they ought
to be.*

'Face it, Leon. You're not a policeman. Never were. You're a ghost.'

70

The day quietened down at Vine Street. In the tucked-away little street and the dark lobby of the police station, the pitch of the world was dampened.

Pym stood behind his desk, wearing the little spectacles that only appeared when there was paperwork on the go.

'Someone called for you, Geats.'

'Hmm?'

'Young lady. Said her name was Bella.'

If anyone could confirm that Benny Brownlow wasn't the Brigadier, it was Bella Gold. As much time as she spent at Chez Renée's peddling cocaine, she'd have known Benny well and could testify that he wasn't the man who had attacked her and Katherine Farrier.

'She leave a message?'

'Said that she'd seen him.'

'Seen who?'

Pym shrugged. 'Dunno.'

'Did she say where she was?'

'Nah. Just that she'd seen him.'

'That's it? Did she sound scared?'

Pym peered over his spectacles. 'I can't be speculating at the hysterics every one of your whores works themselves up into, Leon.'

'Well, Jesus cocking Christ, Sergeant Pym.'

He hurried out into the street. Too early to check the clubs for Bella; he figured she wouldn't be far from her man, nightlife and narcotics maven Gerry O'Brien, and headed for his club, Never Been Kissed, off Golden Square. An elderly cleaning woman told him that her boss had been picked up by the police for dealing. Geats phoned Vine Street and Pym confirmed that O'Brien had been given six months, but had no record of Bella Gold being arrested.

Geats recalled her telling him she lived in Connaught Village, and it didn't take him long to find her place on a little mews near Marble Arch, but neighbours told him she was gone. O'Brien had given the court an address nearby, on the curved neoclassical terraces of Norfolk Crescent. The great five-storey piles with their porticos and pilasters were teetering on the brink of disrepair, many split into flats and boarding rooms, but O'Brien had rented one intact. Even had staff, whom Geats found packing up when he got there.

Upstairs, a young maid complained bitterly that O'Brien had been jailed owing her several weeks' wages, and Bella had stuffed her best frocks in a suitcase and hightailed it with a disreputable-looking man who claimed to be the police.

'She look afraid of him?'

'Not of him, I don't think. Frightful state she was in last night, though, a right hullabaloo there'd been. I don't like to speak ill of her, but I'd say she'd gotten herself in some fisticuffs in a pub somewhere. Looked more than happy to go off with this fella this morning, this policeman.'

'Anyone else been by?'

'Has there. Like a revolving door down there, *clients* of hers turning up. All indignant that she ain't here.'

No problem dobbing her employer in now she wasn't getting paid. Geats thanked her and headed downstairs. If the killer had turned up pretending to be a copper, Bella would have made a fuss before she went with him. He was beginning to suspect Lander's involvement in this, which didn't bode much better for Bella's prospects.

In the downstairs hallway, a dapper gent was peering into the front lounge. Looked like if he were thrown at a wall, he'd stick there. Was it a face Geats recognised from the Soho scene? All the years in the clubs and dives, all the hustlers and whores, the freaks and fiends, the ruffians and Ruperts. And in the end, for what?

'I know you?'

The dandy stepped back in alarm.

'Uh, is Miss Gold here?'

'What do you want with her?'

He glanced back at the front door, still open. 'Perhaps I'll just be on my way.'

'Another bit of posh looking for a fix, eh? Cocaine, is it, keep you going nights? Or opium? Need it probably for a war wound. Dull the pain.'

'I've obviously made a mistake.'

'I'll say. C Division, Vice, shit-knocker.'

'Oh God.'

Geats marched up and stuffed his card in the man's face, walking him backwards into the corner behind the front door. Crumpling into a heap on the floor, hands clasped together in front of him, he was almost in tears.

'What? Speak up?'

'Please, sir. I beg mercy of you.'

Any other day, Geats would have run this type of bleating vermin in without a second thought. Muss up his hair, ruffle his fine threads. Lose him in the cells for a night or two, learn him just how far he could fall. Now, though, he couldn't even get excited about maybe cracking some skull along the way.

He leaned down over him. 'It's your good fortune to have caught me in something of a liminal phase. Betwixt and between.'

Confusion in the dandy's face.

Holding the front door open, Geats booted him in the rump.

'Get out of my sight, you snivelling quimmy.'

Almost tripping down the steps trying to get away, the man vanished round the corner in blind panic. What was it to Geats if dopers wanted to get high? He was done with that shit. The only thing left he could think to do with his rank now was clear Benny's name. Someone was making sure nobody could unstitch the work done to put the killings on the big man. Other than Bella, there was one more witness Geats knew for certain had seen the Brigadier in person – wife-beater and maligned mattress-shitter James Allen Hall.

Breaking into his room in a Charing Cross doss-house, Geats initially thought the man was dead. Lying face-down in a pool of vomit, Hall was victim only to crimes of his own hand. Geats boiled the kettle on the small stove in the oddly shaped room, then hauled Hall into the one armchair and poured tea down his throat, topping him up with what remained of his gin to ferment some measure of coherence.

'Jesus, who am I supposed to have murdered now?' Hall said, picking chunks out of his beard.

'The police think they've got their man. This Brigadier.'

'Official apology will no doubt be in the mail.'

'They think he was a giant homeless former sailor with shell shock who fell to his death from the gods in St Martin's Theatre.'

'Would it be unfair to be sceptical about how good you lot are at your work?'

'You don't recognise that description as the man who let the room from you?'

'He was an average-sized gent. About my height. Walked with a limp. Always smartly dressed. Expensively. His suits looked like they were worth more than my entire life totted up.'

'Hall, the contents of your stomach are often worth more than your entire life totted up.'

Sitting in a scruffy suit soiled with his own sick, he was in no position to dispute this.

'Come on,' Geats said. 'Get washed. We're going down the nick to clear this up.'

71

Vine Street was deserted.

A young constable was in Sergeant's Pym's place and barely looked up from his paper. Upstairs, nobody sat at the detectives' desks, and the Clubs & Vice office was empty. Geats deposited Hall in a chair at the centre of the detectives' pen, and they both sat in the quiet. All that moved were the shadows tracing the progress of panes of sunlight across the floor.

'Rare demonstration of common sense from you, Geats, keeping your head low these past few days.'

Geats stood when he saw Superintendent Dalton in the doorway, buttons rubbed to a shine. He gestured to Hall.

'Who's this, then?'

'This is one of the few people who saw the killer in the flesh.'

'Loads of people saw the killer in the flesh, both alive and dead.'

'Mr James Allen Hall here sublet the Lexington Street room to the killer. A man who was the same height as him and who walked with a limp.'

'That proves nothing, Geats,' said Nutty Sharpe, appearing behind Dalton.

'It proves Ben Brownlow didn't rent the kill room.'

'He had someone else pay for the room. So what?'

'The description Mr Hall gave me of the man who rented the room tallies with what Bella Gold remembered about the man who attacked her. A man who walked with a cane and had a thing for leather strops.'

'My understanding, she thought the man had doped her, so her recollections are to be questioned.'

'She's in the club Ben worked at every night. You don't think she'd recognise him? None of this adds up.'

'Why don't you bring this Miss Gold down here too, then? See what she has to say for herself.'

Geats laughed. 'Well, I would, sir. But I can't find her. She's cleared out of where she was staying, and nobody's seen her.'

'You lost someone, Geats?'

He turned to find Lander at the other end of the office.

'Only a witness,' Geats said. 'Could be worse. Could have lost a partner.'

Lander's boiled smile paled below his raging eyes. Sharpe stepped forward.

'Inspector Lander, see Mr Hall to my office and take his statement.'

'I brought him in,' Geats said.

'I'm leading this investigation, Sergeant. It was my men who brought a stop to Brownlow's carnage. We'll take it from here.'

Geats looked at Dalton. 'Sir . . .'

'This is Flying Squad's brief. Why I brought them in.'

Lander smirked. As he went to pass Geats, he showed the neck of a pint of gin in his pocket.

'Yes, let's see what Mr Hall remembers.'

Geats brushed into him, speaking in a low voice out of earshot of Dalton and Sharpe.

'I was there when it happened. You should know your boy died like a coward.'

Lander's hands were up around Geats's neck before he could slip out of the way, and the two of them scuffled, knocking files and an empty cup off a desk.

'What is this?' Dalton cried, getting between them.

Geats grinned at Lander. 'Remember how your boy loved his confessions? I know you. I know what you are.'

'Enough!' Sharpe cried. 'Inspector Lander, see to Mr Hall.'

Brushing himself down, Lander steered Hall into the Clubs & Vice office, where he would be soaked in gin and encouraged to give a rambling and nonsensical account of his dealings with the Brigadier.

'That man is your evidence that Brownlow was innocent?' Sharpe said. 'A degenerate. A wife-beater, a sodomite, a chronic alcoholic. What sort of man is that to rely on?'

'An eyewitness. Sir.'

Sharpe shook his head sadly. 'Do you even know how he's doing?'

Geats looked puzzled.

'Your old partner. Your friend. Sergeant Cassar. Wonder why the station's empty? Because the coppers who care are at Charing Cross seeing he's all right. Perhaps you should join them.'

Geats snorted.

'Yes, perhaps wiser to steer clear, being as you were trying to help the killer. You're a disgrace to the uniform.'

'Perhaps I should think about another line of work. A bookmaker, maybe.'

Sharpe stared flatly at him. 'Think I'll go and help Inspector Lander wrap this case up.'

The door to the Dirties' office banged shut behind him.

Dalton, hands behind his back, raised his chin. 'You spoke to Brownlow at one of the murder scenes, didn't you, Geats?'

'Max Kassel. At least we know he didn't do that one.'

'Back then, you were pretty certain he wasn't involved.'

'Right now, I'm pretty certain he wasn't involved.' Geats sighed, and Dalton sighed louder. 'I can get him, sir. It's all being brushed under the rug here, but I can find the actual killer if I'm simply allowed to—

'For heaven's sake, man, give it up. We found—'

'With the greatest of respect, Superintendent, you don't know what you're talking about. As far as the streets go, you never have, and you never will.'

'I understand that you've been through—'

'You don't understand a thing about this. None of us do. That's the joke of it all. But if you believe Ben Brownlow was anything to do with it, then you're even less of a copper than I thought you were.'

'Look, Sergeant, I won't stand for this any longer.'

Geats took his warrant card out, dropped it on the desk.

'You won't have to.'

72

Every way he believed the world to be, it was not.

Yet he was years from understanding that, so by confining him to a hospital bed with a mangled leg, two dozen constables and detectives around him drinking from bottles, life seemed to be providing Cassar with a thrilling apogee.

He was the hero of Vine Street.

The killer was dead.

Rumours of past indiscretions were immediately dispelled.

There were even whispers of the King's Police Medal, distinguishing himself by risking life and limb in bringing a halt to a notorious foe.

He'd woken up in tremendous pain, two days after his accident, but seeing Billie sitting by his bed he maintained a brave face. All the same, he took everything the doctors offered him.

A fixation plate had been screwed in to reset the various pieces of the bones in his lower leg, though the doctor had cheerily informed him he would in all likelihood remain bipedal, bar some horrendous infection setting in, and he was hopeful there would be no long-term muscle or nerve complications.

Thinking about his prognosis would only deflate his boisterous mood, so when his colleagues from Vine Street and Scotland Yard appeared, smuggling in boxes of booze, he mixed his morphine with a little ale and swam through the days, Billie closely monitoring his intake so he didn't comatose himself.

Bed rolled into the centre of the otherwise unoccupied ward, he received guests like an ageing sultan, laughing and singing with his new votaries.

Bottles were opened.

Cigars were lit.

Doctors were locked out.

Nurses were chased around the beds.

Wiping his chin, holding his hand and knowing when to chase off the troupe so he might get his rest, Billie mothered him in a fashion both would believe a suitable foundation for marriage. Her regental authority was never questioned, and even the new commissioner bowed to her courtly air when he visited.

Cassar was made.

He was one of them.

And all it would cost him was the loss of his self.

73

Geats eventually made his way to Charing Cross Hospital.

The celebrated copper who fell from the gods had his own ward, and it felt like the whole division was there, air thick with smoke and raised glasses. Behind a half-pulled curtain, Boyle was in repose on a bed with a young nurse, working up an idle friction. Everett sat trouserless on the floor drinking warm ale and bottle dregs, unfussy about the tributes he took.

In striped pyjamas, Cassar lay propped in his bed at the centre of it all, injured leg hoisted aloft. Shoes off, garters showing, Billie sat beside him. With his head tilted back, she poured a pint down his gullet, and there was much hooting when it ran over and down his chin.

Hand on his shoulder, she cleaned him up with her handkerchief, the pair of them laughing. They both saw Geats at the same time, eyes catching across the ward. They had reasons to celebrate.

Catching a killer.

Closing a case.

Being alive.

Reasons to be so reprehensibly cheery.

Geats turned his back and walked out on the whole lot of them.

Part Three
BLITZ

1963

74

Birmingham.
Bollocks.

75

Every spare moment for a month spent there.

Early mornings driving up.

Nights in a fleapit B&B on Varna Road, tatty sheets and chipped crockery. Garret room he can barely stand in, kids out front all hours stealing bricks from the garden wall.

Picks it because it's a semi with an overgrown yard next to it, corrugated-iron fence barely standing. Owner says it's no-man's-land, and he's free to park there. Gully running behind the houses comes out at the far end. Two ways in, two ways out. Good and bad, but if trouble comes, he prefers having options to having none.

Most of the houses are bedsits, popular with the working girls. He checked with the local nick when he arrived, telling them he was off duty, looking for the daughter of a mate who'd done a bunk. Probably on the streets. They told him what was what.

Balsall Heath ends at the river, but even Edgbaston disowns Varna Road, offering it to the Heath as an annex. Everything across the river is open for trade. Balsall Heath Road, Clevedon Road, Court Road, the girls standing in doorways and outside shops.

The girls are all white.

The ponces are all black or Arab or Pakistani.

Punters hold their tongues, the old hate giving way to the need for cunny.

The trade has its own metropolis, the Kashmir Coffee Bar the beating heart. It takes him a few visits to shake off the suspicious glances, let the girls get used to his face. A few approach, and he refuses politely.

Maybe later, love.

Brassic right now. After payday.

He gets to know the ones who're around a lot, and their men. Many of them partner up with their pimps, have kids with them, cram into Victorian terraces carved up into bedsits or one-beds.

Third time he's up there, he chances the photograph of the unidentified woman. Oxford City Police had it taken, head bandages off and hair positioned to hide the wounds. He has hundreds of copies. Gives them the sob story: girl legged it from home. Not even interested in forcing her to come back, just wants to be able to tell her folks she's all right.

Doesn't get a sniff. Nobody knows her, but he isn't getting the impression they're lying to him or hiding anything. Most of them take a good look, show their mates, little gaggles up and down the street talking it over. Face doesn't ring a bell.

One, Elaine, lives on the same street he stays on.

Walks her back one night; she's not had a good evening. Going home short, which she'll have to explain. He knows her fella, a Yemeni by the name of Habib, sees him around the Kashmir. Knows he gets busy with his fists, so offers to make her night easier, cover the cost of a Greek.

Late, the street is still busy. Lorries are parked up, their drivers in seeing someone. A woman sits in the bay, curtains pulled behind her. Waiting for trade. The glass is broken: a large, almost perfect circle that frames her head. She ignores him when he walks by, seeing he's with someone.

Elaine insists on making him tea.

'Habib won't be back till two or three. Neighbour has kid. They'll be fine for bit.'

He sits in the armchair in the bay window, and she brings out a tray with two mugs and a couple of tea cakes from a packet. He hasn't eaten all day and peels back the red and silver foil, taking a bite.

'Feel funny just taking cash. Sure you don't want . . .'

He taps his ring.

'Christ, if that disqualified my punters, I'd be eating out gutters.'

He laughs, finishes his tea cake.

'Some of girls reckon you're police, even with story about your friend's daughter.'

'I am.'

She stiffens.

'But not round here. Down in Kent. London before that.' He shows his badge.

'Sergeant Mark Cassar. What's that, then? Cassar?'

'Maltese. My old man.'

'Dunno that we got any of them round here. Just about everything else.'

She slides across the bed until her back is against the wall, ankles dangling off the side. Flattening her feet, she spreads her toes and peers at them.

'Need nails doing. I hate feet, even my own.'

'Get it done in the shop. Claim it on expenses.'

She laughs. 'Aye, if I paid taxman, I probably would. Rita used to do it, in room upstairs. When you first said about looking for missing girl, I thought maybe you meant her. Until I seen picture.'

'What happened to Rita, then?'

'No idea. Come here from Coventry, probably four years ago. Then, must be six or seven months ago now, she ups and leaves. No goodbye, no nothing. Wasn't day went by we didn't talk.'

'Must be women moving on all the time.'

'Some go home, if they have one. Or you have drugs now. Number I've seen falling into that, especially young ones. But Rita left all her stuff, from what we could tell. Landlord ended up binning it. I thought something fishy had happened, but nobody saw nothing.'

He sits up on the edge of the chair.

'She didn't have a fella, this Rita?'

'Yeah, she had one. Malcolm. Great galoot from Barbados. Has himself four girls and can't keep an eye on a one of them. Gives it that he'd had enough, told her get lost as she wasn't earning. But that's just so other girls wouldn't worry.'

'Any others like Rita? Disappearing just like that, no explanation.'

She makes a face. 'You get so many trying it for a few nights, can't hack it. If you've never done it and don't know score, it can be hard those first times. Especially if you don't have anyone looking after you. But Sheila was a funny one.'

'Funny how?'

'She weren't here long, but she settled in, you know? Everyone liked her, and she got a man pretty quick. Moved in with him, down on Gooch. Place over fruit and flowers shop. Gerald's. You've got radio guy on first floor, and they was up above that. He's still there, Ronald. Has Gill now. Christ, who hasn't?'

'And she vanished, Sheila?'

'What am I like? Yeah, she was working, and they was just down road from where they lived. He popped back to grocer's next door, and when he come back she's gone. So he thinks she's found a punter, see, but she don't show again, so he goes home. Nothing.'

'This was recent?'

'Sheila was before Rita, now I think about it. Couple of year ago, probably.'

'And she hadn't packed a bag?'

'Ronald went police. Only you can imagine how that went, pair of them with records long as your arm.'

'They didn't spend too much time on it?'

'Whole task force set up to look for her, what d'you think?'

He leaves a sheaf of photocopies of the picture of the quarry woman with Elaine, for her to hand out on the street. His gaff is just up the road, but he walks down to the park and does one last loop. Down

Cheddar and back up Court and Clevedon to the Balsall Heath Road, along to Varna again.

The girls humour him, nod and a wink. They're all faces he's spoken to before, but they take a few pictures to give to others.

He gets an idea of it in his head now. The Brigadier on the streets, watching the trade, talking to them maybe to see who has family and who doesn't.

Jesus, doing exactly what he's doing.

Dawns on him he's asking the wrong questions. Someone must have noticed him, must have seen him with women. Taken at least three of them, looks like. Can't do that unnoticed.

Should be asking about *him*.

76

A week later and he's got himself in a predicament.

'You some kinda *pre*-vert?'

The pimp lays a hand on his chest, pushes him back against the wall of the café. Jamaican accent, but enough Brum is layered beneath for it to be obviously affected. He's seen the man before, and knows he's been seen by him. This is theatre.

'I was—'

'Why you bother her?'

The girl chirping in now. 'He was asking about dead girls.'

'Why you want to be doing that?'

'Missing girl. I was asking about a missing girl, not dead.'

A finger prods his chest. 'Don't wanna hear about no missing girls.'

It's late afternoon, and he's stopped for a bite in a café run by a Hindi chap who never seems to sleep. Some of the girls get a tea there before work, and meet back there in the small hours. Seeing a new face, he shows her the photograph of the quarry woman, and now there is a second man with the pimp and it's spiralling.

'Who's this?'

'He asking about dead girls.'

'Dead girls? What for? You fuzz?'

'Friend of mine, his daughter is—'

A knife makes an appearance, a stiletto flick in the second man's hand.

'Asked if you was police.'

Grabbing the knife hand, he twists the ponce's wrist outwards, making him yelp and drop the blade. Kicking it away, he backs towards the door, thick with condensation.

'This doesn't need to go any other way. I'll be off.'

There's a grocery shop next door, yuca roots stacked like firewood on a table outside. Two mothers rhubarbing, prams with little faces looking out filling the pavement. He turns the other way, but they're coming out after him.

Matter of pride now.

The Balsall Heath Road is only yards away; get as many people as possible in the vicinity. Then he sees him, standing outside the furnishings store on the far corner, looking in the window. A constable.

He jogs across the street. 'Sorry, Officer?'

'Sir?'

'Wonder if you could help. I'm not from the area, I travel for work. I'm in a B&B on Varna Road, but I got a bit turned around.'

'For work, of course, sir. You're not far. That way, and it's, let's see, one two three four, fifth on the left. Though it goes both ways.'

'I'm sure I'll recognise it from there. Thank you very much.'

'Worries, sir.'

He glances back; the pimps are scarpering. No point hanging around, though. Hurries along the road, head down. Exactly what he didn't want to do, make enemies in the streets he's working. Been asking around about the Brigadier, about a man who himself had a lot of questions. That raises more suspicions than a missing girl, though. Wonders if he's wearing out his welcome.

'Mr Cassar!'

Elaine waves at him from across the street. Watching for traffic, he nips over to join her.

'Call me Mark,' he says. 'Mr Cassar is a little formal.'

'Been looking for you all over. Got someone you need to meet. Think she knows your friend's daughter.'

Taking his hand, she leads him back the way he's come and slips into a thin alley leading to a bombpeck behind Clevedon Street where houses damaged in the war have been cleared. Uneven land, strewn with litter and the jetsam of life. A wheelless pram, the wire frame of its hood shorn of fabric. A car door. Milk crates. Kids have built themselves a fort against a fence, planting an abandoned door in the earth on its side, trellising perched on it.

'Over here.'

There are no gardens. The houses back right onto this wild brown site. She drags him through a rear door into what was once a kitchen but is now just another bedroom in a working house. A grubby-faced kid plays on the floor with wooden blocks that look hand-painted. A thin, wiry woman, his mother presumably, sits on the bed, all nerves. He thinks she's on something.

'Fella I told you about. This is Mark. Mark, this is—'

'No names,' the woman says.

'He's not—'

'It's all right, Elaine,' he says. Gestures to a dining chair in the corner. 'May I sit?'

'Suit yourself,' the woman says.

He does.

'I'm police, but I'm not on duty. Working something in my own time, to help a friend. Anything you tell me is strictly for my ears. No statement. No testimony. Nothing official. Just information.'

'I don't know if it's her.'

Elaine huffs. 'You said—'

'Well, I don't know.'

'You don't have to be sure,' he says soothingly. 'Just tell me who you thought it was. Ruling someone out is just as useful to me.'

'Looks like Christine. Only, it's the eyes. In your picture she looks like a user, and Chrissy weren't.'

'It's a bad photo. It was just the most recent. Go on. This Christine . . .'

'She went by Mary on the street. Dunno why she changed her name –
what's the point? Coppers get you, gotta give your right name anyways.
Think she was nervous about it still, about being known for a tart.'

'Where did you know her from?'

'Well, she lived upstairs, didn't she.'

'In this house?'

'Sure. Only for a couple of weeks, then she was gone. Just went, left
everything up there.'

He looks at the ceiling. 'Her stuff still there?'

Looks at him like he's simple.

'Sold it, didn't I.'

'What about papers, or identification?'

'Didn't find nothing like that. Flogged the clothes and stuff, binned
the rest.'

She's lying. Covering for keeping any cash she found.

'You know her full name?'

'Nah. Just Christine. Chrissy. Mary by night.'

'She ever mention family?'

'Said her mom was dead. Said she went on the game after that –
she'd always lived with her mom. Kidderminster, I think.'

'Your missing girl, she from Kidderminster?' Elaine asks him.

'No.'

Not technically a lie, since by not existing she doesn't come from
anywhere. But he doesn't want to leave a trail, so it's better they believe
this Christine just vanished.

'Shit. Really thought this was her.'

'That's definitely Chrissy,' the woman says. 'Three moles on her
neck there.'

He looks closely at the image. 'They moles? Might just be because
it's a copy of a copy.'

'Well, they're where her moles was.'

He takes out a fiver, leaves it on the side. Her eyes beam onto it and
she can't look away.

'Thanks anyway.'

He jerks his head at Elaine and they leave.

'Was that her or not?' she says, as they walk back to the Balsall Heath Road.

'Your friend seems pretty certain. There's a chance the girl was going by a different name, had made up a story about this dead mum in Kidderminster. Like she said, using a different name on the street. I think she was covering her tracks.'

'Asked around about man you mentioned, likes it rough with cane or stick. Nothing stuck out. Only fella been hanging around acting weird is you.'

He laughs. 'Good job I'm not working undercover, then.'

They reach his boarding house on Varna. He fishes out a tenner and gives it to her.

'Blimey. Get you far as you like, that.'

'For your help. I appreciate it, Elaine.'

'What do you think happened to her?'

He shakes his head. 'Nothing good.'

1941

77

London. No place for cartographers.

Nightly fires consumed homes and shops and churches and monuments, streets turned to ash and rubbed away like slough around wounds. Alive, restless, ceaselessly shifting and springing up anew amongst the destruction. The grey city of stone and granite was slowly turning the colour of clotted blood.

It had begun already. The night music. The flash of incendiaries, the umber glow of fire in the distance. From the street, Geats watched dark strings of smoke unravel into the night above the domed rotunda of the old Anchor Brewhouse.

'Leon.'

Babe Mancini was nervous. He flitted in and out of the warehouse, a modest brick building behind Tower Bridge, once stocked with goods unloaded at the wharfs, now the scene of blacker markets.

The war had brought a new order of things, the old protection days a thing of the past for the gangs. The Sabinis were gone; interned in camps as enemy aliens along with most of the Italian muscle they had flooded London's streets with. Babe's natural advantage was he barely existed on paper; born to Italian immigrants who trusted only the Church. Last man standing, de facto chief of what remained of the Sabini mob.

Wanting to expand, to take advantage of the natural opportunities of war, he had set up the petrol deal. Waiting for the first delivery, he was having kittens.

'Leon, bombs falling on top of a petrol truck don't seem a great idea.'

'Let's go inside,' Geats said, leading him back through the doors into the dim loading space. 'Bombs fall on us, it isn't going to matter much if there's a petrol truck here or not.'

It was supposed to be low key. Petrol was the most precious of resources, and they couldn't afford to draw any attention. Two gunmen hid in the shadows on the floor above, otherwise it was just him and Babe.

Leon Geats. Erstwhile sergeant and head-cracker out of Vine Street before departing the force under a cloud. Way the streets sang, he'd missed the whore-killer on his own patch. Befriended him, even. Big, slow Benny. The killer the world didn't know, but the streets did.

Babe had instantly seen the possibilities. Geats knew every nook and cranny of Soho, every face, every voice, every trick and ruse. He was a valuable asset for any gangster. And then there was the humiliation of it, the copper turned criminal for coin. Babe enjoyed that part the most.

'Sit down,' Geats said.

Babe sat on an empty forty-four-gallon drum and immediately stood.

'They should be here.'

'Driving through the city during the day is bad enough. At night? Who knows what streets that were there yesterday are still there tonight.'

'I don't like waiting.'

'Be some luck if they got hit by a bomb.'

'*Tocca ferro!*' He touched the gun on his hip. 'Don't even joke.'

The way he paced about, pitting the night with every passing second, Geats ignored him.

'I don't like new places,' Babe said. 'Or new people.'

'That's why we're here. You want we should have them come to our warehouse? That'd be nice. Might as well put signs up outside.'

'Don't get funny. I've told you about funny.'

'Funny is Sunday morning Mass without an umbrella.'

'What—'

'Hey, listen . . .'

Babe cocked an ear.

Geats nodded. 'Yeah, that's them.'

He swung the barn-style doors open wide and a Bedford tanker truck turned into the short yard outside and eased inside the building, two sweethearts sitting in the cab. The driver leaned out the window.

'You Mancini?'

Geats shook his head, jerking his chin towards Babe.

'You got the cash?'

'A cheque, we thought. Got it all made out.'

The man stared at him. 'You can't have the truck.'

'You don't say.'

Geats looked the truck over.

'You got a pump on this thing?'

The passenger spoke with a soft Scottish accent. 'Other side. Hand pump.'

'Hand pump?'

'Only the new ones got the powered pump,' the driver said. 'You think I can just drive one of those off the base?'

Babe stepped nearer. 'What's he saying?'

'Fucking hand pump.'

'*Mettitelo nel culo.*'

'You putting it in them?' The driver pointed to the rows of metal drums.

'Yeah.' Geats nodded.

'Just the two of you? Because this ain't our affair.'

'No. Don't trouble yourselves.'

Babe clapped his hands and the pair from upstairs descended the open staircase in the corner. Geats tipped over an empty drum and with his foot rolled it across to the back of the truck.

As the other two set about fixing the hoses in place for the pump, Babe sidled up to him.

'I don't get it.'

'What's to get?' Geats said. 'We pump the stuff out. If it's full like the man said it would be, it fills eighteen drums with a little swill left over. They're selling to us at double retail, so we mark it up to four times on the street. Honestly, not worth the effort, you ask me. We should be getting some of them plates to print the vouchers. That's easy money.'

'Nobody did ask you. I mean going to church without an umbrella. Why's that funny?'

A car skidded onto the forecourt, its headlights unslotted and beaming brightly through the still-open doors.

'Flying Squad! Don't move!'

Geats dragged Babe down behind the drums, out of sight.

One of Babe's boys, an excitable type with an acne-pocked face, took up his iron and fired into the blinding light, only to be cut down immediately by return fire.

'*Fottiti nel buco del culo di tuo padre!*' Babe roared, standing with his gun out, spraying shots all over the place.

Geats rolled out from behind the drums and scooted under the back of the truck. Realising that sitting under eight hundred gallons of petrol in the middle of a gunfight wasn't his wisest idea ever, he scrambled for the far side of the warehouse, tucking in behind a brick buttress.

The driver tumbled out of the truck and made a break for it. Incredibly, the copper seemed to be alone, one man crouching behind his car, firing over the bonnet. Slowly but purposefully, he moved around the vehicle and walked into the warehouse, behind the occasional shot.

Babe ran round the back of the truck, outflanking the copper, and streaked out into the street with the other gunman, the pair of them disappearing into the night, leather soles clapping down the pavement.

The second man from the truck, the one with the Scottish accent, was up between the cab and the tank, perched on the pump box with a gun. The copper hadn't seen him. From the other side of the truck, Geats watched his feet inching forward. Only a few more steps and he'd put himself in front of the man's muzzle.

As he did, Geats looked past the shooter and saw the copper's face, saw it was Mark Cassar, and without thinking raised his own gun and shot the Scotsman in the back of the head.

Cassar swung round, gun pointed through the gap in the truck at Geats.

'Leon.'

'Hello, Mark.'

Cassar didn't lower his piece. 'You want to put that gun down?'

'This gun?'

'Uh huh.'

'One I just saved your life with?'

'That's the one.'

Geats lifted his finger from the trigger, pointed the gun upwards before placing it on the floor at his feet.

'Kick it away now.'

'In case I get second thoughts about this and kill you after all?'

'Just in case, yeah.'

Geats sent the weapon skidding under the truck.

Cassar edged round the truck, gun still trained on Geats. 'Well. We seem to have ourselves a bit of a pickle here.'

'How about we just go our separate ways and pretend it never happened?'

'How about you put your hands on the wall over there.'

Geats spread them and Cassar patted him down, removing a knife, the wad of cash that was to pay for the fuel, and a pair of lead-loaded gloves.

'Still favour the heavy hands, then.'

He counted the money.

'Hundred and fifty quid.'

'He does five gallons to the pound, and knocked a tenner off on account of wholesale, like.'

'Who's he?'

'No clue. What I was hoping to find out. You must have followed him here.'

'The driver, yeah.'

'All on your own?'

'Work better that way.'

'How is it in Flying Squad now? No Minter. Sharpe retired. Any sign of Lander?'

'He transferred.'

'Course he did. Who is this bloke you were following? Army?'

'Yeah.'

'Fuel's not, though.'

'No.'

'Let's see who, then.'

Geats sauntered over to the dead man, hanging down from behind the cab of the truck, and went through his pockets.

'You forget you're no longer on the job, Leon, and in fact are actually under arrest.'

'Yeah, yeah. Look. I thought he sounded Scottish.'

He handed Cassar an identity card.

'Pumpherston,' Cassar said.

'East Lothian. It's the refinery where the oil from Eakring goes.'

'They drove it all the way down? Just one truck?'

'I expect it's a drop in the ocean of what they're diverting.'

'Turn round.'

'What?'

'Go on. That's it. And here you go.'

Bracelets snapped onto Geats's wrists behind his back.

'You serious?'

'I heard the stories about you. Disgraced copper, hiring out to the Italians.'

'Disgraced? That's rich coming from a schnip who didn't even know he was part of a cover-up. Benny Brownlow. You idiot.'

'Sorry, mastermind. Black-market petrol? You're no better than a traitor. I'd be within my rights to put a bullet in your head where you stand.'

Geats looked at the acne-scarred hood Cassar had gunned down.

'I believe it, too. You never used to be one for the violence. Guess Flying Squad has done its job.'

'Who was it ran out of here? Mancini?'

'Work it out yourself.'

'Get in the car, Leon. Jesus Christ. I mean, what exactly am I sup—'

A deep rumbling shook them where they stood.

'Over near the railway,' Geats said, spying plumes of orange-lit smoke to the south.

'That's close. We should get out of here.'

A huge blast across the road knocked them both off their feet, high explosives falling from the skies through the roof of a house and blowing it outwards. Clumps of broken brick peppered the street, a dust cloud curling off the smashed building and engulfing them. Geats rolled onto his front and squeezed his eyes closed. Brick dust got in everywhere, your eyes, your mouth, your lungs.

As the cloud passed, settling into a mantle of ashen powder, he saw someone stumbling towards him.

'You good?' Cassar yelled.

'Bloody shoulder.'

He unlocked the cuffs. 'Popped it?'

'Don't think so.'

The warehouse was at a T-junction with a residential road, the sixth or seventh house down taking the direct hit, the fire jumping to other homes now. The heat stunned them even at a distance. A telegraph pole that had survived the blast was beginning to smoulder.

Cassar shielded his eyes from the smoke. 'Christ. We should help.'

'What you going to do, blow the fire out?'

'There might be people.'

'We can't get near the place for now. Besides, there's eight hundred gallons of petrol here, Mark. How about we secure that first. You know, not let a bad situation turn catastrophic.'

Cassar dragged the two bodies to the back of the warehouse as Geats cleared up the pump and stowed away the empty drums. Then he shut the doors, locking the place up.

'Get in the car.'

'Just let me go, Mark.'

'You must be joking. You're coming in, or I'm shooting you.'

Geats got in the car and Cassar took him to Tower Bridge nick, all of five hundred feet away, round the corner and next to the magistrates' court.

'Detective Inspector Cassar, Flying Squad,' he told the sergeant.

'Up in the world,' Geats said.

'Need you to hold him for me until morning.'

It was remarkable where a nod and a wink from the Sweeney got you.

'Mark, do me one thing.'

'What?'

'I have . . . there's someone who needs to know I won't be back.'

'And?'

'Let me make a call. Ten seconds, no longer. Old times' sake.'

Cassar nodded at the sergeant, who lifted a phone from under the desk.

'Number?'

'Gerrard 5050.'

The sergeant dialled, checked it was ringing and handed the receiver to Geats.

'Frank Arkwright. Tower Bridge.'

Cassar snatched the phone from him. The line was dead.

'What was that? Code? You playing silly buggers?'

'I was letting them know I'll be back late.'

Cassar turned to the sergeant. 'Don't let him talk to anyone until I get back here tomorrow. I don't care if Churchill himself comes knocking for him.'

'Sir.'

The sergeant took Geats's arms and led him to the cells.

'See you tomorrow, Leon.'

'You will.'

78

Cassar awoke alone on the cot in the other bedroom. Amount he slept in there now, there wasn't much other about it.

He could hear the kettle downstairs, smell something on the stove. Washing in the small bathroom next door, he headed into the large bedroom at the front to get fresh clothes from the wardrobe. The flat was set across two floors above a butcher's, and he could hear the morning trade below. The curtains were open, and he looked down on Berwick Street.

The twenty-foot crater left by the September bombings had become part of the scenery; nobody had experienced anything to compare the bombing to, so it was simply accepted as life now. Produce stalls ringed its edge, and through the rubble and upended earth grew wild flowers not seen in the city for centuries. The acrid, bitter smell of yellow ragwort. The sweet racemes of tiny white bells hanging from lilies of the valley.

New life where there had been destruction.

Old life was whittling away, however. Quite aside from the businesses that were bombed out, others had shuttered permanently as things got tighter all over, and the prospect of clothes rationing promised to hit Berwick Street especially hard, with all its tailors and dressmakers and haberdashers and milliners.

The situation wasn't without its opportunities, though.

Dressing quickly, Cassar pulled the stool from beneath his wife's dresser and positioned it under the hatch in the ceiling that accessed the eaves. He retrieved a cloth-wrapped bundle and quietly replaced the stool. In the other bedroom, he found the wad of banknotes he had stashed beneath the mattress the previous night and added it to the money in the cloth. A little over three hundred and fifty pounds.

A year's salary in his hand.

He pocketed the cash and trotted downstairs to the lower floor, where Billie was plating up his breakfast.

'Hi.'

'Morning. Got your eggs all ready.'

'Thanks.'

'You didn't come to bed.'

'I wasn't back till late. Didn't want to disturb you.'

'I don't mind being disturbed.'

Laying the plate and a mug of tea before him, she sat at the table across from him. He shovelled a couple of forkfuls of scrambled eggs into his mouth before stopping to consider them.

'This is eggs.'

'Well done, dear.'

'Not from a packet.'

Billie grinned and winked. She wasn't much of a winker, lopsiding her whole face in exaggerated effect.

'Well, how?'

'I found an egg man. You know the big garage behind the Plaza?'

'One that got hit?'

'They haven't used it since, and this fellow has taken up in there. Keeps hens. Has loads of them. Place is filthy, absolutely stinks, but he has eggs by the basketful. I got as many as he'd let me take. I'm going to bake a cake later.'

Cassar nodded and clumsily forked up another mouthful.

Billie went on. 'We really should keep our own hens. It would be good to have a reliable supply of eggs.'

Glancing about, he tried to guess where in the kitchen she was planning a coop.

'What did you get up to last night, then?'

He twirled his fork around in a meaningless gesture. 'Just keeping an eye on a couple of spivs.'

Nothing good would come from bringing up Geats before he knew what was really going on there. He had always been on the fringes of things, but hijacking petrol for the Italian mob was out there even for him.

'I got a chicken from Tom downstairs.'

'He trying to dip out of the rent?'

'No, not at all. I think he appreciates the deal we did with them on the amount, and he likes giving me nice cuts or a bird here and there as thanks. I'm going to roast it. Have a proper meal for a change.'

'I'll probably be late again tonight.'

'Right. Well, chicken's good cold too.'

'I should be going.'

'I bumped into Mr Pyke.'

'Oh?'

'He's next door. Said he'd be there until lunch. He wants an answer.'

'Does he now?'

'Maybe we should just forget it, Mark. Having this place is wonderful enough, and the rent from the butcher's is a boon. There's no point stretching ourselves.'

'I've got it all sorted. I'll speak to him.'

He darted upstairs to clean his teeth and pomade his side-part. On the way down, he barely stopped to peck Billie on the cheek before he was out the door.

Their home was somewhere he was spending less and less time. Conversation broke out like skirmishes in a tepid war. Voices were never raised, it was all very civilised, but it usually ended in the same way – Cassar agreeing to whatever was suggested, feeling that if he couldn't please his wife, he might at least quell her.

Cupped hands to the window of Mrs Gal's dress shop next door, he peered inside. Mr Pyke was at the counter, talking to the old dame herself, no doubt trying to coax a competing bid out of her. Cassar opened the door, setting off the bell.

'Mr Cassar,' Pyke said. 'Your wife wasn't sure when you'd be around.'

'I'm a rascal. Never know when I'll pop up. Hello, Mrs Gal.'

The dressmaker gave him a cagey look. 'Inspector.'

'I was just going upstairs, Mr Cassar,' Pyke said, finger pointed upwards.

They left the shop and went up to the flats. The top floor was occupied by a young woman who worked for a particularly uninteresting branch of government, whilst the other one was empty. Pyke unlocked it and showed Cassar in as if revealing Ali Baba's cave. The walls were grimy and peeling, and the seat of the sofa had fallen through.

He stood at the window. 'Look, I don't want to rush you on this matter, but I have my own situation to think about.'

'Three hundred.'

'Mr Cassar . . .'

'Cash. Right now.'

'The building has to be worth—'

'The building has a bomb crater outside it and the shop next door is half collapsed. There are clearly structural problems. I know this because my own place has damage, and you were closer to the blast. These things are insidious. I was in Mayfair last night, one of the streets that was hit about the same time as us last year. Well, this house took its time, but it collapsed yesterday. And they'd been living without gas as the lines had been cut. Someone lost a fortune there.'

'I have to get out. My wife has gone to her family in Staffordshire. We're going to get a place there.'

'I'm taking the risk here. God knows, these places might come tumbling down on our heads. And if they don't, who's to say what Jerry will drop on us next?'

'Three hundred, though.'

'All right. Look, I spoke to my father-in-law. He lent me a little extra; I was going to use it to fix the place up. But maybe I can stretch to three hundred and twenty.' Cassar produced the cash and began counting out the notes.

'Three hundred and twenty, then.'

'I have a solicitor. He'll contact you later today.'

Mr Pyke shook hands as amiably as a man could when he'd just been flagrantly stitched up, and Cassar left, driving back to the warehouse near Tower Bridge. With the 20 mph limit and fresh damage after each raid, he rarely drove the same route anywhere twice; buildings and whole streets vanished overnight, changing the city's layout by the day.

Any time he crossed the river, he felt fortunate for having moved to Soho. The West End had mostly got away with the war so far, the east and south of the city bearing the brunt of the bombing.

The houses on the residential street leading away from the warehouses were in a state. One fire truck remained. Although the flames appeared extinguished, some of the rubble smoked still.

Cassar turned onto the forecourt of the warehouse and found the doors open and Geats sitting out there in a deckchair, right in the middle of the empty space.

79

'What the hell is this?'

'Morning, Mark.'

'Where's the tanker? And the drums?' Cassar lowered his voice to a hiss. 'Where are the bloody bodies?'

'I took care of all that.'

'How are you even here? What happened at the nick?'

'Oh, my boss called up and had a lovely chat with the super.'

'Your boss?'

'Yes. Turns out my boss is your boss's boss. He's pretty much everyone's boss's boss, really. You might know him. Herbert Morrison.'

The Home Secretary. Things were beginning to make sense.

'What are you involved in, Leon?'

'Everything. That's my job. Involving myself in everything.'

'I know you're not Special Branch. I thought that when I first heard stories about you after you left Vine Street, but nobody at Scotland Yard knew you.'

'Yeah, they won't know me.'

Geats was always looking for a rise, and Cassar wasn't going to give him the pleasure. 'Did you leave anything for me here?'

'There wasn't much to begin with.'

'What's upstairs?'

'I don't know. This was just a rendezvous.'

Cassar loped easily up the stairs, Geats panting after him – when it came to his body, he might have let a thing or two slide – and found the first floor as empty as the ground.

'There's nothing.'

'You know what's interesting? There were three main elements to this mess. One: the dead bodies. Taken care of, no need to thank me. Two: the petrol. Taken care of, no need to thank me. Three: the money with which to buy said patrol. That one's nowhere to be seen. You remember that pile of cash?'

'You didn't find it?'

'No. And the M Division boys at Tower Bridge didn't have it either.'

'Must be one of those mysteries, never to be solved.'

'Like who killed Jeanette Cotton.'

'Don't start all that again.'

'Mark Cassar. Money Mark. Flying Squad's finest.'

'You got something to say?'

'Funny, I thought I was saying it. Maybe I need to be less subtle with you Sweeney chaps.'

A commotion in the street caught their attention. Cassar opened the window and leaned out.

Geats hovered behind him. 'What is it?'

'Dunno. They're moving people away from one of the houses that was hit last night.'

'Probably looking to collapse.'

Firemen were still urging residents across to the other side of the road as the front of the house calved off like ice from a glacier, a wave of brick dust erupting to fill the street.

'Jesus,' Cassar said.

Geats whistled.

When it settled, the rear was still standing, opened up like a doll's house with the rooms exposed.

That was when the screaming started.

Pointing at something on the first floor, a woman let loose a seabird shrill, others joining in more muted revulsion. Geats clattered down the stairs and hit the street in what passed for a run. By the time Cassar caught up with him, he was already directing the firemen to get a ladder up to the first floor.

Cassar spotted what the fuss was about: protruding from beneath the boards of a first-floor bedroom were the legs of a woman. Firefighters were already up there, easing her out of the space she'd been wedged into. People flitted about, talking of ambulances and first aid as if she might still be breathing, nobody asking the obvious question of how on earth she had got under the floor.

Rooting about in the rubble, Geats dragged out a wooden door, positioning it at the foot of the ladder so they had something to lay her upon. She wore only a slip, and Geats pulled it down to protect her modesty as she was passed down the ladder from outstretched hand to outstretched hand until she could be placed on the makeshift stretcher.

The crowd stood around her, all of them porcelain white where they'd been caked in dust, their hair, clothes, everything.

'She's dead,' Geats said. He touched her face. 'Not for long, though. But . . .'

Cassar leaned down. 'What?'

'She has head wounds, serious ones, but they'd begun to heal. If they'd happened in the blast, there'd be more blood. It looks like someone treated her already, way before last night. Days, maybe weeks ago.'

Something else had caught Cassar's eyes as they lifted her down, though. The backs of her thighs, and the deep cross-hatching of vicious whip marks that scarred them.

80

Sir Bernard Spilsbury stared at the naked corpse on his slab, then at Geats and Cassar. He shook his head.

'I thought you two had settled all this business years ago.'

Geats choked on a laugh.

'We're not sure what's going on,' Cassar said.

'She was shot, I can tell you that.' Spilsbury pointed to the head, no longer bandaged. 'Entered here, just forward of the ear, and exited high up here. The injuries have been treated and bandaged at some point, and there is stitching at the entry wound.'

'A suicide shot,' Geats said.

'Why bandage her, then?' Cassar said.

'Death wasn't instant,' said Spilsbury. 'She survived the shot, and someone has done a pretty good job of patching her up. Superficially, anyway. It would have taken a major surgical intervention for her to live, and even then her chances would have been slim with the trauma she suffered, but in terms of what you might call battlefield medicine, it's not a bad effort.'

'Can you say how long ago the gunshot was?' Cassar asked.

'From the wounds, I would say a week at the most.'

Leaning down, Geats squinted into the hole in the woman's skull.

'Any idea what sort of gun?'

'From the entry, pretty small calibre. A twenty-five, maybe a thirty-two.'

'So, like a Ruby or a Walther PP? A pocket pistol?'

'Something of that size, certainly.'

Cassar frowned. 'What are we saying? It was suicide? Or it was murder?'

'That, Inspector, I cannot say. As Geats observed, the angle of entry is consistent with a suicide. Equally, it wouldn't be difficult for someone to make it appear that way. And there was a certain level of violence suffered shortly before her death, although the nature of it, it could have been consensual.'

'The whipping,' Geats said.

'Yes. And it's your old friend the razor strop again. I recalled you suggesting it before, with that body found under the floor in Soho. I tried out a few, and there are a couple that match almost exactly. The wounds definitely suggest a leather instrument of that size.'

'It's not suicide,' Geats said. 'The strop? Buried beneath the floor? This is our boy.'

Cassar hooked his arm and pulled him aside.

'All joking aside, Leon, how can it be? It was Brownlow. We put it to bed.'

'Flying Squad put it to bed. Nutty Sharpe put it to bed. Lander put it to bed. You put it to bed. I never did. Why do you think they sang a different song to the press? Didn't tell anyone about Benny Brownlow? Why do you think the body under the floor went missing? Why do you think I turned my badge in?'

Frisked by the past, Geats's eyes brimmed with a child's fury, the anger knocking years off him. Such was its ardour, a creeping doubt wormed into Cassar's mind.

'And the gunshot?' he said. 'None of the others were shot.'

'I don't know. There are enough similarities that it can't be coincidence, though.'

Spilsbury coughed politely. 'She was most likely a prostitute. If that helps matters.'

Geats dampened his glare. 'How'd you know?'

'Signs of infection. Traces of silver nitrate. Some tearing. And her lungs were not in terrific shape. A history of rough intercourse, venereal disease, and spending a lot of time outdoors.'

'You'll send the full report to me at New Scotland Yard?' Cassar said.

'Of course.'

'And do me a favour. Ask around your pathologist pals, see if there have been any others that raised suspicions. Bodies found in the rubble, but maybe there was some doubt as to how they ended up there.'

'You think it's the same man as before? That there will be other victims?'

'I'm thinking that if this is the same killer as '36 – and it's a big if – then whatever interrupted his killing is over, and this might not be his first victim since he started again. If he likes hiding bodies in floors, it's not like the city is short on collapsing buildings recently. All this destruction provides cover for his tracks. He's smart, and he'll have learned from previous mistakes. He probably knows how to disguise injuries to make them less suspicious.'

'He didn't in this case.'

'Maybe he hadn't finished with her yet.'

Geats was still seething as they left, sitting in the car in silence. Cassar turned the engine on and then off again, letting himself drift into Geats's muteness.

'You just left,' he said eventually.

'I jumped before I was pushed.'

'I meant us. Me. Billie.'

'Wasn't me who stopped going to the clubs.'

'You know what I mean.'

'We don't have to make more of it than it was. I hadn't seen you in years before Max Kassel was murdered.'

'You're sulking like I've done you wrong somehow. You say we were mistaken about Benny Brownlow back then. Okay, let's say we were. There's obviously a lot of things that you knew that you didn't tell me, so how is it my fault?'

'I can walk back,' Geats said, opening the door.

'If he's still walking the streets killing women, then we need to stop him. For real, this time.'

Geats sat back, letting the door close again.

'We need to talk about this, Leon. You need to tell me what I'm missing.'

'I've been out all night, what with you putting me in a cell and then needing to clear up our mess.'

'You're fortunate I hadn't got round to telling anyone in Flying Squad that I'd busted the raid.'

Geats sneered, head cocked to one side. 'Fortunate. Sure. I suppose you were planning on telling someone about the hundred and fifty quid, too.'

'Leon . . .'

'I have things to do. People to see.'

'Later, then?'

'Where?'

'Come round for dinner. Billie's roasting a chicken. I know she'd love to see you.'

'Yeah.'

'It's on Berwick—'

'I know where it is.'

Cassar nodded. 'You really think this is the same guy?'

'We didn't get him, Mark. And they don't stop killing until someone gets them.'

81

Geats jumped out at Piccadilly Circus. It was noon, and the streets were packed. Though people hid themselves away from the bombs at night, despite the not infrequent daytime raids, they scuttled about fearlessly in the light.

Hovering outside the Troc, he made sure nobody was on him before slipping into the alley leading behind St Peter's. The great secret of number 4 Sink Street was that the front door was never really locked, but the handle was on the hinge side, so you had to turn it and push the other end. That had kept the wolves at bay for years. Of course, any wolf who did get in would never get further than two or three steps.

In their office on the second floor, he found Harrison staring with Sphinx-like inscrutability into the smouldering hearth. Geats sat across from him and waited.

'I'd rather we not have to involve the Home Secretary too often,' Harrison said finally.

'Flying Squad were on the driver.'

'Your old friend Mark Cassar. He didn't make anything official, though. Other than detaining you for the suitably vague breach of the King's peace.'

'That was just about me and him. Old stuff.'

'Who dropped the bodies?'

'One apiece.'

'How did he get on the driver?'

'Tip-off. He didn't know it was petrol, or where it was coming from.'

'We need a lid kept on all of that until we identify everyone involved. Oil is becoming scarcer by the day. Reserves are depleted and we're struggling to keep up with essential demand. We're going to start dyeing approved stock red so it can be immediately identified.'

'Cassar won't spill the beans.'

'It would be nice to be sure of what he knows.'

'I'm meeting up with him later.'

'Good.'

'He's in a flutter about something else.'

'Oh?'

Geats had thought about this and knew he had to tread carefully with Harrison, given the frame job on Benny Brownlow had been his doing.

'Dead whore.'

'What is it with you two and this sort of thing?'

'Body has whip marks. Reminded him of the previous case.'

'I dare say that sort of thing isn't conspicuously uncommon.'

'She was hidden beneath floorboards. The pathologist said a razor strop was used, just like before.'

Harrison pondered that coincidence, staring at the dying embers.

'It's not inconceivable that it could be the same killer.'

Had to give him credit for the pure brass. 'Really?'

'The Germans hired someone to take care of a compromised agent, and in all likelihood tasked a bravo to do it. Someone who wasn't unfamiliar with a spot of killing. Stands to reason that sort of person might acquire the taste.'

'Yeah. Stands to reason. Whatever's happening, Cassar has invited me for dinner. I'll get close to him again, steer him off.'

'Yes. Very good.'

Harrison stood slowly, smoothing his suit and buttoning his jacket.
'I'll be gone the rest of the day. Do try not to get arrested again.'

'I make no promises.'

Geats watched him walk out of the office. The rest of the floor had been substantially rearranged since he first came to work there five years earlier. Walls had been knocked through or rebuilt elsewhere, offices furnished for administrative staff, and a small room kitted out for a switchboard operator. That was where Harrison had gone.

Peggy, the usual operator, left the room and went to the galley kitchen at the rear. He did it from time to time, made calls directly from the exchange rather than his office phone, so nobody could listen.

A few minutes later, his footsteps pattered down the stairs and Peggy returned to her post with a fresh tea. Geats sauntered in after her and leaned against the back panel, wires hanging out of the trunk-line jacks.

'Morning, Peg.'

'It's almost one o'clock.'

'It's morning in spirit, though.'

'It was definitely morning in spirit when you called from Tower Bridge nick at three a.m.'

'You handled it marvellously.'

'What do you want?'

He leaned in conspiratorially. 'He's having an affair, isn't he?'

'Who?'

'You know jolly well who.'

She glanced at the door. 'You know I couldn't possibly talk about that.'

Geats reached out and nudged it to with his foot.

'You'll get me in trouble, Leon.'

'It's just that he seems so . . . I mean, I can't even imagine him . . . you know. Coupling. With a woman.'

'*Leon.*'

'It is a woman, isn't it?'

'Of course it's a woman.'

Geats pulled a chair across and sat down beside her.

'Is she married? Is it all very clandestine? Is she someone important? Blimey, is it the queen?'

Peggy slapped him on the shoulder.

'I don't know who it is. Stop bothering me.'

'But somebody must know. The mystery is killing me.'

'All I know is she lives in Kent somewhere.'

'Kent?'

'I think so. I was accidentally reconnected once, after his call.'

'Accidentally. Of course.'

'It was a hotel at the rail station in Faversham.'

'Faversham? He's having an affair in Faversham?'

Peggy nodded, her eyes alight. 'And I saw a train ticket once. Same place.'

'Who on earth has affairs in *Faversham*?'

'I think it's romantic.'

'You would.'

'Usually, you can tell when he's going.'

'Yes. It's very subtle, the way he says, I won't be back today.'

'No, I mean in the morning. You can smell him.'

'Like a dog in heat? Can't say I've ever picked up the scent. Really, Peg, you're wasted in here. That sort of ability, there must be some better task for you in the war effort.'

'His cologne, silly. But today he wasn't wearing it. Must all have been a bit last-minute.'

'Came over him sudden, like. Bit of afternoon delight.'

Harrison was well gone when he got downstairs, but Geats stored the information away. Faversham. Something to look into at a later date. He always liked to have a picture of what his boss was getting up to.

It was a two-minute walk to the Yard. Punters gathered outside the Windmill, the curtain rising at midday to accommodate early performances so their audiences and chorus girls wouldn't be out till all hours.

He kipped in the first-floor flat now that Clara was gone – although gone only in the sense of being dead, as the million pieces of her sat in an urn on his mantelpiece.

The day she died, he'd left the window of her flat open. She'd been in the hospital several weeks and admonished him daily to air out the flat so it wouldn't be stale on her return. Rain reminded him, and he'd hurried back from the office to pull it shut. As he'd opened the door, a bird swooped down and crashed into the inside of the pane, bouncing through the open gap and skidding across the wooden floor.

He'd picked it up carefully, thin and fragile little soul, and nestled it in a turbaned towel on the windowsill, unsure if it was alive, and if it was, whether it was injured beyond recovery. Splashing water into a saucer, he had half an idea to feed it, but returned to watch it hop jaggedly along the sill before diving off the edge. Dashing to lean from the window, he saw its wings open and watched it soar out through the mouth of the Yard before rising to disappear in the glare of the sun.

He hadn't even shut the window, just took off running all the way to the hospital, huffing gracelessly up the stairs to Clara's ward, where between breaths he recounted the whole experience to her.

She had stared at him.

'Suddenly seemed important I tell you about it.'

'Leon, you need to find yourself a wife.'

Last thing she ever said to him. Memories sometimes came like that, plaguing him like flies about his head.

He washed and shaved in the shared hallway bathroom, and in a clean shirt went up to his old flat on the top floor. Knocking, he didn't wait for a response before going in. Garments in various states of cut hung from the picture rail along the hallway. A party of mannequins stood tightly in the living room, draped with fabrics of every stripe.

'You here?'

Nell popped up from the floor somewhere, pins sticking out between her lips. She spoke through them.

'Where were you? We were supposed to have breakfast.'

'Got detained. Fancy lunch?'

'Have to pop into college.'

'Did you ask about—'

'I think they're going to shut down pretty soon. Round the corner got hit the other night. Pretty bad, too.'

'Maybe we should think about sending you to—'

'I'm not a kid.'

'I'm not saying that.'

'And I can already cut dresses better than most of my tutors. If they close down, I'm going to make things to sell in the markets myself.'

'For as long as you can still find material, anyway.'

'Most of this stuff is cut from old garments.'

'Everyone will be wearing old garments soon.'

'I'm going to offer to make them glamorous new things from their stuffy old things. There is no reason why we can't look fabulous just because there's a war on.'

'Don't touch any of my old things. I look fabulous enough as it is.'

She narrowed her eyes. 'How about dinner when I get back?'

'I'm going out for dinner.'

'You're what?'

'Out. Dinner.'

'Why? How? With whom?'

'Friends.'

'Leon Geats, you don't have any friends.'

'Well, they used to be friends. I don't know what they are now. I'm told they have chicken, though. And for chicken, I'm prepared to befriend anyone.'

'Breakfast tomorrow, then? Assuming you don't get detained?'

'It's a plan.'

'I'll want to know all about these so-called friends of yours, so get your lies straight.'

82

The road hung empty.

Market stalls were truant, shoppers few and far between, every other shopfront boarded up from unrepaired bomb damage or because the owners had gone out of business. Geats jumped off the pavement into the street, gutters strewn with stray salad from the day's hawking. A kicked apple arced into the crater, splashing down in the pooled rainwater.

A tardy few examined the slim pickings left in the butcher's shop window, wondering how far their rations would stretch. The war was more than bombs dropping, and Soho was gradually falling victim.

Cassar opened the door.

'Wasn't sure you'd show.'

'And miss roast chicken? You must be joking.'

The air was thick with it as they climbed the stairs. Geats and Nell tried to eat at least one meal together a day, but usually threw together whatever they had. His work afforded him access to much more than they could get in the local shops, but they seldom went to the bother of cooking a proper meal like they'd had when Clara was still with them.

'I've got some pretty good single malt.'

'Wouldn't say no.'

Cassar jerked his head towards the kitchen. 'Go say hello, and I'll pour them in the other room.'

Billie had her back to him, tending to pots on the stove. Hanging back in the doorway, Geats watched her a moment. Her feet were bare and she stood with one ankle crossing the other. The room was baking from the oven, and she lifted the hair from the nape of her neck and wiped away the damp.

'Hey, Bill.'

She turned, glancing down at her pinny.

'You're early! I haven't changed yet.'

He pointed to the stairs. 'I can go back down and kick some apples around, return later?'

Grinning, she threw out her arms and hugged him like a bed at dawn.

'Hiya, chum.'

'I'm not sure if you know this, Bill, but you're in a kitchen. Cooking. With an apron.'

'It's not too late for me to poison your serving.'

'Smells like I'd die pretty happy.'

Standing back, she appraised him before punching him on the arm.

'Where have you been? What have you done? What's wrong with you?'

'You're not a copper any more. I don't have to answer your questions.'

'Mark hasn't told me anything. I only found out you were coming an hour ago.'

'I don't answer his questions either.' He lowered to a whisper. 'Imagine how that maddens him.'

'Heard that,' Cassar called through.

They had polite drinks in the front room. The world changed in increments: the pumiced conversation of estrangement; the souse of bloodied water in the gutter outside, the butcher tossing his bucket before closing up; finally, the pulling of thick curtains for blackout, cloistering them in shared understanding, wed against a common foe.

Billie served dinner, and by the time they'd wiped the grease from their mouths, glutted with chicken and flushed from drink, it was like the old nights at Chez Renée's.

'It was too cheap to turn down,' Cassar said, explaining how they'd bought the building. 'We were renting the upstairs. There was a small mole-faced chap down here—'

'Mr de Polnay,' Billie said.

'Yes, some kind of artistic type. He left when the bomb dropped – you've seen the crater?'

'It's a beaut,' said Geats.

'But I reasoned, what are the chances of another dropping on us? That one must have been a mistake. I know they like dropping them on civvies now, but they must prioritise areas with *some* strategic value. Soho has nothing worth bombing in that sense. Not like the east, with the docks.'

'The owner was also worried, I take it?' said Geats.

'He wanted out immediately. The place took a bit of damage, and two doors along had to be pulled down completely. There's a slight tilt, but nothing that can't be buttressed. I offered him two hundred, and he took it. Complete madness. We went from paying rent to collecting an income from the butcher downstairs and enjoying a two-floor flat. I tell you, there's a killing to be made buying up properties in London with all this going on. It's like money falling from the sky.'

They retired to the front room, having prepared themselves for the more serious business.

'The house where the body was, you find the owner?' Geats said.

'It was derelict. Damaged last year by bombing to the street behind. That part of Bermondsey, between the railway and the river, you got the wharfs and warehouses of Shad Thames. It's been bombed to shit.'

'Ideal place to hide a body.'

'Leon, you need to tell me what I don't know.'

Geats glanced at Billie.

'Tell us,' Cassar corrected. 'Only fair Billie knows. You lied to her too.'

'I can't tell you everything. Some of it even the Home Secretary doesn't know.'

'Benny?' said Billie.

Geats shook his head. 'Never hurt a soul. Frame job.'

'He can't have been completely innocent,' Cassar said. 'We found—'

'You found what you were supposed to find.'

'But the photos and the flex and the leather razor strop . . .'

'Yes, just exactly the right things.'

'If it wasn't him, why did the killer stop at four?'

'He didn't. He stopped at two. There wasn't just one killer.'

'Start at the beginning,' Billie said. 'Josephine Martin.'

'Kassel and Lacroix's people-smuggling ring had been identified by German intelligence as a way of getting assets into Britain.'

'Spies?' Billie said.

'Yes. They were already being watched before Josephine Martin was killed.'

'Her death was to do with that?'

'No. At the same time, nothing to do with that whatsoever, a gang of rival foreign pimps were establishing themselves in the West End. Kassel and Lacroix didn't know about them. Nobody knew about them. They sent someone to kill Martin, as she looked after all of Kassel's new girls. The idea being to spook the girls and maybe scare Kassel and Lacroix into moving on.'

'But they turned on each other instead,' Cassar said.

'Yeah. Which worked out even better than the other ponces could have hoped.'

'Some pimp killed her, then?'

'Not exactly. They had people working for them. Coppers.'

'Christ,' said Cassar.

'Gets better. You knew them.'

'Minter and Lander? Shut up.'

Cassar was getting het up, shining with a thin liquor sweat.

'They killed Stilts too,' Geats said. 'She knew about these other foreign pimps, and they found out she had spoken to me. That was my fault.'

'Come on, I've seen what those two were capable of first-hand, but I can't believe they just outright murdered two women. Leah . . . that scene was . . . that was butchery.'

'Minter did leave right after that,' Billie said. 'Always thought that debt story was sus.'

'I don't know about this,' Cassar said.

'Minter confessed the whole thing to me,' said Geats.

'When? Before he fled?'

'He never fled. He told me before I killed him.'

'Jesus, Leon. You know what you're saying here? That you killed a serving police officer? An inspector, at that, for God's sake.'

'He was a murdering piece of shit who I caught trying to kill a child. So I ended him.'

Cassar stood up and went to the curtains.

'Christ, I wish I could look out a window. I need another drink.'

'Bottle's empty,' Billie said.

'There something in the cupboard. Rotgut.' He went to the kitchen to search it out, leaving the other two alone.

'The child Minter tried to kill,' Billie said. 'That was Nell?'

Geats nodded.

'He didn't . . .'

'No. She was unharmed. Physically, anyway.'

'Is she still with you?'

'Yeah. Yeah, she goes to the trade school. Turning into a talented dressmaker. She has my old flat, and I stay in Clara's.'

Billie laughed. 'You and Clara? That must be . . . oh.' She faltered as it dawned on her. 'Oh no, Leon. When?'

'Couple of years ago.'

'I'm so sorry.'

'I found gin,' Cassar declared, tripping back into the room with a bottle in each hand. 'And bitters. Which together I'm sure make . . . something.'

Tongue fixed in the corner of his mouth, he crouched in front of the low table and with high elbows poured a dose of each liquid into their glasses, never the same twice, some mad gallipot.

Listing, he handed them their glasses.

Billie held hers aloft. 'To Mark Antony and Cleopatra.'

Geats clinked glasses. 'Merrily we go to hell.'

They both stared at Cassar, for whom toasts were a trial too far. He frowned.

'Jeanette Cotton? That wasn't Lander?'

Geats shook his head. 'No. That was the person we called the Brigadier. Cotton, and the woman we found under the floor.'

'And that's the man who's back killing again?'

'You don't see it?'

Cassar arranged himself ditheringly in his armchair and downed his glass in one. In his state, he couldn't be sure of anything.

'The girl under the floor, her body went missing,' Billie said. 'There were rumours at the time that it was something to do with the funny people. Spies, national security, all hush-hush. And now here you are, working for God only knows who.'

'Yes. Here I am.'

'The stories were true?'

'I couldn't say.'

Geats refrained from detailing the business of the dead Abwehr agent, not just because it was a matter of national security, but because he was beginning to suspect Harrison hadn't been entirely forthcoming with him about the situation.

'Are you opening a murder inquiry into the woman you found last night?' Billie said.

Cassar shook his head. 'Yes. No. Not officially. I've listed her as bomb dead for the moment, until we see where we are.'

'The scene was destroyed,' Geats said. 'There wasn't much to go on.'

Cassar drank himself snorey. He paled and sat straighter in his chair, pre-empting some unpleasantness. Billie caught on. She tried coaxing him upstairs, but he barely made it to the kitchen in time for a splashy respite in the sink. Returning, he smiled serenely and fell into slumber, wheezing like a steam engine.

Billie sat on the sofa beside Geats.

'He doesn't drink that often. Was never good with it.'

'I remember.'

'He always tried to keep up with you at the clubs.'

'That wasn't about me. He was figuring a few things out.'

'Still does a lot of figuring.'

'But it took you a lot less to work it all out.'

She smiled brightly, wearing it suddenly like armour.

'Breaking his leg was the best thing that ever happened to him. The other men respected him, catching the Soho Strangler. The fact that it never became public knowledge only helped him more. It was a secret, shared only by coppers. It made him, for a while at least.'

'When did you leave the force, Bill?'

'Soon after you disappeared. Had to. They didn't allow married women. Some who had been married before the rule, they were fine. But I knew if we married, I'd have to resign.'

Geats leaned back. Billie in the kitchen; Billie out shopping; Billie doing laundry. *Everyone becomes something other than what they believe they ought to be.*

Maybe she read his mind.

'I'm going back, though. Superintendent Peto has clearance to attest married women who were previously police, as they're so short of bodies on account of the war. I haven't told Mark yet, but I don't think he'll mind. Apparently there isn't a WPC at C Division at the moment.'

Geats shook his head. 'Savile Row.'

The Vine Street station had been moved to new premises, the old building now housing the Aliens Registration Office, which saw an avalanche of activity in Soho.

'He believes you, you know. Mark. About the killer.'

'Yeah, he's falling over himself to agree with me.'

'It's all I heard about when he got in this afternoon. I can already see it in him. He'll be on this day and night. He's mad is all, that you didn't tell him everything back then.'

'He's Flying Squad. The enemy.'

She laughed, nudging his knee with hers.

'I was mad too, you know. You could have told me. How did you get to a place where you thought you couldn't trust me?'

'I didn't want to put you in danger.'

She moved her knee away. 'Can look after myself.'

'Nobody could look after themselves against that lot. I only got out alive because I had help from . . . I don't know – a friend? Of sorts. Bill, Minter came to my home to murder Nell. He came to the flat with the express intent of killing a child, on the off-chance that she had witnessed something. Which she hadn't, not in any way she could remember properly. I only just got back there in the nick of time. Then there was the body to sort.'

'This friend of yours helped you with that, too?'

'They're a person with some authority.'

'A person you work for now?'

His was a silence of confirmation.

'Did Nutty Sharpe know about Minter and Lander?'

'Knew they were bent. Christ, who wasn't. I don't think he knew they were destroyers of women and children.'

'What happened to Lander?'

He shrugged. 'I don't know. He was shuffled off quietly somewhere before the war. I suppose he ended up serving. Any luck, he's buried in a field in France, or the African desert.'

Cassar dragged in a great stuttering breath and ripped out a yawning snore before farting. The pair of them looked at each other and laughed silently.

'Christ alive,' Geats said. 'How doesn't he wake himself up?'

Billie glanced at her husband, a cryptic look passing over her.

'What?'

'You said they were all bent.'

'I could always trust Mark to be Mark. Money Mark Cassar. He wasn't going round strangling women, I knew that much.'

'Different now, though. We bought this place, and the building next door. No way to deny it. But he's looked after me.'

'Thought you didn't need looking after.'

'That's different. It's not about need, Leon. It's want. The want to have someone by your side. A friend. An accomplice. Someone you make a team with, face whatever comes. He gave me that.'

'And he's doing well. An inspector now.'

'He works alone a lot. The others shy away from working with him, and his boss lets him dig into pretty much whatever he wants to. Kind of reminds me of how you used to be. I wish he were home more. He stays out all hours sometimes, I don't know if it's work, or . . . I worry about him.'

'I'm not going to dob him in, Bill. Whatever he gets up to, the money is better in your hands than Babe Mancini's. Graft is practically a way of life in Soho.'

'Not with you.'

'Only for purely selfish reasons. I never wanted to be in hock to anyone, in case I ever got the opportunity to crack their heads.'

She laughed, harbouring a little snort, and looked to see if he'd noticed. He had, and when she turned to him, he kissed her quickly; then, when she didn't pull away, he kissed her again. She pressed into him, a sharp, stubborn kiss as if making some point. He liked her thin lips and pulled the bottom one between his own, enjoying the daft beat of his heart.

There was a careful pause, filled with things he didn't understand. Billie knocked off her drink and picked up the other glasses.

'I didn't realise the time. Himself won't be in a good mood in the morning after a night in the chair with a skinful.'

She hurried into the kitchen and he heard water in the sink. Gave her a moment before going through. He stood close, but not too close, and waited for her to turn. Waited for her to speak. She didn't. He cupped her face. They kissed again and touched each other, and he felt anchorless with possibilities.

Then she turned her face away.

'I'm sorry.'

'Bill?'

'I can't. You should go.'

She fetched his coat, avoiding his eyes. He kissed her goodnight in a gentle fashion and turned the hallway light off so it wouldn't show when he let himself out the front door.

Finding himself in a manly state, he adjusted his trousers and turned back towards the doorway quickly when he saw a warden approaching. The old chap watched him carefully but said nothing. There didn't seem much for him to be doing in Soho that night. When he had passed by, Geats hovered around the crater for a spell, waiting for the thing to moderate itself, being disinclined to compromise himself further than he needed to by blundering into someone else during an artless attempt at concealing his erection.

He could see a fire raging to the south, St James's Square perhaps. Bright citrine smoke bloomed up, the odd spark, but at that distance he couldn't hear the sounds, the bone cracks of buildings losing their fight. From where he was, it was like seeing the war from the outside.

83

Geats maintained an interest in Cassar from a distance.

Billie's comments about him staying out at all hours intrigued him. Clearly, she doubted he was working, but he never saw his friend at any of their old haunts around Soho, and wondered if his habit of taking a taste on the job was getting him into murkier waters.

He wore clear eyeglasses without lenses, a hat with the brim low and a scarf pulled high about his chin, and disappeared into the passing streets as he followed Cassar. Often, he was at Scotland Yard as he said. Occasionally he sought out a quiet pint alone in a pub, or took long rides on the Tube lines that popped up above ground in the suburbs.

Only once did anything of interest happen. Having left a pub near Russell Square (which, as far as Geats could discern, he had gone to only because it was nowhere near where he worked or lived), Cassar walked haphazardly through the streets. Geats wondered if he'd had one too many, and then feared he had sensed he was being followed and was looking for his tail in shop windows.

It began to dawn on him that Cassar himself was following someone, though. Keeping his distance, not wanting to blow what might be an operation, he trailed his friend down into the Tube, onto the Piccadilly line heading west. The train was busy and chaotic. The line eventually going above ground, the long windows not only had blast nets but were painted black, with only a small diamond left clear in the centre through which to identify stations. Custom was for the nearest passenger to yell out the name.

Geats boarded the next carriage along and stood by the guard's controls, from where he could look through the door to where Cassar sat. At first, there were too many people to single out who Cassar might be following, but the further west they went, the more the crowd thinned out.

When they emerged from the tunnels, the lights were shut off to observe blackout and Cassar could barely make anything out in the dimness. The doors opened at Barons Court, glib darkness giving way to full moonlight. He was still there, sitting across from him in his uniform and looking straight at him now. High cheeks lent years to the soft, smooth face, the kind of recreant pleading in his eyes that told Cassar he'd have to make the first move. And he would, as soon as there were fewer others around, but the promise of the thing was tangible.

Out past Ealing Common, the carriage emptied of all but a few shadowy figures down the far end. It was the sort of ill-lit heaven where fleeting friendships formed, lasting no longer than the end of the line, or just their rigidity.

At Park Royal, the young soldier surprised him, springing across the aisle into the seat next to him. A second lieutenant, freshly ranked and raring to go.

At Sudbury Hill, the soldier cupped his chin like a tiny bird and kissed him.

At Rayners Lane, Cassar had the soldier's trousers unbuckled in a frenzy.

At Ruislip, someone stepped off the next carriage along, no more than five yards from them, and the soldier slipped down to his knees.

Coming into Ickenham, Cassar's head jounced against the window where he lay back, eyes closed, thinking how much better, how much freer his incaution in these dark cars was than the Jermyn Street baths where he sometimes had young actors go down on him.

By then, Geats had crossed the platform at Ruislip and was already aboard a train back to the city, no longer worried about Cassar.

84

Weeks passed before Geats saw Cassar again.

His attempts to trace Babe Mancini's black-market contacts proved fruitless after Babe took a knife to a fist fight with two-bob hoods Eddie Fletcher and Harry 'Little Hubby' Distleman, who were foolhardy enough to try running a racket on a racketeer. After nearly severing Fletcher's arm, he plunged the blade into Little Hubby's armpit, and he was done for on the steps of a Wardour Street club.

Geats pressed his claim on Babe at the highest levels of government and arranged for a sweetheart deal whereby if he pleaded guilty to manslaughter, he'd serve a hugely reduced sentence. He intended to bargain further for information on Babe's contacts. But the man was convinced of his natural rights to self-defence and took it to the jury, who, even after a sympathetic summing-up by a cooperative judge, saw only another Italian mobster and found him guilty of murder. Appeals had stacked up as Geats tried to game the system all the way to the Lords, who ultimately refused to overturn the conviction, putting Babe's fate in the hands of the hangman.

In between his judicial adventures, Geats kept himself amused by monitoring Harrison's comings and goings, drawing the switchboard girl Peggy into cahoots with him so he had the latest on his boss's affair in Faversham.

In the early evenings, he often attended the last show at the

Windmill, especially when they had a featured diseuse. His favourite was Dela Lipinska, and he was at a show of hers the day Cassar came to see him.

Geats always sat at the back, away from the raincoated regulars who huddled in the front rows where the air was close and the views more veterinary. He was as grateful an admirer of the nude tableau as the next commando, but for him the songs were really the thing.

A sultry and mischievous performer, Dela sang of street tarts and bawdy adventures. The mackintosh brigade huffed and puffed through her fully clothed numbers, willing on the arrival of the somewhat less coy feature acts.

Geats, though, was in love.

Dela sang in Polish, and the ribald subject matter didn't perturb him as he barely understood a word. Closing his eyes and letting her voice wash over him, for just a few moments he could believe he heard his mother again, deep in her cups and crooning along to her gramophone.

He tripped home on light feet, heading up to Nell's flat for his dinner.

She opened the door suspiciously happy with herself.

'Your friend is here,' she said.

Geats's immediate reaction was to wish he had a gun.

'Evening, Leon,' Cassar called out.

'Mark. I don't—'

'You didn't tell me you'd switched flats.'

'No. Well . . .'

'You've been to a show, haven't you?' Nell said. 'You have that relaxed look.'

'That's more or less accurate.'

'He stops in at the Windmill,' she explained to Cassar, the two of them having a good titter.

Geats hadn't told Nell about Dela Lipinska and the way she reminded him of Clara, as channelling his late mother through burlesque shows wasn't something he had fully unpacked yet in his own mind, lest he be impelled to monkhood.

'Graham Greene gives them a good write-up,' he offered.

'Probably part of some elaborate dig at Noël Coward,' Nell said.

She had Cassar standing in for her dummies, wearing one arm of a winter coat as she worked on the roll of the shoulder with her pins.

'Stay very still,' she warned him.

'This a social call, or a second job to pay that mortgage?' Geats said.

'It's business.'

'Don't mind me,' Nell said.

'Not for young gir—ow!'

'Sorry.' She withdrew the pin from his clavicle.

Geats showed him downstairs to his own flat, fetching them both drinks.

Cassar sipped slowly. 'I understand I had a few too many last time I saw you.'

'I always preferred you after a few jars.'

'Well, Jesus, Leon. Why don't we just carry on kicking each other in the balls.'

'You identify the dead woman yet?'

'No. I spoke to the sergeant at Tower Bridge, talked around the subject of missing whores, but nothing shook loose. I received word from Spilsbury, though.'

'New evidence?'

'Better. New body.'

85

Overnight, it rained.

Geats walked, as he usually did, finding London easier to navigate by foot. The shifting gradients of a city under siege, the erasure of streets and buildings; such was the subsidence of war.

The walkway on Hungerford Bridge was always packed, so he headed for Blackfriars, a more pleasant route. A handful of men were at work on the new Waterloo Bridge, which he was convinced would take a direct hit as soon as they opened it. Temple was on fire again, as it seemed to have been since the autumn. What was London? It wasn't quite a battlefield, though it looked like one. Armies didn't clash there, but death was dropped from above, and the only thing it didn't alter was the Thames, the great pulsating artery keeping the city alive.

Literally, at times.

Gawkers lined its banks, watching as boats pumped water from the river and launched it in great arcs to douse the flames, like blood routed to the scene of infection. Some of them on the way to work, some of them living rough; the Embankment was home to all colour of reprobates.

Cassar was already at Southwark mortuary, at the bottom of the gardens of St George the Martyr. Together with the pathologist, Dr Keith Simpson, he was hunched over a desk examining a spread of photographs detailing wounds to a dead woman.

'There's no body?' Geats said.

'She was removed for burial,' Simpson said. 'We couldn't identify her. The house had apparently been unoccupied, according to neighbours. The owners had sheeted everything over and moved to the country to see the war out. Nobody knew of anyone staying there. The body was badly burned, and suffered crush damage when the house fell. The head in particular.'

'She'd been shot?'

'At the time, it didn't occur to me. With the condition of the body, it didn't stand out. But I took photos because something just didn't sit right. See this?'

He pointed to a photograph, a close-up of a destroyed human head, half the skull missing.

'That crescent-shaped notch on the edge of that part of the skull? I didn't know what it was, although it did seem artificially caused. With the whole house basically coming down on top of her, the skull was so crushed there was no way for me to reconstruct it. But when Sir Bernard told me about his case, this one immediately came to mind. It certainly now seems possible it might have been a small-calibre bullet hole. What looked like pieces of bandaging were embedded in the injuries.'

'Spilsbury thought the other woman's wounds had been bandaged at some point,' Cassar said.

'There's something else. The top half of her body was very badly damaged, but her legs were intact. They had bruising and lacerations consistent with being struck repeatedly or whipped.'

Sifting through the pictures, he found shots of her legs.

'A leather strop?' Geats said.

'Yes. Something of that width.'

'You didn't think that was suspicious?'

'People indulge in all sorts of amusements. If I dedicated myself to everything I saw that was suspicious, I'd never get anything done.'

'How long do you think she'd been dead?' Cassar asked.

'Oh, she was alive when the building collapsed. There was no decomposition, and she suffered substantial blood loss from the wounds she received in the bombing.'

'Was she beneath the floor, do we know?' said Geats.

'No, she was in a Morrison shelter on an upper floor. That's what protected most of her body from being crushed. The end of the cage was ruined, which exposed her head, but the rest of her was preserved when the upper floors came crashing down on top.'

'And no other bodies were found?'

'No. She was alone.'

'She got into the shelter herself?'

'Well, there's no way to determine that, but if she had received a gunshot wound to the head and someone had treated it, as the bandage suggests, then it's entirely possible she had been incapacitated. There was bedding found with her, and she had soiled herself. That could have happened anyway, the injuries she had, but the state of her clothing certainly doesn't rule out the possibility she had been in the shelter for some time before the bombing.'

Cassar walked to a map of London on the doctor's wall. 'Where was this exactly?'

'Here, just south of the railway.'

'That's not far from the other body,' Cassar said.

'Straying from Soho,' Geats said. 'Going to where the bombs are dropping.'

Simpson gathered together the photos and notes.

'These are copies for you. I've spoken to other colleagues. Lone women, eighteen to fifty, with head trauma, I've asked them to pass any notes or photos they might have to Sir Bernard.'

86

Picking his way through the ruined streets of Bermondsey, Cassar was roused by marauding with Geats once again, though they were less partners than a twofold guiltiness. Reunited in picking up the tragically sharp pieces of a job they'd badly botched.

Having believed the case had been brought to a conclusion, if not ever officially closed, he hadn't given it a second thought in the intervening years, other than the unconscious acknowledgement that it had shaped his path in the police.

Geats, however, must have considered it from time to time, knowing as he did that they'd been wrong. That must have swelled within him as a tumour might. Yet here he was, no less of a grousing old bastard than he'd ever been, but first through the breach, unquestioningly at Cassar's side.

The street where the body had been discovered was a Georgian terrace of half a dozen four-storey homes, the lower floors with incised stucco facades. The middle pair had taken a direct hit, collapsing their fronts, and fire had spread, causing widespread destruction. Windows black and empty like skull eyes, the floors behind them fallen through into the semi-basements. It had never been clearer just how hollow a city was.

'End one there,' Cassar said. 'It was the third floor, but they all collapsed into the lower ground.'

The front door was missing, and there was no floor inside; the stone steps led up to the short porch and a pit of rubble. A few beams, charred and groaning, clung uncertainly to the walls, otherwise they had a clear view to the sky above, the roof consumed by the blaze.

The coffin-shaped Morrison shelter protruded from the piled bricks and timber that filled the basement, but was unreachable from the front door without hazardous climbing.

'Downstairs,' Geats said, pointing to the lower entrance beneath the front steps.

The door was open, and the area outside the window was heaped with cleared rubble where firefighters had searched for survivors amongst the ruins.

Cassar peered up through the wrecked house.

'Don't fancy spending too long down here.'

'With you on that.'

Geats clambered carefully up to the shelter, making sure of his footing at every step, and looked inside.

'Anything?' Cassar called.

'No. Nothing except for some blankets. It's strange, though.'

'What?'

'It's fully enclosed. Someone has riveted a hatch door to the side that is usually open. The blast sheared the end off, but there's a hasp secured with a padlock. On the outside.'

'She was locked in?'

'Looks that way.'

As Geats slid back down the mountain of wood and plaster on his heels, Cassar spotted some papers and scattered photographs near the wall and went to investigate. He had to look at them three times before he believed what he saw.

'Jesus.'

'What is it?'

He handed the pictures to Geats: skin shots of young women in various poses. They were charred, some burnt beyond identifying the models, but others were almost complete.

'Recognise them?' he said.

'The chaise longue. And those thick drapes.'

'They're the same as the pictures found in Benny Brownlow's room.'

'And the material we took out of the Domino Milk Bar. It's the exact same studio set-up. That little guy we found in the vaults beneath the milk bar, he was the photographer.'

'You remember his name?'

'No. He had a place near the baths on Marshall Street, where he took the pictures. He went down for the smut, though. God knows if he's still there.'

'Something to look into. If our man bought photos from the milk bar . . .'

Geats was kicking about the rubble near where Cassar had found the photos.

'Here,' he said, holding up a badly dented biscuit tin. 'Buried beneath all this, must have saved it from the fire. There's dozens of them inside.'

'My God, he was keeping her alive here.'

'The dead woman?'

'Remember the Tower Bridge body? She'd been shot and someone had treated her; someone with medical training, Spilsbury thought. But she died, so he hid her in an empty building. Shad Thames, only a matter of time before more bombs fell there. Maybe he was going to go back, smash up her head and take her to a bomb site, make it look like she was killed in a blast.'

'But he was beaten to it by the Luftwaffe. Some irony in that. We might not have realised she was murdered otherwise.'

Cassar looked up at the Morrison shelter. 'I think this is where he got the idea. This was before Tower Bridge, right? Months ago. He shoots her in the head, bandages her up, and she somehow survives. He keeps her in the shelter—'

'Which is pure luck, because the family had it installed before they abandoned their home for the countryside.'

'Right, but the point is, he returned to this place. He had his photographs stashed here. And then it's bombed.'

'Which isn't the disaster he first thinks it is, as it covers up the murder.'

'Exactly. So he tries to repeat the trick. The Tower Bridge body, he stores it in a bomb-evacuated building, waiting for another bombing to take advantage of. Use Jerry to hide his kills.'

'But the building collapses before he can make arrangements.' Geats examined the photographs again. 'Look at these images. The women look doped, or asleep. All of them.'

'That's his thing? He likes them unconscious?'

'Might explain the gunshot lobotomies.'

Both knew what the other was thinking. He would try it again with other victims until he achieved the desired outcome: a living, breathing, vegetative prisoner.

87

Marshall Street was a tight road to nowhere, almost always resting in shadow. Up past the public baths, at its northern end, it turned into a tighter cobbled place where a congregational church had proved so popular it now housed several industrial workshops, lathes and presses humming away with the same air of sombreness.

The school built opposite at the same time had also ceased operations and was now a warehouse, except for the photography studio housed in the grand third-floor gable.

Geats pointed to a nameplate beside the door. 'Fowler. That's him. Mind if I do the talking?'

'By all means.'

Fowler opened the door at the top of the stairs and immediately recognised Geats.

'Oh God. What do you want? I've done nothing wrong.'

'I very much doubt that, Mr Fowler. Might we come in for a quick word?'

Fowler held the door open. The studio was large and bright, sun flooding in from the south-facing gable window.

'You did a year over that business I rousted you for, didn't you?'

'Ten months.'

'Managed to hold on to this place?'

'I paid the rent in advance.'

'Profitable enterprise, making grot with little girls.'

'I have other money.'

'You do look the type does this for the juice rather than the dough.'

'I don't do that any more.'

'No. No, course not. Roaring trade in family portraits and whatnot.'

Geats threw a selection of the biscuit tin photographs on a table.

'Your handiwork?'

Fowler hesitated.

'Pretend for a moment this isn't a trap, and that your cooperation would go some way to repairing your reputation with the various law enforcement agencies in this city. From that of a grubby pornographer and chickenman to something approaching the kind of citizen who I would never consider throwing face-first out that window that they might splash on the cobbles below.'

'Jesus Christ,' Fowler said, shrinking back.

'When did you take them? Around the same time we arrested you?'

He shook his head.

'No, these are on a different stock. More recent. Probably two years ago.'

'Just before your retirement from such filth, no doubt.'

'You still sell them through Babe Mancini?' Cassar asked.

'I'd like to help, but you're putting me in a tight spot.'

'Babe's in the Ville,' Geats said. 'He goes to the rope tomorrow. You can spill all you like on him.'

A pause while Fowler drifted out of focus, no doubt weighing up the ramifications on the one hand of speaking out of turn, and on the other of the kind of misunderstandings that led to being tossed out of windows. In the end, such decisions always boiled down to the same hunch – life was cheap.

'He sold them through the mail,' he said. 'Started doing that after losing stock in raids on the shops.'

'How's that work?' Cassar said.

'Punters sign up. They send money, and we send back the pictures.'

'From here? You have lists?'

'Babe took care of it. I gave him the prints. He liked having the names and addresses.'

'Blackmail,' Cassar said.

'You still do this for him?' said Geats.

'Not since that business with Little Hubby getting knifed. Everything's gone quiet since then.'

Geats spread out some of the photos. 'These kinds of shots, with the girls looking all daffy. Did people order them? Like, commission jobs?'

'You could say you wanted to receive ones like that, but we took 'em like that regardless. Made the girls easier to work with.'

Cassar slapped the little man so hard one of his shoes flew off. He looked up from the floor in bewilderment.

'You get a pass here, on account of the information. But it's a one-time thing. Flying Squad will be keeping an eye on you, and you don't even want to know about this crazy bastard.' He jerked a thumb at Geats. 'Who he works for, they don't even got a name. Receipt of a blow to the chops would be the least of your concerns.'

Geats confirmed this. 'Spectrum of my activities begins with a reduction of consciousness and runs to entire existences vanishing without so much as a batted eyelid. Understand?'

Fowler nodded like something was broken.

The stairwell echoed with their hyena cackles as they ran down to the street. Cassar tossed the biscuit tin in the boot of his car.

'We need to talk to Mancini.'

'Can't be me,' Geats said. 'I was in with his mob for almost six months. He sees me and realises I was playing him, he'll go loopy.'

'Yeah. We need a softer approach. I know just the man for the job.'

88

'That's more like it,' Geats said.

Billie trudged into the lounge in her uniform, throwing her hat on the sideboard and dropping dramatically onto the sofa. She eyed him curiously.

'The constabular get-up, I mean.'

She closed her eyes. 'You'd think there'd be too much to worry about with the war for people to be up to no good, but there's more crime now than I ever remember.'

'War is chaos,' Geats said. 'And chaos is the natural locus of thieving and skulduggery. The streets can't be as much fun without me, though.'

'There's certainly less drinking and skulking in dark corners.'

Cassar pulled the thick drapes, one last peek out the thin gap as wardens were already on the prowl outside.

'We need you for something tomorrow,' he said. 'I've cleared it with your super.'

Billie's nose twitched. 'You two dragging me back into your murder business?'

'You're going to prison,' Geats said.

'Oh good. Might get some rest.'

'See Babe Mancini.'

He outlined the plan, the information they needed about the smut postal service Mancini provided.

'I should wear my uniform, or a gown of some kind?'

'A gown?' Cassar said. 'You're a police constable. We need this on the level.'

Geats grinned. 'Always with the dressing up.'

Billie stood. 'D'you suppose the old wardrobe still exists somewhere?'

Taking her hand, Geats invited her into a twirl beneath his arm.

'Dancing shoes await the lady, resplendent in silks and finery.'

Cassar had forgotten how much it annoyed him, the pair of them babbling away like he wasn't there, even more now she was his wife.

'That collection of tarts' frocks?' he said.

Geats was aghast. 'How dare you? We procured evening wear from only the most exclusive dens of iniquity.'

'The madams of Mayfair,' Billie chimed in.

'The bawds of Berkeley Square.'

'The fishmongers of Farm Street.'

Cassar could see he'd only made things worse.

Billie was animated now. 'You could have got anyone from Flying Squad down there to talk to him. You want me because I'm a woman, and you think he might look favourably upon that, last hours of his life, bit of sport, so forth.'

Geats shook his head. 'You being a WPC is the thing. If I know Babe, that'll provoke a stronger response.'

'Hard to look fetching in it, but whatever you say.'

'Your uniform will do nicely, Constable Massey.'

'Constable Cassar,' she said.

That threw off Geats's thinking.

'We should talk through what to ask him,' Cassar said. 'How to broach the topic.'

Geats was staring at the untouched drink in his hands.

'Leon?' Cassar said.

'Hmm?'

'You with us?'

'No. Yeah. I've had an idea. Someone I should go and talk to, in case this doesn't pan out with Babe.'

'And tomorrow?'

'You two can figure the details. I'll see you both at Pentonville, bright and early.'

Getting out of the flat as quickly as possible, he walked briskly down to Shaftesbury Avenue. It seemed relatively quiet up above, only the distant clack of gunfire accompanying him. Through Piccadilly and along into Mayfair, people were venturing out tentatively to enjoy themselves, anticipating a hail of bombs at any second.

Albemarle Street was a wider, grander cousin to the back streets of Soho, lined with imposing Georgian terraces. Serendipitously located in the basement of one of the area's few concrete buildings, the Medusa Club had opened its doors every night through the war so far, to a Mayfair set who dressed up but partied down. Along with the best jazz acts of the day, it often hosted writers and poets reading their more risqué works; a photograph hung somewhere in the club of Henry Miller holding forth about a prostitute called Germaine, with a drunken Dylan Thomas and T. S. Eliot in attendance.

Garfield was standing at the bottom of the basement stairs in a dicky bow. He looked Geats up and down.

'Afraid it's evening wear only, sir.'

'Garfield, it's me.'

'Strictly enforced policy.'

'Geats. Leon Geats.'

'Out of my hands.'

'You don't remember me?'

'I remember that the last time I saw you, Flying Squad goons shot up the club on Lisle Street, then hunted down Benny and killed him, and spread the word locally that he was some type of crazy murderer, so we had to close down Chez Renée's because nobody would go there.'

'Oh.'

'And I remember the look on her face when she thought about you, and what I really don't need is to have to clean up a dead copper tonight.'

'I'm not a copper any more.'

'That will make the task less of a worry.'

Simone appeared at the door behind him, wearing a gentleman's dinner jacket, her short hair in smoothed peaked lines tweaked over one ear, the back cut up in soft shingles. It was all set off by a look suggesting she was in no mood to play.

'This sorry motherfucker.'

'Wotcha,' Geats said. 'Wondered if I might come in for a spell. Class the joint up a mite.'

Simone shook her head in amazement. 'Been a while, Geats.'

'I try to avoid Mayfair when I can. Reputation to uphold.'

She nodded for Garfield to let him pass.

The basement stretched back beneath the twin property behind, on Old Bond Street, making for a surprisingly large club. The decor was elegant and expensive, yet on the small stage burlesque girls performed a striptease.

Simone showed him into an office with a window that looked down the length of the club.

Geats took a seat. 'I'm not sure if this is a step up or down from Renée's.'

'I don't get raided as often.'

'No. I'll bet. Who pays for it? Jack Isow still backing you?'

'Jack has always been a good friend.'

'I thought he was selling salt-beef sandwiches out of a café after his spell inside.'

'What is it you want, Geats?'

'Five years ago, when the killings were happening—'

'Thought we were done with that. Everyone told me it was Ben. Told me so many times, I had to close Renée's and start from scratch.'

'You don't think Ben killed those women any more than I do. There have been developments.'

'Developments? That what you're calling dead women now?'

'Do you remember anybody at the club who was a bit odd? Specifically, anyone who had a medical background.'

'There was one guy was real odd.'

'Yeah?'

'Used to come in almost every night, just sit in the corner on his own, watching everyone else enjoying themselves. I think he might have been a police officer . . .'

'Funny.'

'It was five years ago. I don't know.'

'You still see any of the old faces from back then? Could you ask about? I'm looking for someone who might have been a doctor, or perhaps had medical experience from the last war.'

'I didn't ask people what they did, honey.'

'All right. It was a long shot.' He pushed himself out of the chair and went to the door. 'It's good to see you doing well, Simone. It's good to see you at all.'

'I heard stories about you. That you left the police, but not really. Became some kind of spook of Soho. That true?'

He said nothing.

'Leon, I might need your help.'

'This a you-scratch-my-back-type situation? You being shaken down? The Italians are all gone, aren't they? Half of the Sabinis have been interned. Who's running protection round here now?'

'No. It's nothing like that. It's . . . more official.'

'Police trouble?'

'Home Office. Someone from the Aliens Department told me I needed to register.'

'You're Italian, so I suppose that isn't a great surprise. I don't think they're going to flag you as a risk, though.'

'That's just it. They told me that because they couldn't find any record of a Simone Calcavecchia, I would be listed as class B, and possibly upgraded to class A and taken to an internment camp, unless I could provide the right documentation.'

'You don't have your birth certificate?'

'No. But even if I did, it don't say Simone Calcavecchia on it. Geats, I'm not Italian. I'm black.'

Geats laughed. 'You're not black.'

'I never knew my father. He was a Creole sailor who stopped off in Cardiff, and nine months later my mother was stuck with me. My name's Clifford. I don't know what his name was.'

'Then why . . .?'

'In Cardiff and Swansea, it wasn't difficult getting gigs as a black woman. You had Spadie Lee and Clara Wason, and a whole host of band members. When I first got here, London was different. I'm light enough to pass, and it made it easier if people thought I was Mediterranean. There was no fuss.'

'But now being Italian is more of a problem.'

'Yeah. And the Aliens Department guy didn't believe me when I said I was black.'

'Probably someone claiming to be black in order to save their skin was a new one on him.'

'What is it you do, Geats? Can you help me?'

'Maybe.'

'But I have to help you?'

'No. I was going to do it out of the goodness of my heart.'

'The girls from back then, I don't see them. They don't work here, and most of them moved on from the club life. I can ask around some of the bands. Anyone who was a doctor, or had medical knowledge . . .?' Her eyes drifted off.

He leaned forward. 'There was someone?'

'Snakehips did a spell at medical school.'

An image from the past, spying through a ceiling hole at Snakehips on his knees, examining a saxophonist at the behest of aristocratic sisters.

'Urologist, if I recall.'

'But Leon, the things this man has done, you can't possibly believe . . .'

He shook his head. 'Doesn't seem likely. I'd like to speak to him, though. You still in touch?'

'I can reach out. And I'll ask around. Garfield might remember someone.'

'That'd be helpful. He's back, Simone. He's killing again, and using the chaos of the war to cover his tracks.'

89

Classrooms in the school where Geats had received Catholic instruction had been broadly similar: wooden floors polished to a shine, dull walls of uniform colour, everything just a little too bright. The brothers would have approved of the execution room at Pentonville.

The pale green walls lent the empty room a sickly hue. The large double-leaf trapdoor was clearly marked out at the centre, and the only other features were the four-foot lever standing beside it and the three two-inch link chains dangling through the hatches in the ceiling from the beam in the gallows chamber above. A rope noose was shackled to the centre chain.

Harrison had arranged for them to have access to Babe Mancini despite the governor's protests. He made his displeasure at their presence known by way of silence.

'We appreciate this, Mr Ball,' said Geats.

Ball sniffed and opened a door leading to the antechamber separating the execution room from the three condemned cells.

'The door must remain locked,' he said, addressing some undefined spot on the wall an inch or so above their heads. 'A guard will be posted outside, and will endeavour to enter as quickly as is possible should anything unfortunate occur.'

Billie glanced at Geats, who shook his head. He and Cassar kept out of sight as the cell door was opened, immediately huddling around the small grate when it was closed again so they could listen.

'You why I've got this?' Babe said, rattling the cuffs that restrained one wrist to his bed.

'I can have them remove it if you like,' Billie said.

'Wouldn't want you feeling uncomfortable. I feel like I know you.'

'I'm C Division.'

'Yeah, but from a while back.'

'I used to run with the Dirties out of Vine Street.'

Babe grinned. 'Leon fucking Geats. What a head-knocker he was. Ended up taking my coin after he was shuffled off the force.'

'Do you recognise this?' She handed him one of the photographs recovered from the biscuit tin at the second murder scene.

'Aye aye. What's this? I've heard of the condemned man being granted a final meal, but this seems a little too amenable.'

'It's your work?'

Babe studied the picture.

'Looks like the ones old Fowler does for me, yeah.'

'I understand you offer a postal service.'

He dropped the photo on the bed beside him.

'How about we cut to the chase here. What is it you want?'

'How many customers do you have?'

'A lot.'

'We'd like to see the list.'

'You need the name of a client? All right, what's in it for me? What kind of deal can be done?'

'Mr Mancini—'

'How badly do you need these names? Only, you might have noticed I'm in a bit of a predicament here.'

'Your appeal in the Lords failed. I'm afraid there's nothing—'

'There's nothing to talk about, then.'

'Look—'

'Pretty lady comes to my cell, morning of, showing me lewd and obscene pictures and asking me to cough up confidentials on my loyal paying customers? I didn't know better, I'd say Geats was behind this.'

He stood up, right shoulder sloped where the cuffs restricted him.

'You out there, Geats? In the shadows like always?'

The cell door opened. Geats nodded for Billie to leave.

'Son of a bitch,' Babe said. 'You was police all along.'

'Not exactly.'

'The raid on the petrol, that was you?'

'Not that it matters now, but no. Flying Squad blundered into it.'

'What are you, then? Setting up some sort of queer roost in my mob. Intelligence? Government ghoul?'

'If you like.'

'I do not like. What the hell have my photos got to do with anything?'

'We're looking for a man, an extremely dangerous man, and we know he used to buy pictures from you.'

'This man one of your lot? An operator?'

'I don't know.'

'But he's dangerous. And you want him.'

'Yes.'

'Fuck you, Geats. Are you why I'm here, staring down the rope? Did you do this to me?'

'I tried to save you, you moron. All you had to do was plead guilty to manslaughter, and they'd have given you a light-touch sentence. Then I'd have gone to work chiselling away at that, bringing it down to nothing. But oh no. You had to plead not guilty and offer righteous indignation in front of a jury who were just looking to have someone like you swing.'

'Well, get me out of here now.'

'Can't. It's gone too far. There's nothing I can do.'

'Then why on earth would I help you?'

'Honestly? I can't think of a single reason. But this man I'm looking for, he's not like you. Or even me. The things he does . . . he's something else. And he needs stopping.'

Babe considered the photograph again.

'Guess I'm going to stretch on the rope anyways. Why not do one good thing before I go, what you're saying.'

'Can't do any harm, few minutes before your maker calls you to account for yourself.'

Babe nodded. 'Kingly Street.'

'Behind Regent Street?'

'Number 23. Upstairs, offices on the top floor. Go easy, now – the boys are usually armed. And, for the love of Christ, don't tell anyone it was me sent you. Still got a reputation to think of, even in death.'

There was a knock on the door and the governor appeared.

'It's a minute to nine.'

Geats nodded. He took back the photograph.

'Babe—'

'Save it.'

Outside the cell, the governor was suddenly chatty.

'Disturbs the whole place for two days. No activities from the time the prisoner is brought to the cell. No movement through A Wing at all; we move the men to B or to the reception hall. All the staff had to be here at half six this morning. The main gate is frozen. We have to screen off the pathways out to the burial field. Won't be back to normal until after he's in the ground, two or three o'clock probably.'

'Distressing for everyone,' Geats said. 'None more so than Mancini.'

'Our Albert is a professional. Best noose man there is. Mancini won't even have time to think about it.'

Two wardens marched Babe through the antechamber to the place of execution. A hood was pulled over his head and the noose secured. When the executioner gripped the lever, the event had taken on a wild momentum of its own, no more than twenty seconds since Mancini had left his cell.

'Cheerio!' Babe said merrily, before he vanished through the trapdoor and his neck was snapped.

90

Cassar visited a friendly magistrate and put together a squad of door-kickers from the Sweeney for the raid. They mustered on Regent Street and at the designated time poured into Kingly Street from both directions and took number 23. There was a stenography and typing service in the ground-floor shop, with a separate door leading to the basement and the upper floors.

Following Cassar and his troupe of jackboots down the narrow street, the instant he saw the building Geats knew they'd been had.

'Christ, stop it!'

'Leon?'

The bruisers rushed the side entrance, thundering up the stairs, banging on doors and shouting.

'This is where the Nest used to be, in the basement.'

'I don't—'

'Moishe Cohen had Little Hubby Distleman run it. The man Babe stabbed.'

'Shit.'

Cassar hurried to the door.

'Sergeant, pull your men back, we've be—'

It was too late.

Gunshots were exchanged upstairs, the cracks reverberating along the halls and down the stairwell. A window smashed, glass shattering on the pavement below. Someone cried out. And like that, it was over.

'Bloody hell.'

Cassar ran up the stairs to the third floor, where armed Flying Squad men huddled round a door. They parted slowly. The window overlooking Kingly Street had been shot out, and a bookcase blasted, exploded paper fluttering in the air still.

Two men lay dead on the floor.

Geats pushed Flying Squad heavies out the way and looked over Cassar's shoulder.

'Christ.'

'Who are they?'

'See him, with the brace thing on his arm? That's "Fair Hair" Eddie Fletcher. Russian Jew. Runs with Moishe Cohen and Joey Franks and the Yiddisher Gang.'

'Jews? This isn't an Italian place?'

'Eddie was at the Palm Beach Club when Babe did for Distleman. Got himself cut up first. Babe sliced him down to the bone; they almost had to take his arm off at the hospital.'

'So this was all bollocks? He just wanted us to hit the Yiddishers?'

Geats laughed. 'It's almost brilliant, when you think about it. No wonder he was so happy when he hanged. Last thing he did was set up the men who got him in the mess in the first place.'

Laughing still as he trotted down the stairs, singing out, 'Cheerio! Cheerio!'

91

The night everything changed forever began with cold baked potatoes and spam fritters.

'This is terrible even for you,' Nell said, peering dolefully at her plate.

'My plan was a fish supper and some bread to make a chip butty.'

'Explain to me then why I'm faced with . . . this.'

'No bread left. Picked up a couple of spuds at Lyons. And the chippy was out of fish.'

'It's amazing I've survived this long in your care.'

'I surprise my own self.'

Tallulah slinked in and out of chair legs, hoping for droppings.

'Sorry, Loolah, no fish tonight.' Nell broke off a piece of fritter and offered it to the cat, who turned her nose up.

'Won't get far with that attitude,' Geats said.

The phone rang, and he sat in the armchair to answer.

'I've been calling you for days.'

'Simone?'

'Where have you been?'

'We don't all work nightclub hours.'

'You *always* work nightclub hours. I have something for you, what you asked about punters with medical experience.'

The case had not been going well. Babe Mancini's execution, coupled with the internment of Darby Sabini, had removed two key leaders from the Italian mob, and the remaining crews had failed to coalesce in their absence. Geats had run down some of the faces he was familiar with, but nobody knew much about the postal smut service. Mancini had kept the paperwork for himself, the addresses potentially valuable blackmail tools. Geats had resigned himself to waiting for another body as the only course of action left.

'Can you come to the Café de Paris tonight?'

'Sure. That where you're going to be?'

'I'm working. It's Snakehips.'

'Good old Snakehips. You tell him I want to talk?'

'His band is in residence at the Café now. I called him up, trying to get him to do a one-off at the Medusa, and we got talking about the old days. I mentioned what you were looking for and he said there was something he wanted to tell you.'

'That's all he gave you?'

'Said he'd only speak to you. Geats . . . if you're going to drag him into something, make sure you protect him.'

'All I'm looking for is information to set me off in the right direction.'

'Set starts at ten. He's never early, though, so probably best to seek him out later on.'

'Thanks, Simone.'

'I haven't heard back from the Aliens Department. I assume I have you to thank for that.'

'Probably they realised their mistake.'

He had asked Harrison to have a quiet word in the right ear at the Home Office, make it known Simone was a friend of the court and therefore not to be bothered.

'Whatever happened, I'm grateful. Maybe come down the Medusa sometime. Drinks on the house.'

'Challenge accepted.'

When he put the phone down, Nell was impatient to quiz him. 'Snakehips? Snakehips Johnson?'

'Old acquaintance.'

'I demand you tell me everything.'

'There was a time when we would run through tunnels together.'

'You do know that most of the time I barely understand half of what you say.'

'You make it sound like that's not by design.'

'We are talking about *the* Snakehips Johnson? The West Indian Orchestra Snakehips Johnson?'

'He wasn't always big-time. Five or six years back, he was singing in Soho dives where I drank. I slipped him away from a raid or two.'

'And you're seeing him tonight?'

'He reached out. Might know something about this case I'm working with Mark. Talking of whom, I should give him a bell, meet him over there.'

'Can I come?'

'Absolutely not. It's strictly business.'

He rang Cassar, and Billie picked up.

'How do you fancy going dancing?'

92

At ten o'clock, Geats hurried down Coventry Street, past the darkened Corner House, and bumped into Cassar wearing a tuxedo.

'You made it. Billie said you were napping. Out all last night?'

'Some of us don't choose our own hours.'

'Uh huh. Where's Bill?'

'She went on ahead, as you said you were going to be there before ten. You'd think she'd know about you and your timekeeping. There she is.'

Billie hovered in front of the door to the stairs leading down to the basement ballroom that housed the Café de Paris. She'd come dressed for dancing in a floral number that played round her legs as she swivelled this way and that. Spotting them, she waved excitedly.

Geats whistled, drawing a look from Cassar.

'Apologies, old sport. Wholly inappropriate.'

The man on the door recognised Geats from a distance and finally waved Billie in, her dress several magnitudes less formal than the Café's usual evening wear. By the time they reached the top of the stairs, she was disappearing from view at the bottom into the small lounge that led to the gallery overlooking the main dance floor.

The set had begun, Snakehips's voice wafting up the stairs to them.

'He didn't give any indication what he wanted to talk about?' Cassar said.

Geats shook his head. 'Must be someone he knew from back in the Chez Renée days. Obviously didn't want to tell more people than he had to, but—'

A huge blast from below knocked them off their feet.

Dust and debris surged up from the club, choking the stairwell and exploding out into Coventry Street in a great mushroom. Geats thought the whole building must be coming down. Blindly he picked himself up from the carpeted steps and bounded down to the lounge area.

'Bill? Billie?'

'Here.'

She was sitting in the middle of the room, shaking the dust from her hair. A shard of glass from a light fixture was buried in her thigh, and she touched it charily.

'Oh dear.'

'Walk that off in no time,' he said.

'Leon . . .'

She pinched the glass between finger and thumb, and he laid his hand on hers and squeezed.

'Don't pull it out.'

He studied the glass, lightly pressing the skin around the wound.

'I don't think it's deep.' He patted her leg. 'Joan Crawford will remain envious.'

Her laugh turned to a sharp intake of breath as the movement jarred her leg.

Cassar burst into the room, waving away the muck still hanging in the air.

'Billie, you all right?'

'Here, Mark,' Geats said.

'What's wrong? Oh dear.'

Billie nodded. 'That's what I said.'

Shrugging off his jacket, Cassar draped it round her shoulders and knelt beside her. He held his hand out to Geats.

'Give me your tie.'

Geats loosened it and pulled it over his head.

Cassar slipped it over Billie's foot and up past the glass, pulling the tourniquet tight around her thigh. As he did so, he said, 'Go check if anyone else needs help.'

Human voices were making themselves heard from the dance floor below them, the extent of the carnage becoming clear. A special constable clattered down from the street with a couple of wardens.

'You folks hurt?'

'Down there,' Geats said, waving them on.

Only one half of the grand double staircase was usable, the other wrecked by the explosion, its iron balustrades bent, blocking the steps. The small stage nestled between the two staircases, but was covered now in rubble and furniture blown off the gallery above. A chair stood atop the piano.

In his white evening jacket, Snakehips Johnson lay at the back, beneath the shredded stage curtains, shrapnel having unburdened him of his head. Guitarist Joe Deniz sat beside the piano scrutinising his ruined foot, from which bone clearly protruded.

The blast pressure had been contained and condensed by the underground chamber, and beneath the gallery whole parties remained at their tables as if awaiting their meals, the shock wave having killed them where they sat. A woman, undressed by the blast, wandered naked among the debris, stunned by her new deafness.

At the far end, tables had been cleared and a woman identifying herself as ATS was organising a triage for the wounded. She said her name was Mardie, and Geats thought she'd make a fine general if such things were allowed.

He guided a man with cuts to his face to Mardie's area, sitting him in a chair with a handkerchief pressed on the lacerations. A wife cried for her husband. A bent trombone hung from the balcony by its bell tube. A scavenger pulling rings from dead fingers was chased off by the constable.

Geats totted up the dead and called it quits at two dozen.

Scores more were injured.

Firefighters and the Heavy Rescue party arrived and set about clearing the scene of unnecessary people. Stretcher-bearers and a medic took over from Mardie, and Geats walked her back up to the street.

'You don't have any shoes.'

Her feet were cut and bleeding.

'They were new and they pinched. My feet were sore, so I left the dance floor. That's when it came through the ceiling.'

A mobile first-aid post had been set up outside: the back of a converted removal van. Geats insisted on Mardie going in and having someone look at her feet, and begged a pair of boots for her from a fireman.

Cassar found him. Billie was sitting on the pavement outside the Prince of Wales Theatre, leg bandaged and complaining bitterly about her dress being ruined.

'Snakehips?' Cassar said.

Geats shook his head.

'Shit.'

Geats watched amused as Mardie took over the first-aid post, directing nurses and wardens this way and that in her giant rubber boots.

'How is it?' Billie said.

'In there? About the same as out here on a bad day.'

'How many?' said Cassar.

'Stopped counting. Thirty, probably. Could have been worse. I don't understand how the damn thing got all the way to the basement. Through the hall of the Rialto above, sure. But how does it then fall twenty feet underground before it explodes?'

'Heard one of the firemen say it found a ventilation shaft. Lucky hit, went straight down it.'

'Lucky.'

The seriously wounded were emerging on stretchers. The dead would be next. Those who could walk stumbled away from the scene bandaged and shaken. Geats considered the wages of luck.

'Here.'

Cassar held out Geats's tie. He took it, dangling from his fingers, stained with blood.

'Thanks . . .'

Stuffed it in his pocket, feeling Billie's eyes on him but resolutely refusing to meet them.

'Christ,' he said, spotting Simone running down the street towards the club. He dashed across the road and intercepted her, leading her over to the other two.

'Kenny Baker told us,' Simone said breathlessly. 'You know young Kenny? Trumpeter. Good one. Plays the cornet too. He's from Yorkshire, but he's been down here playing with George Chisholm. He's RAF, plays with the Squadronaires.'

She was wearing a trouser suit without the jacket, and Geats put his own coat around her.

'Simone, you're shivering.'

'Kenny was coming to the Medusa, I said he could get a jam. He was passing by when the blast happened. He ran to tell us. Leon, what happened? Is Snakehips all right?'

Geats wrapped her up in his arms.

'Tell me.'

'I'm sorry.'

'No . . .'

He felt her face against his neck.

'How about we get you home.'

Cassar helped Billie to her feet. 'I should get you inside, too.'

'How are you on that leg, Bill?' Geats said.

'Pit and the Pendulum.'

Geats cast around the place. Wardens and constables had blocked off the road from Piccadilly Circus to the end of Coventry Street, but an adventurous few were still braving it, including a telegram messenger on his BSA. Geats flagged him down and discussed the principles of defence of the realm, making sure they saw eye to eye.

The lids on the sidecar were raised, and Geats lifted Billie and Simone into the tub. The less brilliant aspect of his plan was him and Cassar having to run behind the bike as it cut into the Soho back streets. They caught up at the corner of Meard Street, where Geats helped Simone out before waving the others off round the corner to their flat.

Simone was quiet. It had been the simplest of things to turn the terror of the early raids into the most ordinary business; days and nights of bombs dropping everywhere became routine. What choice was there? But life was quickly shaken up when one of those bombs landed on someone you knew.

Geats thought to put her to bed. Hot-water bottle; woolly socks; rear-flapped boiler suit at hand should the sirens sound. It was a hectic night. The sky was alive with fire and tracers, and he mooted the idea of seeking shelter immediately, but she didn't want to leave.

She tossed aside the hot-water bottle and grabbed a bottle of gin. When he closed the curtains, she opened them again, so he flicked off the lights.

'What is the point now?' she said, gesturing to the lambent flicker of bombfire across the window panes.

Stepping out of her trousers and pulling her shirt over her head, she lay naked atop her sheets and watched the shrieking darkness rain down as she drained the bottle. Geats didn't know where to look. He felt the tie in his pocket, the stickiness coming off on his fingers. Murmured his excuses and went to leave.

'Stay, Leon. Come here.'

He lay beside her, and for a long while they did nothing but watch the city burn. He rubbed his fingers together but knew the blood was still there in the dark. When finally she undressed him, she did so with the precision of a hunter gralloching a deer.

Eyes thick and impure, pulling on him with wet grip. She'd chewed up twice the men Geats was, but began gently, soothing his clenched jaw, kissing his eyes. The need to forget was too great, though; she scratched his shoulders, and he cried wildly when she gnawed on a nipple.

He snorted through flared nostrils. Twisted fingers into her furls and yanked. Burrowed his nose beneath her arm, inhaling deeply and licking the damp skin as wadded tufts tickled him. His tongue rimmed her navel, parted her toes, his teeth found the softness of her hips and the rough of her heel. Lust's shapes hiding between incendiary flashes, their room as open to the world as the flaming sky was to them.

Afterwards, his neck throbbed for a good while, the gin on her breath eddying softly into the room. There was an erasure of all thought, and the surety that came with that was, Geats believed deeply in that moment, the thing all life should aspire to.

93

Women with no names.

No lives.

Defined only by their deaths.

It was ever thus.

Spilsbury found another one, the body already destroyed but with all the hallmarks of their man. No bandaging this time, but serious head trauma and found in the rubble of a house in Finsbury. A rover; back on his old side of the river, but further east now.

Babe Mancini dead.

Snakehips Johnson dead.

Searches of their homes and related properties turned up nothing pertinent. The medium 'Hellish' Nell Duncan was contacted, but neither could provide her with anything of interest.

One rainy afternoon, Billie called with a lead. Behind Berwick Street was a small mews crowded with warehouses and workshops. The upstairs of one building was used by a Jewish tailor and his wife, who was a dress-shop madam, to store their fabrics. The stables beneath housed a shtiebel. The tailor had called the police on one of his employees, a seamstress who he claimed had been pilfering wool from him.

At the woman's flat on Frith Street, they found a small room stacked with what the tailor estimated to be almost five miles of textiles.

'You know what this is? I could outfit over a thousand gentlemen with this wool. Eight years I employ you, for what? So you could steal from the very first day? Timeless goyishe back-stabbing.'

The true tragic figure of the whole affair, however, was the felonious seamstress's husband, who through no fault of his own was suddenly found to be in possession of materials of the most obscene variety as a result of the police search. Materials that were clearly the product of Babe Mancini's smut-peddling ring. Holding out for an entire thirty seconds of interrogation, he gave up the address where he had mailed his payment.

Geats met Billie there, a slight shopfront on Cecil Court, a narrow cut-through between Charing Cross Road and St Martin's Lane.

'Looks empty,' he said, nose pressed to the glass.

'Was an antiquarian book dealer. Moved here from Enfield a few years ago, but cleared out when the bombs started dropping. Didn't want to lose his stock in a conflagration, so went back to Enfield.'

'Devil and the deep blue sea. Landlord?'

'Working on it. We think he's—'

Geats put in a door light with his elbow.

'Oops.'

The shop was slender; a window at the back overlooking a yard had been papered over. The walls were bare, floor clear apart from a faint carpet of dust. No footprints – it had been empty for a while. Stairs led down to a basement and a room protected by a hefty door.

Billie rapped on it. 'Solid steel.'

'Used to be the heart of the film industry, before the war. All that nitrate stored up, fire safety was an issue.'

'Handy for security now—oh.' She turned the handle and pushed it open. 'Unlocked.'

Filing cabinets, empty drawers hanging out, lined the walls, which were soot-stained, as was the ceiling. Open film canisters lay around like dirty plates, their contents removed. A steel drum stood in the centre. Geats peered inside, finding ashes and the molten remains of celluloid.

'Kept their own films here. Paper records too, probably. Burned everything.'

Billie reached into a drawer and plucked out the charred remains of a single photograph, still recognisable as the creature Fowler's work.

Geats laughed.

'You have to hand it to Babe. As a dead man, he's made more of a bollocks of us than anyone drawing breath ever did.'

94

The summer saw clothing rationed, and Nell took up residence in Mrs Gal's dress shop in the building Cassar owned next door to his and Billie's home. She provided what she called haute couture repairs, and offered bespoke new garments cut or altered from a huge range of quality old pieces she had been collecting for years. Her deft renovations proved extremely popular with locals.

Geats maintained his interest in Harrison's habits.

One July morning, Harrison placed calls directly from the switchboard and excused himself for the afternoon, Geats watching from the window as he strolled out of Sink Street.

'Off to Victoria, is he?' he said, leaning in the door frame to the telephony office.

'First class on the Chatham main.'

'You get a whiff of him?'

'Oh yes. Walking round in a cloud of cologne. Don't know how he expects nobody to realise.'

'No. Me neither.'

If Harrison really was having an affair he wanted nobody to know about, then nobody would know. Geats had no intention of playing silly buggers following the man halfway across Kent, ducking out of sight and risking being seen. Whatever Harrison was hiding, he was doing it in plain sight. Geats had no doubt he was going to the

Railway Hotel in Faversham, and banked on anyone who knew about it also suspecting he was having an affair and so not bothering to look into it beyond that.

The next morning, so as not to create a paper trail, Geats arranged to hitch a ride on a freight train heading for Dover on the Chatham main line, jumping off as it slowed through Faversham. He carried the road bag he always kept ready at his flat, and when he arrived at his destination, he walked with a stiff leg and the aid of a stick; his usual way of pre-emptively fending off questions about why he was roaming around freely instead of serving his country dying at sea or among the dunes.

Directly across from the station was the hotel. There was no way Harrison would use the place for any kind of sensitive rendezvous unless it was friendly. Intelligence would have cleared the owner, who would receive a stipend for making a room available; it was probably permanently booked. Asking in there for someone fitting his boss's description would ring immediate alarm bells.

Opposite the station stood a grand Georgian house, double-fronted with bow windows, a motor shop in one half of the ground floor. A sign painted on the brickwork on the side of the house pointed to a garage round the back and offered cars for hire and a taxi service.

Behind the counter stood a middle-aged woman with thick hair that looked as if it required drastic shaping to get it into its current composition. She wore a sulk, but hastily rearranged her expression when she noticed Geats.

'Hello there, love.'

'Morning.'

'Something I can help with?'

'I really don't know. I saw the sign painted on the side of the building . . .'

'Taxi or hire car?'

'Either, really.'

'Well, we don't have any vehicles to hire at present.'

'Ah. The taxi?'

'Off road currently.'

'That's a shame.'

'Not much use anyway, amount of petrol we have. Good for a couple of local runs at best. Nothing like the business we'd ordinarily do with the station right there. But that's war for you.'

'It is a terrible inconvenience.'

'Between you and me, we ran the thing on pink paraffin for a spell. Got a garage round back, see. My husband's a wonder with the engines, and still had it purring.'

'But not now?'

'Mort Lancaster was driving it at night, and discovered he couldn't see the trees quite as well without headlights.'

'Must have skipped his carrots.'

She tittered politely.

'You looking to get somewhere special, love? Can see you don't fancy a long walk.'

Geats raised his stick. 'Norway.'

'Our lad's in the RAF.'

'Godspeed. In truth, I'm not sure where I'm headed. If I could take you into my confidence, since returning with this leg, I was found a civil service position. Good steady work, and thankful for it. But I felt as if I could contribute in some other way still, and have been conducting a few private inquiries. For the most respectable people only, you understand.'

She nodded keenly, sensing scandal or some other delight.

'Friend of mine, good man. He died at Trondheim.'

'Oh.'

'He had a letter I brought to his widow, and I told him I'd look out for her if she needed anything. Well, she met a gentleman, or he seemed a gentleman. Nothing outwardly improper, and it wasn't a rushed thing, but these aren't times to be alone.'

'Certainly not.'

'Only, she's starting to have suspicions about him. Work trips, you see. He says he's government, essential for the war effort, though nobody I know can find any trace of him.'

'Don't like the sounds of him.'

'Now don't get me wrong. Could be on the up and up. Could be working for something they don't make public; I know how it is. But he does seem to spend a lot of long afternoons in a room over at the Railway Hotel there.'

'Long afternoons?'

'Upstairs room. Doesn't spend the night.'

She tutted. 'Poor woman.'

'Why I asked about the taxi, see. If maybe your driver remembered bringing a woman here.'

'You want to ask Fred behind the bar there.'

'Thing of it is, if they go there on the regular, he probably wouldn't want to jam them up. No slight on him. They're loyal customers as far as he's concerned. And I don't want to tip my hand, least of all because I might yet have the wrong end of the stick. It's one of those careful situations.'

'Yes, I can see.'

'Of course, she might be local, which means my taxi idea would be kaput anyway.'

'I couldn't imagine anyone round here getting themselves tangled up with a married man.'

'From what I've managed to find out thus far, I believe she might be foreign . . .'

A teenage girl emerged from a door behind the counter with a steaming cup of tea.

'Who's foreign?'

'Joyce!'

'Mum.'

The girl weighed Geats up.

'Get you a cuppa, mister?'

'I'm fine. Thanks for the offer.'

'There's that Polish one,' Joyce said, taking a loud slurp from her cup.
'Polish one?'

'Out Throwley way, near where the Harrises live.'

'The Baron Harris,' her mother explained. 'He lives at Belmont House. Five mile or so south of town.'

'I'm a land girl,' Joyce said. 'Day off today. But I've been on a farm down that way. Some of the girls who come from further away, they live there. When we have a dance here in town, Bert takes them back with Bessie.'

'Bessie?' Geats said. 'She's the Polish one?'

'No, silly. Bessie's his horse. He has an old governess cart and runs them home in the dark.'

'Bert does a bit of that,' her mother agreed. 'Suppose you might call him something of a taxi driver.'

'And there's this Polish woman he brings into town. He told us, says she's dead sophisticated. Comes here once a month or so. Always smartly dressed. She was here yesterday, matter of fact.'

'Over at the hotel?'

'Yeah.'

'You know where she lives exactly?'

'Not exactly, but Bert said it were somewhere near the woods. Big house for one lady, he reckoned.'

'That'll be the old Harris place,' her mother said.

From his bag, Geats produced a map and spread it out on the counter. 'Whereabouts would you say that is?'

She pointed. 'There. Bit of a hike for you, though.'

'I'll make out. Thanks for your help.'

Playing up his gimpy leg, he hobbled out of the shop and across the rail tracks. In London, he could stick out a thumb and pick up a ride in no time, empty seats being an enemy of the war effort. Faversham had considerably less traffic these days. He was half a mile out of town when he heard horse hooves, putting a bit extra on the leg for sympathy's sake.

The farmer pulled up, cart piled high with hay, and told him to jump aboard, taking him to within a short stroll of where he was going. Geats showed him his camera, said he was looking for birds. Pretending to be an inquiry agent had already created a mess Harrison would have to deal with; locals thinking this woman was a man-eater. There'd be a reckoning, and it wouldn't be pleasant.

The house was hidden from any road by surrounding trees, and he approached it the long way round through fields, so as to remain unseen. A Georgian manor, it had the castaway look of a place someone had happily allowed to be requisitioned just to get it off their hands.

Settling down in a dim copse with a view of the rear of the house, he spied through his camera lens. It was a couple of hours before she emerged, wearing working clothes and brandishing a trowel, setting about the rose beds. He took pictures and left as quietly as he had come, catching a passenger train back to London before dark.

At Sink Street, he developed the photographs himself. Harrison was still in the office, sitting at his desk.

'Where the hell have you been? Running about with Cassar again?'

'No. Something else.'

Geats closed the door.

'Remember '36? The business with the dead spy?'

Harrison caught himself before he spoke. Calculations running through his mind: a day after a visit to Faversham and Geats brings this up. He already knew it was coming before Geats put the photos on the desk.

'I wondered if you could tell me how someone who was found dead under a floor, and whose corpse we stole from the coroner, is alive and well in the countryside and pretending to be your Polish mistress?'

95

'I'm going to have you sent to France,' Harrison fumed. 'I'm going to have you parachuted in right on top of Paris.'

'It is her, then?'

'Jesus Christ, how did you find her? Did you follow me?'

'I followed the breadcrumbs you dropped, this affair story to give cover to the truth. Then I poked around in Faversham until I found her.'

'Poked around?'

'Might be a handful of locals who think there's a marriage-wrecking Pole living nearby.'

Harrison made a call.

'It's me . . . No, listen. Pack a bag . . . Not the hotel. I'm coming to get you. Soon as possible, a couple of hours probably . . . I'll explain when I see you.'

He replaced the handset with deliberate precision.

'You have no idea of the trouble you've caused me. And how did you . . .' He trailed off, looking towards the office door, imagining he could see through it to the switchboard room.

'Don't even think about doing anything to Peggy.'

'We need people working here we can trust.'

'You concocted the cover story of an affair, so don't hold it against her that she believed exactly what you wanted her to believe.'

'Didn't expect her to tell all and sundry.'

'She didn't. I already had the scent, and I'm the only person she ever spoke to about it.'

Harrison didn't look convinced.

Geats wagged a finger. 'You think I'm causing trouble now, that girl loses her job and I'll blow up your entire existence.'

Harrison stared at him, waiting for him to fill in the silence. Geats put all the photographs and the negatives on the desk and sat down.

'I'm not going to tell anyone. You'll have to move her, and that's unfortunate, but you should have told me. Especially as you knew it impacted something I had been investigating. There are women dead, and the reason they are dead is because you provided cover for their murderer.'

'Jesus, Leon, millions are going to die across this continent, and you're worried about a few—'

'Few what? Whores? Yeah, who gives a damn?'

Harrison slumped down in his chair.

'You know how this works. Hard decisions based on priorities. She has proved an incredibly valuable asset for us. She's important, if we're going to win the—'

'Win the war. And what about the next war? Or the one after that? Where do we draw the line on this kind of thing?'

'There is only one war. It is never-ending and contains multitudes. We call it the world. It began when we crawled out of the swamps and stood upright, and if it ever comes to a close, one way or another it will be with fire, and there will be nothing at all after that.'

'Save the mystical bons mots for the greenhorns. You must have thought it had worked out so well. You had the perfect story to leak to the Germans, and then the killer seemingly stopped, so you had the perfect story for me.'

'It was serendipitous.'

'What if he had carried on killing?'

Harrison shrugged. 'It wouldn't have mattered. Not in the larger picture.'

'There is no larger bloody picture. *This* is the larger picture. Me. You. Us. Everyone. You do what you can for people and—'

'I don't have the energy to argue this with you, Leon. I did what I thought was best, and I still believe I did the right thing. But now I have to go and make sure the little good that did come from that right thing is safe and continues to be safe. Five years, she's got by just fine. And you ruin it all in one day.'

Geats got to his feet. 'You really believe millions are going to die?'

'Probably, yes.'

'Then what was the good that came from what you did?'

'What?'

'If millions are going to die anyway, what was the good? This has to be more than a game.'

96

Billie was on about her chickens again.

'The flat roof out the back, on top of the shop. Has to be fifty square feet. Build a coop out there, plenty of eggs every day.'

Geats tucked into the powdered egg omelette she'd cooked.

'This is lovely, Bill.'

'Mmmovely,' Nell managed through a mouthful.

Cassar shook his head sadly. 'Place will smell of chicken shit twenty-four hours a day.' He could already imagine a toxic whiff of things to come.

Billie nodded. 'Eggs, though.'

It had become a regular thing, Geats and Nell coming over. Cassar didn't mind really, as it meant he didn't have to find excuses to be late so he might dodge dinners alone with Billie, and the constant battle to fend off swallowy silences that matured between them. There was at least some semblance of a marriage to be found at the dinner table now, although an outsider would be hard pressed to decide who the husband was.

Nell jabbed her fork into her food. 'These are better than real eggs.'

'We'll have none of that talk,' said Billie, widening her eyes in mock horror.

'I don't care who hears it. Magic egg powder is the best.'

'Leon, what have you done to this girl?'

'She's entirely a product of herself,' he said. 'I take no responsibility.'

Nell dug him in the ribs with an elbow and in laughter their joy was illuminated by the flash of Billie's camera.

'That's a good one,' she said.

Cassar wondered what it would take for him to look that happy, the kind of captivating delight that attracted camera lenses. He thought of the scuffed old dance floor at Chez Renée's.

Geats jerked a thumb at Nell. 'This one tell you how good she's doing?'

'She's our hero,' Cassar said, sincerely. 'Clothes being rationed, Mrs Gal was talking about shutting the shop. Now people are flocking there.'

'She doesn't even care any more that I'm not really Jewish,' Nell said, another great wodge of omelette going in her mouth.

Geats shrugged. 'What are you talking about? Your mother was Jewish. You're as Jewish as me.'

'That's what I mean.'

That wasn't unfair, Geats reasoned.

When they finished, Nell helped Billie with the washing-up, and Geats followed Cassar into the lounge, told him about Harrison's spy and the fiction he had concocted around the body found beneath Jeanette Cotton's floor.

'Who was she, then?'

'Another tart, most probably. Foreign. No family. Not missed.'

'We heard the stories, that she supposedly was a German agent. It made it easier, as we could link Benny to the first and last killings—'

Geats scoffed.

'Thought we could, at any rate. If the killings were nothing to do with spies, then this Brigadier character – what's his major malfunction?'

'The girl in the floor was his first. He'd planned it – renting the room for three days from Allen, using the suitcase to hide the body. Cover it in lime to speed up the decomposition. Problem was, his execution wasn't up to scratch. Wrong kind of lime, damage to the mattress drawing Jeanette Cotton's attention. He has to kill her to shut her up.'

'But then he stops.'

'Spooked by the attention the killings got? The press were furious with stories of a new Ripper, four dead women, connecting deaths he had nothing to do with. The woman under the floor, he'd planned that out. He'd been working up to it – we know what happened with the young governess, and there were probably other incidents with local brass we don't know about. But then the Cotton killing happened, not in the way he liked these things to go down. Maybe ruined it for him for a while. Or perhaps there's some other reason.'

'He was in jail?'

'Or he went away. Abroad, or lived elsewhere. Or the circumstances of his life changed.'

'This medical angle of yours; he could have been at school. Or moved to a different hospital or practice. You know what, we should hit the streets again. Question the working girls.'

'It's different out there now than it used to be.'

'Exactly. Flashing their little lights on and off in doorways. I'm not even sure some of them are brass in the strictest sense. But we could ask them about doctors. About rough trade.'

'Mark, you need to dial it back. We messed this up once, but getting obsessed with it isn't going to do anyone any good.'

'What other leads do we have?'

'I think Snakehips knew him. Maybe from medical school.'

'How's that?'

'Simone told me he trained to be a doctor for a while. Dropped out to pursue his music.'

'Ooh, Simone.' Nell danced into the room with two steaming cups of tea and handed them out. 'All he goes on about now, Simone this and Simone that.'

'I've never once talked about her to you.'

'No, but I can tell you want to.'

'Talked about who?' Billie said, passing a cup to Nell and drinking from her own.

'His girlfriend,' Nell said.

'She's not my girlfriend.'

'No? You sleeping at the Yard tonight, then?'

Geats took a long drink of hot tea.

'Ha! Exactly.'

'Who's this?' Billie said.

'Simone,' Nell said in a sing-song voice.

A frown creased Billie's brow. 'From the Medusa?'

'Leon's been seeing her. Mostly between dusk and dawn.'

Geats put down his cup. 'Jesus, Nell.'

'Hey, I encourage this behaviour. I've been telling you for years you need a woman.'

Cassar watched Billie desperately seeking Geats's eyes, and him stoutly avoiding her look. Their marriage was little more than an affiliation, in truth, yet some counterfeit proprietary tugged at him. The itch of shabby pride.

Billie excused herself to fetch the pudding, a prune sponge to serve with the tea. She thickened the water the prunes had soaked in with Bird's to make too much sauce because she knew Nell would want extras, as she did with anything sweet.

When they were finished, Nell delighted Billie by showing her how to replace the broken heel on her evening shoe with a cotton reel, Geats getting in on the mirth by raising the possibility of adding lifts to his own boots.

'That's one of my most popular mends in the shop.'

Then the *coup de grâce* – stewing in self-imposed exile in the corner armchair, Cassar was caught unawares by Nell presenting him with a package neatly wrapped in hand-decorated brown paper.

'What is it?'

Geats hooted. 'Such revelations are the culmination of unwrapping gifts, Mark.'

Pulling at the paper with bashful hands, he found his favourite coat, relegated to the wardrobe these past months as he'd worn the lining into a torn and ratty mess that hung like old spiderwebs.

But no longer.

Re-lined with brilliant blue silk embroidered with gold cranes in an Oriental style, it looked better than it ever had. He stood, holding the jacket wide open to take in the full effect of the intricate golden birds.

'Nell . . .' His voice was tear-clogged and snagged on the way up.

Nell was bouncing. 'Try it on.'

His arms slid luxuriously into the sleeves, and it fitted as well as it ever did, trim round the waist. He laughed. A giddiness swarmed him, as with impending danger, or the koan-like verve of his hairier dalliances in the cottages of Covent Garden.

He thought he often had it wrong, that this was a group of people with whom he did belong. A group he could call home. If he'd known in that moment the things that were to come, he would have fought to wring every drop from it he could.

97

Geats walked Nell back to the Yard. She was buzzing from the reaction to the coat – and the celebratory gin Billie had smuggled her – and chatted breathlessly the whole way.

He stole a few hours' kip before walking round to Simone's about three. She had got in just before he knocked, and was still changing out of her hostess suit. He asked about her day and she said her friend Henry had been in.

A writer, he was obsessively terrified of death, and yet had signed up to the Auxiliary Fire Service. Packing his wife and son off to the country, he grew lonely and despondent in his fear, and was increasingly drinking to cope. A few weeks earlier, Geats had been in the Medusa and Henry had drunkenly involved himself in the burlesque, ending up sitting on the fat naked shoulders of a solidly put-together dancer as she walked him up and down the club, her chalky white jiggle not half as obscene as the demented grin on his face.

'Christ, did he behave himself?'

'He took the film from a magazine photographer's camera and dropped it in his rum, smoked a cigarette with me in my office and said he was in love with me, and then wished he was in Burma.'

'I think they amount to much the same thing.'

She threw a shoe at him.

It was warm and they lay naked in bed. It was a lively night, the rumble of distant action, but she dozed off in his arms immediately. Geats was certain he'd never sleep again.

98

Knocking awoke him.

Simone was up, sitting on the edge of the bed pulling on the legs of her siren suit.

'Another raid?' he said.

She shrugged groggily.

He glanced at his watch; they'd been in bed less than an hour. He touched her shoulder. 'Let me get it?'

She nodded.

Stepping into his discarded trousers, he pulled them up with a jump, opening the door shirtless to find Billie standing there. Her gaze slid past him, finding Simone's naked back; witnessing the reality of it for the first time. She riveted her eyes back on him, a hurt in them, but one enveloped by sadness.

'Billie. I—'

'I remembered, from the night they hit the Café de Paris.'

'You remembered.'

'They called Mark. You need to come.'

'They? Who they? Is Mark all right?'

'Yes, it's not—it's the Yard.'

For a moment, Geats thought she meant New Scotland Yard.

'Leon, a bomb hit your building.'

His throat thickened. 'How bad?'

He saw then that she had been crying, had tried to wipe it away before she knocked.

'Oh God.'

'I'm sorry, Leon.'

'Oh Christ.'

He walked back into the flat, went to the window as if he might catch a glimpse from some impossible angle. Smoke ravelled blazingly red into the sky, unspooling across a city aflame, wrapping it in its arms, smothering some and stirring others. There could be an exhilarating freedom to night if you weren't assured to make morning.

'I'm sorry,' he said, to nobody in particular.

There followed a period of things happening at a pitch he couldn't quite process. He was running in the road, shoes but no socks, shirt buttoned at irregular intervals with the tails flying. Billie got lost behind him somewhere. He'd never run so hard. It wasn't far, a few hundred yards at most, but he couldn't have told you which streets he took.

The Windmill and the pubs were untouched, but flames escaped the windows of the building cornering the mouth of the Yard. The basement clubs had erupted, punters spilling out into the street, drinks a-slosh and fags in mouths, firefighters and wardens trying to battle through them to the scene. Their survival inconveniently interrupted by the efforts to save the other buildings.

One of the tin hats stopped him going into the Yard.

'Not in there, mate.'

'I must.'

'I'm not being difficult, it's just not on. The whole—'

Geats lifted him beneath his arms and deposited him off to one side, making his way around the S-bend of the Yard and stopping dead. The front of their building was gone; rather, it amounted to a pile of rubble that filled the yard like scree at the foot of a mountain, sloped against the still-standing back wall, patchworked with the decoration of different flats, including Clara's floral wallpaper and his own billiard-baize green.

Men stood in the mess, throwing bricks out with their hands. One had a torch. From their grim looks, he knew they hadn't found anyone alive. Geats tried to reconstruct the building in his mind, imagine it falling, but he had no idea how such a thing would unfold. Nell would have been on the top floor. Would that have helped?

He scrambled up the mountain of ruins, bricks and timbers falling away beneath his feet as he climbed. A man shouted at him, then left him to it. He was certain he would recognise something, a belonging or piece of furniture, but everything had been whisked into bland and unidentifiable destruction.

Miaow.

'Loolah?'

The cat shook herself off and rubbed against his leg, seemingly oblivious to what had happened. She was white with powder and darted her tongue in and out to rid her mouth of the stuff.

'Where the hell did you come from?'

Miaow.

On all fours for balance, he crabbed about atop the twenty-foot heap, finding an opening: a slender shaft burrowing down where a fallen beam still held up the ribs of broken joists.

'Torch! Who's got a torch?'

The men below halted their work, looking up.

'You found something?'

'There's a way in. A cat got out.'

'A cat?'

'I think I can hear something,' he lied.

'Here, catch it,' a man called out, and tossed up his torch.

It was a bulky lamp-like thing, with a front screen that dipped the light groundwards. Geats shone it down into the hole. It was tight, and narrowed further the deeper it went. Maybe six feet down he could see the taps of his bathtub; it was on its side, forming a small chamber he thought he could get to.

The shaft was at an angle, and he squeezed in head-first. It was awkward, and meant supporting his weight with his arms, but the space was so constricted he wouldn't be able to see anything feet-first. Having left his tie at Simone's, he removed his belt and used the lamp's clip to hang it in front of him, his belt around his chest and the screen removed so the light was full beam.

The heat and dust were stifling, and he sweated bullets from the effort, which didn't help with seeing anything. The bath was resting on joists, beneath which was what appeared to be a solid mass of brick rubble. He tried to bend his arms and ease himself into the tub, but could no longer take the strain and lurched face-first into it, cutting his head.

'Blast it.'

Pausing to get his breath, he mistakenly let his thoughts wander, trying to conjure how he might think back on this later, if he ever made it to a later. But his mind was mum. There was a blankness beyond his present predicament, no way forward making itself readily available to him. He fostered doubts the world outside that heap continued to exist.

Opposite the tub, floorboards stood on their end with darkness behind them. Some hidden space. Tugging and pulling, he couldn't shift them, so spinning round and bracing his back against the bottom of the bath, he kicked out at them. They weren't going to splinter or break, but after several good goes he loosened whatever they had nestled into enough that he could work them to one side, opening a small aperture he thought he might fit through.

'Nell? Nell?'

Someone called from outside, but he couldn't make them out. The fallen building shifted slightly, the rubble a living thing, and the thought that he would trap himself at its heart was all-consuming. Wedging his head and shoulders into the channel behind the boards, he shoved off the tub with his feet and wormed his way further in, pushing concerns of how he might make his way back out from his head.

'Nell!'

Contrary thoughts held court: that the girl was clearly dead and couldn't reply to him, and the expectation that at any second he would hear a clarion call from her, safe and miraculously unharmed in some pocket among the debris.

Neither was quite true.

'Leon?'

Wavering, her voice was curdled by the heavy dust in what air remained down there. He kept tight-lipped, fearful his mind was contriving the voice he so wanted to hear.

'Leon?'

'Nell? Nell, I'm here. I'm here now. Where are you?'

She coughed and spat and he swam through the million loosened parts of the building towards her and found her head, seemingly disembodied yet with blinking eyes and lips trembling.

'Nell?'

Her focus fixed on him. Face and hair white as a shroud, and not from the dust alone. A dark streak ran off her chin, and as if by way of explanation, she coughed up some more blood.

Hurriedly he dug away at the wreckage around her, at first believing she was buried upright, but then he spotted a foot up behind her, and figuring out the angle that made that possible cleared up how dreadfully knotted her body must be.

'Leon.'

'Does it hurt, sweetheart?'

'No.' She moaned.

'See what we can do here.'

He scooped away more rubble, trying to find somewhere to displace it.

'Can't feel a thing,' she said.

Her eyes closed.

'Nell?'

She licked her lip. Reaching out, he pressed a finger to her neck, the pulse he found amounting to a rumour at best.

'Loolah,' she gasped.

'I got her. She's out there with the wardens and rescue crews, every bit the tart.'

The heap shook again, everything sliding a few inches into a tilt.

'Leon, you need to go.'

'Go? Where on earth would I rather be?'

A smile battled onto his face, masking his despair. Scrabbling more broken bricks and handfuls of dust and fragments, a desperation took hold of him. They were beneath tons of fallen building, with little hope of extricating Nell. And even if he could, the shape of her under all that didn't bear thinking about. A dark wonder she had survived at all. The thought took hold that it was only the rubble pressed down on her that was keeping her in one piece.

Amid the waste, he found fingers, marked with little cuts and needle pricks, otherwise intact but unmoving. Squeezing them, he got nothing back in return.

'Guess this means we'll be able to get a new place,' he said. 'Maybe Mark and Billie can put us up above that shop of yours. Short commute. Or we could move to the suburbs. I think we could be suburban people, given some practice. Have a garden. Grow vegetables, keep some chickens. Imagine what Loolah would make of that. We could get to know the neighbours. I could get a car and, Christ, there might even be a place to park it.'

Clutching the lifeless fingers, for she had been gone a while, he crawled just a little further in and kissed her nose and kissed her brow and held her face for a bit. The moment was so large that he had the odd sensation of being pushed aside by it, so immediately and irreparably had it bisected his life into before and after. It had only been a matter of seconds, yet he could no longer properly imagine the world as it had priorly been. It was as if she had never been alive, and the yawning absence of her was all he had ever known.

Shouts from above roused him. Fearing the men might think something had happened to him and attempt a rescue, he struggled back out of the tunnel into the small bathtub chamber and flashed the light up the shaft.

'I'm all right.'

He climbed unsteadily, hands reaching down to help him up and out into the bright morning sun, bestowing and disorienting all at once. He remembered leaving early shows at the cinema, exiting the dark theatre into daylight and feeling as if he knew secret things that the people sweeping along the streets did not.

'Anyone down there?'

Geats looked at him for a moment and didn't say anything.

'Anyone alive in there, sir?'

'No. Not any longer.'

Scooping up Tallulah, he slid down the heap that had once been his home. Billie approached him, fingers at her lips.

'She wasn't in any pain. She said that.'

'Leon.'

He looked back at the mountain of ruins and it suddenly struck him as the craziest thing.

'I'm glad I saw her.'

Tallulah miaowed, and he scratched her chin.

'Would you be able to look after her, Bill, do you think?'

'I . . . of course.'

He handed her the cat.

'Thanks ever so much. And can you tell Mark that I'm sorry.'

'Yes. But, sorry for what? Leon, where are you going?'

'Something I must do.'

99

Sink Street already knew, as it always did.

Peggy met him on the landing outside his office and grabbed him in a hug. He patted her arm. Harrison was in, and from Geats's appearance, clothes dirty and dishevelled, he saw at once the whole thing.

Geats knew what he needed. Had it all mapped out before him.

'You can send me to France now,' he said.

Harrison had a better idea, and called a friend of his to make the necessary arrangements.

In training Geats demonstrated an aptitude for certain kinds of work and was sent to Achnacarry in the Highlands. By the end of the year, he was part of a commando unit conducting raids along the Norwegian coast, engaging Gebirgsjäger in house-to-house combat and killing as many Germans as he could.

There was no future in it, and that was just fine.

Part Four
CARTHAGE

1963

100

The radio is tuned to a commercial station and 'She Loves You' plays, Sergeant Helm half singing along. He drinks from a bottle of Coke that has sweated rings onto the Formica tabletop. The windows are open, but the breeze is warm.

'This place is unbearable.'

'Sergeant Cassar, back from the Midlands. *Yeah yeah yeah.* You a Beatles man?'

'Prefer jazz.'

'Jesus, might have known. You do look a fright, you know.'

'Just drove down from Birmingham. Hotter than a bastard.'

'Been up there much?'

'Every week since I was last here.'

Helm chuckles. 'And find much?'

'Found your girl.'

Helm stops drinking, looking at him over the bottle still pressed to his lips. He swallows, puts the Coke down slowly.

'You sure?'

'Found enough for you to find her, anyways. Name's Christine. Lived in Kidderminster with her mother, until her mother died. Went on the game and moved to the big city to be a bigger player. Vanished without trace, leaving all belongings in her bedsit.'

'Kidderminster? I'll give Worcestershire a bell.'

While they wait for a call back, Helm sends out for fish suppers. The batter is good and crunchy. They sit at his desk eating and discussing what it means if they know the woman's name.

'If there's a connection with the assailant, might give us an in,' Helm says.

'There won't be.'

'You sound certain.'

'This thing I'm looking at, it goes back years. I can't tell you how many he's done, because we never found them all, but it's a lot. He picks them because nobody'll miss them. Nobody sees them. He's been doing it for a long time and he's gotten very good at it. He must have watched, figured out who the likely targets were, but none of the girls round Balsall Heath remember him.'

'Sounds like a ghost.'

Detective Inspector Madison joins them, pinching chips.

'You think this is her, then?'

Helm shrugs. 'Cassar's witness was convinced, but we'll see what Worcestershire say.'

'Posh twats,' Madison says.

Helm nods.

He doesn't get their references. 'How's that?'

'Got themselves a stately home for their HQ,' Helm says. 'Requisitioned during the war and the council took it on after. Family get taxed out, boss?'

Madison shrugged. 'Bet it's not hot as a horse's crack in there, though.'

'If it is her,' Helm says, 'wonder if she has other family. Distant or something. She's going to need caring for.'

'Pity Lady Redesdale just passed. She'd have known what to do with a girl with a hole in her head.'

Helm and Madison laugh, much to his confusion.

'What's that mean?'

'Nothing,' Madison says. 'Just a locals' joke; don't get defensive.'

'I didn't mean like that. Seriously, who's Lady Redesdale? Name rings a bell.'

'Dowager Lady Redesdale, as she was at the end,' Helm says. 'Mother to the Mitford sisters.'

He nearly fucking dies.

'The Mitford sisters?'

'Family place is in Swinbrook, not far from the quarry where they found our girl. But her daughter, Unity, she shot herself. Half the family were fascists, and rumour was she was having an affair with Hitler and tried to do herself when it became clear war was unavoidable. Only she cocked it up and survived.'

'Oh Christ.'

'What?'

He shakes his head. 'Long time ago, when I worked Soho, we crossed paths. She liked the clubs.'

'I'll bet.'

Worcestershire call back. They like the quarry woman as a Christine Long. Story they tell matches nicely with the Birmingham story – born and grows up in Kidderminster, father dies when she's a toddler. Lives with her mother, Mary, until she dies just after Christine's seventeenth birthday. Struggles to make ends meet and goes on the game. Ups sticks to Birmingham for regular trade, nobody hears from her again. A WPC at Kidderminster confirms the photo is Christine.

He scribbles the details down on the paper bag his fish came in.

'You have no official cases?' Madison asks.

'No.'

'And the murders you know of were in London during the war? Nothing since?'

'That's right.'

Madison can see the case stretching out over the horizon and wants nothing to do with it.

'We'll say this. We'll say, unless concrete evidence comes up that this is a deliberate attack by a serial offender, and unless the Met contact us to share information, we're going to put it to bed. Found out who she is, the NHS will do what they can for her.'

Helm is unhappy. 'But boss, Cassar has—'

'Cassar has feelings and intuitions. But Cassar doesn't have shit in the way of actual evidence or even an official investigation. Isn't that so, Sergeant Cassar?'

'That's right, sir.'

'So. Until otherwise.'

Helm walks him to his car.

'You get anything, you ring me. Boss doesn't want his feet in the mud, but that girl deserves better than this.'

He gets in his car and heads back to Kent.

Officially . . .

No murders.

No investigations.

No chance.

But he has one thing. The Mitford sisters.

That can't be a coincidence.

101

Shepherd's pie for tea.

'Thought you'd be another night,' Lottie says.

'Told them I was missing my girls too much and they could stick the final day.'

'You did not.'

'No, I did not. It was Birmingham, and I couldn't stand it. Even coming back to you lot was preferable.'

She digs him in the side with her elbow and he wraps an arm round her, pulling her close. He feels he's going to cry and holds her tight, fighting his eyes.

'Dad?'

Kisses her on the ear. 'Love you.'

'Love you too,' she says.

'What about me?' Marse says.

'Yeah, you're all right.'

'Pepper, drinks, who's looking after the table?' Billie says from the oven.

He makes faces she can't see and the girls giggle.

'I know what you're doing, Mark Cassar.'

He gets up to fetch the pepper and glasses, stealing a kiss from Marse on the way. The pie is good and he forces down more than he should after his fish lunch. Afterwards, all of them sit and watch *Z*

Cars together, Lottie curled up against him one side, Marse with her head on his shoulder the other. Billie watches from the armchair, smiling. Then he makes them sit through *Sportsview* as Frank Bough struggles to find the highlights from a goalless draw between Everton and Inter Milan on an unseasonably bitter night at Goodison.

The girls turn in and Billie joins him on the sofa.

'You all done up there?'

'Up there, yes.'

'Found something, then.'

He gets his satchel, produces the paper bag he took notes on. Still smells of vinegar.

'Remember back in the thirties, the first killings. There was all that rumpus with Oswald's Blackshirts, clashes between the Italians and Jews.'

'Fun times.'

'The Mitford sisters.'

'Blimey. Yeah, at . . . what was the place?'

'Chez Renée's.'

'The one who married Oswald, and the younger one. She tried to kill herself.'

'Yeah. Gunshot. Side of the head. Survived.'

'I don't get it.'

'The woman found at the quarry, that was only a few minutes from where the Mitford family home is.'

'Gunshot wounds to the head. You think there's a connection?'

'I think I wish I'd paid more attention at the time. Unity Mitford shot herself in 1939. She's shipped back here, recovers somewhat, and lives a few more years. Firstly in Swinbrook, and then she's sent away because her behaviour was causing concern. Local gossip in Oxford is that she was seducing fly boys from the RAF base, which, given her form with the Germans . . .'

'And it wasn't until the second lot of killings, during the war, that the bodies showed up with head wounds.'

'Might be nothing. But given that the Mitfords have turned up twice now, it's probably worth a closer look. I just don't know who to ask.'

'I do.'

'Yeah?'

'Simone.'

'Simone-from-the-clubs Simone?'

'Uh huh. She knew everything that went on in her dives. She might have heard something about them.'

'Christ, haven't seen Simone since . . . I wouldn't even know where to find her. Especially after everything that happened.'

'She still sings.'

'How'd you know?'

'There was a thing in the paper about her a couple of years ago. Remember that fiasco at Beaulieu?'

'The jazz festival?'

'Crowd turned a mite obstreperous. Things got out of hand.'

'There was a riot.'

'Teddy boys up from Portsmouth.'

'I heard it was true jazz fans trying to prevent Acker Bilk getting on stage. Doing the Lord's work, you ask me.'

'Memphis Slim played. First time he ever left America. Simone was a backing singer, filled in at late notice. There was a piece on her, how she'd gone back home and was singing there, in a club and casino.'

'Cardiff. Fancy a dirty weekend away?'

Billie blows her lips.

'You better handle this one on your own, don't you think?'

102

The club is in an imposing four-storey Victorian villa faced in Pennant stone. Casino on the upper ground floor, with private rooms above, and a side entrance leads to the nightclub on the lower ground floor.

He arrives early, hoping to speak with the staff.

Doorman is an Italian type, doesn't know who he's talking about.

'No Simone working here.'

'She's a singer.'

'I know the band. No Simone. Sure she didn't just do a few nights?'

'There was a thing in the paper about her, couple of years ago.'

'Ah. I've only been here a year. Maybe she's moved on?'

'There anyone I can talk to?'

'Owner's not here, but Cyril runs the floor. He's been here donkey's.'

In an upstairs room at the back, a small office, he meets Cyril.

'Simone Clifford, yeah. Had to let her go.'

'Oh?'

'Yeah. Shame, she was a great singer, and I liked her. But it was getting out of hand.'

'What was?'

'Her habit. Look, I'm a cosmopolitan gent, I understand people like a pick-me-up or a lay-me-down, but you've got to remain professional about it, don't you? I can't have birds overdosing in the dressing rooms.'

'Right. No. Most inconvenient.'

'Exactly.'

'Any idea where she is now?'

Cyril leans back, appraising him.

'You know her, you say?'

'Long time ago. When she was in London, she ran some joints for a fella called Jack Isow.'

'Yeah, I know Isow.'

'I was a regular back then, but I haven't seen her since the end of the war.'

'You know Butetown?'

'Nope.'

'Down on the docks. Tiger Bay, they call it. Mongrel place. There's a dive down there, the Ordinary Seaman.'

'Classy kind of joint.'

'Last I heard, that's where she was.'

He takes a cab, the driver knowing the place. Looks like a church hall with the windows bricked up, barely even a sign outside. You either know it or you don't. In the small lobby, the doorman sits on a wooden chair. Young, still has some growing to do. Probably only six foot five.

'You a member?'

'No.'

'Members only.'

An older woman appears behind the doorman (he thinks she's a woman), giving him the up and down. He gives it back.

'You've got a glare could cool piss, darling.'

He takes it as a compliment.

'Sometimes you can join on the door,' she says.

'I know Simone.'

'Who's Simone?'

'Cyril at the casino told me she came here after he fired her. Simone Clifford. I knew her, twenty-odd years ago. She's a singer.'

His voice trails off. They know exactly who he's talking about.

The doorman and the old lady look at each other.

'Hold on,' she says, vanishing.

Comes back shortly with someone else in tow. Sequinned dress, long black hair hanging over her face.

He smiles. 'Hello, Simone.'

She brushes her hair back, takes him in with a sneer.

'Oh,' she says. 'Thought you were dead.'

1946

103

The Yard looked the same as the last time.

Perhaps some of the rubble had been removed, the crater dug out, but heaps of it still filled the space. The rear wall of his old building clung on desperately, like a tombstone. The elements had seen to Clara's floral wallpaper, now a colourless shade of biscuit, but at the top his billiard green remained, if somewhat duller than it once had been.

Tugging his bag higher onto his shoulder, Geats made for a boarding house he had known on Old Compton Street, a place for theatrical types that wasn't quite as grimy as Soho's other establishments. He found it just where he'd left it, though under new management. Same threadbare carpets and drapes, same sheets as there'd ever been, but a new spirit of despair. He paid for a week and left his bag in the room.

The neighbourhood was a lonely place. Aside from the odd fenced-off patch, the buildings were largely untouched, but something was missing. Its marrow diminished. The lifeless eyes of empty Berwick Street shopfronts, its rag trade a thing of the past. Even in open establishments, windows were boarded up where they'd been blown in and never replaced.

Estate agent signs beaked out from every other first-floor window, offering freeholds for sale. Lining the kerbs, a few marketeers persisted, but the gaps between them were bigger than the stalls.

Paltry offerings.

Punters thin on the ground.

A brazier smouldered, an old boy with barking shoes warming his hands, rolling toothless gums.

A gold-rush town after the boom.

The butcher was still there. A barber had opened next door, though they had no sign over the entrance and the faint lettering of Mrs Gal's dress shop where Nell had worked was still visible.

He rang the bell for the flat above the butcher. It was February and he could see his breath, stamped his feet against the cold. Billie opened the door with a face on her like she'd seen a ghost.

'Hello, Bill.'

Grabbing his lapel, as if making sure he really was standing there, she pulled him in and wrapped her arms round his neck.

'Thought you were dead, chum.'

'They tried.'

She tightened her hold and he heard her give a little gasp as if fending off tears. He was very aware of her in his arms, her hair in his face, the smallness of her shoulders. It must have been the longest they had ever been in physical contact, except maybe that one time after a few drinks, with her husband asleep in the other chair.

Standing back, she looked at him, hands at her mouth in prayer.

'Can't believe you're here. Just . . . appeared.'

'My flair for the dramatic is what makes me interesting.'

'You tell yourself that.'

She dragged him upstairs, noting his stiff leg.

'I went to war, you know. They shot me.'

The kitchen had seen a lick of paint, but was otherwise as he remembered. Billie placing a cool damp cloth on her neck while cooking; Cassar fumbling around for bottles of booze; Nell helping with the washing-up. A happily ordinary place.

Billie put the kettle on.

He made a face. 'Nothing stronger?'

'Might have a bottle somewhere.'

'I'd kill for a snort of Scotch.'

'You'd have to. Best I can do is rum.'

She made tea anyway and served him a short glass with it. He drank it eagerly, then started when he felt something brush his leg.

'Good God. Tallulah, how are you, girl?'

Tallulah miaowed and ducked away from his touch when he leaned down. She stretched and sat across the room, her back to him pointedly.

'Going to have to work hard for forgiveness there,' he muttered.

'How long have you been back?'

'Oh, at least three hours. Long enough to get a room and grab some oysters off old Walshie.'

She laughed. 'The first thing you did was get oysters?'

'NAAFI didn't serve them, for some reason.'

'And were they good?'

'Not as good as the idea of them, but that's the way with most things.'

He cocked his ear to a sound from the front room.

'Mark here?'

'Nope.' She couldn't keep the smile from her face.

'Well, what then? Another cat? Tallulah, have you been very unladylike in my absence?'

Tallulah didn't dignify that.

'Come on,' Billie said.

Opening the door to the living room, she stood back as first a small hand gripped the door frame, followed by a small person. She stared up at Geats, regarding him with deep suspicion, before looking to Billie.

'Marcia, this is Leon.'

'Eyon?'

'Close enough,' he said. 'Hello, Marcia.'

Unconvinced, she toddled back into the living room, where, in the centre of a wooden baby pen standing beneath the windows, a younger child lay.

'And that's Charlotte,' Billie said.

Geats leaned over the pen and the baby grinned up toothlessly.

'Pleased to meet you, Charlotte.'

She babbled and batted joyfully at his offered finger.

'They're beautiful.'

'Help settle us down, was the idea.'

'And did they?'

'They helped me. Didn't help the marriage.'

She sat on the sofa. Weighing up the armchair, he eventually perched himself at the other end of the sofa, which didn't have a lot of middle between the ends.

'You walked the old neighbourhood, then?'

'Ghost town out there.'

'Thought about selling, but who'd buy now?'

'Still, got the two shops and the flats next door. Must be doing all right.'

'When they pay.'

'Trouble?'

She shrugged. 'The shops are fine. Some of the tenants – one of them, really.'

'Where's Mark in all this?'

An opaque look crossed her face. Marcia charged unsteadily towards her, caroming off her leg and crashing onto the seat of her pants, laughing convulsively.

Billie took her hands and lifted her to her feet. 'Whoops-a-daisy.'

The child turned and chuntered off back across the room, watched from the floor by her younger sister.

'You stopped writing letters,' she said. 'Did you get mine?'

He had written to let her know where he was after he volunteered, and again after the success in Norway. Then came disaster at Dieppe, where he was one of only a handful who survived. The tattered remains of the unit recuperated in Dorset, where he became entangled with a young widow from Bincombe, and a troop of police officers arrived to fill the shoes of the dead.

The remainder of his war was a relentless stream of operations that looking back had the quality of chapter headings in old books.

One – in which Geats leaves England for Gibraltar, from where he infiltrates Spain with bronzed skin to watch for Nazi incursions.

Two – in which Geats crosses the sea to Algiers and on to Suez, from where he storms the beaches of Sicily.

Three – in which Geats takes the town of Cassibile, before again suffering terrible losses saving the Ponte dei Malati bridge.

Four – in which Geats lands on the Italian mainland at Bari and takes the port of Termoli.

Five – in which Geats returns to England and takes part in the Normandy landings, his unit obliterated attacking the Merville battery.

Six – in which Geats rests after eighty-three days of continuous action, and is folded into another unit, leading the assault on the frozen town of Linne.

Seven – in which Geats crosses the Rhine and takes the town of Wesel, capturing hundreds of German prisoners of war.

Eight – in which Geats crosses the Elbe and takes the town of Lüneburg, witnessing the German surrender on the Timeloberg.

Nine – in which Geats is shot by a seventy-one-year-old terribly nearsighted pork butcher, in a brothel above a rabbit-breeding club in Lübeck.

Ten – in which Geats is honourably discharged, having been mentioned in dispatches and awarded the Distinguished Conduct Medal with a bar.

Mail had chased him round the Continent and eventually caught up with him during the occupation of Lübeck. He hadn't known how to reply. The wad of letters, secured with twine, was one of the few items he had brought back home with him.

'Got them in bunches, mostly. I was on the move a lot.'

'Normandy?'

'Eventually.'

'I read about you in the *Gazette*. More than once.' She examined her hands in her lap. 'I read it every day.'

'Bill, where is Mark?'

She stood sharply, growing agitated.

'Billie?'

'He's rarely here.'

'Rarely here? What does that mean?'

'He's gone for days. Comes back to eat and get clean clothes and then he's off again. During the war it wasn't too bad. I think he was almost happy. There was . . . I don't know. A freedom? Something liberating. With everything else there was to worry about, nobody paid much attention to what he got up to.'

'And now the old laws are being enforced again.'

She looked at him carefully. 'He was beaten up on the Tube not so long ago. Really quite badly. It shook him.'

'He's still Flying Squad?'

She nodded. 'Plus his second job.'

Geats frowned.

'Your killer of women.'

'Christ, he's still working that?'

'Never stopped.'

'Where does he stay when he's not here?'

'I don't know. We have another place, on Peter Street. One of the flats, he says it isn't habitable, but . . .'

'That's just round the corner.'

'I've never gone there. If I didn't find him . . . God, if I *did* . . .'

She shrugged and turned to the window, hugging herself.

'How long since you've seen him?'

'Almost three weeks, this time.'

'Is that unusual, to be gone that long?'

'It used to be only a few days, but more recently . . .'

'I'm sorry.'

'It's fine. I deal with everything. I've dealt with everything for a long time. The properties were always in my name anyway, just in case. With the tenants, though, when they don't pay – I mean, a woman going round and asking. You can imagine.'

'Do you want me to look for him?'

'He'll come back eventually. Always does. Pops in like he saw me that morning. Kiss on the cheek. Hot meal. Change of clothes. Then he'll be off again.'

'Well, what about these tenants? I can pay them a visit. Say I work for you. I was going to grab some grub near my digs, and I can come back a little later, when people will be in.'

'He's always in.'

'Well, then. I'll go now. Quiet word in his ear.'

'I'll tell you one thing, you're not going anywhere for grub. You'll eat right here. I'll cook dinner and we can talk it over.'

'All right. I'd like that.'

They mostly talked of other things at the table, and had the kids with them, who were always prepared to do something that would stall the flame of conversation from flickering out. Geats got the pertinent details of the tenants and had Billie write a short letter that outlined his 'employment' for when he spoke to them.

He approached the topic of Mark only tangentially, through his ongoing investigation into the killings.

'He ever identify any suspects?'

She shook her head. 'Not that he told me. He tried at one point to get Flying Squad involved again, but they weren't buying it.'

'Any idea how many more victims?'

'He rarely spoke about it in detail. There was one that he was certain about; she was in the papers. A woman found alive with serious head trauma. She'd received medical treatment, but the bullet was still in her head. The doctors said she was in a vegetative state. She only lived a week or so after they found her.'

'She was dug out of rubble?'

'No. You know St John's church, near Parliament?'

'Sure. Took a direct hit not long before I left.'

'The ruins are still there. The four sides are standing, and the towers, but the roof fell in. They cleared it all away and it's been open to the skies ever since. That's where they found her, lying on the stones of the old floor in the middle. It had rained, and she'd been there a few days. Had pneumonia.'

'Jesus. How long did they think she'd survived since being shot?'

'About two weeks, from the wounds.'

'His finest work, so he put her on display.'

'That's what Mark believed.'

'Did they identify her?'

'No. Her picture was in the newspapers. No mention of the circumstances, just a plea for help. Loads of responses, but none that panned out. Mark thinks he gets to know them, chooses women who don't have friends or family. Nobody who will miss them. Refugees, too. He had a theory that he picks up lone girls hitch-hiking. You know what it was like during the war, everyone being encouraged to pick people up. Spent months talking to young women about men who'd given them rides, but it came to nothing.'

'Was she the only one?'

Billie shrugged. 'I know he spoke with Spilsbury and the other man a lot.'

'Simpson.'

'Yes. They got photographs and notes from other pathologists for him. Often, they couldn't be sure. Mark thought the killer had become skilled at covering his tracks, disguising the gunshots as crush injuries. Honestly, it feels lately like he's just using the whole thing as an excuse not to be here. Can tell himself he's running round the city at night looking for a villain.'

'He keep that stuff here? The pathologists' notes and photos?'

She shook her head.

'At this Peter Street place you mentioned, maybe?'

'God, you haven't even been back a day and you're getting dragged into it again.'

'Finding Mark can't do any harm.'

'Good luck. He's been trying to find himself for years.'

With the children in bed, they sat anxiously in the lounge, fortifying themselves with rum. Unmoored from the interference of toddlers or the doings of errant husbands, an unfocused quiet grew between them. The last time they had sat alone on the sofa he had kissed her, and even after four years at war he couldn't begin to imagine where that courage had stemmed from.

Billie felt it too, past intimacy that returned insurgently with a cringe. Felt it so wincingly that she was compelled to detonate more ardent emotions in order to get past it.

From the sideboard, she dug out a sheaf of papers.

'I have these. I – we – weren't sure what to do, after the bomb. They buried the bodies out near Ealing. I think you can arrange for her to be moved now, but when everything was going on, that's what they did.'

'Oh,' he said.

He stared at the documents detailing the interment of Eleanor Martin in the City of Westminster (Hanwell) Cemetery.

'I thought you might like to visit.'

'Yes. Visit.'

'I know you're not sentimental that way, but after leaving so quickly . . .'

'No, I appreciate that. Thank you. Thank you for taking care of it. It was unspeakably selfish of me to leave like that.'

'I understood.'

He couldn't tear his eyes from the papers, was unsure what to do with them. They didn't seem to want to be put down.

'They didn't recover anything else,' she said. 'Belongings, or whatever. I wasn't sure about . . . that is to say, I know Clara was . . .'

He suppressed a laugh into a hiccupy squawk. 'Was sitting on the mantelpiece? Keeping a beady eye on affairs.'

'They said they couldn't retrieve her.'

Now he laughed out loud. 'What on earth would she have made of that? Christ, the rubble is still there. Perhaps she's waiting for me to fetch her.'

'She wouldn't be happy with anyone else doing it. Certain miseries are reserved for sons.'

They snickered together and refilled their glasses.

'I've got something else, too.'

'Blimey, Bill. What more is there?'

'This is better, I think. I hope.'

It was a photograph, Geats and Nell at the table in the next room. A candid moment of joy, the sight of which quite fractured him. He brushed a tear from his cheek as indifferently as he might wipe his nose.

'I'm sorry, I didn't mean—'

'No, it's fine. It's better than fine. I don't have any pictures of her. Any pictures of anyone at all. There were the few Clara had on the side – my father in his uniform, and one of them together. That was the only one I had of her, and it was taken before I was born. They were lost in the bomb. I dreamt once that I forgot what she looked like – my own mother! – and it's been one of those back-of-the-mind worries ever since, that Nell too would fade. But this is just fine.'

He pulled her into a hug, one of those moments with an elegance that was proof it was the right thing to do. The only thing.

'Leon, you shouldn't stay in digs. Only one of the flats is occupied next door. Stay in the other one.' She gauged him with thrifty eyes.

'I'm not sure how that would look.'

She slipped her hand around his, let it rest there like a promise.

'It'd look like you were my tenant, and that you worked for me. Handling the other tenants and whatnot.'

'I've paid a week upfront. But after that . . .'

Her hand departed as easily as it had arrived, the promise missing its moment.

'Yes, after that,' she said.

104

The building next door was a mirror image of the one Billie lived in. She had a key for the street door to the upper-floor flats above the barber shop, and Geats accompanied her down the narrow corridor and up the first flight.

'How do you want this handled?'

'What we'll do, I'll speak with him and you just . . . stand there looking like you. I'll explain you'll be taking over dealing with any issues, and I think he'll get the message.'

'What's his name?'

'Baldwin.'

'Did he serve?'

She shook her head. 'He's in his fifties, I'd say. Looks older, though. Health problems.'

'Real or imbibed?'

'He's a drunk, and a Bolshevik.'

'Wonderful.'

'There's another thing – some of my mail ends up here by mistake. He's not always prompt in passing it on.'

Baldwin took a while to open the door. Billie knocked several times and they heard him shuffling around in there, before Geats gave it a good thumping.

A bulbous-nosed dipso answered the door in a ratty smoking jacket, thinning hair wild and climbing away from his head, the smell of cheap gin and tobacco escaping.

'What? Who are you?'

'Mr Baldwin, it's me. Mrs Cassar.'

He looked past her as if she had no right to exist, eyes fixed on Geats.

'So?'

'You're two months behind on the rent. I'm not unreasonable, but we need to work something out. Come to an accommodation.'

'I spoke to your husband,' he said, not looking away from Geats.

'When was that?' said Billie.

'The copper.' He waved a hand. 'Some time ago.'

'My husband isn't the owner of the property, Mr Baldwin. I am. And it's me you should have spoken to.'

'Irregardless.'

His eyes dropped to her for the first time.

Billie straightened her back. 'I'd like to come to some arrangement now, Mr Baldwin. Some schedule of payment.'

'Send the copper round. I'll talk it through with him.'

He went to close the door, but Geats slapped a hand up against it.

'Who are you?' Baldwin said.

'Consider me an extension of Mrs Cassar.'

Baldwin looked amused. 'I know the returning rabble are in dire straits, but—'

He didn't finish his thought as Geats kicked through his shin, sending his legs flying backwards so he fell sharply onto his face.

'Leon!' Billie said.

'He's fine.'

Grabbing a fistful of that wild white hair, Geats dragged the man across the front room on his arse, lifting him up and tossing him down onto his sofa, which groaned under the impact. He dropped onto his haunches, so he was at the same level.

'Mrs Cassar is a reasonable woman. She employs me to be otherwise.'

Whatever Baldwin read in Geats's eyes reflected as something else in his own – dread. Billie saw it, and sat beside him on the settee.

'Now then—'

Baldwin just about threw at her a half-dollar he'd clawed from his pocket. He pointed to the crooked sideboard that sat beneath the window and she nodded. Struggling to his feet, he hobbled over, weight on his leg paining him. Billie shot Geats a look and he shrugged.

'Couple of quid,' Baldwin said, counting out more coins. 'Two guineas a week, so . . .'

'That covers this week,' Billie said.

'I can pay more each week . . . I can pay—'

'Why don't we say three pounds a week, Mr Baldwin? Couple of months and you'll be all paid up.'

He nodded enthusiastically.

The room was an odd kind of mess. There were papers and clothes everywhere, but arranged in neat piles rather than strewn around. Every available surface was covered. Geats flicked through a stack of letters and found several addressed to Billie.

'Any more like this lying around?'

Baldwin scratched about among his piles, pulling a few envelopes out here and there. He looked around feverishly for more.

'It's all right, Mr Baldwin,' Billie said. 'You find the rest and just drop them through my door.'

'Yes. Yes. I'll do that.'

Geats left him with a glare that said he'd better make sure he did.

In the stairwell outside the flat, he shook his head in disbelief.

'Let the sod off lightly. Bet if I shook his mattress down, I'd have found a tenner in there easy.'

Billie stared at him and carried on staring, the kind of hawkish scrutiny that he couldn't continue to hold. He looked at his feet.

'What is wrong with you? I asked you along to help me work something out, not crack some head.'

'Coughed up, didn't he? And we got some lost mail.'

'You dragged an old drunk across a room.'

'Bill, if you didn't want that to happen, why did you ask me to help?'

'God, even back in the bad old days you wouldn't have gone at someone just over that. What's happened to you?'

'Nothing.'

'I can't have it like it was, Leon.'

'Like what was?'

'You, putting boot to door and breaking skulls. I remember that ponce Fluke, when you threw him out a window after he . . .'

She tailed off, remembering now exactly what he had done, and seeing Geats remembered it too. Nell, doped and tiny, lying terrified in that bed.

'I'm sorry,' she said. 'I didn't mean to—'

'It's fine. Hundreds of tragedies each day in the city.'

'Different when it's family.'

'Yeah.'

'Listen, come back to mine. I'll make us some tea.'

'I should get going.'

'All right.'

'I'll get round to the other premises tomorrow morning. No head-cracking, I promise.'

'Come for your lunch?'

'Sure.'

At the boarding house, ice had formed inside the window. The meter only took shillings, and he had none. Climbing under the blankets fully clothed, he draped his heavy coat over himself, pulling it up about his ears.

In its pocket, he found the photograph of him and Nell. That raucous head-back laugh of hers. Together they shared a halo of happiness so unalloyed that he could no longer believe such moments occurred. They seemed like gifts, but he couldn't conceive by whom they might be bestowed.

Pulling his duffel from beneath the bed, he dug about inside until he found the bundle of letters from Billie, secured with twine, and slipped the photograph among them.

A spring thawing of the winter snow was bringing to light all sorts of things that had been pushed to the back of his mind by the hazard and immediacy of war. Through his fighting years, he hadn't once considered the possibility of returning home alive, let alone how he might go about living again if he did.

On those rare occasions he had thought fleetingly of his previous life in Soho, it had seemed like a different world. Now the opposite was true – it was remarkable how quickly the place was impressing itself back upon him as home. It was the war that felt like a different world, a fever dream he had suffered. He could readily believe that he had never left London at all, but rather something had left him. Something deep inside now departed. Was Billie right: had it changed him?

He couldn't even begin to put a number on the men whose lives he had taken. He'd been a specialist. A creeper. A throat-cutter. A man the enemy would tell stories about. But he'd always been capable of violence; tossing Fluke out that window hadn't kept him awake at night. He'd been surprised how little it had cost him. During the war it had become his sole purpose; he not only never thought twice about it, he embraced it. Back home, it was something he'd have to keep an eye on.

He fetched a pullover from his bag, another night layer. The unheated room wasn't much better than snatching sleep beneath frozen trees during the harsh Dutch winter. He'd help Billie get on track with her tenants, and then look for a job. Get his own place, and a good supply of shillings for heat. Christ, if that wasn't what civilisation boiled down to in the end, he didn't know what.

But first, he had to find Cassar.

Get the gen on the Brigadier's doings.

105

First thing the next morning, Geats dropped in at the barber's and the butcher's in the Berwick Street properties, introducing himself with Billie's letter, letting them know where he was staying and that they should contact him with any problems. Both were good tenants and he didn't expect any surprises from them.

The Peter Street place held more promise. Billie said she suspected Cassar stayed there, but she had never visited; he had clearly established it as his own territory and Geats hoped it was where he was running his investigation from.

A modest shopfront, a couple of doors down from the mouth of Walker's Court, with two floors above. A rug merchant leased the store, the window piled high with rolls of his wares, more stacked outside during business hours. Geats decided to try the upstairs first.

Billie had a key for the street door, but nothing for the flats above. It was split into two, one on each floor, but there was little sign of regular use. The top storey was unlocked and appeared derelict, bare floorboards exposed, some missing even. The only furniture was a cushionless settee and a small three-legged table, on its back like a wounded tortoise. The rear room overlooked a narrow, unpleasant yard.

The first-floor flat was locked, but didn't put up much of a fight. There were signs someone had lived there, but perhaps not for a week or two; dirty plates in the sink were beginning to cultivate exciting

new growth. The furniture was spartan: an armchair and a mattress in
the front room, a stove and a small table with one chair in the kitchen.
A dresser held some tinned food. There was nothing to identify Cassar
as the occupant, however, and nothing about the murders.

Back downstairs, Geats locked the street door and ducked into the
rug shop.

'Help you, sir?'

He produced Billie's letter. 'Just a quick hello, really. I'll be acting
for Mrs Cassar in relation to the property.'

'Oh. And Mr Cassar . . .'

'Well, you know what he's like. Sometimes he's around, sometimes
he's not.'

The man made a face like he knew very well.

'So, the shop and the basement are all yours, and it's just Mr Cassar
upstairs.'

'Yes, indeed. Apart from the small room downstairs, that is.'

'The small room?'

'At the back of the basement. Mr Cassar has a room there. He
comes and goes sometimes, but gave me a bit off the rent for its use, so
I don't mind.'

'He has his own keys to the shop, then?'

'Sure, sure. Never a bother, though.'

'You mind if I have a shufti?'

'By all means. Down the stairs there and right through to the back.'

The basement was filled with countless rolled rugs, a path between
the precarious stacks leading to a chained and padlocked door. Geats
tugged at it uselessly. He'd need more time to get in there.

Upstairs, the rug man was measuring out a staircase runner.

'All in order?'

'Aye, appreciate that. Just to get a feel for the properties. I'm staying in
a place on Old Compton Street for the moment. You can reach me there
if you need anything.' He left a note with the address scrawled on it.

'Right you are.'

The man wouldn't have any problems. Whatever Cassar was giving him off the rent to use that small back room would make it worth his while putting up with most things.

Geats had lunch with Billie, who he suspected was going stir crazy in the flat with the kids. The butcher had given her a bundle of increasingly scarce sausages, and a light and airy toad-in-the-hole was served. She even made bread pudding for afters. Geats hadn't eaten this well since before the army.

After midnight, he went back to the Peter Street flat, job bag over his shoulder. Cassar hadn't returned. Opening the kitchen window, he kept a quiet watch on the rear of the Wardour Street buildings that backed onto the enclosed yard at the centre of the block. Satisfied that nobody was watching, he clambered out and eased himself down until he hung from the sill, dropping onto the stone floor below.

The back door to the rug merchant's was ill-fitted, rattling in its frame. It was nothing for Geats to slide his knife into the gap and force the latch. By torchlight he made his way down into the basement and snipped a link in the chain on the back-room door with bolt-cutters, rattling it through the eyelet of the hasp it secured. The door scraped open along the concrete floor.

When he flicked a switch on the wall, a single hanging bulb came on. The room was the full width of the basement, but only about six feet deep. A table and chair stood in one corner.

It was what he saw on the walls that horrified him.

The whole investigation was up there: a map of London with dump sites marked; pathologists' photographs; newspaper clippings. The small table was laden with files. Cassar had been busy, but so had the Brigadier.

Cassar had identified more than thirty victims.

106

Geats sat at the table to read.

There was more material than he could possibly sort through in one night – stacked against one wall were almost two dozen reverse telephone directories that Cassar must have liberated from Scotland Yard, along with reams of maps, borough property and rates records, university enrolments and police occurrence books.

The detective doesn't witness the crime himself. He gathers evidence and testimony and confession, sometimes second- or third-hand, and glues it all into a tapestry. He is a collagist. He is resigned to his art.

A lot of it was annotated in unreadable shorthand, but Cassar had made copious notes in exercise books, and Geats scanned through these quickly. When he was finished, he went back through them more thoroughly, taking notes of his own.

Cassar had been talking to working girls, not just in the West End, but in Southwark and the East End around the docks too, interviewing them and tracing possible sightings of the Brigadier. Billie had been correct: he had written extensively on the theory that the killer was picking up hitch-hikers, and many young women had confessed to accepting rides for favours.

Copying down names and places and any details he thought pertinent, Geats filled a spiral notebook. Unsure how early the rug merchant got in, he made certain he was out by four o'clock, replacing the chain and padlock with ones he'd brought with him.

Easing the rear door closed, he heard noise above. Someone in the flat? The noise had been hard, man-made; like something wooden being moved, perhaps even a door. Shinning up the drainpipe as quietly as he could, when he got to the sill he noiselessly raised the kitchen sash and peered into the darkness. He didn't want his weight on the pipe for too long. Slowly and carefully he swung one leg and then the other through, pausing to crouch and listen when he was safely inside.

No lights were on.

He could hear nothing.

Had it been his imagination? Or the wind, or urban wildlife, or one of the million other tiny orchestras that played the city at night. He remained in place for several long minutes, until he was satisfied nobody was in the flat.

Rising on light feet, he moved forward towards the small lobby between the kitchen and the front room. A floorboard keened loudly beneath his boot, and as he glanced down in admonishment, a figure charged from the front room, driving a shoulder into his chest. Geats grabbed at him, but he was off balance and fell backwards, crashing into the dresser, the odd assortment of crockery and tinned food tumbling down on top of him.

His ribs flared agonisingly from the impact, and he rolled away, protecting his head from any follow-up attack. The man sat astride his back, pulling his coat up over his head so Geats couldn't move. He struggled fruitlessly, until the weight lifted off him. He heard feet clatter down the stairs as he got up on one knee, battling to put a lid on the pain and suppress the urge to throw up.

'Mark.' It came out like a puff of dust, his voice all but lost in the battle to draw in breath without it feeling like his ribs were skewering his lungs.

By the time Geats got down to the street, he was nowhere to be seen. They were at the short end of Peter Street, and he could easily have fled into Wardour, or gone the other way and cut through Walker Court to Brewer. Anywhere you looked, Soho was a town of nooks and crannies.

He lumbered back up to the flat and flicked the lights on. A plate lay in pieces on the kitchen floor and a cup had lost its handle. The doors to the lower part of the dresser had been opened by the impact, one of them torn from its top hinge and hanging askew. The contents were scattered.

Most of it was junk that he scooped up and stuffed back in haphazardly. A folded piece of paper caught his eye because of the tiny print on it.

Examining it closer, he saw it was a page from the Bible.

16 Hereby perceive we the love of God, because he laid down his life for us: and we ought to lay down our lives for the brethren.

Unfolding it carefully, he continued reading.

17 But whoso hath this world's good, and seeth his brother have need, and shutteth up his bowels of compassion from him, how dwelleth the love of God in him?

Opening it up completely revealed that it contained a small amount of cocaine, probably the remnants of half a gram. Cassar had indulged when he first became acquainted with the club scene ten years earlier, and continued use might explain his bizarre behaviour.

Someone's idea of a joke, wrapping the flake in Bible verses. It did present the possibility of tracing the seller, however, and thereby finding Cassar, or at the very least one of his haunts.

107

Geats slept late.

He decided not to tell Billie about his encounter in the flat the previous night, or about the cocaine. Not until he found Cassar and knew exactly what was going on. Why had he reacted like that? Why had he run? It was possible he hadn't recognised Geats in the dark, but he thought it was more than that.

Fleeing your own property was odd, as was staying away from your wife and children for weeks at a time. What Geats had seen in the basement smacked of obsession. Years at it now, tracking potential victims, talking to possible witnesses, trying to know the mind of a killer. That kind of compulsion could do strange things to a man; add the coke and you had a combustible situation.

Dressing, he realised his wallet was missing. He thought back to the scuffle the night before, his jacket being pulled up about his head.

'Damn it.'

His small cash roll was stashed in his duffel, and he peeled a few quid off. He went to a Danish joint for lunch and had for his money the best pea and ham soup in the city, with beer pancakes and jam. At a thrift store, he picked up a very acceptable suit, old but in good nick and slim-fitting in that early-twenties jazz style. The woman behind the counter, who had been a nurse during the war and had opened the shop to help returning servicemen, explained that a wealthy patron had donated it after her husband died when a V-2 collapsed a railway bridge on his taxi. She had a whole rack of his clothes out back and was introducing them gradually into the stock as they were of such quality.

Feeling dapper, Geats walked the streets that night. He recognised none of the girls, and none of them recognised him. He hadn't expected to be greeted like returning royalty, but it felt like a different town. He'd been gone too long. He hung around Cambridge Circus hoping to find a familiar face, but none came. A couple of girls approached him and he demurred, until one told him to get lost as he was scaring off the paying punters. Tossing a few pennies in the hat of a blind man sitting outside the Granby, he wandered down Shaftesbury Avenue and along Piccadilly.

On Albemarle Street, he discovered the Medusa had changed names and Simone had moved on. He stayed for a few drinks and a trumpeter told him he thought there was a Simone hostessing and singing at a club on Denman Street, but she was black not Italian, and that he should tell the doorman that Zebra had sent him.

He found the Florida Keys club on the second floor of a building stuffed with joints of various stripes. He remembered the place under a different name from when he lived in the Yard, round the corner. A shutter window in the upstairs door opened and a dark face studied him.

'Zebra sent me,' Geats said.

The man was unmoved, but looked familiar.

'Garfield, that you?'

The furrowed brow uncreased and the door opened. Other than his cropped hair, the doorman didn't look much different to the last time Geats had seen him, manning the Medusa.

'Geats.'

'Good to see you, Garfield.'

'You say Zebra sent you?'

'Saw him over at what used to be the Medusa. Told him I was looking for Simone.'

'She here.' He looked over his shoulder. 'Supposed to be members only, and we ain't touting for no new 'uns, but old friends always welcome. Bar through there. She find you.'

It was hot and dim in the small panelled bar, and Geats ordered quickly so he could find himself a spot. The dance floor was dimmer and not much bigger. He slipped in behind a check-clothed table in a corner where he could watch the comings and goings and enjoy the band, which had a tin-drum edge to it. Coats hung on the chairs, half-empty glasses on the table, and he suspected its occupiers were out there jazzing.

'Always in the corners.'

He hadn't recognised her. In an elegant white gown adorned with a large black bow at the bust, her hair worn high and tight, she favoured Billie Holiday. He stood up.

'You look good, Simone.'

'Yes, I do.'

'A drink?'

'Join me in my office. I have to get ready to go on shortly.'

He followed her through to a warren of private rooms behind the stage, not unlike the back rooms at Chez Renée's. Her office was ten-by-ten, with a desk/dresser and two settees. While he was deciding where to sit, she ambushed him with a sharp slap, his cheek burning with her anger.

'I suppose I deserve that.'

'And more.'

'I had to leave.'

'You think I don't know that? It didn't have to be so immediate. You could have said something. Just leaving me in the middle of the night, I thought you were dead. The report of the building falling, I couldn't find out anything more. If your friend hadn't thought to drop round a few days later—'

'My friend?'

'The one who came that night. The married one who was in love with you.'

'I'm not sure that's—'

'Oh, button it.'

He sat down, still rubbing his face.

'Don't be a baby.'

He pouted. 'I'm not. It smarted.'

She poured them drinks, a respectable single malt.

'Hey,' he said, taking a sip.

'Snaffled away the best stuff from the Medusa before we were raided.'

'They shut you down?'

'Gave sufficient warning. Couple of the burlesque acts got a little too . . .'

'Rambunctious?'

'For lack of a better.'

'Jack Isow still backing you?'

She nodded. 'This is a sort of placeholder. We have grander plans.'

'Oh?'

'Jack did very well in the war.'

'I saw his little salt-beef-sandwich shop isn't so little any more.'

'The GIs lapped it up. He's thinking about opening a club underneath the restaurant. A legitimate one, licensed. He's a player, owns a lot of property now.'

'That what the new look is for?'

'After you got the Aliens Department off my back, Jack helped me out. Got a lawyer who tracked down the right records. Things are different now. So much damage, so many dead, the idea of a black hostess isn't so strange. The clubs were filled with black GIs the last few years, and there are mixed black and white bands playing all over now. But you didn't come here for any of that.'

'Oh?'

'Come on, Leon. You telling me I was your first stop after getting back?'

He took another sip of his drink.

'Didn't think so. What are you looking for, then?'

'Cassar.'

She dropped wearily onto the settee beside him.

'Of course.'

'You see him at all?'

'Didn't for years, but recently he's been around the scene more. He's a bit of a pest, truth told. Bothering the girls, asking about this killer of his.'

'You don't believe it?'

'I believe you two believe it. I don't know. The city was being bombed. Tens of thousands died.'

'Thirty of them look like his work. Maybe more.'

'Thirty? How is that possible?'

'He's clever. I told you before I thought he was a doctor, something medical. Cassar had pathologists on the lookout among the bomb dead. These are just the ones he found. The number of bodies that were coming in at the height of the raids, God knows how many were never properly examined. The killer is skilled in disguising the injuries, making them look like the kind suffered in collapsed buildings. He also hides them in hazardous evacuated buildings, hoping they'll collapse.'

'Do you think Snakehips knew who he was? When he wanted to see you that night?'

'Maybe. Someone must know. I think Cassar is on to something. He's acting strangely, staying away from home and avoiding me. It's like he's crazed with it.'

'You think he has a suspect?'

'I think I need to find him before he goes fully off the deep end.'

'He drank in the Medusa for a spell, earlier in the war. Told me about you, the dispatches. You part of the landings in France?'

'Yeah.'

'He said you were at Dieppe before that, when it went wrong.'

'Yeah.'

A pall of silence fell over them. Geats finished his drink, aware she was watching him closely. He had in his pocket the folded-up Bible page and offered it to her.

'Cocaine.' She examined the page, turning it over. 'Hmm.'

'You know who deals like that?'

She nodded. 'A long time ago, sure.'

'What do you mean?'

'It's how Bella Gold used to wrap her flake when she sold at Chez Renée's. She had a reputation for good coke, and this is good coke. The Bible pages were her signature.'

'You think someone's copying her?'

'Mite obscure for a tip of the hat. Bella hasn't salted the clubs in a decade. Who'd even remember?'

'Someone who was involved?'

'You know who I have seen knocking around – Gerry O'Brien, used to be Bella's bloke.'

'Thought he went down.'

'Only a short stint, but he dropped the bottle parties after that. Had his own money from the family, anyway. But the last six months or so, he's been around a few of the clubs again.'

'I wonder if he still knows Bella. Cassar would have wanted to talk to her; she was attacked by the killer and survived. He'd doped her, though, and she couldn't describe him in anything more than the broadest terms. I always thought she might be dead, as she vanished right after that mess with Benny Brownlow. She could have confirmed Benny wasn't the killer, so it was in someone's interests to shut her up.'

'She left the streets.'

'Cleaned up?'

'Not exactly. Went to work with a friend of yours.'

'Oh aye?'

'Queenie Gerald.'

It all fell into place in an instant.

'Lander,' he said.

Being part of the fit-up on Benny, Lander would have wanted Bella out of the way. Snuffing her was a risk, but Bella could always be bought. Offer her a way off the Soho streets – working for Queenie Gerald looking after the protected brothels owned by the Messina brothers meant a steady income and no more busts for solicitation or distribution.

'You know these Maltese, the Messinas?'

'By reputation.'

'Think they'd stand for her supplying O'Brien in the clubs?'

'They don't like anything that attracts the attention of police who aren't in their pocket. But Bella always was a soft touch when it came to O'Brien.'

'He sell in here?'

'Nobody sells in here. Garfield slung him out, and he ain't a member. Probably you'll find him in Mac's.'

'The rehearsal rooms?'

'Above that. Not much more than a couple of pool tables really. The GIs liked it, so it was wall-to-wall women.'

'And now?'

'Musicians still dig it, so O'Brien does okay there.'

Geats got up.

'You going to come back?'

'You going to let me?'

'Might.'

'There you go.'

108

As he was a stone's throw from Sink Street, Geats decided that before seeking out Gerry O'Brien, he'd drop in on old friends and see what Harrison had to say for himself.

He stood in front of St Peter's for fully ten minutes, not quite being able to work it out. The alley leading to Sink Street was gone. Not just gone, but he couldn't even figure where it had ever been, the church being abutted on either side by the Trocadero and Scott's. Had the alley actually run *through* the church? He went inside, but there was no passage out the back of the building.

Round the corner on Shaftesbury Avenue, he entered the Trocadero. The place was heaving, and nobody noticed him slip into the staff area and take a service elevator up to the top floor, where the kitchens were.

Finding a small terrace at the rear of the building, he tried to look down on Sink Street.

Only it wasn't there.

The department hadn't just moved; the entire street, buildings and all, was simply gone, the space filled with what seemed to be the rear of the Lyons Corner House.

Nagging doubt that it had ever been there at all crept into his mind.

109

Shaking it off, Geats walked round to Mac's, opposite the Windmill Theatre. It was mere steps from the entrance to the Yard, but he'd never drunk there.

It lacked something compared to the Keys, didn't feel vital. Men crowded round the pool tables playing, and women crowded round them watching, but it felt like a place of commerce rather than community.

A thin corridor led to the cloakrooms, and he found Gerry O'Brien leaning against the basin. The flicker of something in his eyes: recognition, if not of Geats specifically then of the possibility of a bobby.

'Not a bust,' Geats said.

'You're not force any longer, anyway.'

Geats held up the folded Bible pages.

'Bella helping you out?'

Things escalated to anger in a flash.

'The Paris connection was mine originally. Helping me out, she's doing what's right.'

'The Messinas know their supply is also hitting the streets?'

'What do you want?'

'Just a chat with your lady.'

'I'll pass on the message.'

O'Brien went to push past and Geats gave him a vicious hook to the ribs, dropping him to his knees.

'You make sure you do.'

Hurrying back through the club, Geats nabbed an unattended hat off a chair and took the stairs down to the street. Wearing the hat low, he huddled in the shadows of an alley between the back of the two theatres across the road, waiting for O'Brien to re-emerge.

Following him down along the Dilly, in tandem they cut away from the park and into Mayfair, up Queen Street. The corner lay in ruins, other houses further down demolished and gone too, their absence like missing teeth. Geats watched O'Brien enter one of a row of Georgian terraces on the unbombed side of the street, a serious-looking gent inside the door. The war had evidently been good to the Messinas.

In the night's dark it was easy to hide in the bomb ruins and wait. The piles of bricks were neater here than in Soho, the bomb sites having been at least partially cleared. When O'Brien appeared again, being strongly encouraged to leave by the doorman, Geats let him go. He maintained a vigil on the site for another couple of hours before Bella Gold came out.

She didn't look so different: a little more Mayfair than Soho, a little less club than lounge. Her dark hair cascaded in soft waves over her shoulders, falling mysteriously over one eye. She scanned the street carefully before leaving on foot. No more Rolls-Royce. Geats stepped out from the shadows, remaining on the other side of the road, and cleared his throat.

Bella did a double-take before stopping and staring, peering out from under that hair. She shook her head.

'Bloody Gerry.'

'Invite me in for a brew?'

'We're not a Corner House.'

Geats shrugged. 'Quick jump in the sack, then.'

'You should be so lucky.'

Her voice was different, rasped in her throat. She looked down at her shoes, turning her toes in and out as she thought. High vamp numbers, kind a waitress might wear, built for walking. He could see her weighing up whether to lead him home or take him back into the house, wondering if that meant trouble.

'Not a copper no more, Geats.'

'Old pal. Looking to reminisce. Nothing our Mediterranean friends need fret about.'

She nodded back towards the house and he followed her through the door.

'It's all right, Claude. He's with me.'

The doorman eye-fucked him all the way up the stairs until Geats moved out of sight on the landing above.

Bella had a two-room suite at the front of the house. A tastefully decorated office, the kind of room a woman keeps to remind men who the boss is, led into an expensive bedroom.

'Thought you'd be above accommodating by this point.'

'I am. I run the place, and the tables upstairs.'

'Tables?'

'Top floor. High-stakes games between gents who can afford to lose. Throw so much down, they get the cunny for free while they're here.'

'Bed's for sleeping, then.'

'There's nothing can't be bought, if the price is high enough. And you'd be surprised what some men will fork out for what isn't advertised.'

'Oh aye?'

'If you have to ask, your pocket ain't deep enough.'

Hanging her coat in a leviathan wardrobe, she reclined on a chaise longue by the window.

'Messinas know Gerry's running around Soho flogging that good French coke?'

'What do you think?'

'Be careful with him, Bella. I got the impression he feels you've hijacked his connections.'

'He was doing so much flake back in the day, it was all I could do to keep the Pigalle source working with us. Him doing bird was the best thing that ever happened.'

'The Messinas bring in weight for their brothels?'

She nodded. 'Punters like it. Girls, too. You don't know what fucking is until you've had a cuntful of cocaine.'

'Who brings it across the Channel?'

'Thought you weren't casing us?'

'Unprofessional curiosity.'

'Comes by mail. Have the new girls receive it. Those who take the risk get their transport costs waived.'

'All heart, those Maltese. And you got in with old Queenie. How's she doing?'

'Dead.'

'Oh.'

'Going on four years now. Lungs.'

'Sorry to hear that.'

'She did well by me. No real cause to, other than she thought I could do the work and needed someone with her.'

'Who hooked you up? Lander?'

She nodded. 'He advised I get out of town for a while. Someone he knew got me on a ship to France. The boys I get the coke from, two Americans living in Montmartre. Stayed with them for a spell. Lander fixed me up with Queenie when I got back.'

'Tidy.'

'This what you're here for? Run-down on what I done during the war?'

'No. You remember my old partner, Mark Cassar? Flying Squad?'

'Christ. Who doesn't?'

'He come round at all recently, talk to your girls?'

'Nup. He don't know about our places. Frankly, I can't believe you found out again. How long you been searching?'

Geats looked at his watch. 'About six hours.'

She laughed. 'You know, I should tell the Messinas to just pay you not to be a pain in the arse. You're likely twice the trouble any of the coppers who take a taste could ever be. Even Lander.'

'He still works for them?'

'You kidding? He runs Vice at C Division. Who better to have working for you than the top man?'

Lander. The sound of his name stoked a primeval hatred inside Geats, but he needed to focus on the matters at hand. There'd be time for old vendettas.

'I don't give a damn about the Messinas. Man who tried to kill you and Katherine Farrier that night, who did the killing that fell on Benny – he never stopped. He's been killing women through the war, hid his doings in the rubble and ruins of the bombs. Cassar's out there alone, looking for him.'

'I've heard stories from girls who come to work for me. Cassar pesters everyone about it.'

'He never came to talk with you?'

'Like I said, he doesn't know about my places. I've never met the man.' She grinned slyly. 'Except when he and his friends sampled my coke.'

'The killer, I maybe could have stopped him ten years ago. If I'd had your help.'

'Oh yeah? Like I had your help?'

'What do you mean?'

She brushed back her rich hair where it cowled one eye. He could see the white shine of scar tissue along her brow.

'You want to see the dentures he left me needing?'

Geats shook his head in confusion.

'After I spoke to you, he came looking for me again.'

'The killer?'

'Found me, too. I called you at Vine Street, but never heard back. Lander came instead.'

'I don't . . . what happened?'

'I was keeping it close to home, after the killings and what you said. Only going to Chez Renée's if someone could come with. Otherwise, I was keeping to the Never Been Kissed. Gerry was inside, but the place stumbled on for a spell on its last legs. That's where he found me. Stupid.'

'He just came up to you? Why didn't you leg it?'

'Had no reason. I never recognised him, half in the bag as I was the previous time with whatever he put in my drink. And I'd already had a bit of dope this night. He was different. Seemed younger, on the wang. I never twigged. He knew the band, and I just figured him for a tip-topper looking for a good time.'

'You left with him?'

'Yeah, but not like that. He wanted to buy. I knew he weren't a rozzer, and he seemed straight-up. Said he knew some well-to-dos who wanted to score, Smith Square set, family of government types. Untapped market, good prospects.'

'Bella . . .'

'Dumb, I know. But he took twenty quid's worth off me there and then. Paid cash. I had more in the office, so I fetched it and he was going to a party nearby. What's the harm, I thought. It was a doss-house round on Brewer, but we were the only ones there. "They'll be here," he kept saying. He had gin and fixed us drinks. It was only then, when my head was swimming, that I started having doubts.

'It was almost a relief when it turned out he was just a punter, offered another fiver looking for a spot of how's-your-father. Wouldn't get you a flash of thigh off me these days, but back then it was shillings if you're willing. A fiver and I'm out my frock in half a jiff.'

'He have his tools with him? Leather strop and that?'

'Well, he says he's rather more into the slap than the tickle, has me bent over a table and is putting some mustard on it with his open hand. It's a fiver, though, and worse things have happened at sea. But then he changes, real quick like. I felt it in the air. There's an old scroll-arm sofa, upholstery all thin and torn. He drags me over, pushes my face into the corner, and he's asking questions, badgering me. "Good girls don't talk," he says. "Good girls don't talk." Wants to know what I've said, and I still don't get it until he stands me up and punches me in the face. Then I knew. Knew who he was. Knew it didn't matter what answers I gave, I just had to get out of there because he meant to put an end to me.'

'How did you escape?'

'His own fault really. Hit me so hard I flew into the table and cleared everything off. Bottle, glasses, the whole shebang. The gin broke and he got so mad, yelling about the mess. I grabbed the neck of the bottle and stuck him with the broken end. Got him on the side and on the arm. Christ, the amount of blood, it was everywhere. He panicked something fierce; you could tell it was different for him when it was his own being spilt.'

'And you didn't need telling twice.'

'Too right. I was up and out of there, left my stuff. Screaming through the streets starkers and all painted red. Wonder I weren't nicked, but no one stopped me. Ran all the way home. Called you right off, left a message, and then started packing a few things. Lander come round not long after and helped me over to France.'

'I'm sorry, Bella. I didn't know that had happened. I went looking for you, but the maid told me you'd already scarpered.'

'It was better the way it went down. Better for me. I didn't want to get caught up in any investigation.'

'You called me, though.'

'For help, Geats. I didn't come looking for you that night at Chez Renée's. You put me in a jackpot, and fair's fair, you should have helped me out.'

'You're right.'

'None of us exist the way we think we do. There's the person we think we are, and then there's the way we exist in the minds of other people. None of us have any control over that. And when we die, we *only* exist in the minds of other people. It's terribly unfair, but that's the way it is. All those women he killed, when you find him and put names to them, all they're going to be is victims of a monster. That's the only way they'll exist in most people's minds. They'll be a spectacle. And if I'd had to go to court and speak against him, I'd have been the same.'

'You'd have been the one who caught him.'

She shook her head. 'I'd just have been the one who got away. The one who ought to count her blessings she avoided ending up another dead whore. There'd have been no credit in it. Maybe for you, but not me.'

Geats, who'd been standing the whole time, sank onto the edge of the bed.

'You're not afraid he'll find you here? Not a million miles from his old killing grounds.'

Pushing herself up off the chaise longue, she approached him.

'It wasn't miles I needed to get between me and him, it was years. He won't know about this place. I don't do the clubs and the pubs no more. I'm here, or I'm at home. If he comes here, he has to get through Claude. And getting through Claude would mean killing him. He gets that far, then I've got a little something waiting for him.'

'Oh?'

From somewhere in the skirts of her dress she produced a Webley pocket revolver, brandishing it like one might a paintbrush.

'All right, Calamity.' Laying a hand on her wrist, he lowered her arm and eased the gun away. 'Where'd you get this?'

'Off a fella I know. Said someone killed a president with it once. Not that exact one, I don't think he meant.'

'It's loaded.'

'Not much use otherwise. He said more than ten yards and you couldn't hit a barn with it, but if a punter is close enough to get in your bloomers, then he's close enough for it to do a job.'

Geats laid the ivory-handled revolver on the bedside table.

'Got another one in the bed.' Kneeling, she pulled out a pouch sewn to the underside of the mattress and flashed the handle of a matching piece from it.

'Someone's going to have a very sorry night sometime soon.'

She shrugged, like: they'll be asking for it. 'I take it you're no closer to finding out who he is, then?'

He shook his head. 'You've just told me more than I've ever found out, I think. Except what he looked like.'

'Tall. Dark hair. Not fat exactly, but soft. Putty-faced and chinless. Then there's his voice, and he has an air – he's well-to-do. His hands have never seen work. Not beyond the beating of a woman.'

'He give a name? Even a false one?'

She shook her head. 'And I never asked. Got his initials, mind. A.B.B.'

'How did you . . .?'

'On his hanky, fancy little design. And they were sewn into the inside of his jacket too.'

'A.B.B.'

He rolled them around his mouth.

Three initials.

Three tiny letters.

They meant nothing to him on their own, yet their mere existence felt revelatory. The first part of some hermetic riddle revealing itself to him.

110

Geats walked back to Soho, through Berkeley Square and following the course of the long-buried Tyburn along Bruton Lane. He had the queer sense of being followed, the prickle of strange eyes on his neck. It was late, and impossible in the dark to spot anyone behind him.

Conduit Street had copped it pretty bad at both ends during the war, and on the corner of New Bond Street several tailors and dress-makers had been bombed out. Half a dozen buildings were in ruins, part of the ground-floor façade of a couple all that remained. The site had been fenced off, but there was a way through to the wasteland behind, which no doubt harboured all flavours of illicit affairs, and Geats slipped in and hurried across the uneven ground, splashing Christ knows what on himself, coming out on the old horse yard for hotels on Clifford Road.

The new police station wasn't far, and he ran hard. Other than the station itself, the whole end of Savile Row was a crater. One might have believed the destruction of British haberdashery had been a stra-tegic goal. It meant there was an open expanse of ground, though, coupled with the coming and going of numerous constables. Geats hung around smoking a cigarette, but no tail made themselves known. It had crossed his mind that Cassar was keeping tabs on him.

Regent Street was well lit. The shops were closed, though a few revellers straggled away from the noisy Piccadilly end. He darted between cars to the other side and ambled along, unable to shake off the grip of paranoia. The New Gallery cinema had emptied out its last showing, but the lights remained on, so he stopped across the street from it and lit another Woodie. A silversmith and a jeweller's had dark shutters pulled down over their windows, but the men's clothing boutique between them had less to worry about from smash-and-grab artists.

In the glass of the angled shopfront, he surveyed the street behind him. A few brass on the prowl, a few gents lighter on their feet for having been prowled; nothing he wouldn't expect of a midnight stroll. Pulled on the cigarette, studying his reflection caught pale in the dark glass, and in his own bloodless face he saw him, standing beneath the cinema's awning, watching.

Geats spun round to see him already on the run, heels disappearing round the corner. Making pursuit, he heard fleeing footsteps out of sight on the cobbles of narrow Heddon Street, usually no more than a glorified alley leading back out further down Regent Street. A crater where bombed buildings had collapsed let out from the street onto Savile Row behind. Losing the footsteps on the dampening earth, Geats stopped and yelled.

'Mark!'

The clatter of iron fencing gave away where he'd cut through, and Geats followed, but there wasn't a soul on Savile Row. He peered over the railings into the semi-basement light wells, but there was nobody in the shadows. A couple of potted gents stumbled haphazardly out of the Albany Club and gave him the once-over before weaving their way down the street.

Geats gave up his search and headed back to Soho.

III

Violent knocking woke him.

It was still dark outside, and he lay still, running scenarios through his mind. After chasing shadows along Savile Row, he'd headed for the Peter Street flat and entered the rug merchant's shop below the same way as before: out the window and in the back door, unlocking the chain he had put on the basement room. He hadn't recalled coming across any mention of the initials A.B.B. when he had sifted through Cassar's notes before, and he didn't find any going through them again.

That was maybe a couple of hours ago. Sliding his Browning Hi-Power from where it slept beneath his pillow, he climbed out of bed. He was naked, having stripped off to sleep in warmth after stocking up on shillings and pumping them into the meter so he could hunker down like a hibernating bear.

On the balls of his feet, he crept across the room.

Edging along, back to the wall, he pressed himself flat beside the door and silently turned the key. Transferring the gun to his left hand, he held it across his chest and took a grip on the night latch with his other hand.

Whipping the door open, he remained pressed against the wall as it swung wide and clattered against the wall the other side.

Billie's head appeared on craned neck.

'Leon?'

'Jesus fucking Christ, Bill. Why didn't you just say it was you?'

He covered himself quickly with the gun, but if she'd noticed his nakedness, her face didn't let it slip. She walked in and stood in the middle of the room, not looking at him or at anything.

'Billie?'

Snatching a blanket from the bed, he wrapped it round himself. There was no chair in the room, so he guided Billie down onto the edge of the bed.

'What's going on? It's . . . what time is it?'

His eyes found hers and brought her back round to the room.

'Mr Baldwin came by.'

Geats stood. 'I'm going to kill him.'

'No. He had money. He paid. And there was post. I told you letters and stuff were going there. He gave me this. He'd had it a few days already. Since before you . . . spoke with him.'

An envelope hung between her finger and thumb.

'I only just opened it, you see. The phone woke me up, and I thought I might as well go through them, and I came to this.'

He took it carefully and unfolded the flap. Inside was a single photograph.

'The calls were for you,' she said.

He pulled the picture out and looked at it.

'Simone. She called three times. About someone called Bella Gold.'

Something inside him fell away, like his core had become detached from his being. Folding down, he collapsed onto the floor in a sitting position with his legs crossed. Examining the photo, he was having difficulty understanding it.

'She said Bella had called and she had seen him and was terrified. I don't know who him was.'

Staring back at him was Cassar.

Only he wasn't really staring.

His eyes were pointed at the lens all right, but there was nothing in them, any glint of humanity dimmed. Mouth open, as if snoring perhaps. A darkness to his hair and down the side of his face; it was poorly focused, but if it wasn't blood, Geats didn't know what it was.

'I . . . Billie . . .'

'It's Mark. I know that. I couldn't decide if he's alive or dead, though. Or what it means.'

Geats looked in the envelope again.

'There was nothing else with it,' she said.

He turned it over. 'When was it posted? What does the postmark say?'

'A week ago. It was posted a week ago.'

It was all falling horrifyingly into place.

Cassar had been taken before Geats even returned to London. The man in the Peter Street flat, the ghost following him through the streets – it hadn't been Cassar at all.

It had been *him*.

The killer.

'What did you—wait, Simone called? What did she want?'

'Who is Bella Gold, Leon?'

'She's a . . . a madam. A brothel madam. She saw the killer years ago.'

'Simone said Bella had called her, that she was frightened out of her mind and saying that she had seen him. Who's him? Is he the man who's done this to Mark?'

'I better go see Simone.'

'She's not there. The last time she called she said she was going round to see Bella and for you to meet her there.'

'Where?'

'I don't . . . I wrote it down. Queen Street, but I can't remember . . .'

'That's fine, I know where.'

'Leon, where is Mark? What's happening?'

'I don't know.'

'It's him, isn't it? The Brigadier?'

'Look, you go home, and . . . no. No, you can't. If he has Mark, he probably knows where you live. Where are the kids?'

'There's a woman downstairs. She's watching them.'

'Good. Good. Right, we need to go. Give me a sec to get dressed.'

He pulled on the previous day's clothes, fixing his pistol into the back of his belt, and they fetched the children from Miss Clerricot, the spinster who had the run of the place and so far had given Geats nothing but suggestive looks.

'We're going to put you somewhere public,' he told Billie, ushering her out into the street with Lottie in his arms. 'Too early for restaurants or cafés. Come on.'

He hustled her through the gloomy streets towards Piccadilly, and up Denman Street to the Florida Keys.

'I can't take the kids into a club.'

'There's an office. You'll be safe here. I can't leave you somewhere I'm not sure of.'

Garfield's face appeared in the door hatch on the second floor.

'She's been looking for you, but she's not here.'

'I know. I'm going to where she is now, but I need to park this lot in her office.'

Garfield set his face sceptically.

'Look, I think Simone might be in some bother, and this woman and—'

'I know who she is. I know who you are, miss. I remember.'

'I need her safe. I need her and the children out of harm's way.'

Garfield sighed and nodded, unlocking the door.

'Go with Garfield. Sit tight. I'll be back as soon as I can.'

Billie nodded and carried the kids inside.

'She told me to stay here,' Garfield said. 'But if there's bother . . .'

'No, you stay here and wait for me to return. Or I might call. But someone needs to make sure Billie's all right.'

It was a little under a mile and just shy of five minutes in a flat run to the Queen Street brothel, the war having made something of Geats in that regard, though not enough that he wasn't shattered when he got there.

The door to the building was ajar, no doorman in sight.

Gathering his breath, he studied the front, remembering other buildings he had stormed in the dead of night. Remembering things he'd seen and things he'd done.

No lights showing.

Five floors and a basement; could be over a dozen rooms. He didn't know the layout, other than Bella's rooms, didn't know where threats might come from.

Door open like an invitation.

Still, he hadn't got this far in life by being smart.

Crossing the road at pace, he drew his Browning as he took the step onto the stubby porch and placed his hand flat against the door, easing it wider.

The hallway was empty, though he could only see as far as the stairs. They rose in the centre of the house, the crooked hallway leading to more rooms behind.

The carpet was rich and spongy beneath his feet, good for dampening any sounds. The stairs looked solid, looked like they wouldn't creak. He didn't need the house conniving against him too.

At the front was a drawing room, studded leather sofas and low tables. Enough light sneaked in from the street for him to see it was empty. The back of the house was a different situation.

He paused where the hall elbowed round the stairs and allowed his eyes to adjust to the gloom. Browning gripped in both hands, he followed it through to an office and a small kitchen, both unoccupied.

Another door opened under the stairs, leading down to the lower ground floor.

As pitch as the cellars in hell, his mother used to say. Something she got from his father, residual Catholicism. He took the steps slowly, waiting for one to betray him.

None did.

The blackness at the bottom was that of a cave; not an inch in front of his nose was visible. Arms outstretched holding the gun, he swept slowly from side to side, waiting to touch a wall.

The hard floor was tiled and he slid his feet along noiselessly until one of them hit something.

He knew what it was from the first touch, knew it was heavy but had the frail softness of a person.

Of what used to be a person.

Kneeling, he felt around tentatively in the dark.

A man, wearing a suit. Not a small man. Claude, the doorman, presumably. No pulse, skin cold as the floor he lay on. Geats searched for a weapon and found none, but did come across a black crackle Zippo in his trouser pocket.

He flicked it alight.

The lower ground floor looked like a cellar, was used as such. Boxes stacked up against the wall. A large sink that looked as if its purpose might be laundry.

Leaving Claude, he returned up the steps, shutting the lighter when he reached the main staircase. Taking it sideways, he kept his back to the wall and held the gun out above him.

The landing was a shifting mass of darkness, ceaselessly black as if alive. Climbing up into it was like walking into fog; he swore he could feel it.

He paused on the top step and crouched.

A form of stasis.

Gradually the outlines of walls and door frames embossed the darkness. The first door was open. He straightened up, giving himself a moment for the blood to return to his legs before he took three quick steps towards it.

A middle room, it had a narrow window that must have overlooked a void at the centre of the house, but thick curtains were pulled across it. Bed against the far wall. Nobody in it.

He moved swiftly to the rear room, larger, but similarly furnished

and similarly empty. He had to rein himself in moving down the landing to the front room, almost breaking into a run.

Bella's suite. She could be in there, with Simone.

Or what used to be them.

Whatever he found in the room, even if it was an abattoir, he had
to keep his nerve, stay sharp. He steeled himself to walk in on a
shambles.

The juice coursed through him. He wanted to shout or scream.
Adrenaline burgeoned a primal howl within him and he concentrated
on suppressing it.

The door was ajar, and swished quietly over the carpet as he pushed
it and crouched in the doorway. Curtains were pulled, and he waited
for shapes to climb out of the black. The desk; chairs in front of it; the
oak panelling; bookcase along one wall.

Rising up, he followed his gun further into the room, making for
the folding doors linking the bedroom. They were concertinaed open,
though he could barely see anything beyond them. The carpet softened his step as he slowly moved forward, nosing into the other room.

The bed looked unoccupied, as did the chaise longue by the
window.

Wardrobe door was open a mite, and it was big enough to conceal
several people.

Or bodies.

Drawing nearer, he stretched one hand out, picturing himself
throwing the door open wide. It was about then that time began to
misbehave, events happening seemingly all at once, so quickly did
they move.

He caught a sudden whiff of him before he heard or saw
anything.

Tobacco.

Booze.

Faint coils riding on the air, licking his nostrils.

Half turning, he heard the gun the same instant he was punched high in the chest by what he felt could only have been a gorilla, clearing him off his feet and onto the bed.

The light cut on like a rapture, blinding him for an instant and returning with a sight of familiar repugnance. Lander stood over him with a gun and a leering grin.

'Waited ten years for you, Geats.'

112

His first thought was that Lander must already have been in the room, waiting for him in the darkness.

His second thought was that Lander was the killer. It made sense: he knew the man was capable of destroying women, and really he had only Minter's dying word that he and Lander weren't responsible for all four of the original murders.

He wasn't sure if he could talk. Shot in the leg during the war, his abiding memory was of the scorching pain, a burning so intense he could happily imagine it had been made of either fire or ice.

This was different.

He wondered if the bullet had passed completely through him. He was hurt in a manner he couldn't pinpoint in any precise way, the pain everywhere at once, as if it were inside him pushing everything else you would usually find in there to the edges, including his voice.

His left arm, the side where he'd been shot, was useless.

Couldn't so much as twitch a finger, which was mildly irritating as the Browning had fallen onto the bed just inches away. His other arm was folded behind his back, and he could feel the fabric of the bedding beneath him.

Lander lifted the Browning, put it in his pocket. Grabbing Geats's foot, he tugged his trousers up his leg and removed the blade from its sheath in his boot, regarding it with something like admiration. A coy smile curled the corner of his lips.

'Always appreciated a man who comes to war.'

Geats gurgled.

That was when the second man appeared, or perhaps he had been there the whole time, Geats being fuzzy on reality by that point. There was a small powder room in the corner he might have sprung from, dragging Simone with him. She looked unhurt.

His straw hair was long and unruly, covering his ears and playing about his collar. Eyes so dark the iris was barely distinguishable from the pupil, giving the impression of being permanently dilated.

Silently he held a knife to Simone's throat, watching Geats curiously. He had something in his other hand, a black package of some description. Abruptly he shoved Simone into a corner and walked out of the room.

Geats tried talking, settled for raising a foot in Simone's direction, the look on his face asking all he needed to.

She nodded almost imperceptibly.

The knifeman returned holding a telephone, wire trailing behind him. Receiver fixed in the crook of his neck, he dialled.

Geats knew smatterings of Italian and French; not enough to converse, but certainly enough to recognise them being used. This was neither, and sounded more like the Yiddish his mother had sometimes spoken when drunk.

The black package was a wallet. The man opened it and read from the identification.

'Leon Geats.'

Geats wanted to laugh. Maybe he *was* laughing. He felt the bed shake beneath him and believed he was either laughing or dying. He'd thought Cassar had taken his wallet, but of course it had been the killer. Or Lander? Were they one and the same? He didn't understand, and at that moment barely cared.

The other man replaced the receiver and left the phone carelessly on the bed. Seemingly disinterested, he toyed with bottles of cologne on Bella's dresser.

'Where is she, Geats?' Lander said.

Geats stared at him. Then looked at Simone, briefly wondering if she was actually there, or if only he could see her and another world was bleeding into this one.

'Bella Gold. Where is Bella Gold?'

If Bella was gone, then the killer had beaten them all there and in a few days, maybe a week, she would turn up on wasteland somewhere, dead or at best absent her faculties.

'When did you plan it? Or was it just opportunity? The big card games on the top floor?'

Geats shook his head, no idea what Lander was saying.

'You think you two were going to waltz off into the sunset with twenty-five thou of the Messinas' cash?'

This time, Geats knew he was laughing; nothing else would hurt that much. He sought out the wardrobe, and with the lights on could see in through the open door, empty hangers where clothes had been removed. Bella had done a runner again, helping herself to the house takings.

He coughed, mangling his words.

Lander leaned in. 'What's that?'

'Good . . . for her.'

'She leave you high and dry? Use you to deal with Claude and then vanish before the split? Typical fanny behaviour. Thought you'd be smarter than to leave your wallet here, though. She throw you one? Thank you for helping her out, you too cuntstruck to realise she was forking your wallet while you ploughed away. Leon, Leon, Leon. Undone by the oldest trick in the book. I'm embarrassed for you.'

He turned to Simone.

'Or is the half-coon in on it too? Used to be your tart, if I recall. You getting led about by the pair of them? Perhaps she could stand a bit of interrogating.'

Geats barked and tried to lift himself up.

Lander pressed the barrel of his gun to the wound in his shoulder and Geats cried out, falling flat.

'Let's not get belligerent now, love.'

The Messina hood said something in Maltese.

Lander ignored him.

'We're out the takings from the games and the cunny, and our top bawd is missing. Bella was a good worker, kept the girls in line. And I don't suppose I'm going to find much in the way of reparations on you.'

The bed sank where Lander knelt on it, pistol pressed to Geats's neck as he fished through his pockets. Geats had full command of his right hand now, hidden behind his back, and was slowly easing it out towards the edge of the bed.

'You haven't even got two farthings to rub together.'

Geats laughed. 'Put the shillings in the meter.'

'My God, is this where your decorated service got you? All these years, and you were always headed to this very spot. Your little missions for Harrison. Running away to war when the building fell on that urchin of yours. Always leading you right back here into my hands. Doesn't it feel like this is how it had to end, Geats? Doesn't it feel like fate?'

He produced the Browning from his pocket.

'This is nice, though.'

Turning the blued pistol over in his hand, he read its acceptance mark.

'Wa-A-six-one-three. This wasn't one of ours. You take this off a Jerry, Leon? Waffen? Only fitting I should put you down with it, eh? You and me, one last trip. What do you say, love?'

The Messina hood had slipped his knife into the high sleeve of Simone's Billie Holiday gown, and she pulled away, shoving him. He backhanded her hard, sending her tumbling into the dresser.

She spat a mouthful of blood at him. 'You hit like a baby. Got a baby dick too, I bet.'

Lander laughed, riling the knifeman, who slapped Simone again. She wiped her mouth with the back of her hand. Hooking one finger into the sleeve of her dress, she tugged it off her shoulder.

'This what you want?'

The Maltese was well into it. Lander less so.

'What I want is for you to watch as I kill your man here.'

Geats shifted himself to the edge of the bed, slowly sliding off and thudding onto the floor.

'Jesus, Leon. You can't even lie still and die right. What is wrong with you?'

Lander knelt down, turning to Simone as he brought the gun to Geats's face. 'You watching?'

When he turned back, he was facing the little Webley Bull Dog from the pouch beneath the mattress. Geats winked. There was just enough time for all that could happen in life to pass across Lander's eyes before he shot him in the throat.

The remaining four rounds he sent into the Maltese's chest in a tight grouping, exploding his heart and killing him instantly.

The smell of the gun filled the room.

Geats waited to catch up with the stillness that followed the shots. Lander spluttered and groped at his neck, blood galloping out of him and up the walls. His eyes never more alive than when faced with the fresh panic of mortality.

For the first time, the magnitude of what was happening struck Geats. The blood everywhere, his own blood. You'd think a pig had been necked.

Simone rushed to his side and took his hand, which was warm still, and squeezed it.

'I'll get help. I'll get help.'

Hooking the telephone wire, she yanked it from the bed and clawed it towards her. He let go of her hand and reached out for it.

'I know a doctor,' Simone said.

He shook his head, wiggling his fingers. She placed the phone beside him, receiver in his hand. Still couldn't move his left arm to dial.

Simone turned the dial towards her. 'What's the number?'

For a frantic moment his mind was blank of the number he needed, before it flowed back like multiplication tables learned as a child.

'Gerrard 5050.'

It rang interminably, until a woman finally answered.

'Yes?'

'I . . . this is Leon Geats . . . blasted code . . . tell Harrison I'm at 5 Queen Street, Mayfair . . . in need of urgent assistance. I need doctors. I need Harrison. I—'

The code Harrison had made him learn interrupted his mind.

'Frank Arkwright. Frank Arkwright. Jesus . . . send people now.'

The receiver fell from his hand.

Simone gathered up his head and cushioned it in her lap, her fingers curling round his. In his good hand he took up the gun once more, pointing it unsteadily at the door.

He figured the man with Lander to be a Messina enforcer, and he'd called his bosses and fingered Geats for this whole palaver.

Muscle could be arriving at any moment.

Or the killer could come after all.

Or Harrison's men could beat them all to it, if anyone had understood what the hell Geats was talking about on the phone.

It had been five years. Sink Street had vanished.

He had to be ready for anything.

He looked up at Simone. Her eyes were more purely white than he ever knew existed.

Around the corner of the bed, through the folding door, he had an obscured view of the door out to the hallway. It was dark, and his eyes were failing. The gun was heavy, and his arm dropped to the carpet. Was there someone out there? The darkness twisted around something, itself taking form, encroaching on the room.

He tried to speak, but his voice was lost.

Shadows moved, and took the shapes of secrets he was privy to.

His sight faded.

And he knew those unspeakable things that throttled the heart.

That the dregs of all horror were the same for everyone, and we called them the world. That they buoyed all life to the final shore.

It came to him as an inner darkness creeping into his vision, devouring it not from the outside but from the centre, a gaping black maw that widened and widened, pressing the world he could see to the hems until he realised it wasn't a darkness at all but was in fact a vast nothingness.

The nothingness from which he had come.

The same nothingness to which all life returned.

113

Geats came to several times and felt so wretched it wasn't worth trying to move or say anything or even bother breathing if it hadn't been something the body seemed to do itself.

A shaded light hung from an elaborate rose on the subtly patterned ceiling. That was all he knew for what seemed like a lifetime.

When he wanted to speak, he couldn't.

A nurse appeared and he managed a growl. She smiled and applied ice packs to his shoulder and chest.

It was excruciating.

It was exquisite.

She checked his dressing.

He tried a smile and drooled on himself.

She mopped it up. 'Rest a while longer.'

He was happy to rest forever.

The room, which was larger than any he had ever lived in, gradually made itself known to him.

Fresh flowers appeared daily.

There was a wall lamp above his bed.

Plush drapes hung at the window, which from the light was south-facing, and an expensively upholstered armchair and pouffe were set out in front of it. On the opposite wall, along from the door, the sun sometimes caught the large mirror on the mahogany dresser.

When he thought he could manage to get a few words out, it wasn't the nurse who came, but Harrison, peering down at him like a specimen in a Petri dish. He looked older than Geats remembered, a fragility to him that he could never previously have imagined. In fact, he looked so awful that Geats feared he had died after all and ended up in some hellish beyond.

'Am I dead?'

'Not yet. Don't think I'm not tempted to authorise it, though.'

He was wearing pyjamas and a gown, which threw Geats as he'd never seen him in anything other than tailored suits.

'The London Clinic in Marylebone,' Harrison said, catching the confusion on his face. 'Private room. Didn't want anyone unnecessary knowing where you were until we got this sorted. Even the doctors here haven't been told who you are.'

'I thought you would have looked happier about winning the war.'

Harrison tutted.

'There is only one war. It is never-ending and contains multitudes.'

'What happened to you?'

'I know what you're thinking. If this is how people they treat look, I'd be better off on the streets. But what I have nobody can cure, so I look as well as could be expected.'

'Winning the war but lost the battle.'

Harrison snorted.

Geats frowned. 'I'm sorry.'

'So am I. Death is a sorry business all round.'

'I went to Sink Street to see you, but it was gone.'

'Sink Street is never gone. It is always exactly where it needs to be.'

'The phone number still worked.'

'Peggy had quite the shock when Gerrard 5050 lit up. It was discontinued as an active number after the last time you killed a police officer. We left it live in case anything resurfaced. Worms, and the like.'

'Glad you did.'

Geats tried suddenly to sit up, as if starting at something, but fell back in agony.

'Shouldn't try that too often. You were shot, you know.'

'I remember.'

'Went straight through, although not exactly cleanly. Made a bit of a mess. Truth told, Leon, the whole affair is a gigantic mess.'

'I was with a woman . . .'

'Miss Clifford.'

'She all right?'

'Far as I know. Not exactly forthcoming with details, and has a somewhat garrulous West Indian gentleman who rather enthusiastically ejected a couple of my men from the Denman Street property.'

Geats laughed. 'There's someone else I need you to find for me. She's in great danger.'

'Willamina Cassar.'

'Is she all right?'

'She's fine. Miss Clifford told me where to find her. I have Mrs Cassar and the children at a safe house in Bayswater.'

'Can I see her?'

'I told her that can wait until you're stronger.'

'I'm well enough to see her now.'

'It's not really a question of your welfare, Leon, but of whether I decide to hand you over to the authorities or not.'

'What for? I've done nothing wrong.'

'Well, C Division aren't exactly over the moon that one of their chief inspectors was shot dead.'

'Oh. That.'

'Yes. That. The fact that Lander was found in the company of a dead Maltese gangster in a Mayfair brothel has mitigated their fury for the moment. Of course, given that he also worked at Sink Street, my own fury is a different matter altogether. What the hell happened? You've been back in the country five minutes and have unleashed absolute carnage.' Harrison lowered himself gingerly into the armchair.

'All this, frankly, is at least partly your responsibility. This man, whoever he is, has never stopped killing. Cassar has identified over thirty women he believes to be his victims. And if we hadn't botched the investigation back in 1936 to cover for your spy—'

'We've been over this, Leon.'

Geats looked away. 'Welcome to actions having consequences.'

'Mrs Cassar showed me the picture of her husband.'

'It was taken before I even got off the ship. I thought he was playing silly buggers, avoiding me but following me in the streets. All the time it was the killer who was tracking me. Followed me everywhere I went, saw everyone I spoke with. I led him right to her.'

'To who?'

'Bella Gold. He was looking for Bella Gold. Must have known Cassar was looking for her.'

'I don't know her.'

'Former Soho good-time girl. She's been running operations for the Messina Brothers.'

'This cathouse-cum-casino in Queen Street.'

'They came up in the original investigation ten years ago. Bella had a lucky escape from the killer, who had laced her and a friend's drinks with something. Then he went looking for her again, and she managed to get away a second time. I thought your boy Lander would have kept you up to date with the gen on this. He was the one who got her out of the country.'

'Let's get to Lander, then.'

'He was on the Messina payroll.'

'Which is precisely why I recruited him. Not for what he might or might not have known about this killer of yours. He was a very reliable source of intelligence on the Maltese.'

'You know what else he was. A psychopath. A destroyer.'

'Yes, yes. But how did he come to die?'

'The killer followed me to Queen Street. Bella Gold had seen him and left a message for me. She decided not to hang around, though. I think she fled when he was dealing with Claude.'

'The dead tree trunk we found in the basement?'

'Yeah. She took all the cash in the place, some twenty-five grand according to Lander, and disappeared. The killer had my wallet; I lost it a few days ago. He left it at the house, made it look like I was involved. Lander and that Messina bravo thought I had cooked up the whole scheme with Bella, and then she'd double-crossed me.'

'Long story short, he shot you, but you shot him better.'

'Basically.'

'We didn't find your wallet.'

'The Maltese had it.'

'Not when we got there. Would Miss Clifford have taken it?'

'I don't see why.'

Geats thought about the darkness animating the room as he lost consciousness. Had someone else been there?

'Is there anyone else who knows what went on at Queen Street, apart from you and Miss Clifford?'

'I don't think so.'

'We need to control the story. You're probably going to have to eat Lander being made into some type of hero, if we can swing it. Cop gives life in line of duty, yadda yadda.'

'The Maltese know. The bravo made a call, told them I was the one did the killing. He and Lander genuinely thought I had killed Claude and ripped them off.'

Harrison got slowly to his feet.

'If you'd been dead when I got to the scene, Leon, the rest of the world would think that too.'

114

Days spent vacillating between consciousness and narcotic stupor.

Unsure if he was in convalescence or custody.

Life felt like a distant rumour.

Death a legend.

The bullet had missed his lung and, according to the doctor, anything else vital. Geats considered their attitude towards holes blasted through him front-to-back obscenely casual. His collarbone had shattered, the ricocheting shot also mangling the shoulder joint on the way out.

The flotsam of war still in his leg ached anew in sympathy for its fellow limb.

His years of lead.

When Billie came, she was alone and sat quietly holding his hand. She laid her head on his belly and wept, and he touched her face, her neck, and saw her very clearly.

He would have to rethink things. This getting killed business was not as straightforward as it had once seemed. He would have to reconsider his whole position.

115

'Mrs Cassar has made a suggestion,' Harrison said.

Sitting in the armchair when Geats opened his eyes. Always a pleasure to awaken to old friends.

'It is quite beyond outrage, but elegant enough to solve most of our problems.'

'Problems?'

'If we tell the truth – that Lander was not only corrupt but a murderer, and that you shot him having already been shot by him and facing certain execution at his hands – the damage to the police's reputation will be catastrophic. If we save Lander and throw you to the lions . . . well, I don't trust our ability to do that without you managing to bring us all down with you.'

'Glad you think so highly of me.'

'There's also the matter of the Maltese. Your gunning down their man and essentially closing the Queen Street brothel irked them somewhat. There's talk of a specialist, the kind of hooray who comes up to you in the street and plunges a janbiya into your guts and is back on a boat to the Mediterranean before your blood's dry on the pavement.'

'At least it's only the most powerful crime syndicate in the city trying to kill me.'

'As for this business of a multiple murderer on the loose, three dozen victims to his name – simply unthinkable. The press must never get hold of that.'

'Is there any word on Cassar?'

'No. Not a single trace. Mrs Cassar is convinced he is dead. Or – and whether this would be the best- or the worst-case scenario I cannot say – he is reduced to a vegetative state somewhere and will certainly soon be dead. I can't say I disagree.'

'What is her suggestion?'

'Quite straightforward, really. That Mark Cassar simply returns home, after a short spell in hospital, and is transferred to Kent Constabulary so he can move out of the city with his young family.'

'I don't—what?'

'Cassar's files would be . . . how shall I put this?'

'Criminally altered?'

'Massaged. Your photo would appear in them. Anyone checking up on Cassar will find you.'

'I'm moving to Kent? What about Simone?'

'You cannot see Miss Clifford. Cannot tell her anything. Nothing will be officially announced, but news of your death will be fed to whatever lowlifes pass as informers at C Division. The Maltese will hear about it.'

'I'm dead?'

'This plan works if as few people as possible know about it. So far, only three of us do. I can handle the paperwork side of things. Everything that exists in military or police files pertaining to Leon Geats since 1936 will be scrubbed. Your time with me, your war record. Your medals.'

'Easy come, easy go.'

'I can swing Cassar a transfer as a sergeant to a smallish station in Kent. It isn't the kind of breakneck policing you usually feel comfortable with, but you'll have other priorities. As far as Miss Clifford will know, Leon Geats will simply vanish, presumed dead.'

'Disappear in a puff of smoke.'

'Leave the city, Leon. Raise a family. Don't die horribly.'

'You really think there's any other way to go?'

116

Was there a degree of inevitability to it?

Seemed that way to Geats. The fulfilment of some long-ago promise that only now in its fulfilling actually felt real, but also felt as if it was always meant to be.

Billie had wanted to sell all the properties, but he counselled against it They let only the Peter Street place go, the rug merchant making a fair offer, and it covered the cost of a new, larger family home and an automobile. The rent from the other properties would provide a generous nest egg.

They took only the essentials, wanting to start from scratch in the new place, though Geats filled several large cartons with material from the Peter Street basement. Couldn't bring himself to let the whole thing go completely, especially as the man whose life he was stepping into remained unaccounted for.

His arm was still giving him grief, so Billie drove them out of the city, following the removal truck. In the back seat, never having been in a car before but refusing to be stunned into silence by the experience, Marcia yabbered away in something like words.

Charlotte howled as if moonstruck for the first half of the journey, before falling asleep in Geats's arms. It wasn't something he and Billie discussed, but the girl never knew him as anything other than her father, and by their first Christmas in Kent, Marcia too was calling him Daddy, and would with surprising ease forget her life in Soho.

Billie couldn't get over the house.

'Look at the garden. The girls are going to love that.'

Tallulah sprayed every surface she could cock her hindquarters at, leaving nobody in any doubt as to whose domain it really was.

For Geats it was a terrifying space that would require the having of a life to fill. Only once had he allowed himself the sprawl of comfort, when he and Nell lived in the two flats on the Yard, and that had come to a crashing halt in the rubble of bricks and death.

Since then, he'd slept in army dormitories, or on the ground, or in holes he'd dug himself, and even the sparse doss-house on Old Compton Street had seemed impossibly large for his existence.

The removal men carted the furniture to the relevant rooms, and when they had gone, he found Billie in the big bedroom upstairs, standing by one of the windows. The children had tuckered themselves out and were sleeping, an oasis of calm in an otherwise hectic day.

Geats sat on the bed.

Their bed? The only other one was Marcia's tiny cot in her room. Charlotte's crib stood in what Billie was calling the nursery. There was so much they hadn't discussed before they made this decision.

Everything, really.

Geats wondered what his name was now. Officially he was Mark Cassar, Harrison having seen to the paperwork. Even had a passport in that name with his own photo. Was Billie going to call him Mark? She'd have to, he supposed, for the children's sakes. And he needed to get used to it for all other aspects of his life.

The plan had been so simple, it felt like a ruse.

An abstract idea.

Sitting there with the mattress giving beneath his weight, it was dawning on him that this was it, from now until the end. Toe-to-heel, he eased his shoes off and swung his legs up onto the bed, lying back.

So began the process by which the pinch of months and seasons became the bite of years and decades, and somewhere just out of his own sight, he became someone other than who he once believed he ought to be.

Became the man who would lie in that bed more than half a century later and die surrounded by such life as he could not then begin to imagine.

Became himself.

Billie turned to him in delight.

'There are magpies.'

Part Five

DESTROYER

1963

117

There's a stand-off outside the Ordinary Seaman nightclub.

'Who is this joker?' the giant doorman asks. 'Who are you?'

Simone sighs. 'He's—'

'My name is Mark Cassar,' Geats says. 'I'm a copper, but I'm here on private business. With Simone.'

Simone laughs.

The giant takes half a step forward. 'I can get rid.'

Simone shakes her head. 'No.'

'You know him?'

'Used to think I did.'

A silence crams in between them, which the old dame breaks.

'Can't stand in the door all night, darlings. You want in, fiver.'

'Five pounds? That's extortionate. What's that, the membership fee?'

'It is for you.' She winks.

Geats ponies up and the giant lets him by. Simone has gone inside, trailing slowly along the side wall of the club so he can follow. The main space is a single long hall with wooden vaulted ceiling, a bar across the far wall. On the opposite side is a low stage, fronted by a dance floor surrounded by tables. The floor is buffed to a surprising shine that you could do your hair in.

Lighting is minimal, and there's barely a soul in yet. The walls feature nautical murals painted directly onto the brick, worn and faded dancing sailors. He follows Simone, skirting round the back of the tables and through the raised countertop at the end of the bar to a changing room behind.

They're met by a tall man as naked as the day he was born, except for his trowelled-on make-up and long feather-cut wig with tall pink head plume. He stares at them, one hip cocked and a penis of such startling girth Geats doubts he could snap cuffs on it.

'Cop what you can for free.'

'Come on, *Mark*,' Simone says.

'This another new one?' says the plumed man.

'No.'

'He won't last. Stanley sees them all off. You see if he don't.'

Through the changing room there's an office. Xeroxes of newspaper articles about the Ordinary Seaman line the walls, pinned photographs of choice acts that have graced the stage.

Simone perches on the desk, leaving no comfortable way for him to take a chair, so he relents and remains standing, wondering why it is he can't get enough of disobliging women.

'This place is something,' he says.

'Marjorie is good to me, and the clientele are interested in the other attractions mostly. They like me for my voice.'

'Simone, I—'

'Twice, you just left me. Think I'd know better by now, but here we are.'

'I'm sorry.'

She laughs. 'Ain't much of a word, is it? Sorry. Sorry indeed. I'd ask what happened, but . . .'

'Probably there's no good answer to that.'

'No. There isn't, is there? What do you want, Leon? What is all this? This *Cassar* shit?'

'He's killing again. I think I can find him. I think I'm close.'

Her grin is twisted, not by her face but by the hatred behind it.

'Always obsessed. I don't care, not any more.'

'I do. He took my friend.'

'*You* seem to have taken your friend. His name, anyway. You take his wife and his children too?'

'After what happened, the Maltese, they believed I was responsible.'

'You were, weren't you?'

'I had to leave. They'd have killed me. There was no way to explain it.'

Simone cackles. 'Isn't that always the way with your messes?'

'I thought the killing was done, but there's been another one. A young woman left on display. She's brain-dead. The doctors are doing what they can, but . . .'

'Why are you here?'

'Something came up. A connection to the Mitford family. I remembered back when you had the place on Lisle Street, a couple of the sisters were there quite regularly.'

'They liked the bands.'

'That one night, upstairs with the saxophonist . . .'

She slides off the desk, turning her back.

'Undo me. I need to change.'

'I can wait out—'

'Just undo me, Leon. It's nothing you haven't seen before.'

But it is.

Unzipping her gown reveals a cross-hatching of pale scar tissue like fish scales across her back.

'Oh.'

'You knew what he liked.'

'I didn't know he had . . .'

'No. You didn't see me again after you passed out.'

He frowns. 'I thought I saw him in the doorway, in the shadows. But they said you were the only person there when they arrived.'

'Your friend Harrison and his spooks. They got there a little too slow. A little too late. He was gone by then.'

'But Harrison saw . . . this?'

She nods.

'He never said.'

'Your man had hidden himself somewhere. Came out after you shot Lander and the Maltese. I was holding you, and I didn't hear him come up from behind. Put something over my head, pillowcase, or fabric of some sort. I don't know how long it lasted. I remember thinking it didn't matter because the time I was with him was all the time I had left. For many years, I thought Harrison interrupted him, but I've come to believe that he didn't make mistakes. If he'd wanted me dead, I never would have left that room. In many ways, I never did.'

The gown pools at her feet and she turns to face him. He looks away and she chuckles.

'How you going to humiliate me more than you already did?'

She sits back against the edge of the desk. Her paraphernalia is in a wooden box and she prepares her fix. Spreading her legs and planting her feet wide, she stretches out the inside of her thigh, finding the deep-lying femoral below her groin. Blindly inserting the needle with practised hands, she stares at him unblinkingly, as a wolf would watch over a carcass, bloodying its snout.

Defying him to look away.

Her face softens and she removes the needle, leaving it on the desk. Pulling on a silk robe, she slides down onto a small sofa at the back of the room, one leg slung over the arm.

'Those two were insatiable,' she says, voice thick with promise. 'The Mitfords. Cock-happy harpies. Went through just about anyone who held brass.'

'And Snakehips?'

'They weren't to his taste.'

'But they had him . . . check prospective partners?'

She throws her head back, laughing.

'They had funny ideas, those sisters. Marching with the Blackshirts by day, sleeping with the jazz boys by night.'

'There was a man, tagged along with them.'

'Followed them like a pup. Yappy little pup. He was in love with the younger one. Besotted with her. It was cruel. He was the one usually on dick duty. Snakehips filled in if he wasn't there. He was some kind of cousin to them. Don't know why he did it to himself. They even paid him.'

'I don't remember much about him.'

'I think that was the way he liked it. He was—'

She halts abruptly, eyes snapping open to look at him funny.

'What?' he says.

'He's who you're looking for?'

'I don't know. Maybe.'

'I never saw his face, when he attacked me. He never spoke.'

'Did Snakehips know him? Could that be what he was going to tell me the night he died?'

She thinks about that. 'They studied together for a while in Edinburgh.'

'Medicine?'

She nods. 'He completed his studies, was a doctor of one kind or another. He recognised Snakehips on the club circuit and suggested the girls use him when he wasn't there. Whole thing was pure theatre. Peering at the man's prick; long as it wasn't dripping like a tap, declaring it safe for use. Got five pounds a prick. Back then, imagine that.'

'You remember his name, this cousin?'

'They called him something . . . it was his middle name. Blake. Yeah, they called him Blake.'

Blake.

A.B.B.

Middle name.

A killer with medical training.

'You going to totter off and find him now? For all the good it'll do.'

'Someone should.'

'Yeah, someone should. Thirty years, people just falling over themselves trying to stop him killing women. How many times did you walk away from it when you could have done more? You're complicit, so how are you any different?'

'What he does, there's hatred there.'

She laughs, screams almost.

'You *all* hate us. Deep down in there, some part of you.'

'No.'

'You've hated us since you were born. Since your daddies hated us. You love hating us. You joke about it with your pals. You think about it when you drink. When you're at the beach. When you see a show. When you flick through back-room grot, or watch stag films. You dream about it when you sleep. You burn with it.'

'That's not true.'

'You ever gone to bed wondering if the person next to you could kill you? You ever walked well-lit streets home wondering if they'll be your last? Because there isn't a woman that hasn't at one time or another. That you don't realise you are part of that is why your world is one way and ours is another.'

He shakes his head.

'No? You don't think there's hatred for women inside you? Then why is it only the dead ones you're obsessed with?'

He glances back towards the door.

'Yeah, you should leave. You should go find him. And there being no hatred inside you, it's not like you're going to kill him, is it?' She laughs silently, shaking with it.

He goes to the door.

'And Leon? Don't ever come back here.'

118

He gets home early afternoon. Marse is working at the bank, Lottie is at college. Over tea, he tells Billie everything he has learned.

'Blake? That was all she knew?'

'Matches with the initials Bella Gold told me at the time. A.B.B. I'm not sure what to do with it, though. Not like I can knock on the Mitfords' door. Hi, I'm enquiring after your cousin, who was obsessed with your late Hitler-loving sister and is a mass murderer.'

'Come with me.'

He follows her upstairs to their bedroom, where more than a dozen dusty cardboard boxes are arranged along the wall beneath the window.

'You've been in the attic.'

'I've been in the attic.'

'This is all of Mark's stuff. His investigation. Blimey, Bill, how did you get all this down?'

'With great difficulty. I know you took notes back then, but he had amassed so much stuff.'

'There was loads I didn't get through. There are volumes of reverse telephone directories he sourced through Scotland Yard. And he even had . . .'

'Had what?'

'Jesus. He had university enrolment records.'

'Medical school?'

'I don't know. I didn't know what relevance they had back then, so I never went through them.'

'Well, then. This'll be just like old times.'

They sift through the cartons until they find what they're looking for – the matricula for the University of Edinburgh, 1930. What they do not find is any record of a Kenrick Reginald Hijmans Johnson.

'Snakehips never enrolled,' she says.

'Doesn't look like it. Simone said his father was a doctor. Perhaps he just told him he had.'

'Then how come this Blake knew him?'

'I don't know. Perhaps he attended under a different name. Either way, look at this.'

She shows him an entry in the matricula. *Alexander Blake Blackborne.*

'Blake. A.B.B.'

'Think that's him?'

'Only one that fits.'

'Now what?'

'Simone said he was related to the Mitfords. The sisters' father was an earl or a baron or something, so this Blackborne family might be old money. I'll look into them.'

At the local library, in the most recent edition of *Who's Who*, Geats finds an entry for a Sir Henry Bertram Blackborne, 8th Baronet of Blackborne and eldest son of the previous baronet, who was killed in service during the war. He has one younger brother, Alexander Blake Blackborne, a doctor in general practice near the family home.

Originally seated in the historic hundred of Cornilo in Kent, the current baronet has a stately manor in the northern Cotswolds, just inside the Warwickshire border, built in the eighteenth century by the last Earl of Knightlow, the marriage of whose daughter to a Blackborne brought an end to the Seton family line. Mention is made of an older house elsewhere on the extensive estate, now demolished, a villa having been built upon its grounds.

The Warwickshire telephone directory yields a listing for a Dr A. B. Blackborne in the small village of Winderford.

Geats stares at the address.

'Got you.'

119

Geats retires from Kent Constabulary.

As Mark Cassar, he had seventeen years in the Metropolitan Police Service, and a further seventeen with Kent. Perfect symmetry. A younger man is waiting for his sergeant position, so they let him retire with immediate effect, the leave he is due serving as notice.

His superiors think it rather sudden, but as a long-term veteran of two forces his decision is respected. Of course, they do not know what he does: that there is one last case to close. One that has been open for almost three decades.

Winderford Park, with its nineteen bedrooms, stands on the high ground of a large estate that encapsulates most of Winderford village and several other hamlets. An almost mile-long yew tree avenue reaches out before it to Seton Lodge, the more modest seven-bedroom villa built near the ruins of the original Elizabethan seat of the family for which it was named.

Geats is a regular visitor, albeit one the occupants of both homes are unaware of. This particular day, he has taken up a position in the woods to the east of Seton Lodge, affording him a view of the front drive and the rear gardens. He wears his old Denison over battledress trousers and rubber-soled boots.

It feels like the war all over again.

A little before nine, Blackborne exits the back door from his kitchen, as he does most days. They're probably a similar age, but Blackborne's neatly trimmed beard makes him look younger. Geats doesn't remember him having it back in their Soho days. In fact, though it's tricky getting a good look from a distance, he can't say he remembers the man at all after all those years.

Moving unseen in the woods, he tracks him down through the meadow to the north of the villa, to the ruins of the old house. Most of the stone was put to use in the construction of Winderford Park, leaving only the foundations and stubby remnants of the plinths. Inside the low and tumbled walls stands an Eccles caravan, which Blackborne enters. This is something of a daily ritual. He stays in there for about an hour, before returning to the villa to get dressed for work. He opens his surgery in the village at eleven.

As he walks through the meadow, any trace of Blackborne's limp evaporates, but as soon as he's back up at the house, it returns. Must have been faking it so long now, Geats wonders if he even knows he's doing it.

When Blackborne leaves in his Jaguar for work, Geats remains in the woods perfectly still for almost half an hour before approaching the caravan. For a week he has watched the man go there each morning and most evenings, but has not the faintest idea what he gets up to.

Hidden by the unkept grass in the meadow, a power line runs from the house to the caravan, the kind of extension cables used daisy-chained together on building sites. Geats steps over a low ruined wall. The caravan still has its wheels, but it is supported by bricks, though they barely keep it off the ground, which bears evidence of flagstoning.

The door is unlocked.

Spring-hinged, it shuts sharply behind him. Double bed at the front, two singles at the rear either side of a drop-leaf table. None of them have sheets or blankets. A few cupboard units, some with doors missing. Nothing in any of them. He tries the lights, but they don't come on. Perhaps the power has to be turned on at the house.

He slides the leg beneath the table to one side and it drops down. The floor beneath it is unremarkable. Curtains are pulled across all the windows. In the hope of stealing a look inside next time Blackborne is there, he unlatches the front window and traps the curtain when he closes it again, holding it open a sliver down one side.

Changing out of his combat garb into everyday clothes, he makes the short walk into the village and heads for the local pub, the Saddlers Inn. If there's a lunchtime trade, it hasn't built up yet. He judges the gent behind the bar to be about his own age; probably saw action in the war.

'Pint of mild, please.'

'Right you are.'

'One for yourself, if it's not too early.'

'I'm the boss, so early is relative.'

'Good man.'

The landlord pours out two pints of mild. Geats stretches his shoulder, grimacing.

'Ta,' he says, leaving coins on the bar as the glass is placed in front of him.

'Got a sore one?'

'Souvenir from Lübeck.'

'Oh aye? Never missed an opportunity to duck, me.'

Geats grins, saluting him with his pint.

'Got two, actually. Took it in the leg and all. Thing of it is, I'd engaged in Norway, Africa, Italy, Normandy, Holland and then Germany, and I get shot in a brothel in Lübeck by a grandpa thought I was after his bird.'

The man laughs heartily. Offers his hand.

'Bernie Wallace.'

'Frank,' says Geats. 'Frank Marker.'

'Got yourself around a bit, Frank. Raiders?'

'Number 3 Commando.'

'Next one's on me.'

'Appreciate that, Bernie.'

'What finds you in this neck of the woods?'

'Thinking about moving out here. Kids are leaving the nest, and life's been good. Wife fancies a change. Having a bit of a recce.'

'Old habits die hard.'

'Too right. Seems a nice place.'

'You looking in the village?'

'Anywhere in the general area, really. See what comes up.'

'Been here ten years meself. Can't complain. Though I frequently do.'

'The wife, she finds herself in need of a doctor's reassurance from time to time.'

'I know the story.'

'What's it like for quacks round here?'

'Just round the corner, Dr Blackborne.'

'Good bloke?'

'Be lying if I said he wasn't a strange duck, but I've not heard any complaints about his doctoring. From a good family. He's the earl's brother, up there at Winderford Park.'

'Roots in the area, then.'

'Well, he was overseas after the war. He has something with his leg, which I've heard tell was his own little souvenir. Come back maybe a year, eighteen months ago. Settled in Seton Lodge, another place on the estate.'

'I hear America's all the rage for the old money these days.'

'He went the other way. Burma, as I understand.'

'Should give him some good yarns for the wife, if she has to see him.'

He stays for a few more jars, swapping war stories and promising to drop in again when he's found himself a place in the area. Won't be dropping in on Blackborne tonight, not with the ales in him. It's eight miles back to Banbury, where his car is parked at the station. He collects his Bergen from the woods and makes leisurely pace, getting there in a couple of hours.

Returning early the following afternoon, he leaves the car in Banbury again and has a restrained run to the woods behind Seton Lodge. He knows the place is empty, but settles down and watches for a few hours until Blackborne returns from his surgery.

It's starting to dim outside when he comes out, flashlight cutting a path ahead of him. Climbing into the caravan, he flicks on the lights. Against the higher ground of the gently sloping meadow, Geats slowly makes a wide arc of the ruins and approaches the caravan unseen from the front end.

Crouching beneath the window, he cranes his neck to peek through the gap where he fixed the curtain. The caravan is empty. He stands and looks through properly, face pressed to the glass. The beds are empty, but a mattress on one of the singles is propped up on its edge.

He settles down behind a tumbled wall in the shadows of the ruins and waits for Blackborne to emerge. He hears the door bang shut, followed by footsteps sweeping through the grass. Waiting thirty seconds longer, when he chances a look over the wall, Blackborne's torch is up near the house.

Drawing his Browning, he opens the caravan door as quietly as he can and steps lightly inside, easing the door shut again. The floor is uneven and the caravan rocks gently underfoot. Though up on bricks, one end is fractionally lower than the other. He moves as carefully as he can.

The mattress has been flattened out again and he lifts it up on its side against the wall. The base of the bed is constructed like a chest, opening upwards to offer storage.

Gun pointed, he lifts the lid.

In the low light, it takes a moment to make sense of it.

There is no floor, just a ladder going down through a hole in the earth to a subterranean chamber. The bricks the caravan is up on make it impossible to see any of this from the outside.

Flicking on his own flashlight, he makes out stone walls and maybe a clay floor.

He steps onto the third rung and descends into the darkness.

120

The ladder is standing on a mezzanine, steps leading down into a hall-way. It looks as if stairs once came down from the surface, and the well has been mostly covered over. Must be the cellars of the old house.

The steps and the floor of the passage are stone, but coated with the dirt of years. Perhaps centuries.

He moves lightly, one step at a time, gun in one hand, torch in the other.

Controls his breath, slow and shallow.

A larger room opens up, stone walls and vaulted ceiling. Walking as though on shards of glass, his steps still echo unreasonably. There are several doorless exits from the chamber, and slipping through one he enters a smaller room with a trolley bed and thick wooden chair. A harness hangs down above the bed.

He finds a box with a power switch and the lights come on, a fes-toon of small bulbs strung around the cornices.

On the wall hang the tools of Blackborne's trade.

A leather strop.

A cane.

A heavy knife with a slightly curved blade. It looks vaguely Asian to Geats's uneducated eyes, and where it has been sharpened, the edge is brighter than the dull flat.

On a table beneath where they hang, a pearl-handled .25 Walther pistol has been stripped and cleaned and lies in pieces. Beside it is a small chest, the lid open. It contains what look like forms of identification. At the front, the buff card covers of driving licences – he recognises the names of two of the missing women he heard about in Birmingham, Rita Donovan and Sheila Tremlow. Behind them are cards of a worn pink, faded photographs of women mounted on them. He cannot read the language, but assumes they are Burmese.

At a rough count there are over fifty.

There are also British national registration cards. Easily twenty brown ones from earlier in the war, and later ones in blue. Geats knows many of the names as victims Cassar identified from pathology records.

Right at the back of the chest are two other items.

Marie Jeanette Cotton's bank passbook.

A letter in an envelope addressed to a Delphine Aldridge. He wonders if that was the woman found in the floor of the Lexington Road address.

Tucked into a sheath inside the lid is a memorial card for Mary Long, mother of the quarry girl, Christine. Too young to have been issued an identity card, and a teenager when her mother passed, perhaps Christine had no documentation, and the card was all she had when he took her.

The first victim and the last victim. Everything in between.

The number begins to harden.

The circumference of Blackborne's crimes takes shape.

Geats examines the wooden chair in the corner. Sturdy, with leather straps fixed to the solid arms. The wall behind has been washed but is darkly stained. This room is where he took Christine Long, and the others who went missing from around Varna Road. This is the chair they were bound to before he shot them.

The box of identifications can be brought to Madison and Helm in Oxford. A live investigation can be built on the Christine Long case whilst the historical murders are looked into.

Blackborne can be brought to light. His crimes named.

Geats's heart flutters with wordless revelation.

More than half his life spent looking for one man, and now it's all here before him.

There's something else inside the lid – another identity card.

His own.

Stolen and planted at the Queen Street brothel to set the Messinas on him, but never found at the scene. Another kind of souvenir. He slips it into his pocket.

An archway leads to an identical parallel chamber in somewhat worse condition – masonry tumbled, ceiling supported by rude scaffolding. It is here he finds the remains.

Nothing more than bones now, folded flat on the floor, clothes draped thinly on smooth femurs and clavicles. Chains bolted into the wall, one sleeve of a coat still caught up, empty where the arm unglued and slipped away.

Hanging open, the coat reveals its lining. Geats opens his mouth to cry out, but no sound comes. Dulled slightly, but the blue silk is still brilliant, the ornate cranes embroidered in gold metallic thread as beautiful as ever. He sees Nell labouring over it, getting it just right; sees the delight when it was presented.

Twenty-two years since the last time they shared a room, he sits on the stone floor beside his friend.

121

The skull has a small-bore entry, no exit hole. The bullet is cupped in the occipital, where the brain has decayed around it.

Touching the coat, he rubs the silk of its lining between his fingers. The room is dry but cold. Another set of chains is bolted into the opposite wall. This is where Cassar met his end just as Geats slid neatly into his life. How many others were brought here? Did they sit chained to that wall, staring at Cassar's bones?

He feels an overwhelming need to explain.

To unburden himself.

He has many times over the past thirty years tried to form in his mouth the names of that thing that has pressed down upon him.

Anger.

Guilt.

Selfishness.

Yet he knows he could no more devise an expiation for it than he could shake off his own shadow.

'Looked for you. I really did. Had hospitals call with any unidentified or strange patients. Went everywhere over the years. Thought I had you in Hartlepool. Description seemed so accurate. Time went by, there was no possible way you could still be alive. And there was no trace of him. Burma, so no wonder.

'Got here with your work, though. The matricula from Edinburgh.

That's how close we were, back in '41. Snakehips was going to lay it all out, put us onto him. Bloody bomb.

'Wonder how many times we were close without knowing it? You must have found him. Must have known, in the final moments. Jesus, I thought it was you following me through the streets, but you were here. Shackled in this cell. Did you know what was coming, or had the bullet done its job?

'The girls! My God, you won't believe how they've grown. Marse is working in a bank. I think she has a young man, which I'll have to have a shufti into. And Lottie is at college doing hair and beauty. She's so excited by everything. Reminds me of Nell. When I think about us running round Soho . . . Christ, at least they've got a chance at a real life.'

He's quiet a moment. With a finger he draws dirt shapes on the floor. His thoughts are disorganised, cascading.

'They don't know. About you, I mean. We decided it would be better. Or easier. I wouldn't know where to begin. You were never where you were supposed to be. Hell, I wasn't either. I saw Simone recently.

'Billie's doing good. Really good. We left the city. Live in Kent. We've been happy, I think we're happy. And let's not pretend that you marrying her wasn't a mistake. An act of cruelty, really.'

He kicks the empty steel cuff, its chain ringing across the stone.

'Damn it all to shit.'

Something snaps under a foot, and before he can push himself up off the floor, Blackborne is standing over him with a fowling gun.

'The Browning at your belt. Two fingers, by the barrel.'

Slowly Geats pinches his gun, lifting it out of his belt and holding it up.

'Slide it over there.'

He does as he's told.

'You came alone?'

Geats scrutinises the face, tries to imagine it without the beard.

'I said, is there anyone with you?'

'I know you.'

'Sure. You led me through a tunnel once.'

'No. From somewhere else, too.'

Blackborne smiles, twists his face into mock beseechment. 'Please, sir. I beg mercy of you.'

Geats pictures it instantly. A quarter of a century earlier, the blubbering dandy in Bella Gold's crumbling townhouse.

'Jesus Christ, I had you. I bloody had you.'

How many has he killed since? All but the first two. All who could have been saved if Geats had been paying attention and not feeling sorry for himself.

Blackborne scoffs. 'You never had me. You couldn't see past your own nose. Back then, and in the Mayfair brothel later. Unconscious and bleeding out. I have to admit I thought you wouldn't make it. But I chose not to end you. You and the negress. She wasn't what I wanted. Both of you live only because I allowed it.'

He glances at Cassar.

'Lived five days, you know. Remarkable. I watered and fed him, mashed up food like for a baby. He suckled the spoon and smacked his lips when it was taken away, like an automaton. Then he simply stopped. Nothing discernibly different about him, nothing alive in his eyes. Just would no longer chew or swallow. Which was a good job, as I had no plan for him. I don't for you, either, but I can't see why this wouldn't work again.'

'I told people what I was doing. They know I'm here.'

'The police? I doubt it. You wouldn't be creeping about in the dark on your own if they knew what you were up to. That wife of yours, though. Or of his, I should say. Yes, I can see you telling her. How old are the children now? I imagine I can find out where the family home is, pay a visit before you're reported missing.'

Without even a glimmer of consciousness, Geats reacts. Fingers finding his friend's skull, he shies it with everything he has, charging in after as it slams Blackborne above the eye. He tackles him to the floor, the shotgun going off somewhere over his head, its sound immense against the stone walls. They land in a heap, and the stock of the gun rains down on his head as Blackborne paddles it wildly.

Trying to deflect the blows, Geats is unable to stop Blackborne getting astride his chest, and the barrel presses down hard against his throat, making him difficult to buck. Clawing at his face, going for an eye, he inadvertently fishhooks the corner of Blackborne's mouth. Forces a second finger in and brings his left hand up, getting two more in the other side. As Blackborne starts to bite down on him, he pulls violently outward.

When it rips apart, Blackborne's face peels not in the way of an orange, retaining shape and consistency as it comes away, but like a cotton T-shirt yanked from the collar, stretching and tearing such that you could never imagine it restored to its former state.

Blackborne shrieks, releasing the gun and tumbling away, hands clutched to his ruined face, skin and muscle hanging in bloody tatters around a ghastly exposed grin.

On him in a flash, Geats strikes with a heavy fist until the pleading eyes are beaten shut, until the piercing inhuman wails fall silent.

Rolling off him, he scurries back against the wall.

It happened so quickly, with such horrifying efficiency, that he's stunned by his own actions.

Bloody bubbles froth in what's left of Blackborne's face; he's alive.

One shot remains in the shotgun, but the rancour of the moment has not persevered. In the quiet company of his own thoughts, he baulks at executing the man.

He retrieves the Browning and slides it into his belt. Taking hold of the chains bolted into the wall opposite Cassar, he tests them; an elephant wouldn't shift them. His punching hand throbs, so he grabs Blackborne by one wrist, dragging him over to fasten the steel manacles. Taking the shotgun, he heads back into the other room, out of sight of what he's done.

Takes stock.

Gauges the new reality.

This place can compromise him. Any evidence of Christine Long's presence – the memorial card, and her blood probably in the brickwork – will raise questions of Mark Cassar. He pictures explaining what happened to Madison and Helm, them seeing the state of Blackborne.

Brother of an earl.

Old money.

Older ties.

The family is established, they know people. And even if the police protect Geats, would the fiction of his and Billie's life together stand up to official scrutiny?

No. Involving the police is not a chance he can take.

This needs to look like something else.

122

In a clockless twilight, he busies himself with the task at hand.

Sitting at the table, he reassembles the pieces of the small Walther pistol. Loading five bullets into the six-round magazine, he slots it into place. He hesitates. The ammunition won't match the bullet in Cassar's skull, so he ejects the magazine and re-inserts it empty.

The shotgun he gathers up, along with the box of Blackborne's souvenirs and the leather strop. Any superficial clue connecting this place to the killings must be cleared out. Beneath the table is a large tan leather overnight bag. Inside are bandages, bottles of morphine, basic surgical instruments. Keeping the Walther, he chucks in the other items, half the shotgun protruding. Any .25 calibre rounds he finds, he sweeps in there too.

Through the archway he can hear noises. No longer capable of words, Blackborne gargles desperately as blood seeps back down his throat. Geats picks out a bottle of morphine.

When he walks through, Blackborne squeals and splutters, pushing himself tight to the wall, trying to protect his face with his hands, but the short chains restrict his movement. His eyes have closed up completely from the beating, blinding him. He looks like the bottom has fallen out of a bag of meat.

He calms down, holding himself still with an ear cocked to any movement as Geats retrieves Cassar's skull and reunites it with the rest of him. He wipes it clean. The bullet has come loose and he finds it rolled into a gap between stones in the floor. Picking it up with the fabric of his cuff, he replaces it inside the skull. He unsnags the sleeve of Cassar's coat from the shackles and lays it down carefully.

Blackborne's breathing is wet and ragged.

'Found morphine next door.'

'Puhluhguhmuhsuh.'

'I'll leave it right here.'

With a *ting*, he places the bottle on the stone floor out of Blackborne's reach.

'It's a shame I beat your eyes shut, because I really want you to be looking at the bones of my friend when it dawns on you what awaits.'

'Nuhbuh. Duhguh.'

The Walther he places near Cassar's bones, and puts his old identity card in the inside pocket of his dead friend's coat. It feels as if he's finally closing off the cycle. Leon Geats will be officially dead. Christ knows what anyone will make of all this if it is found, but the truth should prove undiscoverable.

He climbs the ladder to the caravan and kicks it back down into the cellars. The pitiful sounds of Blackborne fade away as he steps outside. The sun has lolled beneath the horizon in his absence, and the frisson of confusion he feels in the silver darkness is precious. The moment holds secrets.

He takes in great gulps of fresh air.

Dragging the power cable out from beneath the caravan, he runs it back up to the villa, wrapping it round his arm into a thick roll. The house is unlocked, and he finds a set of car keys in the drawer of a sideboard in the entrance hall. He stows the cable in the boot of Blackborne's Jaguar Mark X, along with the leather bag from the cellars.

The caravan comes off its bricks easily enough, but it's a tougher job moving the thing on deflated tyres. Hauling it along by its tow bar over the uneven ground takes everything he has; guiding it across broken flagstones to a break in the ruined walls. His hand still aches from the fight, making everything that much harder.

Out in the meadow, the long grass snags up the wheels and axle. He spins it round and uses the slope to roll it backwards, so the tow bar doesn't dig into the ground. On the steeper ground it gathers its own momentum and runs away from him, nudging gently to a halt against a tree on the flats down at the bank of a stream. A long way from any road, and out of sight from the main house, he hopes it'll go undisturbed.

Among the ruins, he sees where heavy slabs were moved to uncover the cellars. Bracing his heels against them and his arms against the low wall, he slowly slides them back over the hole, dropping them snugly into place between the other flags, burying Blackborne and Cassar. He scatters lose detritus over the scene.

Sitting atop the sealed entrance, for a long while he listens for any sound below. There is none, or none that can be heard.

Up at the house, he finds Blackborne's bedroom and pulls a suitcase down from above the wardrobe, packing some clothes. From his initial reconnaissance of the estate, he knows that the stream, a tributary of the Stour, widens into a pond or small lake, not far from a quiet lane.

He drives the Jaguar there and hauls the cable to the pond, tossing it in and watching it sink. He throws the overnight bag in after it, except for the box of identifications, which he keeps.

Wearing Blackborne's coat and hat, he drives to Leamington Spa and buys a train ticket to London Marylebone. Having removed the coat and hat, he disembarks at Banbury with the suitcase to fetch his own car. Near home, he stops at woods and buries the case far from any beaten path.

A little before dawn, he puts his key in his own front door. He checks on the girls, both asleep in their rooms. Billie is too, but he doesn't want to disturb her. He slips his coat back on and sits in the chair by the window.

He doesn't remember falling asleep.

123

As a boy, he dreams of the sea.

A ship hulks against the moon, impossibly large for the small cove, and he walks broken keys of light across the water to the wooden vessel and descends through a hatch to the decks below. Sometimes he finds himself with men who he knows not by name or sight but by something more, and other times is purely alone in the blackness of unlit passageways, where eventually he always ends up.

There is only one way to go, and that is on through the dark and into the deeper dark, hoping to find that which he is looking for but could never name.

Always, he awakens before he does.

124

Afternoon before he comes to. He doesn't remember his dreams.

Billie asks nothing, waiting for him to volunteer his story. She cooks him breakfast for lunch. The knuckles on his right hand are swollen, possibly broken, and he manoeuvres the fork awkwardly with his left.

Afterwards, he shows her the box of documents and tells her everything that happened, everything he thought while it was happening. At some point, he cannot go on.

Three decades with one purpose in mind, and now he has reached the edge of his obsession to glimpse what lies beyond.

And there is nothing.

No justice.

No relief.

No sense of fulfilment.

It is not the finding of something other than what he seeks that bothers him; it is that there is no finding whatsoever. His life isn't a battle cry, but the echo of a mad howl that he didn't realise was dying over the years until he arrived at the silence.

Billie is less abstractly minded on the issue.

'Will anyone find them?'

'I don't know. Stones were cut to size to fit over the entrance to the cellars. I pushed them back into place and you wouldn't see it was there unless you knew. I don't suppose he would have used it if he thought anyone else knew about it.'

'And there's nothing to connect you to the place?'

'I removed anything that can be tied to Mark Cassar. The landlord in the pub would probably recognise me, but he knows me by a different name.'

'How badly hurt is Blackborne?'

'Very.'

'Can he last long?'

He shrugs. 'There's no water. He has lost a lot of blood and the chains mean he can't move much. Two or three days, he'd be doing well.'

'Then it's done. We tell nobody of this.'

'All those women, though. Someone should know. There are people who deserve to know. Families.'

'Yes, there are. But how would that work? Are you going to turn yourself in?'

He shrugs, and she shakes her head.

'You're not going to martyr yourself now. I won't let you. The time for acting honourably passed when you couldn't restrain yourself. Anything you do now would only be out of guilt.'

He looks up, face pained, like a small boy chastised by his mother.

'Let's be honest here, Leon. This isn't about the women.'

The name jolts him. He hasn't heard it on her lips for years.

'If it ever was, it hasn't been for a long time. It's about you, and it's about Mark, and it's about proving yourselves men. Well, have you? Have you made yourself known?'

He isn't sure what this is. He expected anger or pity, but this is worse because it is quite probably true, and so little of life ever is.

'There should be some justice for them,' he says meekly.

'Justice isn't for the dead, it's for the living. The dead don't care; they're dead.'

He nods. 'And what about him? He's down there—'

'No, he's not.'

'Sorry?'

'Alexander Blake Blackborne packed his bags and drove to the station and got aboard a train and fled. That's what the evidence will say, until the day someone goes down into that hole.'

Geats can't think of anything to say. She places a hand on his forearm.

'He killed an unimaginable number of people. Including Mark. This is a terrible situation, and one there is no good way out of. So, we take the least bad. I need you here with me and the girls. I can't have you going away.'

Heavy with tumoral guilt both for what he has done and what he has not, he sinks in his chair. She pats his arm.

'Say anything else, did he?'

'No. What do you mean? Like what?'

'About why he did all of this.'

'Jesus, Bill.' The thought has never occurred to him.

'Was it just about the Mitford woman? With the gunshots . . .'

'Nothing's ever about one thing. He'd already killed before then. Whatever he felt for her, that only honed his method.'

'Then why?'

'Think there's a reason could ever satisfactorily answer that question?' he says, recalling all too vividly those things he himself felt in the immediate aftermath of taking lives. Things he will never tell her about.

She fetches their first-aid box from the cupboard and takes his injured hand. He winches as she stretches out the fingers, testing the knuckles here and there with the pads of her thumbs. Fetching ice from the chest freezer, she applies a pack to his hand with a sigh that tells him he should have done this the previous night.

After fifteen minutes, she sets about wrapping the hand in a light bandage to stabilise it, frowning with concentration.

'He said he'd come here.'

'What?'

'He knew about you and the girls. Said he'd pay a visit.'

She finishes the bandage.

'You need to keep it elevated if you can.'

Disappearing into the hall, she returns with a silk scarf, which she ties into a sling. He loops it over his head and cradles his arm in it. She adjusts it to her satisfaction, before touching his face.

'There hasn't been a single day when I've regretted what we did. Mark was gone, and anyway . . . I love our life. Our girls. Our home. And I know who you are. The things you've done. I thought we were past all that, since the war. That thing inside that drives you, Leon, you have to change it. Fluke, Minter, Lander, Blackborne. I don't need overwhelming gestures. Violence and death. I don't want you to kill for us. I need you to live for us. Every day. I need you here to make breakfast for in the morning. I need you at the table for tea. I need you to pick the girls up or drop them off. I need you to sit on the sofa with me and watch television. I need someone at my side, my best friend. I need a dedication to all the little things, because they're what our days are made of. And what do we have but days? Run them consecutively and you get a life. Can you do that for us?'

Nods that he can, but still savours within his heart the lingering traces of quiet majesty lent by the killing of bad men.

He cakes brutal sentimentality over the taste.

He is a ghost. Forever looking backwards, haunting his own life in the name of another. A ghoul, a spectre, he has been wearing a mask for years, behind which Leon Geats was lost.

If he had perished in the war, his death would have been a recorded fact. A noticeable loss. As it is, it happened in increments, day by day, piece by piece, a disappearance so quiet that even he didn't notice there was nothing of himself left.

He cannot recall the last time he felt like a person.

She takes his good hand, and he allows himself to be led upstairs and put to bed.

125

Dark outside when he awakens.

His feet are cold. About the only thing he is sure of with age is that the older he gets, the colder his feet get.

Some flickering light at the window. He gets up and draws the curtains, greeted by a bonfire in the garden. Billie out there with the girls, roasting foil-wrapped potatoes in the embers.

When he joins them, Lottie fetches him a cup of tomato soup, made from their own garden. She's happy, the fire playing in her dark eyes.

'I've retired,' he says.

Lottie frowns. 'Dad, why?'

'Done enough. Done too much. I wake up these days and all I want to do is stay at home and annoy you.'

Marse walks over and he pulls them both close.

'Should have done it years ago,' he says.

Billie fishes out the potatoes with iron tongs, splits them and drops in lashings of butter to melt. They sit in deckchairs and eat contentedly. He must learn that this is what life is, the things accumulating as he trundles along that if he's not careful he'll only catch glimpses of in the corner of his eye.

In the flames, burning away, he can see the edge of the small chest that held the identifications.

2002

126

Opening his eyes, he thinks it's Lottie in the chair beside him, a young woman again.

'Hi, Grandad.'

He licks his lips and swallows his own spit, and it is sweet.

'Hello, pet.'

So much like her mother. Speak of the devil. Lottie comes over, touches his hand. He smiles.

'Been looking all over for you, Fiona. She annoying you, Dad?'

'Only in the best way.'

'I'm not annoying,' Fee says. 'Grandad, the police were here.'

Lottie nods. 'Yes, Mum says they want to take you away.'

'Won't get me without a fight,' he manages.

Wheezing now. Lottie places the mask carefully over his face and turns the oxygen on.

'Comfy?'

He nods.

'Grandad, who's this?'

Fee has a picture in her hand. Billie found it a few weeks ago. Cleaned it up and put it in a frame, set it beside his bed. He looks to Lottie, who removes the mask again.

'Her name was Nell.'

'Who was she?'

'Someone I used to know. An orphan.'

'It looks old.'

'During the war. 1941. She was killed not long after, in a raid.'

'Oh. God, that's awful. Sorry.'

'Your grandmother took the picture.'

'Really?'

'Is that the flat in Soho?' Lottie asks.

He nods.

'I don't remember that. Marse used to say she did, but I don't think so.'

'It's a café now,' Fee says. 'Downstairs. Me and my friends had lunch there. Told the waitress my grandparents owned the place, to get free food.'

'You didn't,' Lottie says.

'Course I didn't.'

'Best investments ever,' he says weakly.

Lottie fixes the mask back in place.

'Come on, you. Your grandfather needs his rest.'

He flitters a hand.

'I'll send Mum up,' Lottie says.

Time no longer sings to him, no longer marks its passing other than in the sky he sees out the window. Yet he feels more alive now than he did for years. He has raised his children, his grandchildren, and loved his wife. All in the name of another man, but he now can't imagine it ever having been another way.

And who is to say?

For he has lived life as Mark Cassar for decades longer than he did as Leon Geats. For longer even than Cassar himself did. There is no longer a line between Geats and Cassar. He no longer knows the difference.

He hears Billie on the stairs.

She shuffles in and sits beside him, sighing deeply.

'Eating us out of house and home.'

Reaching over, she slips off the mask.

'You hungry?'

He shakes his head.

'I've made chicken soup. You'll have some later. The police were here again, those two young ones. We're going to have to speak to them; they don't seem to be for giving up. I told them to come back in the morning, that you're better in the mornings.'

'You'll be here?'

'I'll be here.'

He nods.

'Good.'

127

Dining chairs are brought up, placed one side of the bed. Billie sits in the armchair on the other, holding his hand.

DS Rathbone crosses and re-crosses his legs, unable to get comfortable. Lottie brings up a tray of tea and leaves them to it. DC Duffy sips quietly at hers.

Rathbone clears his throat. 'We apologise for the intrusion, Mr Cassar. We'll make it as brief as possible. Just a few questions.'

He nods, the mask amplifying his sorry breaths.

Billie can read Rathbone's mind. 'I'll take it off if he has anything to say.'

'Of course. Good. Well then.'

Rathbone looks to Duffy, as if deciding he isn't the man for the job. Duffy sits forward on her chair.

'Mr Cassar, does the name Blackborne mean anything to you? Alexander Blake Blackborne.'

He shakes his head.

'This would have been some time ago. At least back to the 1960s, and possibly before then.'

Makes a show of looking up to the ceiling, racking the dusty stacks of his mind. Shakes his head again.

'He was a general practitioner in Warwickshire in the sixties. May have lived in London before that, in the thirties and during the war.'

'How would my husband know him?' Billie says.

'His remains were found alongside those of Leon Geats. The circumstances of their discovery lead us to believe the deaths were
suspicious, although we can't be certain if any other parties were
involved.'

He makes a noise, looks at Billie.

'I think we're both a little confused, Constable,' Billie says.

Rathbone jumps in. 'As far as we can establish, nobody has seen
Blackborne since some time in 1963. His surgery closed rather abruptly.
Nobody ever reported him missing, however. We've located family
members, none of whom ever met him, and their understanding is
that he went abroad at that time. He had previously lived in Burma.'

'But you found him with Leon,' Billie says.

'There is no record of Blackborne leaving the country in 1963. No
record of him ever doing anything again. He simply vanished without
trace, until his body was discovered. We think, therefore, it is likely he
died in 1963.'

He smiles, but the mask obscures it. Never reported missing. He
scoured the papers for weeks, months after that day in the cellar, and
there was never a single story. An earl's brother missing, it was unusual.
He believes someone in the family knew exactly what Blackborne was,
never tried too hard to find him. Or perhaps they found the scene in
the cellar and thought it for the best. Sealed it right back up again and
left time to deal with it in its own way.

He shakes Billie's hand and she removes his mask.

'And what of Leon?' he says.

'We're not entirely clear on what happened. Leon Geats suffered
injuries consistent with a self-inflicted gunshot wound. The gun was
found at the scene, with a single round apparently fired.'

He tries to say something, but his breath fails him. Billie replaces
the mask.

'You're saying Leon killed this Blackborne and then shot himself?'
she says.

Rathbone sits back. 'I'm saying it could be construed that way. The bodies were found in the cellars of a very old building that had been demolished many years ago. Centuries, in fact. Some low ruins remained. New owners sought permission to build a swimming pool and summer house, and the ruins were about to be cleared. The earth gave way beneath a heavy digger, revealing cellars nobody had known about. That's when the bodies came to light. The chamber was relatively dry, and they were completely skeletonised. No weeds or plants had grown among them. We can tell the age of bones with a great deal of accuracy, which can help identify victims. However, telling exactly when they were killed is much harder. Almost impossible in these circumstances.'

'We have a few unanswered questions,' Duffy says. 'Leon Geats's clothes seem to date from the war. Possibly earlier. But Blackborne's date to after his return from Burma, in the early sixties. There is evidence that one or possibly both men were chained up in the cellar at some point.'

Rathbone speaks again. 'Mrs Cassar, you said you hadn't seen Leon Geats since the war.'

'That's right. Well, just after: 1946.'

'We checked the *Gazette*, like you suggested. We did find a Leon Geats mentioned in dispatches. We double-checked, though, and there is no service record for him whatsoever. It's possible it was lost, though someone at the Ministry of Defence told us it looked more like it had been scrubbed.'

'What does that mean?'

'That someone had removed it deliberately.'

Billie nods and rolls her eyes like she was expecting something like this all along. 'The funny people.'

'I'm sorry?'

'Spooks. Spies. The funny people.'

'Yes. Is that a possibility?'

'It wouldn't be a surprise to learn Leon had got himself caught up in that sort of business. But he never told us about it.'

Mask keeping him quiet, he shakes his head in firm agreement.

Rathbone slaps his hands on his knees and glances at Duffy. 'Well . . .'

Duffy puts her tea down and stands. 'We appreciate you both speaking to us.'

Billie gets to her feet.

'What will happen to the remains?'

'That's a decision for the coroner,' Duffy says. 'If they give the go-ahead for a burial, would you like to be contacted?'

'Yes, if that's possible. I don't like the idea of him being buried by strangers.'

'We'll let the coroner know you'll be willing to make arrangements.'

'Thank you.'

Billie shows them downstairs, and he can hear her saying her fare-wells, the door clunking shut. Her footsteps coming back up.

'Well,' she says. 'That's that.'

He pulls the mask down around his throat.

'Not reported missing.'

'No.'

'Someone knew what he was.'

'Someone always does.'

'Won't be long before there's nobody alive who knows.'

There is regret in his voice, and she picks up on it. He has come to believe the women's stories should have been told; so many of them just erased, here and overseas. He also knows he hasn't always believed that, not really. For years it was about him, the story in which he was the leading man. And somewhere inside him, a part of him still believes that. Looking back, the way he feels about it is how someone feels about their working years once they are retired.

'At least he won't be remembered,' she says.

But killers always are, one way or another.

128

Through the course of the day, his family pop in and out.

Lottie with her husband, and Fee with her younger sister Jackie. Marse turns up, widowed now, and tells him her two, Mark and Jess, will be coming by.

'Jess has a new man. I'm quietly excited about this one.'

Everyone senses it, that there isn't long.

He doesn't say much. Can't say much. The mask stays on all the time. At one point they're all in the room with him – his wife, his daughters, all four grandchildren. The secrets that bind them together are known only by him and Billie, and soon will be known by nobody at all.

He awakens, not recalling dropping off.

Shadow of that hulking ship bleached into his retinas; he knows he had the dream of his childhood that he never knew the ending of. Knows now he never will, as there is no end to the deeper dark, save what keen light you spark yourself. Knows if life is a story at all, its only meaning is us.

Billie is at the window. He has something to say, and it takes him a moment to build up the breath for it. She takes his mask off.

Coarse, barely audible. 'Thank you.'

She winks. 'You bet, chum.'

Her eyes return to the window and he wonders if birds still pick scraps from bones, then everything is gone. Life isn't etched, but is painted – on untamed stone that will erode in no more than an epoch or two.

Only the dead see the end of war.

Credits

Dominic Nolan would like to thank everyone involved in the production of Vine Street

Editorial
Toby Jones
Bea Grabowska

Copy editor
Jane Selley

Proof reading
Helen Norris

Audio
Hannah Cawse

Design
Patrick Insole
Cathie Arrington

Production
Tina Paul

Marketing
Joe Yule

Publicity
Rosie Margesson

Sales
Becky Bader
Chris Keith-Wright
Frances Doyle
Izzy Smith

Legal
Kirsty Howarth

Contracts
Helen Windrath

Special thanks are extended to: NBarr, for everything and a little bit more; Russ, for spiritual guidance and refusing to pose for likes; Amelia Hodgson and everyone at The Bent Agency for all their hard work; Victoria Selman, for essential Vix's Fixes; Maddalena Fuzzi at Mio Piccolo Formaggio Consultants Inc., for her patience as I wildly mangled her mother tongue.